CHAPTER ONE

20 December 2006

In the old days, when they were both working, Åke Melkersson liked to get up an hour before his wife — she was more of a night person — just to indulge himself for that hour with a cup of coffee and the crossword in the morning paper. A quarter of an hour before they were due to leave, he would wake Kristina; she would get dressed more or less in her sleep, then stumble her way to the garage and collapse in the passenger seat with a blanket over her knees. She would sleep all the way to the timber factory gate, where he would get out and she would drive the short distance to Hjällbo and the post office where she had worked for so many years.

In the afternoons she would pick him up at the factory gate at twenty to six, every day except Thursday when she arrived two hours later after meeting her sister at Dahl's for coffee and cakes. And so on Thursdays he would have a shower at work instead of when he got home.

Since Kristina retired he had had the car to himself, and had been forced to rent a space in the factory car park for the first time in twenty-seven years. Sixty kronor a month it cost him. At first he had thought about leaving the car in the free car park down by the holiday cottages and walking the last bit of the journey. It wasn't the money that annoyed him. It was just so penny-pinching on the part of the company.

Anyway, now he didn't need the space any more. He had paid until the end of the month, but he wouldn't need it after today — his last day at work.

The realisation had coursed through his body like an electric shock when the alarm clock went off. For a second he had considered calling in sick for the first time in many years, pretending that he had been struck down by a nasty bout of the flu in order to avoid the obligatory cake and the laboured speech from the director.

A frozen branch had caught on the dining room window during the night and was stuck fast in the rime. December hadn't been this cold for a long time. He lingered over his empty coffee cup and thought that this was the last time he would spend an hour like this: sitting alone in the early morning, by the soft light of the Advent candles in the holders Kristina had inherited from her family.

He decided to set off a little earlier than usual so that he would have time to empty his locker before work started; he stood up a little too quickly and knocked over the glass of milk which had been dangerously close to the edge of the table.

When he got in the car it was almost half past six. The first hesitant snowflakes fell from the lingering night sky

2

and landed on the windscreen. He switched on the wipers and watched them sweep the snowflakes away, hypnotised by the movement.

Kristina had been saying for days that it was going to snow, warning him that the roads would be slippery; they were always at their most treacherous just before it snowed. And you can always tell it's going to snow when the air tears at your skin and ice particles form on your face, invisible but feeling like frosted glass.

It was those five years that made the difference, the fact that she was five years older than him. It had been an issue when they decided to get married almost half a century ago but the age difference had levelled out over the years, and for most of their marriage they had hardly noticed it. Now it was making itself felt once again. Kristina had turned seventy in May, but he thought it was the lack of social contact that had changed her, rather than the encroaching years. That was what had made it easier for anxiety to tighten its grip.

Was that what happened to people who retired? People like us, he thought for a second, who no longer have anything to do. Who have long ago exhausted every topic of conversation and established that the pleasure gained from the various activities available barely compensated for the effort involved.

The last hill, the steepest, had been gritted. That was the only advantage of the shocking amount of building and the mass influx of residents during the 90s: the roads were gritted during the winter. From being the back of beyond, the area had suddenly become highly desirable. One pastel-coloured house after another had shot up with impressive speed. The potholes left by last year's deep frost needed filling in, however, and Åke grimaced as the undercarriage of his old Opel Astra jolted. It carried on banging rhythmically beneath his feet as he took the bend at Johansson a little too quickly and felt the tyres lose their grip on the surface of the road. No, the new highways agency was in no hurry to get the holes filled in. After all, the younger generation drove around in enormous cars with tyres to match.

As he pulled out on to Göteborgsvägen, which was still deserted, early risers were starting to switch on the lights in their kitchens. The windows of the houses showed up as soft yellow points of light in the midst of all the blackness. He braked and let the six-thirty bus pull out from the stop. As usual it was almost empty.

Bang-bang-bang. It sounded like the exhaust pipe.

The bitterly cold morning was hardly conducive to the idea of pulling over and waiting for the next bus. It wouldn't be daylight for a long time yet. Åke decided to chance it, hoping the car would make it as far as work, then he would drive straight to the garage in Lerum at the end of the day. He could ask Christer to take a look at it.

Happy with his decision he increased his speed as much as he dared on the twisting, icy road. The sparse street lights showed the way over the hills to Olofstorp like a string of beads. In a way it felt good to have something specific to do when he left the factory for the last time, with his personal effects in a cardboard box on the seat beside him. Like a kind of assurance that

4

life didn't end there, that there were still things that wouldn't be done if you didn't exist.

Kristina's prediction of bad weather came to nothing when the snow stopped falling just as suddenly as it had started. He switched off the windscreen wipers and turned on the radio so that he wouldn't have to listen to the banging from underneath the car. *Bloody old heap*. He was now passing through Olofstorp: the school, the nursery, shops, the folk museum, and then the street lights came to an end and he was once again on a deserted road. He was trying to get rid of the mist on the windscreen while simultaneously struggling to find a frequency on the radio when suddenly the car decided enough was enough. A deafening clatter made him swear out loud. He managed to manoeuvre off the road at the petrol station, which was closed, rolling the Astra under the roof, which seemed to float freely above the self-service pumps. With one more curse, he breathed out. He was grateful that the exhaust pipe — it had to be the exhaust pipe — had fallen off here, and not on one of the pitch-black stretches of road between the villages.

He took out his mobile and weighed it in his hand for a moment. The thought of ringing Kristina and asking her to find the number for a breakdown truck or for Christer, then spending another half-hour calming her down, wasn't exactly appealing. He would have to find another solution.

In the boot he discovered an oily piece of rope with which he was able to do a reasonable job of tying up the exhaust pipe — that should enable him to drive to the nearest garage. Buoyed up by having coped with the challenge so far, he acted on impulse and drove along the gravel track into the countryside instead of carrying on towards the town. The track crossed the river Lärje over a narrow stone bridge, then continued to slice its way among the hills. Åke was taking a chance. A few years ago he had driven their grandchild out to a friend's house somewhere around here and he had a vague memory of a garage by one of the farms a short distance past the bridge.

Perhaps his memory wasn't quite as reliable as it had been. Each curve revealed only fresh stretches of road running between deserted fields and meadows. He was glad that dawn was beginning to break. There was no guarantee the garage would still be there, of course, he thought, regretting his impulse just as the car rounded a bend and the full beam of the headlights illuminated a dilapidated old barn. The house opposite wasn't exactly in tip-top condition either, but in the yard in between stood a considerable number of dead cars. The place was run-down, that was obvious, but the iron sign proclaiming THOMAS EDELL — VEHICLE REPAIRS AND SCRAPYARD was still there.

It was a relief to park the rattling car in the yard between two scruffy pickup trucks. The silence that followed felt almost sacred. He got out and stretched his legs, took a couple of deep breaths, inhaling the bitterly cold morning air, and gazed up at the greyish-white wooden house. There were no lights in any of the windows. However, bright light was pouring out from a metal annexe attached to the barn — a garage, with its doors wide open.

It was gone seven o'clock by now, and he wasn't surprised to see that someone was already busy in the workshop. Real grafters make an early start, that's what he had always believed, although it was a little odd that no one seemed to have noticed his noisy arrival. Everything was as silent as the grave. He cleared his throat and shouted a greeting as he walked across the grass.

The floor of the workshop was covered in tools, but there wasn't a soul in sight. A Nissan Micra up on the ramp was obscuring his view, so he took a few steps further inside.

"Hello there!"

Where the annexe joined the old barn there was a chaotic office made of white plywood screens; that was empty too, but a radio was playing away to itself almost inaudibly. He stood there nonplussed for a moment, then managed to make out the sound of *Soothing Favourites*. Then he realised he was late for work, late for his own leaving party, and this place was obviously not manned, despite all the indications to the contrary. He stepped outside again and decided to walk around the house just to make sure there was no one there who might help him. He didn't really want to drive that rattling heap much further.

Afterwards he would recall that a feeling of unease gradually crept over him. Perhaps it was the thought of the director and being late for work, but there was something else as well, something indefinable. He almost had a heart attack when a black and white cat shot out of an open cellar window, yowling loudly. The next moment he saw the man, lying spreadeagled on the ground where the gravel path continued around the back of the barn. He didn't need to go any closer to see that the man had been run over, probably several times. The whole of the lower half of his body had been more or less . . . destroyed.

He's only half a man, thought Åke Melkersson, a hysterical, terrified giggle rising in his chest. He's flat, half of him smeared over the gravel. He thought back to the cartoons of his childhood, in which characters were always getting run over by steamrollers, ending up as flat as pancakes. There was never any blood in the cartoons, but there was blood here, collected in a hollow in the gravel around the man's head, like a gory halo.

Then Åke did what the characters in the cartoons never did: he walked backwards and threw up. He wiped his mouth on the sleeve of his jacket, then he threw up again all over his trousers. *I can't go to work like this*, he thought irrationally before he stumbled back to the car and reversed out at high speed, making the exhaust pipe come crashing down again; it dragged along the ground all the way back to the main road.

When he finally reached something that could with a little goodwill be classed as civilisation, he pulled over at a bus stop. With trembling hands he keyed in the emergency number.

Afterwards he sat for a while in the car with the window down, hoping that the cold air pouring in would stop him from fainting. The policewoman's voice had been matter-of-fact, gathering information. This had helped him to calm down, and to come to his senses sufficiently to offer to drive back to the scene of the crime; he could wait there to be interviewed by the police, instead of giving his home address and telephone number. He didn't want to worry Kristina unnecessarily, least of all in a situation like this.

The traffic, increasing as usual as the time approached eight o'clock, also had a calming effect on his nerves. He turned the heater up to maximum and picked up his mobile once again.

CHAPTER
TWO

Andreas Karlberg was sitting at his desk in the police station watching a magpie that had obviously taken a wrong turning and ended up on his windowsill. Its feet made a muted tapping sound as it moved across the metal ledge. The small coal-black eyes stared straight into his, then the bird seemed to take fright and flew away.

Karlberg had other things on his mind. He was pondering whether he was a man of integrity, a man who knew how to draw suitable boundaries around himself, or whether he was just using this as an excuse for behaving like an egotistical pig. In the top drawer of his desk lay a popular psychology book entitled *Energy Thieves*. He had found the book lying on his doormat in a padded envelope on his birthday a couple of weeks ago. It had turned out to be from his ex, whom he hadn't seen for months. *On your 34th birthday. To someone who ought to learn how to say no. Good luck, love from Marie.*

His first impulse had been to ring her up and ask her what she meant, but he realised there was a risk that she would immediately see this as an opportunity to explain at length why she had left him six months ago and he wasn't sure he wanted to know. Not any more, not when the wound left by the broken relationship had started to heal.

Presumably it had something to do with his job. He worked too many hours, too many evenings, was too preoccupied with the job. But he couldn't agree that he had a problem when it came to putting her before other people. If you had the chance to be there for a friend, he still thought you ought to do so. Even if it meant you often found your weekends taken up with helping someone to move house, giving someone a lift to the airport at some ridiculous hour or lending money to someone in a tight spot.

Good luck, Marie had written. He presumed she was encouraging him to practise the art of saying no, and he had actually taken her seriously. Not that he had since become notorious for saying no, but he had started by carefully evaluating every situation where he would previously have said yes without a second's hesitation. Like yesterday evening, when he had stood in the queue at the supermarket checkout watching the woman in front of him puffing and blowing as she unpacked a mountain of food from her trolley. She had suddenly turned to him and asked, somewhat apologetically, if he would mind loading her shopping on to the conveyor belt while she went to the other end and started packing it into bags. It would speed things up, she said. And she might well be right, he had thought, glancing in confusion from his prawn baguette to her enquiring expression, and back to his baguette.

"No, I'd rather not do that," he heard himself say.

"No?" said the woman, surprised, as if he'd had THE GUY WHO ALWAYS HELPS OUT tattooed on his forehead.

"No," he said firmly, running a hand nervously through his light blonde hair. The woman's face turned dark red. Now he suddenly saw with painful clarity the checkout assistant's embarrassed smile, the woman's crushed expression; in the end she had managed to pack away all her Christmas food shopping and had lumbered off with her bags. To catch the tram, no doubt — she wouldn't have a car. She was probably a single mother with several children.

He ought to ring Marie and boast about what he'd achieved. And he might have done if he hadn't heard on the grapevine that she'd started dating again. A market analyst, whatever the hell that was.

He was brought back to reality when Inspector Christian Tell stuck his head round the office door.

"You're here, great. We've got a body in the Gunnilse area. He's been run over, but the old guy who rang in thought he'd been shot as well. In the head."

A short while later they had passed the county governor's pastel-coloured house in the old town and put the grey concrete buildings of the northern suburbs behind them. One outlying district of semi-detached houses and rows of terraces had given way to the next, finally tapering out into the smaller communities: Knipared, Bingared, Linnarhult. Between these lay undulating grazing land. It always surprised Tell that the city was actually so small — it only took half an hour to get out into the countryside.

After a drive at breakneck speed along a bumpy gravel track they finally pulled into a farmyard. A police van was parked by the entrance, and representatives from the local force seemed to have already made themselves at home. Tell growled something inaudible.

Karlberg took a deep breath and cleared his throat.

"So where's the old guy who called in?"

"I suppose he's on his way back."

Tell lit a cigarette and opened the car door.

"Apparently he panicked and took off, not surprisingly. Then his car packed up and he got stuck on the main road. He knows we want to talk to him."

Karlberg took several deep breaths to slow down his pulse after their high-speed drive. The feeling was always the same when you went out on a case: you wanted to get on with it, and yet you also didn't. Open that door, walk round the corner of that house. Violent deaths were not unusual in his job but outright executions like this one, at least according to the emergency call, were not exactly something they came across every day. They had discussed in the car whether it might be the result of some kind of gang warfare, but it didn't fit the context. Not here, on a farm, in the middle of nowhere. A drunken brawl perhaps, one neighbour losing it with another. Although there was no sign of any neighbours out here, just fields and forest.

"They're certainly not living on top of one another," he muttered as he heard the sound of a car in the distance.

"OK, let's get started."

Tell had already taken a few rapid drags of his cigarette, stubbed it out in an empty McDonald's paper cup and set off towards one of the uniformed officers. The police surgeon's car turned in and drove up on to the grass, followed by the crime scene team. The investigation was under way.

CHAPTER
THREE

Nine minutes before the telephone rang Seja had switched the alarm clock to snooze in case she fell asleep again. One foot in reality, her gaze fixed on the cracks in the painted ceiling, one foot still in her dreams. She jumped when the clock emitted its vaguely encouraging beep, followed swiftly by the shrill sound of the telephone. The noise drilled into her skull, and for a moment it startled her. The meagre daylight seeped in through the gaps between the curtains, but the cottage was still in darkness.

The old copy of *Rekordmagasinet* fell on the floor as she rolled out of bed and dashed across the cold wooden floor.

"Hello?"

"Hello. Were you asleep?"

"Who is this?"

"Your neighbour. Are you up and about?"

"Åke, is that you?"

She sighed to herself. Since Martin left she had been grateful for some contact with her next-door neighbours. It gave her the feeling that she wasn't entirely alone with her fears during all those dark nights; she could peep through the curtains, and even if the only thing she could see was the fir trees silhouetted against the night sky, she knew that behind those fir trees there was a peat bog and another little house where Åke and Kristina Melkersson lived.

It was true that Åke could be a bit too chatty in his old man's way, and annoyingly flirty, but they had developed a comfortable relationship; it was quite pleasant to meet someone by the mailboxes in the mornings. She had also enjoyed being around to help Kristina during the day while Åke was at work. It was often something small, such as bringing an item back from the shops or posting a letter. Seja suspected that Åke was grateful for the sense of security this gave him, despite the fact that her involvement with his wife was comparatively limited. On a couple of occasions he had even, with a certain amount of embarrassment, offered to pay her for coming round. Which, of course, she had declined, equally embarrassed. She was on her own after all, and despite the fact that she was halfway through a training course to become a journalist after several years of aimless study, she had oceans of time at her disposal. However, being woken up in the morning by Melkersson was definitely a step in the wrong direction.

"What do you want, Åke?"

"I need your help. I've got into a bit of a . . . well . . . an odd situation. To say the least."

He sounded stressed.

"What do you want me to do? Where are you?"

"Pick me up outside the ICA supermarket in Gunnilse. My car has broken down, but that's not all.

16

I'll tell you about it when you get here. I don't really want to talk over the phone. I'm hanging up now."

"Åke!" she yelled down the phone. "I'm going nowhere unless you tell me what this is about. What's going on? Has the car packed up? Why don't you just ring for a breakdown truck?"

He lowered his voice.

"Listen . . . A man has been murdered. At a garage not far from here. I found him. He's been executed, shot in the head, that's what must have happened, there was so much blood. But that wasn't all, Seja, he'd been run over. He was completely squashed. Someone has . . . You have to drive me there, I promised the police and my car's completely —"

"Åke! The police? What —"

"I'm hanging up now."

Click.

He was very pale, standing there in front of his old Opel. Seja pulled in next to him and pushed open the passenger door.

"Jump in. And explain yourself."

An acrid smell surrounded Åke as he slumped down on the seat.

"I only wanted to ask him to take a look at the car."

He seemed to be concentrating on his breathing.

"For God's sake, you tell me there's a body in a garage, and for some unknown reason I'm on my way there. I just don't understand why — you could have called a breakdown truck. Or a taxi."

"Left here. Don't you understand, Seja? I'm too old for this kind of thing. I need a bit of support."

She didn't say anything. The first rays of the sun hit the wing mirrors and dazzled her as she took the bend a little too fast. Åke grabbed hold of the handle on the roof and gave her an inscrutable look. She swallowed and thought about how she had rushed off without taking the time to feed her horse or let him out into the field. She couldn't be away for too long.

She often got annoyed when she was afraid. It seemed easier to be afraid and angry than afraid and merely weak. Easier to be driven by an idea than to allow chance to make a fool of you. The sense of excitement, because it was there too, came from her nightly reading of fifty-year-old crime reports in *Rekordmagasinet*. She had found the pile down in the cellar, left behind by the former owner of the cottage. She had intended using them for the fire, but instead had become caught up in a wealth of old-fashioned and innocently formulated articles about long-forgotten crimes. They interested her, giving a picture of how society had changed or perhaps of the general fascination for the darker side of mankind. Recently she had started to think about using them as a basis for her undergraduate dissertation: a historical overview of crime journalism. Or perhaps this was just an excuse to avoid getting down to the reading she should be doing for her next exam. Right now the thought of the grainy black and white pictures and the sensational headlines gave her a reassuring sense of distance from the current situation.

She was thirty years old, and had only recently decided what she wanted to do with her life — or perhaps the realisation that it was actually possible was something new, for the writing had always been there, so much a part of her that she had hardly even considered that it could become her profession. So far she had only managed to get published in insignificant contexts: she had sold a short story to a monthly magazine; done a brisk report in the local paper about a long-distance ski club that was celebrating an anniversary; carried out an investigation into local procedures for clearing snow. She was happy just to be paid for her writing.

At that moment she caught sight of the place. There was no doubt that this was where the crime had been committed. A collection of cars was already blocking the entrance to the yard, and she had to park by the side of the road a short distance away.

It was an old farm, the paint flaking. A sign was swinging in the bitter wind: THOMAS EDELL — VEHICLE REPAIRS AND SCRAPYARD.

An electric shock ran through her body. Her heart beat so fast it felt as if her chest was actually vibrating. Her hands started to shake and she had to take a deep breath in order to regain control of her body.

Åke didn't seem to take any notice; he was completely taken up with his own anxiety. He got out of the car and, with as much composure as he could muster, walked over to a group of what she presumed were plain-clothes police officers. Her mind was racing feverishly. She couldn't hear what was being said, but

Åke was directed towards a man who was over at the side of the yard, staring down at the ground like a tracker dog.

She opened the car door and stepped out. All around her was a hive of activity, but she could see no sign of the body. Her heart turned a few more somersaults in her chest. Driven by a strength she neither understood nor could analyse, she walked towards Åke and the man in the coat. Her neighbour didn't turn around when she stared at his back. *Help me now, Åke. Help me be allowed to stay here and see the body. I can't explain why, it's too complicated; I just have to do it.*

The police officer caught sight of her and she took a tentative step in his direction.

"Excuse me, but I assume you'll be wanting to question me. I was with Åke when he found the body."

She pretended not to notice Åke's surprised expression.

"And you are?"

"I think there's been some kind of misunderst—"

"Seja Lundberg," she interrupted, her voice sounding reasonably steady as she met the officer's gaze. He had a finely chiselled face: with its straight slender nose and thick eyelashes it could have been regarded as feminine had it not been for his bushy eyebrows. Seja thought she caught a hint of his breath: coffee and cigarettes, a trace of mint.

He extended his hand towards her.

"Inspector Christian Tell. Right. Melkersson here told me that you found the body just after seven, then drove up to the main road to telephone us. Hmm . . ."

He's wondering why Åke gave the impression he was alone. Seja was already regretting her stupid lie.

"That seems about right," Tell went on after a brief pause. "The emergency call was logged at seven thirty."

He seemed a little distracted, raising his shoulders up towards his ears and shivering as if he had just noticed that the temperature had fallen well below zero overnight. It was hardly surprising that he was frozen. His coat was much too thin for the weather, a typical city coat, perfect for someone who only moved between his apartment and the car, the car and work.

"I'll see if I can find somewhere inside where we can talk. It's too bloody cold out here. If you'll excuse me."

Seja nodded mutely after he had turned on his heel. She got the idea that she had met the man before, in a completely different context. *There's something ludicrously familiar about him.* The thick black eyebrows that met in the middle and didn't seem to match the ash-coloured hair, which fell below his ears. The deep voice and the accent: broad Gothenburg to start with, but a real effort had been made to tame it. She recognised the voice and thought she knew from which evening the memory came.

They had just moved into the cottage. She was due to pick up Martin from the pub at the central station; he had been bowling and had gone for a few beers afterwards with a friend from Stockholm who was staying over. Both the guys were pretty drunk, very drunk in fact, loud and not at all interested in going home with her. She had grown tired of nagging them and had considered driving back on her own and leaving them to their fate, but instead she had sat down crossly on one of the bar stools while they ordered another beer and a shot each. The man who resembled Christian Tell had been sitting next to her, and had made a comment on her unfortunate situation, half amused and half sympathetic. She remembered that she had found him attractive and had been embarrassed at being so feeble. At just sitting there, sweaty and furious with her jacket on, waiting, like a dog, once again placed in the box labelled nagging old bag, while Martin was the one who was such fun, so ready to embrace life. The one who was absolved of responsibility because there was always someone else to shoulder it, the martyr who yet again would come tiptoeing along with the Alka-Seltzer the next day, doggedly tidying up, cleaning up, picking up the pieces of something that had been fun but wasn't any longer.

She was brought back to reality as Åke grabbed hold of her arm. She pre-empted him by whispering, "I thought if I said I was in the car with you I'd be allowed to stay. Otherwise I would have had to leave."

He seemed to have regained the power of speech.

"Do you realise what you've done? You've lied to the police in a murder case, and dragged me along with you. Now we'll have to carry on lying and —"

"Please, Åke . . . I can't explain."

It was hopeless. Åke's expression made it clear that he had no intention of listening to her. Instead he bent down to pick up some rubbish as if he too were part of the police operation.

"Excuse me, but could you identify yourselves?"

A uniformed officer placed his hand on Åke's shoulder. Seja realised that her options were limited at this point: she could either keep digging herself into a hole, or she could hold up her hands, apologise and be told off and sent away. A part of her wanted to disappear before she was found out. It must be breaking some kind of law, surely, poking around a crime scene like this? But another part of her wanted to stay, wanted to see before it was too late. See the dead man before they carted him off.

It was like the morbid fascination that affects people driving past the scene of an accident, but it wasn't only that. She came closer without actually making a conscious decision to do so, her legs moving of their own volition, taking her round the side of the barn. A group of men and a woman were crowding round a figure dressed in dark clothing who was lying in an odd position on the gravel.

Her camera phone was burning a hole in her pocket. Seja forced herself not to look away. She took a few steps closer. Somewhere behind her she could hear Åke being told off for having destroyed evidence by picking up a chewing-gum wrapper. She heard the words murder investigation uttered in a stern female voice. It didn't concern Seja. Only this body concerned her.

A moment of confusion arose when she finally saw the man's face. She ransacked her memory, her mind racing. He didn't look the way she remembered him. She felt both relieved and disappointed at the same time.

She wouldn't have dared to sneak out her mobile if it hadn't been for the fact that she was even more afraid to encounter the dead body without some form of protection. She shot from the hip, and each time she pressed the button she expected one of the uniformed officers to come rushing over and grab the phone. But it didn't happen, and as long as the button was clicking between her and the glassy eyes, half-covered by a milky film, she could cope.

Close his eyes, for fuck's sake. The words leapt into her mind and the thought surprised her.

The navy-blue Helly Hansen sweater was similar to the one her father had often worn under his jacket during the winter. The blonde hair was drenched in blood; it had stiffened and darkened. "Close his eyes," she repeated in a whisper, and she could no longer hold back the tears.

Tell reappeared. For a second he met her tear-filled eyes with an intense questioning expression before waving Åke into a police van parked by the side of the road. She ran across the grass, feeling that she had been caught out.

In the van there was a Thermos flask on a folded-down table, along with a stack of plastic cups and some broken ginger biscuits in a tin with no lid.

"Coffee?"

Seja nodded mutely, although her stomach was churning. Christian Tell busied himself serving the coffee. His hands had a calming effect on her; they were broad, and in the light from the steamed-up window she could see the fair hairs on the back of them. He wasn't wearing a wedding ring.

"So . . . you made the call, Åke. Is it OK if I call you Åke?"

Åke nodded. He still looked pale.

"Did you know the victim? Who he was? His name?"

"No, no idea. Edell, I mean that's what it says on the sign."

Tell turned to Seja. She shook her head.

"OK, so your call came in at 07.49, Åke. By that time you had found the body and driven up to the main road."

Seja couldn't bring herself to look Tell in the eye. She left her steaming cup of coffee where it was — her hands wouldn't do as they were told, they were shaking and would have given her away immediately. And yet she couldn't do the obvious thing and tell him what had really happened, that she hadn't been there when the body was found. She was painfully aware of the shapeless black heap just a few metres away. The corpse. She carried on staring down at her red chapped hands.

Tell went on: "I need to know, as accurately as possible, what time it was when you arrived at the garage and found the body."

Åke cleared his throat.

"Er . . . I, or rather we, left home — we're neighbours, you see — at half past six. I know that for sure because I saw the six-thirty bus at the stop."

Happy now because he had managed to be helpful, give concrete information. Then he frowned.

"I was driving quite slowly, of course, because as I said there was something wrong with the car. The exhaust pipe fell off up by the petrol station. It must have taken me a while to tie it back on. Twenty minutes, maybe. Then I looked — I mean we looked for the garage . . ."

"So you did know the place?"

"No . . . well, I knew it must be around here somewhere, if it was still open. I'd only driven past it before, seen the sign, and that was a few years ago. I usually go to Christer. Or sometimes I go to Nordén & Son in Lerum. I've always —"

"So that was all the two of you did: you drove up to the main road and made the call. So can we make a rough guess that you found the body say ten or fifteen minutes before you called?"

Åke nodded again.

"Yes, I think I — I mean we — sat at the bus stop for a while, but it can't have been long. Just to gather my thoughts. I mean I was in shock, you understand. I realise I should have stayed here, of course, until you arrived, but . . . I wasn't even thinking. I just wanted to get away. It didn't even occur to me that I had a telephone with me. I haven't had one long, but my wife —"

"It's perfectly fine, I realise the first impulse is to get away," said Tell reassuringly. Åke seemed to relax slightly. He took a gulp of his coffee and crossed his legs.

Tell leaned forward.

"I want you to tell me exactly what happened, as accurately as you can. Did you see anything in particular? Did you hear anything? Did anything seem odd? Whatever comes to mind."

While Åke Melkersson took his time formulating his reply, Tell spotted Karlberg chatting to the doctor who had certified the death. The medics were getting ready to move the body into the ambulance, and Tell considered asking them to wait. He would have liked to go over the way the man was lying one more time before they moved him, but decided to let it go.

Reluctantly he turned his attention back to the disparate couple in front of him, just in time to see Seja cast a pleading look at Åke. She shrugged her shoulders.

"I didn't really see anything other than what Åke has already told you."

"Can we just go through it once more, Åke?"

"The house looked empty but the door of the workshop was open. There was a light on inside. I went in to have a look, I called out but nobody answered. The radio was on — *Soothing Favourites*. I usually listen to that myself."

"Good. That's something else. And where were you, Seja, when Åke went off to look for help?"

"In the car. I stayed in the car, so I didn't see . . . the dead man." *If you're going to lie successfully, say as little as possible.*

Tell nodded slowly. When she didn't go on he turned back to Åke, who picked up where he had left off.

"I decided to take a walk around and see what was happening. I mean it seemed as if somebody was there, or had been there not long ago."

Åke pointed in the direction of the yard by tapping on the van window.

"And then I saw him. He was just lying there. I could see straight away that he was dead. I didn't get too close . . . then I think I . . . brought up my breakfast. It happened so suddenly, I mean you don't expect to find someone, not like that . . ."

"It's perfectly understandable, Åke. Perfectly understandable."

Tell had taken out a notebook and started jotting down some points. The colour had come back to Åke's cheeks, and he had regained his confidence. He risked a question.

"I was just wondering . . . He'd been shot, hadn't he? Someone shot him and then ran over him?"

Tell glanced up from his notes and pushed his fringe out of his eyes.

"It's up to the pathologist to establish the cause of death. But he's definitely been shot, so we can assume that's what killed him."

He took a packet of cigarettes from his inside pocket and shook one out with an apologetic smile. Seja noticed he had a crooked front tooth, which made him look younger.

"It's not acceptable to smoke anywhere these days, but if you don't mind I'm going to have a couple of drags."

He smiled again, slightly embarrassed, and turned away to exhale the smoke, which immediately filled the small space. Seja felt her nausea welling up, like a delayed reaction, and suddenly she was enormously and irrationally irritated with this ugly, attractive, smug man who clearly thought the world was there for his convenience, although he did stub out the cigarette after two drags.

"So, back to your story . . . Åke, you said the car broke down and you couldn't drive it from the bus stop where you made the phone call. So the car you arrived in just now, that's not the one that broke down?"

"No. I had to leave the Opel up there by the road. I didn't have anything else to secure the exhaust pipe with."

"I understand. But the person who came to help you, I presume that person was driving the dark blue Hyundai you just arrived in?" He looked out through the steamed-up window. The Hyundai was in full view a little way off. "Who does the car belong to?"

He's looking at the registration number.

"Me," said Seja quickly.

Her impulse was to stand up and walk out.

"So someone borrowed your car to come out and pick you up. Did you drop that person off somewhere, before you came here?"

Åke gasped for breath a little too loudly and nodded.

"Exactly. In Hjällbo. It was my wife, Kristina. Her sister lives in Hjällbo, so I dropped her off there. We dropped her off there."

His face was now quite red, and a vein was throbbing in his temple just below the edge of his fur hat. Seja was just about to put a stop to the whole charade by explaining what had really happened, that she was to blame because she was so insanely curious, that she had wanted to write a crime report or just to see a dead body, but then Tell closed his notebook.

"I noticed that the back seats were folded down."

The comment broke Seja's train of thought.

"I had horse fodder in the back."

She knocked over her coffee cup, which contained only the last few dregs. A thin stream ran towards the edge of the table and dripped on to her knee. Christian Tell passed her some toilet roll.

"Where was Kristina sitting?" he said.

"Kristina?" said Seja stupidly.

Tell nodded.

"Where was Kristina sitting, if you were driving and Åke was sitting next to you and the back seats were folded down?"

Seja wiped her trouser leg with exaggerated care. She sighed when the silence became too much for her.

"Nowhere," she admitted. "She wasn't with us. I lied because I didn't want to leave Åke alone."

Tell nodded tersely.

"Right, let's start from the beginning. And let's have the truth this time."

CHAPTER
FOUR

1993

Once upon a time there was a workhouse close to a mountain lake; apart from the house there were only gravel tracks covering the forest landscape like a spider's web.

The red three-storey house with its high stone foundations still sits there on the edge of the forest. The lake still reflects the clouds when there is not a breath of wind. The gravel area in front of the house is just the same, apart from the fact that three cars have been carelessly parked there, their paintwork dulled by the dust from the road.

On the side of the minibus it says STENSJÖ FOLK HIGH SCHOOL, and something else that has been eroded to the point of illegibility. And it is also Stensjö Folk High School that is filling up all the rooms. She will soon be familiar with the history of the house. She will also find out that it is boiling hot in the summer beneath the roof beams — she will be one of the few who do not leave Stensjö during the summer break. In the winter an open fire burns in the common room on the ground floor, but its warmth does not find its way up to the boarders' bedrooms. The electric radiators are of course turned up to maximum, but they barely keep the worst of the cold at bay.

It has taken Maya almost a whole day to get there, travelling by bus and train up through the country. It is a cleansing process: she is leaving Borås with its suburbs and outlying areas and the strategies she has so far employed in order to get by. No one knows where she is going, well, her family does, but no one in her circle of acquaintances. As far as they are concerned she has disappeared in a puff of smoke. Perhaps she is letting people down, but no one would be able to take her to task for that. After all, it is a well-known fact that morality is closely linked to the risk of discovery.

She is not quite eighteen, and three years seems an absolute eternity. No one will even remember her when she goes back, if she ever does go back. All the people to whom she has been so closely bound during those turbulent teenage years will have entered the adult world they know so little of as yet. A world they want to forswear, nevertheless, as if it were a matter of life and death. They think they are defending themselves against the boring, middle-class mentality of adulthood, but in fact it is their childhood they are fighting against.

The idea of flight has always been like a balm to her soul, often with the help of drugs: hash, trips and amphetamine bombs rolled in scraps of cigarette paper and swallowed with a glass of water. Now she is running away with the feeling that this is her last chance. That she is jumping on the last train to somewhere completely unknown. It is terrifying, but not as terrifying as what she knows is waiting if she stays in town: the meetings with stiff-necked social workers; the youth centre with its employment training programme because she dropped out of grammar school; in the long term, a residential facility for young people.

And she would continue to pretend to fit in with her friends while at the same time feeling a marked distance that only she seemed to see: those last few inches of closeness that were simply not there. She had chosen the security of the gang because she felt even more of an outsider with everyone else. And her circle of acquaintances has at least formed some kind of fixed point, even if it is more apparent than structured. They have made something of having grown up in the wake of prog music, freshly plucked from both the hippie movement and punk; they have been political in those contexts where it attracts attention, running the gauntlet at every opportunity to demonstrate, going barefoot or sitting cross-legged on the streets in the town centre. But the drugs have a definite tendency to take over.

She has never been afraid of ending up an addict; the drugs were to make her happier, to enable her to stay awake at night, to have the courage to be against something or for something. She has never been afraid of getting hooked on them, only of getting hooked on the rest of it — never being able to move on, suddenly realising one day that she has forgotten what she was for or against, that the revolt has faded into everyday life and she is no longer streetwise, just bloody stubborn. She has always been afraid of being pathetic.

She is sitting in the buffet car on the train to Stensjö, writing in her black notebook. It's an ordinary black book with a red spine, although she has stuck a newspaper cutting on the cover: Ulrike Meinhof, a black and white prison photograph. Beneath the picture it says, *This book belongs to Maya.* On the lined pages are her poems.

She writes a great deal but keeps very little. If her words frighten her once the heat has died down, she burns them. Even as she sits on the train she scrutinises and crosses out old words in a frenzy of shame. And yet the poetry she keeps is painfully unstructured, self-centred and obscured by powerful unidentified emotions. As if to force some future reader to feel the mood of the author rather than his own. It is mostly about love, because she has devoted the years since leaving junior school to believing that she is constantly in love, among other things.

A middle-aged ice cream maker tries to strike up a conversation with her in the buffet car. He asks almost straight away what she does for a living, and she tells him she is unemployed. It sounds more mature than saying that she has dropped out of school and hasn't yet decided what to do with her life. He waves vaguely in the air as if to say it's nothing to be embarrassed about.

"I've got money, but I don't think I'm better than anyone else because of that. I'm just as happy talking to a company director as to someone who's out of work and has a ring through their nose," he says.

He invites her to share one of the tiny ridiculously expensive bottles of wine they keep behind the counter. She accepts his offer. After a glass of red he gets personal and wants to talk about his ex-wife. She soon loses interest.

"I'm just going to the toilet," she says, and goes to sit a couple of tables behind him. The lie, when he discovers it on his way back to his seat, doesn't seem to bother him. Perhaps he's used to it.

She starts a letter to her mother. She writes that growing up has been *the very opposite of an Oedipal child's great fear*. Her father has never even existed on paper, and so there was no united parental front to make her feel alone and excluded. Instead her anxious mother, desperate for approval, wanted to carry her daughter close to her heart; to keep her like a child as yet unborn. Intimate. Like a partner. *Mum. I have to put some distance between us in order to be free of you*. In her mind's eye she can see her mother opening the envelope as if it were a great event. As if she had been waiting for the moment when she would finally understand her daughter. As if she had spent years wondering.

But deep down Maya knows that her mother has not spent years wondering, despite all the arguments and reconciliations. Not really. Her mother has had enough to cope with just looking after herself.

In the notebook Maya has scrawled on page after page, words that have somehow burned themselves into her mind, embarrassing and full of overblown emotions. It was a significant part of her adolescence, this revelling in her emotional life. Constantly giving every Tom, Dick and Harry information about how she is feeling, which is not so different from her mother, in fact. She has frightened off a whole load of potential boyfriends in this way. She spoke with such insight about angst that the supervisor at the youth centre contacted the psychiatric service. He was afraid she might be suicidal. Which, after some consideration, she feels she wasn't really, not at that particular time.

Out in the wilds she is picked up by the minibus at a bus stop with a shelter on the narrow tarmac road. The bus to and from the railway station evidently runs just twice a day, once in the morning and once in the afternoon, and is the only way to travel to the school if, like Maya, you have neither a car nor a driving licence.

The end of August brings the heat of high summer when the sun is at its zenith. The evenings have begun to grow cooler as autumn approaches. In her suitcase is a blank calendar boasting of a fresh start, her nicest clothes and a mishmash of things representing the room she had as a girl and her earlier life. Being seventeen means that every step is for ever.

Her stomach is churning. Apart from that she is stone-faced behind the black-painted eyes and lips. She is wearing black jeans, a black long-sleeved sweater and Doc Martens. She took the ring out of her nose at the railway station, only to put it back in ten minutes later.

It is difficult to decide how she will behave until she has observed what the others are like.

Most of all she is afraid of having to share a room with someone. That is also the first thing she asks the woman who pulls over in front of her on the empty road, just as she thinks the school bus is going to drive past her. The woman responds with an inscrutable smile, if indeed it is a smile. It makes Maya feel embarrassed because she has forgotten to introduce herself. She realises then that it is the borderlands that are the most difficult.

Being angry and rebellious is easy; being well-behaved is something she knows all about. If you're a girl and you've grown up in a small town, gone through school before the equal opportunities programme kicked in, you get to be good at making room for other people. Standing with one foot in each camp in front of a woman who is ten years older than you, with cropped hair and a leather waistcoat worn over paint-stained dungarees, with that smile and that indulgent expression — that's the difficult part. She thought her appearance would protect her. Instead she wishes she could turn back the clock. She wants to be a blank sheet of paper coming to this new situation, with nothing to fall back on.

The woman throws Maya's bag into the back of the bus. She has a pale rose tattooed on her upper arm. It looks as if something had been written on the leaves of the rose, something that has almost been erased. Down the side of her neck winds the shape of a black snake. For a second Maya thinks it looks ominous.

Next to the main building a handful of smaller cottages are scattered over the lawn. High above the roofs are the tops of deciduous trees, their trunks so gnarled and thick that you probably couldn't put your arms all the way round them. Maya has no idea what kind of tree they are. She wonders if there is a garden round the back, and feels a sudden impulse to become a child again, to run around the corner and have a look. Maybe hide deep inside the leafy greenery. Instead she stands on the gravel, rooted to the spot.

She stands there until Caroline comes back and takes her by the hand, leading her on her way to her first day at school. Through the brown doors and up the stairs to the attic, where the boarders' rooms lie. Maya switches off the bigger picture, as she always does when she feels stressed, and silently adds together the details. Stains and scratches beneath the shining surface of the varnish on the staircase. The black snake on the neck. Long snakes of scar tissue winding their way up the inside of Caroline's arms, towards the crease of her elbow.

Maya just goes along with her.

CHAPTER
FIVE

2006

The fried cod eaten in haste, along with countless cups of coffee and several ginger biscuits during the course of the morning, had left a stale taste in his mouth. Tell had intended to top up his cup yet again when he discovered to his annoyance that someone had removed the coffee maker from the kitchenette. Instead, a huge apparatus had been placed in the corridor, and apparently countless drinks could be ordered through this machine. He hadn't even heard of most of them.

"Vanilla macchiato. What the hell is that?"

Renée Gunnarsson, one of the indispensable office staff, was walking by and patted him on the back.

"Aren't you up to date with all that kind of thing, Christian? You're a city boy after all. Don't you go to cafés?"

"Not recently," he muttered, pressing a button at random. You couldn't go far wrong with café au lait. The machine started grinding coffee beans, and finished off with a long drawn-out hiss as the foaming milk covered the top of the paper cup like a blanket.

"At last, a proper coffee machine!"

Karin Beckman's eyes were sparkling like a child's on Christmas Eve. She immediately started to run through the list of choices.

"Café chocolat, Café mint, Café au lait, Café crème, Macchiato, Latte . . ."

"And you call that proper coffee?"

Bengt Bärneflod joined the more or less admiring group surrounding the machine. For once, Tell nodded appreciatively at his older colleague. They had worked together since Tell joined the squad fourteen years ago. A sudden awareness of the passage of time made him punch Bärneflod playfully on the shoulder.

"Come on, Bengt, for God's sake! Who wants to live in the past? Of course we need café au lait in this place!" He took a large gulp and pulled a face at the chemically sweetened drink.

"Right, I'm going to find our good old coffee maker. Where the hell has it gone, anyway?" Bärneflod looked at Karlberg with a challenging expression as he stuck his head out of his office, as if he were personally responsible for the removal of the old machine.

"OK, we've got a murder on our hands, in case you haven't noticed," Tell said. "Conference room in five minutes, please."

He clapped his hands impatiently like a PE teacher, and could just imagine them all rolling their eyes behind his back as he walked away. Tough. It was part of his job to get people working.

Ten minutes later Karin Beckman drew Tell's attention to his unconscious but probably extremely irritating

40

habit of clicking his ballpoint pen, by placing her hand on his wrist. He *was* stressed, anxious inside, as he always was at the outset of a murder investigation.

He looked around the room, examining his colleagues in what was inaccurately known as the murder squad. They still hadn't finished joking about the finer points of the coffee machine or the bag of buns in the shape of animals that Karlberg had chucked down on the table with some embarrassment. He'd obviously been baking with his niece.

Bengt Bärneflod, sitting to the left of Tell, looked increasingly tired with every passing day, and Tell often caught him doing crosswords during working hours. He was also increasingly prone to expressing less than sympathetic views on immigrants. These days he constantly maintained that everything had been better in the old days, *when you could sing the national anthem without the risk of treading on someone's toes.* And he hardly ever took the initiative any more. But he was good in a critical situation. The slowness that got on Tell's nerves the rest of the time served him well then, for he could persuade any lunatic at least to listen, if not to be entirely reasonable.

Beside him sat Andreas Karlberg, who in contrast to Bengt never expressed a single opinion about anything. He was ambitious and well intentioned, but was often like a weathervane in a strong breeze.

Karin Beckman was experienced and had been a promising investigator before she had kids, Christian Tell thought bitterly — although naturally he would never dare to be so politically incorrect as to say this out loud. Dead on five o'clock she dropped whatever she was doing and went home, quoting some law and the union. On top of that, both her daughters were still at nursery school, and she was off almost every other day looking after one of them because they were ill. At times he had completely given up counting on her as part of the team. But to look on the bright side, things could only get better from now on. The kids were growing up, after all, and she was hardly likely to have any more; she'd already turned forty.

She was a good police officer, though, when she was working. He had to admit that. And she was good in sensitive situations. She had a good knowledge of people, a competence when it came to psychological issues. Sometimes that kind of insight was lacking in the squad. And she had almost finished the basic psychotherapy training she had been undertaking for the past two years. It would be good for the squad to be able to rely on her full time again.

As far as Michael Gonzales was concerned, Tell hadn't really had time to form a definite opinion. He had only been working with the squad for about a year, and hadn't yet been involved in any major investigations. Gonzales was the only officer who had actually grown up and still lived in an area that was over-represented in the crime statistics — it was something he had mentioned in his initial interview. Tell probably hadn't been the only one to think that the squad might be able to make use of his contacts and experiences, even if this was an idea somewhat coloured by prejudice. In fact, Gonzales' contacts with the underworld would turn out to be negligible; on the contrary, he appeared to be miraculously naive. Even though he had legally been of age for ten years, he still lived at home and had no plans to move out, as far as Tell could discern. The high-quality service provided by Mrs Gonzales wasn't something he intended to swap for a bachelor pad with piles of dirty dishes and laundry. However, he seemed to be sufficiently intelligent to understand that he couldn't count on being treated like a little prince in any other context. With endearing self-awareness he told them what had happened when he got into the police training academy — Francesca Gonzales had wept for over a week out of sheer happiness, until the neighbours had told her in no uncertain terms to pack it in.

In any case, Gonzales was a diligent officer, ready to learn. He was also a textbook example of positive thinking, which was not to be sniffed at in a job like this.

Tell turned his gaze back to Karlberg. Perhaps it wasn't fair to think of him as a weathervane. It was more that he had a subtle ambition which, if Tell were to make use of the self-awareness he had acquired during his forty-four years, didn't threaten Tell's own ego. Karlberg worked quietly from his own hypotheses, which were frequently well thought out, without making a fuss about it. He sneezed loudly and wiped his nose with the back of his hand in some embarrassment.

Leaning against the door frame stood Chief Inspector Ann-Christine Östergren, dressed as always in black: velvet trousers and a polo-neck sweater, contrasting sharply with her instantly recognisable white frizzy hair, which stood out like a curly halo around her lined face.

She was a good boss; the squad were in agreement on that, even if they all had different views on what made a good boss. She knew what she was doing and had plenty of experience after spending almost her entire working life as a female police officer in a male-dominated world. During the six or seven years she had been in her current post she had built up a strong sense of trust among her colleagues, despite the fact that in the beginning there had been gossip that she had moved because of irreconcilable differences in her previous job.

What Tell appreciated most was her clear readiness to rely on her team, the ability to delegate tasks and responsibilities without constantly feeling the need to check up and make adjustments according to her own views. There was an unspoken agreement between Tell and Östergren: as long as he did his job and made sound decisions, he didn't need to keep running to her to check every step he took during an investigation. And that was just the way he liked it.

Östergren cleared her throat, and just before she began to speak Tell caught sight of Beckman discreetly raising her eyebrows in the direction of Renée Gunnarsson. Renée sat in on the initial meetings so that she would know the direction the investigation was going to take; this was because part of her job involved dealing with telephone calls from the press and anxious members of the public. It would be Christian Tell's decision as to how much should be revealed and which questions should be passed on to the investigating team.

Gunnarsson rolled her eyes at Beckman in return. Tell suspected that this silent exchange of views was to do with the fact that Östergren was standing in the doorway rather than sitting down at the table like the rest of the group. Tell was annoyed with Beckman and Gunnarsson's attitude. Instead of being so ready to criticise her, surely they ought to be supporting their female colleague? But wasn't it often the case that women were most critical of other women?

"OK, listen up. As you all know a man has been found dead, in all probability murdered, on one of the minor roads between Olofstorp and Hjällbo, in Björsared to be precise. I say in all probability because we're still waiting for the report from the pathologist, but given the fact that he had been shot in the head, we can assume that was the cause of death. He was also — probably after death, but we're also waiting for confirmation on that — run over several times by a vehicle. Most likely a car."

Östergren took off her glasses and held them in front of her for a moment before rubbing off a mark with the sleeve of her sweater.

"The location is under the jurisdiction of the Angered police force, and I have already been in touch with their chief. He's promised to give us as much support as he can in the form of manpower and local knowledge. Unfortunately it's obvious they've got their hands full at the moment — a whole load of arson attacks and some kind of burglary boom over the past few weeks. We have therefore agreed that they will step in as and when they are needed rather than giving us an officer on a permanent basis. To begin with we will work together on the routine matters: door-to-door enquiries, checking for any similar crimes, anyone on release from psychiatric care — I'm sure you get the idea."

She nodded in Tell's direction.

"Christian Tell will be coordinating the operation. The whole team will get together for a follow-up meeting next Monday, or whenever Christian decides it's appropriate. Anyway, you can talk to them about all that, Christian. Over to you."

She put on her glasses and left with a tense smile. Although he couldn't quite put his finger on it, Tell thought he perceived an uncharacteristic distance in Östergren. He wondered for a moment if something had happened in her private life. But Ann-Christine Östergren wasn't the kind of person you would tackle about something like that. If she wanted to talk, she would.

"OK, so we have a dead man, executed and run over. According to the electoral register one Lise-Lott Edell and one Lars Waltz live at that address. We haven't been able to get in touch with her yet, but hopefully a more thorough investigation will tell us where she is and how we can get hold of her. Karlberg, you and I will head straight over there after this meeting. There are actually two companies registered to Lise-Lott Edell: the main one is a fabric shop in Gråbo, and then there's Thomas Edell's vehicle repair workshop and scrapyard. The latter operates from the scene of the crime."

Yet another loud sneeze from Karlberg frightened the wits out of Bärneflod, who was doodling psychedelic patterns on his notepad. Karlberg didn't look good at all. Tell had managed not to notice that his colleague had been coming down with a cold over the past few days, but now you couldn't miss it: Karlberg's nose was glowing like a beacon, and his eyes were covered with a fine network of red lines. Beckman wasn't slow to put Tell's thoughts into words, although diplomacy wasn't her strong point.

"Bloody hell, Andreas, you look rough. Shouldn't you be at home in bed?"

Karlberg shrugged his shoulders. It was the best he could do to avoid a discussion that often caused bad feeling. On the one hand there were those who came to work whatever state they were in due to an ambitious attitude to work, but also to police pay and benefits and a general shortage of money. And then there were those who chose to stay at home to minimise the risk of passing on the infection to their colleagues. Over the years these differences of opinion had developed into a matter of principle.

Karlberg pulled his fleece more tightly around his shoulders and gratefully accepted the packet of tissues Beckman pushed across the table. Tell took a sip of the sweet, cloying coffee before he went on.

"For the time being we can proceed with the hypothesis that the man lying in the yard is Lars Waltz.

47

Please note that this is only a hypothesis. He had no form of identification on him so he could also have been an employee. We've sent the body off to Strömberg and will have a verbal report as soon as he knows anything. I don't need to tell you that this investigation is our top priority."

He scratched his head.

"We'll make a start on door-to-door enquiries as soon as possible, working with the Angered police. Beckman can take care of that, along with Gonzales. The gravel track follows an arc, parallel to the main road. Call at every house in both directions up as far as the road. It's possible we might have to go round again once Strömberg has established the exact time of death, but it won't do any harm to ask people twice. The first time they're too shaken up to think clearly."

Bärneflod was drawing matchstick men in his diary when he felt Tell's eyes on him.

"Bengt, you can look after things here until we have more to go on. Look for anyone else who might be involved, as many people as you can find. As soon as you've got a list, start sorting them into groups. Relatives, employees and so on. Call me on my mobile then we can decide together how to tackle things."

"Are the technical team out there at the moment?"

"Yes. They're not exactly cheering, but the tyre tracks are pretty clear, so we might get something from those. There might be fibres too. There's a chewing-gum wrapper — the old guy who was first on the scene picked it up — but to be honest, the probability that the murderer decided to have a piece of chewing gum while he was waiting to murder Waltz isn't strong."

"Not to mention the chance of finding a decent fingerprint among all the rest on a wrapper from some newspaper kiosk."

That was Bärneflod's contribution.

"Exactly. Talking of the old guy, one . . . Åke Melkersson." Tell read from his notes. "And his neighbour Seja Lundberg, we need to take a closer look at those two."

"Why?"

The sharpness in his voice gave away how offended Bärneflod was. He ought to be grateful to escape shitty jobs such as knocking on doors while the rain was lashing down, but he seemed to feel that Tell was doing more than looking after Bärneflod's creature comforts by leaving him out of the main investigation.

"Because they were first on the scene. And because they lied."

Tell stood up a little too quickly and managed to knock over his chair, which fell backwards with a crash.

"OK, let's get a move on."

He turned to Karlberg, who already had his jacket on.

CHAPTER
SIX

It was as if a sigh passed through the plane as it landed.

At last. Lise-Lott Edell realised every muscle in her body had been tense ever since they left Puerto de la Cruz. Next time she flew she was going to take a taxi out to Landvetter instead of leaving the car in the long-stay car park. Not that she travelled a great deal; it had been eight years since her last trip abroad. But that was exactly why she should have been able to indulge herself with a whisky or a Martini on the plane to calm her nerves. Her fear of flying certainly hadn't lessened over the years.

"You look as if you've seen a ghost!" said Marianne when the plane finally came to a halt. Marianne had seemed completely unmoved by the fact that the plane was sufficiently high up in the air for the earth to look like an abstract map of itself. She had even said that she loved flying, as if sitting on a plane was the next best thing to being able to fly under your own steam. A feeling of freedom — filled with expectation about the coming holiday, or sated with tales to tell, memories to cherish.

Her pronouncements might have had something to do with the fact that she *had* had a drink, or a couple to be accurate. Not that this particularly bothered Lise-Lott — if you were on holiday, you were on holiday. But there was no doubt that Marianne's fondness for a tipple had made Lise-Lott look like a Sunday school teacher. And there was no doubt that the nightcap in the hotel bar after they'd done the round of all the pubs and clubs had been one drink too many for Marianne. Every night.

Despite this, Lise-Lott was more than happy with her trip, and grateful that her friend had eagerly agreed to come along when she had suggested as late as the previous week that they should take a last-minute holiday in the sun. After all, Lars could never get away because there was just too much work in the winter. And the few short weeks in the summer had a tendency to disappear while they mowed the lawn and fixed things in the house that had been waiting all year. The thought depressed her.

There wasn't really anything wrong with the way they felt about each other. They loved each other and still had plenty to talk about, and they still wanted each other — if only they had time to talk or the energy to make love. It was stupid, really: two people burying themselves in their work to the extent that they had no time to live.

They had only been married for six years, but with Lars having two jobs and Lise-Lott getting the fabric shop up and running, which had been a dream come true but had cost so much in terms of time and energy, they had already begun to drift apart. She recognised the signs: Lars fell asleep downstairs on the sofa in front of the television more and more often. She would hear him nod off and drop the remote on the floor. When she got up in the small hours to go to the toilet, the war of the ants would have taken over the television screen. He didn't always bother to have a shower before he came to bed after working on the cars, and the smell of oil and petrol put a definitive stop to her interest in marital relations.

He was also spending an increasing amount of time in the darkroom, developing his photos. That was his second job, even if the line between job and hobby was only a hair's breadth when the activity in question took up time without actually generating any money. In the 80s he had published a book of photographs which received very good reviews, but these days it was mostly a case of commissions from the local council, pictures for brochures and that sort of thing, which brought in a little extra cash. He had tried the advertising industry for a few years and had done fairly well as an art director before he developed an allergy to computer screens and, with considerable relief, was forced to abandon his ambitions on that front.

But photography was still the activity closest to his heart. Apart from that he really only wanted a job that would bring in money and wouldn't make any more demands on him than he was prepared to meet. He wanted to be able to work less so that he had more time for his passion. At least that had been the logic when he gratefully agreed to run Thomas's old workshop. It was just that the hours in the workshop on top of the hours in the darkroom turned out to be far more than a full-time job, which was something he perhaps hadn't reckoned with.

Lise-Lott no longer had any idea what he was developing in his darkroom. That was the saddest sign — the fact that he had stopped taking photographs of her. When they first met she had been his favourite subject. Lise-Lott in bright sunlight, Lise-Lott when she'd just woken up, Lise-Lott slightly tipsy, her eyes seductively half closed. She had loved it, once she had got over her initial shyness of course.

That was the price they'd had to pay for fulfilling their dreams and combining their work with their interests: they had to work all the time. But it was fortunate that Lars had the workshop to provide a steady income, fortunate that Thomas had left her the workshop and that she had been so stubborn, or perhaps so incapable of doing anything, that she hadn't sold it straight after his death. It was also fortunate that she had met Lars and that he had been handy with cars.

She thought about how lucky she had been, and this put her in a better mood. Despite everything, Lars was a real catch.

A middle-aged widow in a run-down house out in the middle of nowhere with a car workshop and no employees wasn't exactly at the top of anyone's wish list, but Lars had seen her qualities. Not only on the inside, but on the outside — his camera had brought out a beauty she didn't know she possessed, and presumably no one else did either. It was also Lars who had persuaded her to follow her dream, who had supported her every time she almost lost heart in the struggle to open her fabric shop. He could make most things seem easy. And with that attitude everything became achievable.

Looking back now, she couldn't understand why she had gone through life being so afraid of . . . of failing, perhaps. She had grown several centimetres in the last few years, she felt. That might have had something to do with the fact that she had shrunk several centimetres during her marriage to Thomas, and that she had rediscovered herself and her self-confidence in the calm waters of a normal relationship with a normal, nice guy. Whatever the reason, she was very happy.

In the car on the way home she decided that things were going to change, and that she was going to initiate that change. From now on they would invest more time in each other. Special candlelit dinners, taking a bath together, romantic weekends at that little hotel in Österlen. She started planning, aware of the soppy grin on her face. It didn't matter, because Marianne was fast asleep beside her, her cheek pressed against the seat belt. She had a red stripe on her temple when Lise-Lott helped her unload her suitcases outside her terraced house.

"Thanks for a fantastic week, Lise-Lott. Can we do it again next year?"

Lise-Lott waved as she drove off. She had a good feeling in her stomach. Christmas wasn't far away, and for once she could hardly wait to make a start on the preparations.

54

She felt a great sense of calm as she made the sharp turn on to the gravel track. She would be home in a few seconds.

CHAPTER
SEVEN

They hadn't needed to break open the front door when they went into Lise-Lott Edell's house that morning; a cellar window had been left ajar. Karlberg was constantly surprised at how careless people were when it came to their hard-won possessions. Mostly people fell into two categories: a minority who went over the top and built walls taller than the house, got themselves a guard dog or a security firm or ridiculously expensive alarm systems; and then there was the vast majority who fastened the front door with a double lock and left the cellar window open.

Perhaps they hadn't thought a burglar would find his way to a house that was as inaccessible as this one. Perhaps all the years in the job had damaged Karlberg.

At any rate, the murderer had found his way here. Karlberg gave an involuntary shudder at the thought.

The neighbour — they couldn't exactly chat over the fence, although they might be able to exchange light signals across the fields on dark winter evenings — had informed them that Lise-Lott Edell was away on holiday.

"She's gone to the Canary Islands — on her own! While her man is at home working."

Yes, they were sure. Lise-Lott had told them all about it when they met in the shop.

"Lars hadn't time to go with her. Lars is the one who runs the workshop these days since Thomas — that's Lise-Lott's first husband — went and died. There's plenty of work because I hardly ever see him leave the place, but she goes past here every day. You can't help noticing, officer, because they have to drive past our house whenever they go anywhere. And if you're as old as Bertil and I you haven't got much to do apart from sit here and gaze out of the window. And there aren't that many people who drive along here these days."

Karlberg had declined coffee and cakes three times before he managed to get away. He could just imagine Tell's reaction if he'd sat dunking cake in his coffee in the middle of an investigation.

"We'll be back to ask you some more questions, fru Molin, probably tomorrow. It's good that you and your husband sit here looking out of the window; I'm sure you must have seen or heard something significant."

He backed out on to the steps and pulled his woolly hat down over his ears. But fru Molin wasn't satisfied. She was wringing her wrinkled hands.

"I mean, we just presumed it was a break-in. But then we saw an ambulance, and of course that made us wonder if something might have happened to Lars. That would be terrible! You shouldn't have to lose two husbands when you're as young as Lise-Lott. You understand, officer — I knew Thomas when he was just a little lad . . . and his father too, in fact. When Thomas died, it was just too much for Lise-Lott, looking after the house and the workshop. I mean she didn't know anything about cars or farming. For a while we thought she would sell up and move away, but . . . It would be absolutely dreadful if anything happened to Lars . . ."

"Thank you, fru Molin. I just wanted to check if you knew where your neighbours were, but as I said, I will be back."

Karlberg tramped across the muddy field, which was already beginning to freeze as the light faded. He could feel fru Molin's gaze on his back for a long time. At the bottom of the field, with a grove of trees behind it, the Edell property stood etched against the darkening sky.

Tell was smoking impatiently at the bottom of the steps when he got back. Karlberg was glad he hadn't spent too much time with the neighbour.

"The woman has gone off on holiday on her own," he informed Tell. "Lars, the husband, runs the workshop, but as far as I understand, Lise-Lott Edell owns the firm; she inherited it from her late husband."

"Thanks, we already knew that."

"Anyway, the neighbours seem to have a fair amount of information. It's probably worth having a chat with them again later."

Karlberg walked past Tell towards the front door, aware that with the mood his boss was in, it was best not to get involved in any kind of discussion. Best just to get on with the job.

An hour later they had gone through some of the mess contained in the kitchen drawers and the small office on the ground floor without finding anything that might help them get in touch with the woman who was supposed to be on holiday.

It was obvious that a woman lived in the house. The outside might have been in need of a coat of paint and the workshop wasn't exactly a statement in style, but the rooms of the house itself were pleasant and tidy.

"You might think the mouse would play while the cat's away, but that doesn't seem to be the case here," said Tell thoughtfully.

Karlberg shot him a questioning look.

"It's tidy. I mean, the husband has been looking after himself here, so you might expect to see a load of pizza boxes and empty beer cans on the coffee table. Or socks on the floor. Or maybe that's just the way I imagine these country mechanics live."

"Mmm. Either that or the wife has only just left. Perhaps he hasn't had time to make a mess yet."

At this point Karlberg realised he ought to have asked the neighbours when Lise-Lott Edell had gone away, and when she was expected back.

Tell didn't waste any time, of course.

"Did the old woman next door say when she left?"

"I forgot to ask," Karlberg admitted, but to his great relief a sigh was the only response. He liked working with Tell, he really did, but at this stage of the investigation, before he found a clear line to follow, a gallery of characters to start mapping, a motive, a suspicion, he could definitely be a pain in the arse.

"She might have run off," said Tell, "got tired of her husband and the whole thing."

"Somebody certainly got tired of him," said Karlberg with a wry smile. "Maybe it was her. Who murdered him, I mean. It wouldn't be the first time a woman has lashed out at a useless unfaithful husband who beats her up every time he's had a drink."

"Statistically it's the men who do the beating up who tend to kill the women," muttered Tell.

"OK, but it's the husband who's lying out there. Or who was lying out there. And the fact that the murderer ran over him below the waist . . . doesn't that suggest something sexual? Symbolically, I mean. Something to do with him being unfaithful? He's been screwing around and she's had enough and she runs over his lower body. Gets herself an alibi by booking a trip and pretending to go away. But in fact she doesn't go anywhere."

Karlberg was getting excited, and he noticed a spark in Tell's eyes.

Most murders were more or less straightforward. In a surprisingly large number of cases the perpetrator was still at the scene of the crime, ready to be arrested or sent to a psychiatric ward or a detox cell, in no condition even to think about getting rid of any clues or running away.

Tell wasn't buying Karlberg's hastily cobbled-together theory, that was obvious, but it clearly put him in a better mood.

"I think we'd better meet this woman and have a chat with her before we put her down as a murder suspect."

"The relatives are always suspects to start with," Karlberg persisted, but his words fell on deaf ears. Tell seemed to be communicating with a higher power as a pair of headlights appeared around the bend in the road.

From travelling at a comparatively high speed, the vehicle slowed and finally stopped ten metres from the entrance to the yard. For a minute or so Tell and Karlberg gazed across at the stationary car, painfully aware of what must be going through the mind of the person behind the wheel.

It was a woman who finally opened the door and stepped out on to the road, her movements endlessly slow: Lise-Lott Edell. Afterwards Karlberg would marvel at the fact that those close to someone who has died always know what's going on, long before the police have informed them and expressed their condolences. Lise-Lott Edell knew immediately that this was not a case of a break-in or criminal damage. Karlberg closed his eyes as the first scream echoed against the wall of the barn. It was going to be a long night.

CHAPTER
EIGHT

1993

She would think back to her room at Stensjö Folk High School as other people think back to their first apartment. In a way that was when she left home, even if she had spent weeks on end staying in town with older friends since she was fifteen. From now on she discounted the option of crashing out at her mother's when everything was spinning too fast, when life kicked her in the teeth. She wanted a new start, and the room beneath the sloping loft with the little handbasin next to the window represented it.

There was a faint smell of damp in the autumn and winter, but the first time she stepped in through the creaking door and gazed across the room and out through the window — you could see nothing but the sky and the tops of the trees — there was an aroma of summer dust and warm wood rising from the floor. There was a little cupboard tucked under the handbasin, and on the opposite wall was an ungainly linen cupboard with jade-green fabric fixed inside the glass doors. The cupboard was empty, but its smell resembled her grandmother's ointment and tiger balm. The only other furniture was a bed; she made it up with the bedclothes she'd brought from home. The bedspread was made up of crocheted stars.

Her early days at the school were terrible. In the evenings she would creep down to the little room on the ground floor and close the door silently, like a burglar. The walls of the telephone room were burgundy, and apart from the phone the room contained only a battered velvet armchair and a small wicker table with a large ashtray made of stone. Maya clutched the receiver and wondered who she could ring back home. She couldn't come up with anyone.

Above all the doors in the building was a sign with the name of the room. Perfectly adequate and perfectly understandable on the ground floor: CAFÉ, COMMON ROOM, OFFICE. On the first floor were the teaching rooms, dedicated to famous names, a daring mixture of film stars, authors, politicians and philosophers. The residential rooms had names taken from space: the narrow corridor was THE MILKY WAY and she slept in GALILEO. The loft was closest to the sky, after all.

Sometimes she would talk to Caroline, but not because she sought her out. On the contrary, Caroline made her nervous with her intense gaze, and Maya was relieved when she went away for a couple of days. At the same time she wondered where Caroline went. If she had a boyfriend to go home to.

The fact that they had any conversations at all was down to Caroline. She was stubborn, refusing to leave Maya in peace with her homesickness. She could see it and would mention it without a trace of embarrass-ment.

"You haven't settled in yet, have you?"

They were sitting at the back, on the steps leading into the garden. Maya didn't want to be a stroppy teenager; she wanted to answer. She longed for intimacy, but suddenly all she could focus on was the ant crawling boldly across her bare foot instead of choosing the longer way round. It was really too cold to go barefoot. The autumn had seized the garden in a firm grip after a few cold and rainy days, and her feet suddenly felt chilled to the bone.

"I didn't settle at first either. I absolutely hated it, thought I'd made completely the wrong choice. And I was scared as well."

Their conversations often followed this pattern. Caroline talked. Maya reacted silently in her mind to what Caroline said but never managed to think of answers quickly enough to come out with them.

"Now I'm celebrating my eighth year here. Hopefully I won't make the decade. You can get stuck in a little lost corner of the world because in the end you don't know what's waiting outside. So it's easier to stay."

"I think it's much more scary here. I mean, in town I knew my way around. I ran away from the whole shitty mess."

Maya said this without looking up. For a moment there was complete silence. Caroline threw back her head and stretched her legs out in front of her. She hummed thoughtfully but didn't speak. A light breeze rustled through the leaves.

"I ran away from the whole shitty mess too, eight years ago," she said finally. "I could see things were the same for you."

A wave of heat flooded up through Maya's chest, staining her throat with patches of red. She cursed her tendency to blush. In order to hide her face she rested her forehead on her knees and wrapped her arms around her shins.

"So do you live here?"

Caroline laughed and pointed to one of the little cottages on the edge of the forest.

"I've lived in that house over there for a couple of years now. Before that it was a studio for the painting and ceramics courses but they're held on the first floor now. For the first few years I lived in one of the attic rooms, but it's nice to have something of your own, a kitchen of your own and so on. It's good to be able to close the door when you don't want company and have a bit of peace and quiet."

"But don't you have an apartment to go to when you have time off?"

"Not any more. I got a place when I finished studying, but it was just standing empty during term time."

Caroline hesitated and seemed to be evaluating Maya with her gaze.

"I . . . I had a few problems before I ended up here. Such a lot happened. I don't really want to talk about it but let's just say that coming here was my salvation in many ways. So in the summer, when I realised that the idea of going away from here made me anxious, I was afraid that . . . Anyway, I got rid of the apartment."

Maya didn't let on that this confidence filled her with joy. She looked at the group of pupils standing outside the former studio, chatting loudly.

"You can't get that much peace and quiet!" she exclaimed.

Now Caroline was hiding her face in her hands. Close by, a squirrel was scampering up and down a tree trunk. Every time it reached the ground it seemed to come a little nearer, as if it were getting more used to the presence of people.

"You see, the idea of sitting by myself in an apartment trying to do something sensible with my life makes me go to pieces. I just haven't got the nerve to do it. Being alone is an art, and I'm no good at it."

Caroline picked up her shirt and her coffee cup.

"Hanging out with other people is an art too," said Maya by way of consolation.

Caroline got up. "Thank you for your kind words; they've warmed the poor heart of an inveterate navel-gazer! Next time it's your turn to lie on the couch."

"No thanks."

Maya rubbed at her frozen arms and shoulders. Cautiously, as if she were approaching a timid animal, Caroline leaned over her and placed her hands on Maya's shoulders, gently at first, as Maya held her breath.

Caroline smelled of smoke and sugar.

66

CHAPTER
NINE

2006

Lise-Lott Edell's slightly sunburned nose and cheekbones glowed in ridiculous red blotches against the pallor around her eyes.

"Breathe," mumbled Tell, gently but firmly bending the shocked woman's head down between her knees. She struggled against him, whimpering as if he were hurting her.

"You have to breathe. In, out. In, out. That's it."

Beckman stuck her head round the kitchen door without speaking, just to show that she had arrived. Tell nodded briefly at her, then knelt down in front of Lise-Lott Edell.

"You're in shock, and you shouldn't be left alone. Would you like me to ring someone? A relative, a girlfriend? Karin Beckman here will drive you if you want to go to someone's house. Or we can drive you to the doctor's. You might need something to calm you down, help you sleep."

She shook her head, and he heard a sob.

"No. No, I don't need a doctor. My sister is a doctor. She only lives a few kilometres from here."

Beckman bent down and placed her hand gently on Lise-Lott's hand.

"I'll drive you over there as soon as you're ready."

With a pang of sadness she noticed the pretty ring on the right hand. A wedding band with a turquoise stone. They hadn't had very long to love each other for better or worse.

"We're going to need to talk to you as soon as possible, Lise-Lott. We can do it now, but if you'd rather not, that's absolutely fine. A colleague and I can go with you to your sister's and talk to you there. Or we can have a chat first thing tomorrow morning. Or we can ring your sister and ask her to come over here."

Lise-Lott shook her head violently.

"No. I don't want anyone coming over to Angelika's with me. I'd rather talk now, get it out of the way."

Beckman glanced enquiringly at Tell; he shrugged almost imperceptibly. Carry on.

"Thank you, Lise-Lott. We appreciate it. The sooner we can sort out the circumstances surrounding this tragic . . . death, the quicker the person who did it will get the punishment they deserve. Just tell me if you want to stop."

"Could I have a glass of water, please?"

Her teeth were clenched so tightly that her temples had turned white. The suntan covered her face like a mask, and Tell realised how far away Puerto de la Cruz must seem right now, the heat she had left behind only a few hours ago. Since then her whole world had collapsed.

"He was planning a book of photographs of the area," said Lise-Lott, nodding towards a pile of prints. She had curled up in the corner of the sofa with a blanket around her shoulders, her hands wrapped around the cup of tea Beckman had produced. "He was fascinated by the landscape around here, the fact that it was so . . . untouched. That it's always looked like this, through the ages."

She gazed out of the window.

"I've heard that the forest over by Kitjärn could be classed as primeval. It was an old man on the council who told Lars; something to do with the fact that no human hand has shaped it . . ."

"I believe Lars wasn't from this area."

"No. I suppose you have to come from somewhere else to notice how impressive the surroundings are out here. Lars comes from the city. Came. From Gothenburg."

Her tears had dried up, but her expression was glassy. Tell suspected that she had taken something to calm her down a little while ago and he couldn't blame her.

"I moved here with my parents when I was a teenager. Of course at the time I thought it was the pits."

A wry smile passed over her face, turning to a grimace a second later.

"He enjoyed life so much. It's dreadful . . . unthinkable that someone . . ."

Tell waited while she pulled herself together, but Beckman got in first.

"That's just what we've been wondering. I know it might be difficult to think about it right now but can you think of anyone who might have wanted to hurt Lars? Someone he's fallen out with, through work or ... Do you know if he might have been doing anything ... suspicious? We have to ask," she said quickly as Lise-Lott looked at her in surprise.

"No, of course not. Who would want to murder him? He was an honest person, decent through and through."

"Take a moment," Tell interrupted. "Even if you have no proof, even if it seems like something completely banal. Has anyone threatened him? Has anything happened recently that you thought was strange? Anything out of the ordinary? Or has he met anyone new?"

The furrow between Lise-Lott's eyebrows indicated that she was trying to think, but in the end she shook her head helplessly.

"No, I can't think of anyone he's quarrelled with. I suppose it would be a customer who wasn't happy with the bill, maybe? I mean something to do with the garage . . .?"

She shrugged her shoulders.

"Lars did have an . . . an argument is overstating it, but he did have some differences of opinion with the person at the council in Lerum who used to give him commissions. Per-Erik Stahre, his name is. Lars thought they had agreed that he would be the first port of call for any photographic commissions for the council, but Stahre seemed to think he had the right to make decisions based on price, and last autumn he gave a big job to someone who was cheaper. It involved taking photographs of a new residential area on the outskirts of the town, and . . . well, it was going to pay quite well. Lars just thought Stahre should have discussed the price with him before he gave the job to someone else. We could have done with the money."

She shook her head. Tell nodded and made notes, but he could feel his spirits falling. You don't murder someone because of a garage bill or a minor dispute at work.

"We'd like you to keep us informed if you think of anyone else who might be of interest."

"His ex-wife. Lars got divorced when we met, and divorce is never much fun. There's always one person who draws the short straw. She didn't want to split up and there was a great deal of bitterness. He has two sons as well — they're only just grown up, seventeen and nineteen."

In Tell's experience people talked more if you asked fewer questions — particularly in the unfamiliar and often frightening circumstances of a police interview — so he let the silence have its effect.

He put down his pen and tapped a cigarette out of the packet.

"Do you mind?"

"No, carry on. It was the house too. She — his ex-wife, I mean — couldn't afford to stay there and she became quite depressed. I can understand her in a way. At her age — at our age — it isn't easy to be left alone."

She laughed, a harsh sound that seemed to bury itself in her throat as she realised she was now in the same situation. Tell lit the cigarette, ignoring Beckman, who made a point of moving away from him on the big sofa.

"When you say depressed," she began, "do you mean in some way mentally unstable?"

Lise-Lott sighed.

"No. Well, she'd had problems with her nerves, as they say, for a while, but . . . There was a time right at the beginning, when she found out where Lars was after he'd moved out of the house. She would ring up during the night and . . . she didn't make any sense. She turned up here once or twice and made a scene. But it passed. After that any contact was mostly to do with things she was disputing legally, their joint possessions. And this is a long time ago. I don't think Lars has had any real contact with Maria for a few years."

"And the sons?"

"Joakim and Viktor. No, not much unfortunately. That was a source of great sorrow for Lars. He did try, but . . . I suppose they thought he'd let the family down. Their mother had convinced them that was how things were, and they were loyal to her. Children usually are. Anyway, they refused to come here, but they would meet up with their dad now and again. At a pizzeria or something like that. Lars did feel guilty because of the boys, it was painful to see. I don't have any — children, I mean. Never had any with my first husband, although we did want them at the beginning. We never found out whose fault it was, and suddenly it was too late."

72

Beckman, who had had her first child when she was almost forty, wanted to protest, but she bit her tongue and instead decided to try to stop Lise-Lott Edell from exposing herself emotionally. It was quite normal for people in a state of shock to start sharing their innermost thoughts and feelings with the police during an interview. Only afterwards did they realise this made them feel even more exposed. Of course it was a balancing act, since a large part of an investigation involved getting people to reveal what they would prefer to hide. But at the moment she didn't believe Lise-Lott had anything to do with her husband's death, and they would soon know for sure once they had checked with the travel agency.

Just as Beckman was about to ask if anyone wanted more tea, a woman in a red coat appeared in the doorway. Her heels tapped across the parquet flooring, and in a second she was by Lise-Lott's side, hugging her.

"Sweetheart!"

She rocked her sister back and forth, tears glistening on her thickly made-up eyelashes. Tell closed his notebook and discreetly stubbed out his cigarette on the sole of his shoe. He cleared his throat.

"We'll need to talk to you again, Lise-Lott, but that's enough for now. My condolences once again."

He met her sister's eyes above Lise-Lott's drooping head, and she nodded at him. She would take care of her sister. They could go now.

CHAPTER
TEN

The paint was peeling off in great lumps and the wood on the window-sill felt like cold, soggy sponge beneath her fingers. The water must have been running down the inside of the pane for years. In the mornings a thin layer of frost obscured the view over the woodpile and the manure heap on the edge of the glade. The windows definitely needed sealing, or replacing.

Seja sighed. She knew nothing about maintaining a house, having grown up in an apartment. Behind her Lukas snorted in the box Martin had managed to build before he disappeared. It was made of coarse, untreated pine with a green door. It wasn't really a stable, but a storage shed in which old man Gren, who had sold them the cottage, had installed his carpentry workshop. The workbench was still there along one wall under sacks of oats and feeding pails. The heater warmed up a radius of a couple of metres.

After a cold night like the last one Seja suffered from a guilty conscience when she opened the door and revealed the flickering light bulbs and Lukas, shaking the straw off the hugely expensive olive-green blanket she had bought at the beginning of November. It was just as cold in the stable as it was outside.

She had spread a layer of straw inside for him, thick as a mattress, and put a rug down outside the box despite the fact that Martin had said she was crazy. As Christmas approached she had even placed a holder with Advent candles in the gloomy little window of the shed. At least it looked cosy, she tried to convince herself, and soon it would be spring again.

Seja slid her arms around Lukas's neck and hid her face in his coarse mane. She didn't really know anything about horses either. Like many others she had started riding lessons as a child, but after her mother had stopped teaching, the family finances had been under pressure. Not that anyone ever came out and said that the riding school was expensive; it was more a question of reading between the lines, sensing the atmosphere when the bills had to be paid and everything that was unnecessary had to go. She had given up riding and stuck to the community piano school and the choir instead. Writing was free too, as was the recreation centre.

As far as she remembered, she hadn't really suffered as a result of being deprived of horses. The fact was that, as a child, the huge animals had frightened her, as had the sharp elbows of the older stable girls. There had been a kind of relief in not having to make the decision herself to step outside the equine community.

And yet Lukas had become hers. Despite the fact that she'd got him cheap (he was getting on a bit), he still took up all her savings and a large part of her student loan each month, not to mention time and commitment, but she had never regretted it.

The day old man Gren showed her and Martin around the cottage right at the top of Stenaredsbacken (he called the place the Glade), she had seen the horse in a vision of how their future would look. He had been standing just where the glade turned into forest and small pine trees clambered up a moss-covered hill behind the house; he was eating grass and drinking out of an old bathtub. Since then she had fenced in that particular patch as Lukas's exercise area. The bathtub was still there among the trees, the surface of the water covered with a sheet of ice strewn with pine needles. At least that part of the vision had come true.

With her cheek pressed against Lukas's warm neck she could usually push away thoughts of Martin, but today it was difficult. In her mind's eye she replayed the scene that had made her so happy until a few months ago. They were sitting in the kitchen of their tiny cluttered one-room apartment on Mariaplan and had spotted a small advert in the newspaper, *Göteborgsposten*: "Cottage, needs modernising, going cheap for quick sale." They had arranged to go over straight away, caught the bus as they didn't have a car, and had reached the end of the line as it was starting to get dark. They had to walk from there to the Glade, up all those hills and into the forest.

A taxi was waiting by the gravel track and an old man climbed out of it on weak trembling legs. Old man Gren. Six months earlier he'd had a stroke, he told them, and it looked as if he was going to have to stay in the nursing home down in Olofstorp, so he'd decided to sell up.

In order to get to the house they had walked past a marshy area, the old man moving with infinite slowness and caution along the track. The cottage had neither an indoor toilet nor a shower. The outside toilet was joined to the shed, and at the back there was an outdoor kitchen with a showerhead and warm water. They got the place for next to nothing.

Many times she had asked herself what had happened. When it had all started to go so wrong. If there had been signs that Martin didn't feel as if he had found his home out here. That it was only she who felt a sense of calm spreading through her body as she toiled up the hill, got to the top of Stenaredsvägen and turned off into the forest, with its powerful scent of earth, pine needles and rotting leaves. There must have been signs, of course there must.

The fact that he chose to stay in their crash pad in town more frequently was one sign. He would be working late, meeting up with a friend, or just felt like a hot bath rather than a shower in the glow of the outside light behind the cottage. Increasingly she found herself alone in the house, along with Lukas and the cat she had acquired when she was buying some things at one of the eco farms over in Stannum. Each time Martin left the cottage, he took a few more of his possessions with him. One morning he drove into town and never came back.

He explained over the phone: he couldn't take the sense of restlessness the place gave him. The silence. The walls were closing in on him. The quiet that she loved was for him like taking a huge stride towards death. The boredom was killing him, he said. *What about me,* she wanted to say, *am I a part of that boredom?*

He had once said that he never understood how someone could live with the same partner for their whole life. Live in the same place, work at the same thing.

"I didn't understand it until I met you," he said, smoothing things over when he saw her surprised expression, but doubt had already sunk its claws into Seja. Perhaps in some way she had sensed that things would turn out like this. Martin was an uneasy soul: he always wanted to be moving on, travelling, meeting new people, trying new things. From this very basic point of view they were different. Internal journeys were enough for Seja, and for those outer calm was essential, a frame within which dreams could flow. Riding in the forest early in the morning, the ice-cold autumn dip in the mountain pool, these were events. This was enough.

Since Martin's disappearance she had developed a close relationship with her sorrow and all its stages. To a certain extent it was a matter of what you did. Most of the time it was perfectly possible to keep that small amount of control necessary to stop her from losing her grip altogether. At least this far down the line, when the sharpest edges of her grief had been worn down. These days her sorrow only made its presence felt at night, and in situations that specifically reminded her of what she had lost.

Several months after clearing out all his things she found the battered red Converse trainers in a box in the stable. She had been searching for fuses; she still hadn't learned that it wasn't possible to do the vacuuming, make coffee and have the computer on standby all at the same time, and suddenly the shoes were there in her hand. Despite the fact that she could hardly even see her hand in front of her in the darkness she knew that there were holes in both soles and that the logo on the ankle was so worn you could barely read it. The memory of a sleety afternoon, scrupulously divided between two different shops selling household goods and clothes, had come back to her. The wet had seeped in through the holes, and Martin's feet had lost all feeling because of the cold, which he had not been slow to point out.

"I'm going to catch a cold, I just know it. I haven't got time to be ill — can't we go home now? What the hell do we need more pillows for, we've already got one each. How much stuff are you going to pack into that little house, anyway? I can't afford all this."

"What you can afford is irrelevant, Martin," she had said. "It's always me who pays when it comes to the home we share. It's a question of priorities. Your priority is going into Gothenburg several times a week and drinking beer. At the moment my priority is this. Fine. For God's sake stop moaning. The only thing I ask of you is that you walk alongside me and pretend to be happy and interested. Just for today?"

Had she said that, felt like that? It seemed to be characteristic of the furious harangues involved in their marital squabbles: the lack of constructive clarity. Over and over again they went off the point, lost their focus in a struggle that, in the end, was all about breaking the other person, scoring points in a kind of verbal combat.

During the shock at being left alone, she ascribed all her pain to this one upsetting fact: that the break-up had been so unexpected. *They'd just bought a house, just made a new start; everything was going so well . . .* As if change should be thought of in terms of children or perhaps marriage. The fact that he had let her down and with that one action destroyed what they had begun to build together was completely impossible to grasp at first. And the idea that time heals all wounds felt like complete nonsense.

However, she had to admit that, as time passed, the ability to have some kind of overview had grown. The pain was still there, but it was fading. In moments of clarity she could look at the failed relationship in a more sober light, remember days like the shopping trip and add to them other, similar days: early evenings in smoky bars with drunken strangers and an array of different beers, Seja waiting crossly by the door with her coat on while Martin struggled with his separation anxiety — just one more large strong one, just one more. But it wasn't really about the booze for Martin. It was more the fear of missing out: those smoky bars with drunken strangers and all those different beers, so much more attractive than the greyness of everyday life and the frightening emptiness of being just the two of them.

She checked the thermometer. It was a little milder, so she decided to let Lukas out for a while. She slipped the halter over his head and led him out on to the grass.

Outside the stable lay rolls of fencing she had intended to use to make an alleyway leading to the exercise area, so that Lukas could move in and out as he wished, depending on the weather. A project that had come to nothing when Martin disappeared — like everything else.

"You don't really need me," he'd said.

Yes I do, she wanted to say. *I bloody do need you.* But she had said nothing. Instead she had cried for a week.

She cried in the mornings on the way to pick up the newspaper from the mailbox. Åke Melkersson had tilted his head to one side, had even been so bold as to offer her the use of their bathroom if she needed it — the message had come from Kristina. And she only had to say the word if she needed help. *A girl like you shouldn't be living in these conditions, all alone in the forest.* He seemed genuinely worried. *And certainly not in old man Gren's cottage. Isn't it cold at night?* When Kristina had instructed Åke to ask Seja at their daily meeting whether she wouldn't like to rent a room in their modern, fully equipped bungalow, Seja had politely but firmly declined. She would cope. Time would heal the wounds. And after all, she had Lukas.

But since Åke had taken her to the place where the man was murdered, she had needed to keep her distance. It was to do with her own conflicting emotions. A sense of unease had taken over, despite the eagerness with which she had begun to describe the scene of the crime; when she got home after being interviewed by the police, she had sat down at the computer straight away. The dead man's eyes still came back to her in unguarded moments, and in her nightmares she was the one lying there on the gravel. But something else was wrong. Part of her was drawn to the place where it had happened. She needed more time. To absorb the atmosphere. Take photographs. She felt a morbid pull towards the junction where one of the roads led to Thomas Edell's workshop. Thomas Edell.

She had tried to deceive that inspector, and she was certain he wasn't going to forget it. Yet she felt guilty of something far more serious than lying. It was the motive behind the lie she was unable to defend or explain. Something had made her want to stay, to see the dead man at close quarters, to immortalise him in her mind. It wasn't only her journalistic ambition; it had something to do with an event that had happened a long time ago, in a completely different reality.

We will contact you again in order to complete your statement, he had said, the detective with the crooked front tooth. And the strong hands.

She had intended to spend the day writing. Her article about dedicated individuals working in various clubs and organisations had ground to a halt, despite the fact that she had chosen the topic herself, albeit with the ulterior motive of perhaps selling it to one of the newsletters produced by local organisations. The work she had put in at the beginning of her training, building up contacts with people who might possibly give her work at a later stage, had to a certain extent paid off.

82

From time to time, although it didn't happen all that often, she was asked to report on the opening of a sports hall, for example. There was fierce competition for even the most trivial jobs, and she hadn't even finished her training yet.

Seja had realised at an early stage that she would need sharp elbows to succeed in a profession where the idea of a permanent post seemed utopian. Sometimes she wondered if she had made the right choice, if a safe position in a boring job wasn't better than a lifelong struggle to do something you enjoyed. When she sat there editing a piece about broken windows in a lighting shop or the result of an enquiry into domestic services, the idea that this was her passion was difficult to sustain. Sometimes she was afraid the urge to write that had been part of her since she was a child — letters, diaries, stories — would simply dry up and eventually disappear amid the constant stress and the need to compromise.

However, any assumptions about her future professional life were no more than speculation; she knew nothing yet, after all. She had embarked on a particular course, and in order to see the consequences of her choice she would have to travel to the end of the line.

The cat rubbed against her shins and Seja was brought back to earth with a bump; she threw the last shovelful of dirty straw into the wheelbarrow and took it round the back of the stable to the manure heap. She decided to leave the horse outside as long as it was daylight; the rain had definitely chased away the worst of the cold and the air felt mild against her skin.

She went inside and changed into jeans and a sweater that didn't smell of the stable, and hid her hair in a scarf. Once again she was lost in thoughts: memories of the dead man tempted her, insisted on attention, were treacherous when she lowered her guard. She was therefore unprepared when fear took her unawares, when it suddenly flooded her body and made her wish that she had never gone along with Åke to the garage. That she had put the phone down instead and gone back to sleep.

Perhaps she ought to drive to the university library to take out some books in preparation for her next assessment, but as soon as she got in the car she realised it was going to be difficult to drive past that junction. Printouts of her fuzzy pictures from the murder scene lay, tucked between the pages of her pad of file paper. She had sat with them in front of her for most of the night, thinking about events that had lain hidden for so many years and about possible punishments for compromising a murder investigation. About possibly stealing a march on Tell and getting more information about what had happened. About other ways of finding things out.

A disturbing heat spread up through her body to her head as she once again allowed the scene of the crime to pass before her mind's eye, excitement and embarrassment alternating with one another. She almost managed to push away the memory of the inspector's expression when he established that she had lied.

She had lied, had already embarked on a particular course. In order to see the consequences of her choice she would have to travel to the end of the line.

She considered going back to the farm, however insane that might be.

The blood was coursing through her body, faster, hotter. More palpable than for a long time.

CHAPTER
ELEVEN

"Bloody kids," he muttered between gritted teeth as he slammed the door of the tack room shut. Out in the corridor the noticeboard was plastered with angry messages like a laundry room in a block of flats: "*When you sweep the stable passageway, do NOT tip the muck into the well. It gets blocked!!!! Whoever stole a bucket of silage from me the other day, put it back by Saturday at the LATEST, or else I'll be talking to Reino about it!!!*"

Reino sighed from the bottom of his lungs. When he decided to do up the stable block on the farm and rent out stables to girls in the area who owned their own horses, he thought it would be an easy way to get a bit of extra income. The building was just standing there, after all. And since his daughter Sara had been nagging him about getting a horse for years, he got the job done, combining business with pleasure, so to speak.

However, he was finding it hard to remember exactly where the pleasure lay in this particular enterprise. Especially since Sara had rapidly grown tired of her horse and had turned her attention to mopeds and the opposite sex. And as far as the extra income was concerned, it certainly wasn't easy money. He had never had to work so hard for such a small amount of money.

The obvious duties of a landlord, for example fixing a leaky roof or a broken fence, were nothing compared with the abundance of additional needs he was expected to meet. And worst of all were the endless conflicts. He had lost count of the number of times he had sat at the kitchen table, squirming uncomfortably opposite yet another sobbing teenage girl.

It was a hell of an effort, a hell of a struggle, but he had spent 70,000 on doing up the stable block, and shutting down the business would be like throwing the money away. Besides which, they needed all the extra income they could get, even if it was only a small amount. Financially, they were on their knees. Gertrud had a bad back and could no longer cope with her job as a child minder, which meant that more than a third of their monthly income had disappeared. And these days farming didn't bring in much money.

Sometimes he thought the only way out would be to move. Then it was the rage that made him carry on working. The rage, and the thought of the little apartment and the unemployment that would be their fate.

And the thought of Sara. He nourished the hope that one day she would have the opportunity to make the same choice he had: to go in for agriculture, even if it was financially impossible to live as a farmer in today's society. If you don't want to live on subsidies, that is.

The rage. That was what gave him the strength to keep going. Not that he was all that old, and he was still as strong as an ox when he needed to be. On those mornings when he could hardly summon the energy to swing himself up on to the tractor, he was fighting against a different kind of tiredness. A feebleness on a completely different level, which neither rest nor a visit to the doctor could cure.

The slamming of the tack room door, obligatory whenever he visited the stable block these days, usually fell on deaf ears, but he had learned that it was necessary now and then to loosen the pressure valve on the brooding, clanking machinery in his stomach, to let out a little burst of rage in the form of a slammed door or screeching of tyres as he pulled away from the stables. The past few years had certainly been bloody difficult.

As Reino slumped on to the seat he met his own eyes in the rearview mirror — a little bit red-rimmed. He ran his hand thoughtfully over his stubble before he turned the key in the ignition and drove off. As he sped alongside the pasture the noise made the horses shy away from the fence.

Through force of habit he gathered the strength to drive past Lise-Lott's house and the workshop, because no horse-mad girl — or even EU regulations, for that matter — had the ability to put him in such a bad mood as the sight of that bitch. Not to mention her new husband, running around like some big girl photographing old buildings or half-rotten trees and weeds.

On one occasion Reino had actually gone over to have a chat with Waltz because every attempt he had made to talk to that stupid bitch had ended up in a row. He had been well prepared, and had even taken a small bottle of whisky to show that he came with the best of intentions. He was willing to resolve the situation in the best possible way for all concerned. After all, his own situation was not financially viable in the long term, and Waltz was in the same position, if you thought about it. As far as Reino understood, Waltz hadn't known much about cars when he got the workshop as part of the package that came with Lise-Lott, so to speak, and didn't know anything at all about farming. If Reino understood correctly, Waltz wasn't even intending to make use of the land that belonged to Thomas's and Reino's parents' farm.

My parents' home, Thomas's parents' home. He sucked on every syllable, but Waltz had pretended not to understand, had just gone on and on about his photography and how the landscape around the farm appealed to him. How happy he was to be living in this particular spot, thanks to the fact that he had met Lise-Lott. Reino had just wanted to punch him, and had laid it on the line so the fool could understand.

"Thomas is gone, and in my capacity as his brother it's my duty to take over the family farm, to carry on with the work — that's the way it should be. I mean, somebody has to do it, and my own place is just too small. It doesn't bring anything in. Lise-Lott knows nothing about farming, and watching her try to keep the car workshop open has been a complete joke. A woman!"

It took all his strength to restrain himself.

"Listen. I grew up here; my father ploughed these fields. As long as Thomas was alive and he and Lise-Lott were running the farm, I had my own projects, but now Thomas is dead I have a right to my father's land. It's obvious. In fact, Lise-Lott had been planning to hand over the farm just before you came on the scene. For a symbolic amount, of course, perhaps in exchange for our place. I mean, what's she going to do with all that extra land — it's nothing but a headache."

He thought his argument was quite well put; he was even generous enough to offer to let Waltz and the bitch carry on living in the house. Theoretically he wouldn't need it anyway; he was quite comfortable in the larger house that was Gertrud's childhood home.

But that skinny wimp Waltz had suddenly turned nasty and refused to listen. In his opinion the person who had a right to the farm according to Swedish law was Thomas Edell's widow, namely Lise-Lott, and therefore it was entirely up to Lise-Lott to make any decisions regarding the house and the land. If Reino wished to discuss her late husband's inheritance, then he would have to conduct that discussion with Lise-Lott herself.

"Besides, I did a bit of work on cars during my military service. I wasn't completely useless."

With that salvo Waltz had turned on his heel and stalked up the stone steps that Reino's father had made because his mother wanted to feel more like a lady of the manor and less like a farmer's wife. The stone steps where Reino and his brother used to sit, dressed in their Sunday best, while they waited for their parents to get ready for church.

The fury had hit him like an explosion inside his head. He had had to exercise extreme self-control to avoid running after Waltz and knocking him to the ground, which wouldn't have been a good idea, bearing in mind that he was busy formulating a legal challenge to his brother's widow.

As usual he got hot under the collar even remembering that conversation with Waltz. But now everything had been turned upside down. When he reached the bend by Lise-Lott's place he slowed down as much as he dared without attracting attention, and drove slowly past the police tape flapping in the faint breeze. The machinery that had been grinding away in his stomach earlier had now fallen silent.

CHAPTER
TWELVE

Karin Beckman was looking at the chain distrustfully. Every time the muscular body of the dog launched an attack, the chain appeared to be yanked to breaking point. She didn't want to think about what would happen if it actually snapped.

"You look a bit pale, Beckman." Gonzales laughed. "You're not telling me you're frightened of this little chap?"

Beckman snorted. "I don't see you going over to give him a cuddle."

She fell silent as the door of the glassed-in veranda flew open with a crash.

"QUIET, SIMBA! QUIET!"

The woman was wearing a dressing gown over jeans and a T-shirt, and her hair was in rollers under a thin scarf. She jerked a cigarette out of the corner of her mouth. Gonzales nudged Beckman in the side.

"I'm more bloody frightened of *her*."

The expression on the woman's face made them explain their business quickly. A little while later they had made it past the Rottweiler. Once it was off the chain, it turned out to be more interested in nuzzling them in the crotch.

They were sitting in a scruffy kitchen, each with a mug of instant coffee in front of them, despite the fact that they had both said no when the offer was made. The woman had taken off her dressing gown and turned down the volume of her powerful voice. The wall behind her was covered in framed photographs of small boys and girls in front of a sky-blue screen.

"Grandchildren," she explained.

Since Beckman was fully occupied with rummaging in her bag, Gonzales nodded politely.

"They're very sweet. Now, if we can just get down to the matter in hand, fru Rappe. The evening of the nineteenth, the night of the nineteenth-twentieth and the morning of the twentieth of this month. We are interested in anything that might have seemed out of the ordinary during that period. For example, did you or your husband see anyone you didn't recognise?"

Fru Rappe stubbed out her cigarette in an ashtray decorated with sea anemones and coughed asthmatically before she replied.

"I suppose this is about the Edells' place? I heard from the Molins that there were lots of cars in the drive and . . . Well, this is a small community, after all, and we do like to know what's going on. I noticed when I was driving past that the place had been cordoned off. Dagny thought there had been a break-in, but I'm not stupid enough to believe there would be such a fuss over a break-in. At least there wasn't when somebody nicked my jewellery box and our telly last autumn. No, Waltz has been murdered, hasn't he?"

The question hung in the air. She was making it crystal clear that she had absolutely no intention of carrying on until she got an answer. Gonzales squirmed uncomfortably. There was something about this woman that he found extremely demanding. His gaze was caught by an enormous Santa Claus on the lawn outside the kitchen window, complete with sleigh and reindeer covered in hundreds of tiny bulbs in all the colours of the rainbow.

"I'm afraid we can't comment on that at the moment, for technical reasons. But we do need your help, in view of the fact that you live nearby and might have seen something."

She shrugged her shoulders.

"I don't know about nearby. I mean, I don't keep a check on everybody who drives past; I can't even see the road all that clearly from the window. But I know a number of cars went past that evening. I think there was an open viewing of a house a couple of kilometres away. Not that people are exactly rushing to view houses around here at the moment, but this was a manor house from the nineteenth century. I know that because the agent, a young girl, got her car stuck in the ditch when she met somebody coming the other way up by Sänkan and Bo, my husband, helped her out."

Fru Rappe started telling them about an occasion in her youth when she had visited this particular manor house, but then she heard a noise from the room next door and broke off. She stood up, raised her huge voice again and bellowed for Bo.

94

Gonzales thought quietly to himself that these people from the country were a bloody sight odder than the Chileans and Yugoslavs who lived on his street. He turned back to the woman. By this stage she had polluted the air so thoroughly with her cigarettes that his eyes were watering.

"Do you know Lise-Lott Edell and Lars Waltz?"

"Well no, I wouldn't say that I know them. Waltz hasn't been living here all that long. I've bumped into Lise-Lott from time to time, as you do in a small place. My husband knew Lise-Lott's former husband's father; they used to hunt with the same club. Lise-Lott married into the farm but perhaps you already know that. Her first husband, Thomas, died of natural causes. I think it was his heart. Not that he was very old, but I suppose it was in his genes. His father died of heart problems too. And I think Thomas was fond of a drink, just like his father. He didn't take a lot of water with it, if you know what I mean. That's the way life is for some people. And Lise-Lott had plenty to console herself with — the farm is quite substantial. Reino wasn't too pleased, of course."

"Reino?"

Beckman noticed that Gonzales was scribbling feverishly and wished she had brought the tape recorder along. Sitting in the kitchen with a dyed-in-the-wool gossip, you were bound to find out all kinds of interesting things. Perhaps even the odd motive for murder.

"Reino. Gösta and Barbro's son. Thomas's brother."

"Right."

"I mean, you can understand it. It's one thing for your father's inheritance to go to the older brother, but quite another to watch his widow drive the business into the ground. Because she's not much of a farmer, Lise-Lott, you certainly couldn't call her that. It would be just as well if she packed her bags and moved somewhere else, to a nice little house — at least I suspect that's what Reino thinks. Not that I've ever been particularly fond of Reino, but I can understand how he feels. I don't think things are very easy for him on Gertrud's farm. It's too small to make a profit, really."

She leaned back in her chair, running her fingers over the edges of a plastic tray.

"You should know when you don't have what it takes. Lise-Lott ought to know. I mean, we did."

She gave a wry smile, revealing a row of yellowing teeth.

"Did what?"

"We moved to this nice little house. Bo had a bad back, and he couldn't cope with running the Rappe farm — it's the first house after the main road, the yellow one. It was in his family for four generations. Our son and his wife have taken it over. You have to step aside for those who have the ability. And we got this house for a good price. Anna-Maria's mother, Anna-Maria is our daughter-in-law, she —"

"Thank you."

Beckman broke in by holding up both hands, smiling at the same time to compensate for the sharpness in her voice.

"That's fine for the moment. If you happen to think of anything else that might be of interest with regard to Lars Waltz, please do get in touch."

She placed her card on the table in front of fru Rappe.

"Wouldn't it have been better to let her carry on talking? She seems to know plenty about the people around here. We might have found out something interesting," said Gonzales. They had established that fru Rappe's next-door neighbours were not at home and were walking back to the car.

"I don't know, but I'm sure you're right. I was actually thinking the same when she was going on, but she just lost me. Who was Anna-Maria?"

"Their daughter-in-law. But more importantly, who's this Reino? It seems he had a motive for killing Waltz."

"But why? It's Lise-Lott he should be getting rid of, surely?"

"Maybe he doesn't want to murder a woman, so he takes the man instead. He thinks she'll be broken by grief, and she'll move away so she doesn't have to live with all the memories."

"Do me a favour," Beckman said and pulled out on to the road. She glanced at the clock on the dashboard. "We've only got three more places to visit. That's the advantage of investigating a murder in the middle of nowhere."

Gonzales cackled.

"True. But there are one or two disadvantages as well. These farmers, for a start. If I was in their shoes, regardless of whether I had anything to do with the murder or not, and if I wasn't mentally subnormal, I certainly wouldn't have behaved as suspiciously as most of the ones we've met so far."

"If you *weren't* mentally subnormal, you say . . ."

CHAPTER
THIRTEEN

1993

As time went by, Maya began to settle at the school.

The actual work was no problem, in fact it turned out to be a source of pleasure. She had dropped out of grammar school in a fit of existential questioning and had caught the commuter train into Gothenburg every morning to hang out in the Northern Station café with a gang of other kids on the loose. They would meet in the morning, scrape together enough for a cup of tea each, preferably Twinings Söders Höjder; then they would sit there with the same infuser, and by the afternoon would always end up drinking "silver tea" — a mixture of hot water and sugar. They wrote on serviettes and in visitors' books, and smoked roll-ups.

The youth centre, which was the only thing on offer to those who refused to study, was totally uninteresting. They were obliged to spend two days in a remedial class and three doing some crap job for no pay. Maya became aware of this after only a week, and not without a certain elitist attitude towards her classmates — boys with bum-fluff moustaches who nicked cars. None of this bothered her as much as the fact that they couldn't actually spell their own surnames. Nor did she feel any kind of affinity with their admiring girlfriends, all chewing gum and bleached blonde hair.

At the root of Maya's aversion to staying on at grammar school, and of her contempt for the unfortunate remedial kids, was a refusal to conform. School was classed as the most obvious form of oppression. And when it came to Maya's mother, she had not merely contented herself with trying to persuade her children to carry on studying by means of bribes, threats and guilt; in addition, she had limited their choice of study options to the subjects she herself would have liked to pursue but had not been allowed. As a general rule, Maya's mother had always found it difficult to distinguish where she ended and other people began.

Up to this point Maya had never realised that learning could be fun; it had certainly never struck her that she had a talent for absorbing knowledge. But it did now. She was praised for her writing in Swedish, lost herself in the study of literature and also, quite unexpectedly, science, which extended before her like an exotic country waiting to be explored. She flicked through university prospectuses and chose unashamedly among completely diverse professions: architect, biologist, psychologist, school teacher.

The social aspect of school life was considerably more difficult. A Maya she had not seen in daylight for several years came creeping out, the quiet and submissive girl who melted into the wallpaper. She was the only alternative to the truculent mask of the past few years. It was like starting afresh, sitting there in class and waiting in agony for the teacher you have had for six months to remember your name.

The students at the school came from different social backgrounds and were all there for different reasons. Many simply wanted a break, to find some peace, or perhaps to find themselves. Some were there to get to know other people, to break out of their isolated existence. At seventeen Maya was the youngest, and she felt ignorant yet also weighed down by experiences she just couldn't share. There was a boy she vaguely recognised in one of the other classes — she thought his name was John. On one occasion he came up to her and asked if she was from Borås. She said no. She would rather be alone than mix the two worlds together — the Maya she had been had no place here.

She kept herself to herself, reading in her room or in the library. She went for walks around the lake. She didn't join the gang of younger students who hung out together in the evenings, sitting on the lawn, playing the guitar and singing, having parties in their rooms as they giggled and drank booze someone had smuggled in. No one was allowed to have alcohol in their rooms.

In fact she found it less painful to be alone than to be the one who was alone. She was perfectly happy on her own, but was almost ashamed when someone from class put their head around the door of the library to find her sitting there with her books: *Are you sitting here all on your own?* As if there were something seriously wrong with her.

Caroline was the one who made her feel just a little more interesting, at least Maya imagined that the others noticed them together. Caroline had an air of independence because of her position at the school; she could move in and out of groups as she pleased. Most of the students seemed to feel privileged to be in her company; only a few whispered that she was a bit odd. Unpleasant, somehow. That she was supposed to have *those eyes.*

Maya found herself reacting with primitive jealousy whenever she saw Caroline talking to one of the others — particularly if it was one of the outgoing, self-confident girls, and she saw them laughing together. Then she would feel inferior, like the seventeen-year-old she was.

That's what Caroline does to people, Maya wrote in her book. *She makes the person she turns to feel chosen, while the person she turns her back on is left shivering in the cold.*

CHAPTER
FOURTEEN

2006

At some point Melkersson had told Seja that in days gone by it was possible to reach the lake, Älsjön, by following designated paths across what was now cleared land where the trees had been felled. As a young man he had had a sweetheart in Lerum and he used to go and visit her by walking through the forests. It wasn't all that far as the crow flies, according to him. Since then the tree-felling machines had churned up the ground, and the paths were unidentifiable. The few remaining trees had fallen victim to storms because of their exposed position, which gave the area an even more chaotic appearance.

The lake was situated quite high up, as was Stenaredsberget. These days local families made their way up by car, but had to take a detour down into the village and back up again via Stora Älsjövägen to the car park. From there they could walk with their blankets and picnic baskets to reach the communal swimming area, with its diving boards, trampoline and a small building where people could get changed.

She and Martin had spent the holiday among the crowds on the sandy beach over on the Olofstorp side.

On the far side of the lake they could see the rocks leading down into the water on the Stenared side, which were wide and smooth with an oval-shaped inward curve that was just perfect for one or two sunbathing bodies. They had swum easily across the lake and lay down to dry off on the rock.

The water was deep there. You couldn't see the bottom; you could only sense it through the weed that extended slimy tentacles right up to the surface in some places.

"We ought to make our way home from here," Seja had said. "I mean, it can't be very far."

Then she realised it wasn't very clever to leave their clothes and the car on the other side of the lake and to plough home through rough terrain in their swimsuits. Besides which, Martin was comfortable. And she never did get him to go out with the red paint and mark the track, although she had gone on and on about it. In the end, after he'd left, she did it herself. It took a day to find her way to the lake, and by the time she did she was covered in scratches and sweating. September was long gone so she hadn't intended to go for a swim, but she did. The ice-cold water flicked at her exhausted limbs.

That had been her reward, along with the flask of coffee she drank on the hillside afterwards, wrapped up warmly in her old anorak. For the first time in ages she had felt a surge of happiness in her chest, like a light but unmistakable butterfly wing against her heart. *To have the courage to be alone*, she had thought. To have the courage. On the way home she had marked out her route by dabbing paint on selected tree trunks and rocks until she could glimpse her cottage through the trees.

She started to ride up to the lake almost every day, once she had sawn up and carried away tree trunks from the buried path. By this stage Lukas knew the way by heart, and when Seja relaxed the reins and leaned back in the saddle, she sank into a meditative state she had never experienced before. The track to the lake became her secret, symbolising her newly discovered and still fragile inner strength, this contradictory state. And God knows she needed it.

"You've changed so much," Martin had said just before they split up. She knew he was referring to the fact that she had embraced life in the country and in the cottage without any hesitation. She had hardly dared to wonder herself what it was about living here that made her feel as if she had come home; she had lived in the city all her life. She had felt if not happy, then at least disposed towards happiness.

Happiness is possible here, she had painted, somewhat pretentiously, on the stable wall just above the saddle hook.

Only once had she visited the small village in northern Finland where her mother was born. She wasn't very old at the time, perhaps five or six, and the summer heat had still been embedded in the tarmac as the family climbed into the scruffy Saab and set off from Gothenburg. Seja was dressed for early autumn. When they were met by the frosty ground and the bitterly cold air, she had had to borrow clothes from

Grandma Marja-Leena. That was the first and only time she met her grandmother. At first Seja had not wanted to accept the borrowed clothes, she had wanted to go around in a work-shirt with the sleeves rolled up like her father as if they both suspected that making concessions to the cold was a sign of weakness. Only when they went off into the forest to help with clearing the ground did he put on Grandpa's warm lined dungarees that hung on a nail in the barn.

Grandpa had died six months earlier. At night her mother talked quietly in the bedroom about how Grandma was going to manage with the farm and all the heavy work. And the forest, which would eventually be passed on to her only daughter. Much later Seja would come to realise that her mother had wanted to move back to Finland, but her father had refused. It was something that remained between them.

Now Marja-Leena was dead, and Seja's mother rented out the land. The house itself was falling into decay. Seja had only fleeting memories of her grandmother and the farm. A sinewy woman in an apron, her hair in a bun at the back of her neck. A grey house and a huge barn in the middle of nowhere. Snow in September. And the forest.

But she remembered other things. These days she would get a lump in her throat at the thought of how her mother had instantly changed as soon as her feet touched the frozen ground. As if the austerity of the earth quickly found its way through the soles of her shoes and established itself in her body, just as the cold had settled in Seja's grandmother's bones and become a part of her. It was obvious in every word, every gesture. Marja-Leena had nodded appreciatively when Seja was so thrilled at having learned to drive the tractor on her mother's knee. That was the only time Seja saw her smile.

Seja remembered the sudden reverence with which she regarded her mother, the practised way in which she went about the neglected tasks around the farm. How she would swing herself up on to the tractor, or drive the animals in front of her with calm assured calls and slaps. Like a cowgirl, absolutely in her element.

Seja's mother had lived in Sweden for thirty years, but still spoke Swedish as if she was constantly forcing her way past some obstacle at the front of her mouth. Weighing every single word so that it would come out right, and yet it was often wrong, poor and lacking in shades of meaning. You could see it on her face afterwards. That what she'd said hadn't turned out the way she'd intended. That she was prepared for misunderstandings.

Seja had never returned to Finland as an adult. No, wait, there was one time. A school trip to Helsinki with her sixth-form class. When Jarmo, the one person in the class who spoke Finnish better than she did, wasn't around, she had to translate all the signs and the menus at McDonald's.

Seja laughed as Lukas whinnied loudly at the sight of the stable. She let go of the reins and slipped her boots out of the stirrups. For a short while her heart felt light.

Then she caught sight of the roof. When the trees were bare of leaves and not weighed down with snow, Åke and Kristina Melkersson's recently completed red mock-tile roof glowed through the branches. She turned away, as if denying the uncomfortable feeling would make it disappear. By removing Melkersson from her mind she could pretend she had never been there on that day.

It was unfair, but ever since she had seen the dead man sprawled on the gravel, the unpleasant sensation that had replaced the immediate shock had increased at the mere thought of her neighbour. All he had done was wake her up and take her to Thomas Edell's workshop and scrapyard, completely unsuspecting.

And there it was, the name. It aroused feelings of vulnerability and a vague guilt that she had never really acknowledged, a guilt that she had wiped from her mind with the excuse that she had been too young, had been suffering from a very human uncertainty. In fact, she was still uncertain about the whole thing. She didn't even recognise that face: scraped along the ground, distorted by pain and the fear of death.

And many years had passed. Many years of letting the past remain where it was, of rethinking, of tidying away, burying, reconciling, defying the uncomfortable thoughts and making them bearable. As you do. There was a great deal from those days that had disappeared — people, memories — rationalised away in the agony of a hangover.

CHAPTER
FIFTEEN

Tell poured himself another cup of coffee from the Thermos Bärneflod had produced from the depths of the police station. An old-fashioned red candlestick had been brought back into use for Advent and was burning beneath the fluorescent lights. Tell closed the window without giving a thought to the fact that Beckman had opened it five minutes earlier. Outside Ullevi a gang of people had gathered after a car hit a cyclist travelling in the cycle lane. Karlberg had established that it was serious; the ambulance and a patrol car had been there for almost an hour.

So far, the morning meeting had mainly been devoted to gathering information. The various facts that had come to light the previous day had been presented. Tell had informed them that over the next few days — nobody mentioned the fact that Christmas was fast approaching — all other ongoing investigations would be put to one side, and every member of the team would work on the murder in Björsared. They all knew that the first few days were critical in solving a case — or not.

The technicians had sent in a verbal report with Magnus Johansson, who had obviously interrupted his holiday to be there. He had informed them that according to SKL, the national forensic lab, the bullet in the victim came from a 9mm Browning HP.

A call from forensic pathologist Ingemar Strömberg was put on speakerphone.

"I don't think I've got anything particularly startling to tell you," said Strömberg apologetically once he had got his headset sorted out. "Lars Waltz died of a gunshot wound to the head, and death was probably instantaneous. He collapsed at the moment of death, most likely falling forward and on to one side, and then someone ran over the body."

"When and in what?" asked Karlberg.

"Some time during the evening or early that night. After seven, but before midnight. You'll have to wait for more exact details until after Christmas. As for your second question, all I can say is that it's a vehicle of some kind, heavier than an ordinary car. A four-by-four, for example."

Johansson nodded in agreement. "Judging by the tyre tracks . . ."

". . . which crushed the hips and the chest, that would be about right." When nobody spoke, Strömberg went on: "The body fell on to its back as it was rammed, then it was driven over again as the perpetrator reversed over it. Perhaps in the madness of the moment he didn't look in the rear-view mirror, but simply slammed the car into reverse and floored the accelerator, with the result that only the lower parts of the body were affected: the kneecaps, shins and feet.

Well, they were splintered really . . . Hmm. I'm putting quotation marks around the word only."

He sounded embarrassed, as if the intellectualised brutality of the job had suddenly caught up with him.

"You mean the main damage happened the first time the vehicle drove over him. When the perpetrator reversed over the body, he just drove over the feet," Tell clarified.

"Exactly. Which might perhaps be regarded as a very minor mitigating circumstance, bearing in mind that he was already dead."

Johansson nodded tentatively.

"Before I forget," said Strömberg. "There was a small amount of alcohol in the victim's body, the equivalent of a couple of glasses of wine. Nothing remarkable, but still . . ."

Silence fell across the room once the pathologist had signed off, as everyone considered what they had been told. Magnus Johansson returned to his handwritten crib sheet, which he intended to hand over to Tell unofficially before he left.

"We found some fresh footprints from the victim's own trainers, size 9. But even if there had been other prints that were equally clear, they could have come from just about anybody who had brought in or collected a car over the past few days."

He scratched his head.

"No sign of a struggle between victim and perpetrator, either on the man's clothes or his body, or in the surrounding area. We did find blue fibres on the gravel next to the victim, but they turned out to have come from the pullover he was wearing."

"OK, what else?"

"Well . . . the blood at the scene of the crime came exclusively from the murdered man. A chewing-gum wrapper in front of the veranda was covered in lots of different fingerprints, so I don't think we can get anything from that."

When Johansson had left and Tell clapped his hands to quieten the chatter that arose, Gonzales put forward the theory that the perpetrator hadn't even got out of his car while carrying out the murder. That he had simply pulled into the yard, somehow got Waltz to come over to the car, then shot him in the head.

"He's a cold bastard, in that case," commented Karlberg, before exploding in a sneeze that made the glass in the pictures rattle. "And clever."

There wasn't anything particularly clever about getting a car mechanic to leave his workshop for a minute. The perpetrator could have sounded his horn and wound down the window, and Waltz would have assumed he was just an ordinary customer.

"Something wrong with the car, of course," Beckman suggested. "He asked Waltz to come over and listen to the engine while he sat in the car and pressed the accelerator, and then, when the victim was close enough, he simply grabbed hold of him and put the gun to his head."

"Which suggests that the murderer wasn't known to the victim," Bärneflod pointed out. "I mean, otherwise he wouldn't have bought the idea of there being something wrong with the engine, and he wouldn't have gone over to the murderer's car."

"What do you mean?" Gonzales exclaimed. "He could have known the murderer really well, he just didn't expect him to put a bullet through his skull. Doesn't it suggest that it *was* an acquaintance, sitting in the car and sounding his horn rather than parking and going inside to look for the mechanic, like a normal person would? Wouldn't Waltz be suspicious if —"

Without managing to conceal his impatience, Tell cut short the discussion. "Can we move on? We don't know if he was suspicious; we don't even know if that's how it happened."

He regretted his reaction at once. An open discussion and speculation might be a way of moving the investigation forward. In addition, Tell ought to be encouraging Bärneflod to keep hold of the team leader's baton.

Beckman had spoken to Lise-Lott Edell at her sister's house in Sjövik the previous day. She reported briefly on the meeting, which had gone on for two long hours, including several pauses for tears and lost threads, due to the strong tranquillisers with which Angelika Rundström had supplied her sister.

The interview had resulted in a grief-stricken portrait of Lars Waltz. Lise-Lott had also agreed to write down the names of some of her husband's acquaintances. Beckman suggested they compile a priority list for these interviews; the key was to get a picture of who Waltz was, and what would make someone want to see him dead.

"I'd also recommend another chat with Lise-Lott later on, when she's more alert. She needed to talk about Lars in her own way yesterday, and it was difficult to steer the conversation. And of course we mustn't underestimate the therapeutic effect of these interviews," said Beckman.

Tell bit his tongue in order to avoid saying what he really thought, namely that Beckman's job wasn't to act as some kind of therapist, but to ask the questions that could help them find the murderer as quickly as possible. Instead he merely nodded, but out of the corner of his eye he glimpsed a meaningful look from Bärneflod, who was less discreet.

For some reason Bärneflod often sought his collusion when it came to new-fangled ideas versus good old honest police work. Tell had no idea why, and to be perfectly honest it frightened the life out of him. He was only forty-four. In his eyes Bärneflod was a comfortable old fogey who was more interested in the past than the present, on top of which he was capable of demonstrating a clear lack of intelligence in many situations. Despite the fact that Tell could easily get annoyed at Beckman's way of breezily relating most things to issues of gender, and despite the fact that he was sceptical about all this talk of quotas and the advantages of bringing a female way of thinking into the police service, Bärneflod's jokes about "bluestockings" and "man-haters" made him feel depressed. He didn't want to find himself in agreement with someone like Bärneflod. For that reason he gave Beckman a word of encouragement. But, to be honest, he also thought it would be a strategic move in the long term.

It had come to his attention that Beckman had had a series of discussions with Östergren the previous year, regarding the macho atmosphere at the station. At first this had perplexed him. Was he a male chauvinist pig without even knowing it?

"I've never perceived the language used in the station as particularly male," he had responded, with a slightly defensive air, "even if it's a bit rough at times. It's more to do with the job. Police jargon, that's all."

He felt perfectly at home with it after twenty years in the job and was tempted to say that if someone didn't feel comfortable in the corridors of the police station, perhaps they should consider a change of profession.

"There's nothing to say that macho jargon within the police service is constructive, or has anything to do with actual work," Östergren had pointed out brusquely.

He chose to remain silent.

"I'm glad Karin Beckman brings such competence to the job and is not afraid to say what she thinks," she went on, "just as I'm glad we have Michael, who is young and green and brings a fresh pair of eyes. As well as Bengt, who is older and has a different perspective. In the same way, I'm glad you have such drive, and Andreas is more reflective."

She tilted her head to one side. Tell had the unpleasant feeling that she wanted something from him that he didn't understand. He pulled himself together and muttered a few words that could be interpreted as agreement. Of course he would keep an eye on the team and smooth the way for both the male and female perspective. It seemed eminently sensible, he just had no idea how to go about it.

After giving their conversation a great deal of thought, he had gone to see Östergren the following week and said that he too was pleased to have Karin Beckman in the team, but that he had never regarded her primarily as a woman, or even a woman police officer, but quite simply as a police officer.

"And a bloody good one, when it comes down to it."

Östergren's expression, which had been tense and concentrated as she prepared the annual statistical report, softened and she broke into a smile.

"Thank you, Christian," she said. "That's what I wanted to hear."

Tell had gone back to his office with the feeling that he'd been given top marks for behaviour by his teacher without really understanding how it had happened.

He was brought back to reality as Beckman rapped the whiteboard with her knuckles. In the centre was a Polaroid photograph of the dead Lars Waltz.

"I've found out a few things about his background . . . Born in Gothenburg in 1961, in Majorna to be precise. Parents separated when he was about ten, limited contact with his father subsequently. The family didn't have much money. Mother worked nights at the Sahlgren hospital as a nurse. One older brother . . ."

She moved her glasses down her nose and leafed through her papers.

"That's it. Sten Roger Waltz, known as Sten. He's seven years older and evidently lives in Malmö.

Unmarried, no children. The brothers didn't have much to do with each another."

"Who's going to contact Sten?" asked Tell.

"I've already spoken to him. They hardly had any contact, but of course he was still very shocked. Off the top of his head he couldn't think of anyone who might want his brother dead. But he also said he didn't really know him any longer."

"Well done, Karin. We'll follow another angle, then we can decide if we need to go to Malmö later. What about his mother — does she still live in Gothenburg?"

"No. She died a couple of years ago."

"Carry on."

"He attended the Karl Johan School, then the Schiller Grammar School. Took a gap year and stayed on some sheep station in Australia. Since his twenties he's worked on all kinds of different things, including car repairs and . . . well, just about anything you can think of. He's done a few courses in marketing, something to do with art, and a one-year photographic course. Developed an allergy to computer monitors when he was thirty after a couple of years as an art director, and was signed off sick for eighteen months."

Beckman drew a somewhat sloping line on the whiteboard and filled in years and headings to represent the different phases in the life of Lars Waltz.

"And then he met Lise-Lott Edell," Bärneflod concluded, throwing his pen down on the desk as if he'd been busy making notes up to that point.

"Well, sort of. He'd actually been married before. Lise-Lott wasn't sure about dates and so on. She's only known Lars for six or seven years. He published a book of photographs at the beginning of the 90s and was evidently working on a new one; it was going to be about the decline of the agricultural area around their farm, from some kind of environmental perspective. Anyway, he ran the car workshop part time to provide an income so that he could carry on with his photography. He got work from the district council in Lerum from time to time, information leaflets, that kind of thing."

A sweeping movement with her arm. She jotted *Lerum District Council* next to the resulting circle and *2000–2006* inside it.

"Is this what they call mind-mapping?" said Bärneflod sarcastically, picking up his pen to carry on with his own notes. Nobody bothered to reply.

"It seems there was some kind of conflict between Waltz and the person at the town hall who gave him work," Tell added.

Beckman nodded. "Yes. But Lise-Lott didn't really know anything. She thought it had all been sorted out."

"Bengt, you talk to him," said Tell, waving his hand in Bärneflod's direction. Bärneflod responded by pointing meaningfully at his watch, but Tell made it clear that he had no intention of stopping for a coffee break just because it was ten o'clock.

"What else? There was an ex-wife and kids."

"An ex-wife and two boys in their late teens."

"I'll take them," Tell decided.

Gonzales sprawled across the desk to reach the whiteboard, groaning with the effort, and wrote *M. G. — Reino Edell*.

118

"He's our most interesting character, as I see it," he said, rapping on the table with the board marker. "He's the younger brother of Lise-Lott's ex-husband and has been involved in a well-documented quarrel with Lise-Lott. I've checked it out, and there are shelves full of legal proceedings to choose from. Well, there are some at least. He thinks Lise-Lott has stolen his inheritance. He's bloody furious, and most people who murder other people are bloody furious."

"Sure, but not everybody who's furious goes off and commits murder," said Bärneflod smugly. "Besides, I can't see what Edell would get out of murdering Waltz — he doesn't have any legal right to the farm."

"No, he doesn't, but he's got a grudge against them as a couple. Mainly Lise-Lott, he's bloody livid with her for clinging on to the farm like a leech. Then all of a sudden Waltz turns up, waltzes in (no pun intended), takes the place of his beloved late brother and seems quite happy to stay on the farm and let the agricultural side go to rack and ruin. Instead he spends all his time screwing Thomas Edell's wife and taking photographs of rusty old ploughs. So of course Reino Edell is going to be angry with this guy. And perhaps he was intending to get rid of Lise-Lott, but instead it's Waltz who's coming towards him and . . ."

"To be honest, I'm more interested in the ex-wife," Bärneflod persisted. "I mean, Waltz just clears off after twenty years of marriage and immediately moves in with a new woman. That's got to hurt, and we already know she was volatile after the divorce. And isn't this a particularly female way of murdering someone?

Shooting the guy and then running over him? It doesn't require any strength, just a decent car."

Bärneflod paused for breath.

"Of course we need to check on the vehicles of anyone who crops up in the investigation, and compare them with the scene of the crime," said Tell. "We'll leave that to the Angered boys."

Karlberg accidentally nudged Beckman, who spilled coffee on the old overhead projector. A fuse blew, and the electric Advent candle in the window went out.

Tell sighed. "OK. We'll leave it there for today."

CHAPTER
SIXTEEN

The passageway between the garage and the outside door sloped gently and was well gritted. As Seja passed the dining-room window she sensed movement. She had been spotted. But she still had to wait while Kristina carefully slid the cover off the spyhole. Seja waved a little wearily.

The lock clicked and the door opened.

"This is really kind of you, Seja. Åke's in town changing a part for some drill or other that wasn't working properly. And I was just about to have a cup of coffee when I realised we're completely out of sugar."

"No problem."

Seja handed the bag of sugar to Kristina, who moved away from the door and waved her inside.

"Come on in. It's all ready; I just needed the sugar."

Seja suppressed a sigh. She had thought it was a bit odd, given that Åke had finished work and therefore had all the time in the world to go shopping. Now she realised the sugar was just a ruse.

"I've got quite a bit to do, Kristina."

Which was actually true. She ought to be studying, ought to be writing the kind of things that would generate some income. Ought to change the rotten plank in the wall of Lukas's box, change the washer in the constantly running shower, which had caused a minor flood behind the house.

But Kristina was already on her way into the kitchen. Seja kicked off her boots, promising herself she wouldn't stay long, wouldn't allow herself to be drawn into anything. Because she had an idea of where this was going.

In the dining room Kristina had laid out cups and saucers and a plate of ginger biscuits and some raspberry cakes. She was pouring the sugar into a bowl.

"You hardly ever come up here nowadays, Seja," she said, lowering herself laboriously into the armchair at the end of the table. "It's mostly you and Åke who meet up. I think one should take care of one's neighbours."

Seja didn't reply. She had made a couple of dutiful attempts to invite Kristina over to her cottage but she had refused politely but firmly, blaming her aches and pains. Seja had the feeling that her resistance went much deeper; Kristina simply preferred not to leave her own home.

Kristina wiped an invisible drop of sweat from her brow as she caught sight of the coffee pot, still standing in the kitchen. Seja stopped her as she moved to get up.

"It's OK, I'll get it."

By the sink she drank a glass of water. There was a pot plant in full flower standing in the bowl, a wax plant. She followed a trickle of muddy water with her eyes.

"The police phoned," she heard Kristina's voice behind her.

This was it.

"They . . . they wanted to speak to Åke." The voice had a falsetto tone.

Seja turned and leaned against the draining board. There was a serving hatch between the kitchen and dining room, which framed Kristina as she sat at the table.

So this is what I'm supposed to do now, Seja caught herself thinking. *Is it my job to calm this woman? Haven't I got enough, dealing with my own anxiety?*

Kristina Melkersson's expression was pleading. The chubby thighs spread wide apart, the hands clutching at the kneecaps, the double chins wobbling — her whole posture suddenly seemed entreating.

"Åke, he . . . he doesn't tell me anything."

Seja walked slowly back into the dining room. "There's nothing to tell."

A little too brusque. She poured coffee and cream into both cups and pushed one over to Kristina. "There was a man at a car repair workshop. He was already dead when Åke got there. Åke called the police. That's all."

"But he'd been murdered!"

Seja avoided Kristina's agitated gaze and fixed instead on a framed photograph that stood on the sideboard: a young woman with her hair piled high, a bouquet held just beneath her chin. A wedding photo. The dimples, Kristina still had those. Apart from that, the years and the drugs she took for her aches and pains had made her face unrecognisable.

Seja tried to quell the impulse to pull away as a swollen hand was placed on top of her own.

"But what do they want with Åke?"

Seja freed her hand on the pretext of taking a sip of her coffee. She had worked hard to leave the image of the dead man in a closed room, carefully separated from everyday life. In time, through the written word, the crime scene would reappear so that she could work on it. Could put it behind her. The synonyms became a constant mantra: *isolate it, put it behind you, deal with it*. Until it was no longer dangerous. She had already established a routine for her work: research through other crime reports. In the early morning when the approaching daylight brought a sense of security. A cup of steaming Rooibos tea, the warmth of the cat on her knee. All the lamps lit. The words tumbling easily across the screen.

Now Kristina's anxiety was upsetting this hard-won balance, touching Seja's shoulders and the back of her neck like a cold gust of wind. The empathy the older woman's fear usually aroused in her dissipated.

"It's just police routine, that's all. He found the body. I should think they just want to go over how it happened. There's nothing strange about it, that's what they do."

She no longer cared about the sharpness in her voice. She wanted to get out of there, so she stood up and forced a half-hearted smile.

"Seriously, Kristina. You need to talk to Åke about this."

124

"But he won't say anything! He doesn't want to worry me, but nothing worries me more than not knowing because then I imagine the worst. And because I know that if the worst did happen, he still wouldn't tell me anything!"

"Like what?" Seja said involuntarily. She stopped and made herself sit down again.

Kristina Melkersson's frown drew a line across the bridge of her nose.

"Anyway, what were you doing there?"

"Kristina . . ."

There was something touching about the woman's utter confusion. It was clearer than ever, the way her fear of a world that was rapidly changing had eaten into her. Seja looked at the wedding photograph again, at the dimples. The timidity.

"Death-watch beetle," said Kristina Melkersson. "No, a world war. Cancer, or the lad dying in a car accident. Or the grandchildren."

"What?"

"You asked me what the worst thing would be."

Seja sighed again. "I really do have to go now. I've got a lot to do. But I can come again. Give me a ring if you need help with anything."

She felt inadequate, but Kristina Melkersson merely shrugged her shoulders. All of a sudden she seemed distant, as if she no longer cared.

Seja rinsed the cups under the tap and put the carton of cream in the fridge before she left. By the time she walked past the dining-room window, Kristina had drawn the flowery curtains, as she always did when night began to fall. It was because of the chandelier. So it wouldn't be seen from outside.

Seja took a short cut across the lawn.

CHAPTER
SEVENTEEN

Beckman tossed the morning paper aside. There was nothing about the murder in Björsared apart from a vague item about a farmer who had been found dead at a garage in Olofstorp and was presumed to have been murdered.

She poured the first cup of coffee of the day in the hope that it would perk her up. Today was not a good day. A miserable drizzle became apparent as the sky lightened, lying like a damp mist over Fiskebäck and the neglected patch outside her kitchen window. She hadn't bothered switching on the rope light running around the patio fence for several days. In addition, the tension pains had come back, shooting out from her spine like poisonous arrows, up between her shoulder blades and across one side of her face, over her jaw and temples, concentrating beneath her left eye. She massaged her temples for a long time, but only managed to achieve a very temporary numbing of the pain. She was coming down with something, all because Karlberg hadn't had the sense to stay at home with his cold.

True, she had been putting up with the pain in the back of her neck and her shoulders for a long time. Far too long. She could no longer remember when she first began to experience the long drawnout process of writing reports as torture, or to put it more accurately, even more of a torture than it had been without the pain. Meetings that went on and on often found her sitting there, working out an excuse to leave before they were over. Sitting still was the worst, but if she was particularly stressed, even her coat resting on her shoulders felt as heavy as lead. As if the stiffness had made her skin sensitive too.

The police physiotherapist was just about ready to retire, an old-fashioned severe woman in a white coat with an unpleasant way of seeing right through a person, in Beckman's opinion.

"It's as if your head is completely separate from your body," she had said as Beckman lay on her stomach, naked to the waist. "You seem to live in a completely theoretical zone. As if you have no contact at all with this body of yours. As if you don't want to acknowledge it. That's why it's protesting."

Beckman had felt embarrassed and annoyed. Was this woman a physiotherapist or a fortune teller? And it got worse as she massaged Beckman's wronged body with alternate hard and soft strokes.

"Unspoken truths often settle in the muscles and turn into pain. Things you want to say, but don't have the courage. Particularly in the musculature at the back of the neck and in the face. Many people experience pain in the jaw and even the teeth. When the mouth refuses to form those liberating words, they gather around it like an indefinable pain that refuses to go

128

away. There are tensions in your body that have turned into inflammations. If you're not careful, you could end up with a chronic condition. It's also not unusual for a person to burst into tears when someone touches them, if they're not used to it. Linking the body to the brain."

Beckman never went back. Instead she went to a doctor and got a prescription for Diclofenac.

"Start doing some exercise," he advised. "It's the only thing that will help. Go to the gym or take up swimming."

She had swum a few lengths after work on a couple of occasions, but concluded that feeling guilty about yet another thing she hadn't got around to was hardly likely to have a positive influence on her symptoms. She had, however, thought about playing tennis with someone, combining usefulness with pleasure and thus avoiding the aerobics culture that frightened her.

Beckman had played a lot of tennis when she was young and sometimes she missed that feeling of physical exertion. The feeling of being right there in the moment. She could ask someone from work, but most of her colleagues' activities seemed to be firmly established.

She couldn't help wondering if Christian Tell played tennis. She really liked him as a colleague. They were compatible, so to speak. Despite the fact that he could sometimes walk all over her, she was aware that he respected her. However, the idea of spending time with Tell outside work bordered on the absurd. It was probably the very concept of Christian Tell as a real individual that seemed absurd, if he even existed. He never talked about his private life at work and it was easier to believe that he didn't actually have anything significant in his life apart from the job. Then again, what did she know?

She wondered for a moment what her colleagues imagined her private life to be like. Presumably she too was perceived as fairly reticent. Had she always been that way? She was suddenly unsure, just as she felt unsure about most things that had happened before she met Göran — had they really happened, or were they just part of a diffuse and distant dream she thought she recalled because others reminded her of it from time to time? And now, since her mother had begun to disappear into the incomprehensible world of dementia for long periods, there was no longer anyone who reminded her directly of these things.

Beckman had got to know the few friends she spent time with after she and Göran had got together ten years ago. At least she had started to spend time with them before she had children and life was transformed into a totally unrealistic timetable with no margin for error.

So she probably was seen as closed in on herself at work. *Integrity* was an epithet she had often heard said about herself. And she liked hearing it — it sounded dignified. But it wasn't a question of character; she had simply never thought that her private life corresponded with the professional person she regarded herself to be, the person she knew others perceived her to be. And the facade rarely cracked.

Once, before she had the children. Renée Gunnarsson had come into work at the crack of dawn and found Beckman in the staffroom, her eyes red from weeping. Göran had been gone for a couple of weeks following a heart-rending quarrel, and in order to avoid being alone in the house Beckman had been coming into work every morning before dawn. She had sat there in the office in the darkest hour, staring at divorce papers.

When Renée turned up with a hug and words of consolation, she had broken down completely. They went to a nearby café before the rest of their colleagues arrived, and Beckman had wept for hours. She explained how lonely she had felt during the years she had lived with Göran, how she had grown less and less like the person she believed herself to be, and turned into someone she neither knew nor particularly liked.

Afterwards she was embarrassed, not because she had shown weakness, nor because she had wept. She was embarrassed because Göran had moved back home again after a few weeks. Because life had gone on just the way it had been before he moved out. And because it was neither the first nor the last time.

No, she would never be able to entrust someone with her private life, except in very small chunks. At least not someone she wanted to go on respecting her. A woman with inner strength — because that was how she wanted to be regarded — was not a reed, bending in the wind, nor a magnet for another person's mood. A person with integrity came to a firm decision and then stuck to it, however lonely she might feel. However much it hurt to have a shared history that suddenly exists only in the past.

Her mobile rang in her handbag. She ran into the hallway and swore as she missed the call. It was high time to wake the children, according to the plastic kitchen clock. The antique wall clock she had inherited from her grandfather had remained packed in a box in the cellar for most of the time she and Göran had been together, because Göran insisted it was ugly. The clock was the first thing she turned to during those periods when he wasn't living at home. As soon as he left the house in a rage with his suitcase, burning rubber as he screeched away in the car, and while she was still more angry than upset, while the feeling of freedom was still more powerful than loneliness, she would hang up her grandfather's clock.

When she thought about it, this silent victory seemed ridiculously sad. Many times she had considered throwing the clock away, just to break the pattern, but she had never done it. The pathetic aspect was not the clock in itself, but the role it played in her inhibited emotional life. She had once screamed so loudly at Göran that the neighbours had called the police, and she had to run and hide in the cellar, terrified that the officers in the patrol car would recognise her.

Evidently these unspoken truths had welded the length of her spine into aching knots.

On the way upstairs she heard loud snores coming from the spare room. He wouldn't be able to take the kids to nursery today either. She would have to take them, and be late for work.

Standing outside Julia and Sigrid's room, she saw that the missed call was from Andreas Karlberg. She rang him back.

"I'm on the way out to Björsared to interview the neighbours," he said over a crackling connection.

"OK, I'll be a bit late."

She closed her eyes. From the children's room Sigrid, the two-year-old, let out a scream of rage. She hated the transition from dreams to reality.

"I'll meet you there," Beckman managed to call out before the connection was broken.

She pushed open the door and was dazzled by the warm golden light of the Advent star. The room smelled of small children.

When they came in out of the cold, the heat hit them like a wall. As they sat on the well-used moss-green sofa, both ailing police officers enjoyed the warmth from the open fire. The Molins' home was just the way the homes of the elderly tend to be: tidy but over-furnished. Full of ornaments that perhaps had sentimental value or just happened to be there. Furniture in varying styles and from different periods. Standard lamps with low-watt bulbs and faded shades. Christmas decorations and a thin layer of dust covering everything. As if the memories of an entire lifetime had been gathered together in three rooms, plus the kitchen and the upper floor. And that's just how it was, in all probability.

The early hour did not deter fru Molin from ceremoniously producing a three-tier cake stand, laden with ginger biscuits, Lucia saffron buns and pastries. She had baked the marble cake herself. Karlberg accepted a slice out of politeness and was just about to take a bite when he detected the faint but unmistakable smell of mould. He put the cake back on his plate and thought it wouldn't be the first time he had spirited away some inedible delicacy while the hostess excused herself on some errand in the kitchen.

Dagny Molin drew her knitted cardigan more tightly around her shoulders as she lowered herself into the armchair opposite Beckman.

"It's cold in here, isn't it? I'll ask Bertil to turn up the heating."

"No, there's no need," said Karlberg, feeling the sweat break out on his upper lip. The fire, which had seemed so wonderfully welcoming at first, was now beginning to eat up the last of the oxygen in the room.

Bertil Molin shuffled forward out of the shadows. He turned up an electric radiator, strategically placed next to the sofa where Karlberg was sitting. Karlberg removed his jacket.

"I didn't think for a minute Lars would be dead," said Dagny Molin when her husband had settled himself in a wicker chair right next to the door, as if he needed an escape route. "When you were here the last time, I mean."

"Well, the picture has become somewhat clearer to us as well since I was last here. But there are still a number of question marks. You already know that Lars Waltz was murdered. We know that the perpetrator arrived by car, which means he must have travelled along this road at some point during the evening or night of the nineteenth. You can actually see the Edell farm from your veranda so we just want to be sure that you didn't see or hear anything you didn't remember the last time I was here."

He spoke slowly and clearly to emphasise the significance of his words. Dagny Molin shook her head.

"As I told you, we were asleep. Our bedroom upstairs is at the back of the house, so we don't hear or see cars on the road. And even if we had, Waltz ran a car repair workshop. We wouldn't notice every single car."

Karlberg had to accept this, of course. He tried another tack.

"Last time you said you knew Edell well. Lise-Lott's first husband."

"Thomas, oh yes! He often spent time down in our basement in years gone by. Sven, our son, had his den down there, next to the boiler room. That's where they used to go. You know how it is: youngsters want to be left in peace. At least when they're growing up. It's the first step away from you — you know you're starting to lose them. And we don't see him often enough these days. Do you have children, officer?"

"Er, no. So you're saying that your son used to go around with Thomas Edell? When was this?"

Dagny Molin smiled, as if she found the question ridiculous.

"Well, they were neighbours. They were the same age, so it was only natural for them to spend time together. When they were little they didn't have much choice, really. It was a long way to the nearest house, and in the old days we didn't drive kids here and there so they could play with somebody else. No, in those days you had to play with what was to hand. In Sven's case that was Thomas, and it was probably no bad thing. They used to love playing out in the fresh air. On their bikes. Making go-karts. You know the sort of thing."

"What about later on?" Karin Beckman interjected. "When they were teenagers."

Dagny Molin seemed put out.

"Well, I don't really know what to say. What mother knows exactly what her teenagers get up to? They had mopeds, they used to go around on those. There were more lads hanging around by that time, from different villages, and God knows I can't remember all their names. When you get to my age you're pleased if you can remember the important things."

She fell silent and glanced at her husband. He had switched on the television, with the sound off. A parliamentary debate filled the screen, and the leader of the moderate party was reflected in the tinted glass of the mahogany bookcase. Dagny Molin's hands moved restlessly for a moment, then she leaned over and made sure the radiator was on. She turned it up to maximum then sat back in her armchair with a sigh of relief.

"He was a bit difficult, was Thomas. I won't pretend otherwise. Sven was always a sweet boy, but easily led. Sometimes I worried that Sven would get into trouble with Thomas, I don't mind admitting that now. Not that there was any bad in him, absolutely not. Nor in

136

Reino. But boys will be boys and they got a bit carried away sometimes. They wanted to experience everything, try everything. I'm sure you know what I mean, officer. You're not too old to have forgotten that sort of thing?"

The heated dust was spreading a suffocating smell of burning. Karlberg felt panic creeping up on him as he discovered that he had lost the ability to blink. His eyelids appeared to have dried on to his eyeballs.

Beckman was quick to take over the reins.

"Exactly what do you mean, fru Molin? Drinking? Fighting? Could you be more specific?"

Dagny Molin squirmed, pursing her mouth.

"Well, there might have been drinking and a certain amount of violence, but they were only young. And Thomas is dead," she said censoriously. "He inherited the farm and he got married before bad luck caught up with him. He turned into a really good man. Sven too."

She brightened up.

"Sven has made a fresh start: he's met someone, and he's bought a business. A mink farm, up Dalsland way. And he's got two children into the bargain, a boy and a girl."

She pointed over towards the piano, which was visible through the doorway of the next room. Between mother and father in a porcelain family of Christmas goblins stood a framed photograph of a boy and a girl. They looked Asian.

"She's from Thailand, apparently, this woman Sven's met. I can't remember her name. We've never met, but Sven sent that photo last winter. I'm glad Sven's found a woman. He needs someone to look after him and he

137

isn't getting any younger. He's a good boy. They were good boys, all of them."

A mantra, thought Beckman. *Good boys*. She kept having to rub her hand across her forehead to stop her fringe sticking to the skin. Without any idea of what was waiting for them, she had put on a cashmere sweater over a much too revealing camisole, and now she could neither take it off nor stand the heat any longer. She got the idea that Dagny Molin was well aware of her torment and was secretly smiling to herself. Every breath she took hurt, as if she were sitting in a sauna, and she could barely keep her thoughts in order.

"What do you know about Reino Edell's relationship with Lise-Lott?" she asked.

Without taking her eyes off Molin she could sense Karlberg's muted surprise. Perhaps he had been thinking of a different approach, but right now she couldn't have cared less. Just as long as she could get out of this suffocating heat, out into the damp December morning and the fresh air before she expired.

Bertil Molin took his eyes off the TV screen for a second and met Beckman's gaze over the cake stand.

"He couldn't stand the woman."

Then he turned up the volume and gave his attention to Rosenbad once again.

CHAPTER
EIGHTEEN

He wasn't looking forward to Christmas; as usual it would be too much. Too much food, definitely too much drink, and above all far, far too much time spent with the family.

When Bärneflod set off from his home in Floda to the town hall in Lerum, he had just seen his wife naked, on top of everything else. By mistake he had walked into the bedroom as she was getting changed and had seen her stark naked. It didn't really do much for him.

Fifteen years ago she had started sleeping in a full-length nightdress in a vain attempt to keep the decline of her body to herself. Not that they lacked a conjugal sex life. It did happen, although not that often, that he would tap her on the shoulder once they had finished watching TV, and then shuffle upstairs, brush his teeth and possibly splash a little aftershave on his face. It was just that Ulla seemed to think her body was in some way exceptional, which it most definitely wasn't. It looked neither better nor worse than the bodies of sixty-year-old women usually do. A little bit droopy here, the odd hollow there, a few wrinkles. But what could you expect? As long as there were no younger, prettier models to turn to, and there weren't for a man of Bärneflod's age and energy, he didn't think it was worth complaining.

But it was different for women. For men their self-esteem was bound up with their professional status but for women it was all to do with appearance. Particularly women like Ulla, whose contribution to the household economy was no more than pocket money. And she'd always been unsure of herself. Afraid of not being appreciated. He didn't see things that way. He'd always taken the view that anybody who didn't like him could leave him alone. Usually the dislike was mutual.

Bärneflod drove past the Solkatten shopping mall and the square, which exuded a 1950s air in beige and pale green, the shop names dating from a time when illuminated signs were something new. Lerum's handful of alcoholics had already settled in the winners' enclosure: four benches in a half-moon shape, the off-licence within easy reach.

A certain satisfaction came over him as he parked his car. He had no intention of paying the parking fee. A handwritten note, *Police Business*, lay in full view on the dashboard. That should scare off the jobsworths.

"Per-Erik Stahre will see you as soon as possible."

The secretary, or receptionist maybe, had forgotten to take off her knitted scarf, which, appropriately for the season, was red. She had a spiky appearance. Presumably she, like Stahre, had had to break her holiday in order to be available to the police.

140

It irritated Bärneflod, sitting in this shabby town hall corridor waiting for some stroppy little clerk who no doubt felt the need to restore the balance of power. He tapped his fingers impatiently. For a moment he considered heading off to the ironmonger's in the mall across the road to buy the hinges he had been thinking about for the new gate. The last storm had torn the old one right off, which was just as well, since it was completely rotten. There wasn't really any need to have a gate in the pathetic little fence between the garden of their semi and the road, but Ulla wanted a gate, so a gate there had to be. In certain matters she was implacable.

The secretary was surfing the net, he could see that clearly from where he was sitting. Chatting with boys online, no doubt, even pretty girls did that nowadays. In his day it had only been the ugly ones who put an ad in the paper or rang hotlines.

There was a large clock above the receptionist's head. The second hand was driving Bärneflod mad. In the end he stood up and took his wallet out of his jacket pocket.

"This is a police matter, as I said. Could you please tell me where Per-Erik Stahre's office is?"

Several seconds passed as the girl's fingers flew over the keyboard. She clicked on "Send" then finally turned to Bärneflod.

"As I said, he's busy at the moment."

Bitch.

"And as I said, that's not my problem."

She rolled her eyes. Then she got up and walked past Bärneflod and down the corridor, her heels clicking on the lino floor. He was right behind her, and the next moment he was standing in front of Stahre, who was sitting at a round table opposite a woman with bright red hair that didn't suit her at all. Stahre was surprisingly young. Bärneflod had expected some old fogey.

"I'm busy at the —"

"Bengt Bärneflod, police. This is a murder investigation."

He shoved his ID card under Stahre's nose.

Stahre looked at his watch for the tenth time in half an hour, drumming his fingers on his open Filofax.

"I don't know what to say. It's all very upsetting, but I still don't understand how you think I can help."

"Me neither. You had dealings with Lars Waltz, and I'm trying to get to know Lars Waltz. There are some people who claim you'd fallen out with him."

"But that's ridiculous!"

Bärneflod's mobile started vibrating in his pocket, but he ignored it.

"I was in touch with Waltz with regard to some photographic jobs for a while, that's all."

"For quite a long while, if I've understood correctly."

"For a few years, yes. It was just a handful of jobs. It may well be that Lars got upset the last few times we were in touch, but I think to say we'd fallen out would be overstating the case."

Bärneflod nodded thoughtfully.

"Why did Waltz get upset?"

Stahre clamped his lips together and gazed out of the window. "I'd broken off our arrangement in favour of another photographer."

"He got the sack?"

"No!" Stahre slammed the palm of his hand down angrily on the desk. "He was freelance. He wasn't employed. We had no agreement to use him exclusively for the kind of job we're talking about. I was perfectly within my rights to choose another photographer."

"But this wasn't just about one job. You said you'd broken off your arrangement."

Stahre sighed and ran his hand through his hair a couple of times. It stood up on his head like a plume.

"If I'm going to be honest . . ."

"It surprises me that you've only just realised you have to be."

"Lars Waltz wasn't a good enough photographer to be worth so much trouble."

"Trouble?"

"He was pretty fond of himself. I hope you understand it goes against the grain to speak ill of the dead, otherwise I would have mentioned this right at the start."

"If everybody followed your line of reasoning, herr Stahre, we wouldn't be able to do our job. So let's hear it. I haven't got all day, and nor have you."

"He was impulsive. He referred to his difficulty in working with other people as artistic freedom, and he was usually in a bad mood. In a work context, that is. I have no idea how he behaved in his private life."

"Go on."

"The type of job we're talking about had to fit within a particular framework. Community information. No room for diversions. Waltz found it difficult to accept that. He wanted everything his own way."

"And when he couldn't have things his own way?"

"Then he'd get very angry." He shrugged his shoulders. "Yelling and slamming doors, I suppose he thought he was eccentric, but he made it impossible. And he was overcharging. There was no reason to carry on using him. As I said, we only hired him as a freelance, we had no obligations. But to say we'd fallen out, I think that's —"

"OK, I get it."

Bärneflod got to his feet and zipped up his suede jacket. In his mind he was bemoaning the fact that people in general, and murder victims in particular, were rarely as obligingly straightforward as you might think at the beginning of an investigation. Some tosser always came along and went against the prevailing view.

"Thank you for your time. I'll find my own way out."

He still had time to go and buy the hinges.

CHAPTER
NINETEEN

The strains of a familiar Christmas song. The Christmas holiday would once again be a disappointment to the children, with the rain drearily pouring over the pavements and gushing down into the grids. Tell changed the radio station to avoid "O Holy Night".

The car park at the police station was lit up like a stage, the street lamps reflected in the wet sheen of the cars. The story behind this completely over-the-top lighting was to do with vandalism and break-ins in the staff car park. A couple of locks had been forced, but it was mainly a case of some kind of symbolic vandalism: slogans sprayed in red, along with dents and scratches arbitrarily inflicted with a baseball bat or a bunch of keys.

It was pretty brave, he supposed, for them to venture inside the police station compound. Skånegatan was manned more or less 24/7. And given that the entire city was full of cars, presumably the fact that these vehicles were owned by police officers had some particular significance.

On one occasion Tell had brought in a sixteen-year-old boy for throwing cobblestones at the police during a violent anti-racist demonstration. He had been amazed at the boy's conviction. He had thought back to his own confused teenage years and realised that he had never in his whole life felt so sure of anything, whereas these kids were willing to fight for what they believed in. Tell was secretly quite impressed.

"At least they believe in something," he had said in the staff room in the aftermath of 30 November, when the city had been ravaged by demonstrations and counter-demonstrations. The statement wasn't directed at anyone in particular, but had certainly been provoked by Bärneflod's narrow-minded comments about a "communist rabble".

It wasn't only Bärneflod who was horrified at young people's lack of respect for social institutions financed by their parents' generation. The media also leapt on the bandwagon of blackening the political viewpoint inaccurately linked to the destruction. Suddenly the entire basis of socialism was synonymous with a gang of aggressive masked lunatics.

"They're the ones we're paying for," Bärneflod snorted angrily, "working our backsides off day in and day out. First of all they're on benefits because the bastards don't want to work, then we're supposed to support the buggers when they decide to smash up half the town. I get angry too sometimes, but I don't start smashing bloody windows, do I?"

Beckman had sighed deeply.

"These kids aren't likely to be on benefits, Bengt. They're middle class with politically correct, intellectual parents, the kids of tree-huggers who've grown up and got good jobs. These anarchists will get an

146

education too, and eventually they'll end up sitting there in a nice terraced house — just not yet. How are they supposed to rebel if not by being even worse than Mummy and Daddy?"

"You seem to be speaking from personal experience," muttered Bärneflod. "I bet you were one of the ones I carted off in the 70s. In a kaftan and sandals. Or perhaps you're too young. Sorry."

He laughed loudly, trying to smooth things over when he realised he'd gone too far.

"All I'm saying is we can't afford to cosset these people. They don't contribute anything to society. Evidently there isn't enough money for schools or nurseries or care homes for the elderly. It's as if you have to be a foreigner or a criminal to get any help. I mean, I've got a lad of twenty-five living in the basement at home, still with no prospect of getting a flat of his own. I'm bloody certain he'd have been provided with a place to live and all the rest of it if he'd been a bit less conscientious. Where are the ordinary decent Swedish kids supposed to go?"

Beckman had stalked off into her office. Tell couldn't remember if he'd carried on arguing with Bärneflod or if he'd just allowed the irritation to chafe at him for a while before it gradually faded away, as he usually did. Sometimes an exchange of views cost a great deal more than it was worth in terms of time and energy. At least he convinced himself that was the case.

Now he heard footsteps outside his office and automatically glanced at his watch. Twenty past six. Because his thoughts had been with Bärneflod, he almost expected to see him standing in the doorway, but it was Karlberg who appeared, which seemed only logical. It was the evening before Christmas Eve. What normal man with a wife and children, even if they were grown up, would choose to stay on at work going through reports? Tell had encouraged his colleagues to go home and start celebrating several hours ago.

"What are you doing here?" he said. Karlberg shrugged his shoulders.

Tell pretended to look stern. "Get out of here. And merry Christmas."

"Same to you."

Karlberg disappeared. Tell realised he hadn't given any thought to how he was going to spend Christmas Eve.

Of course he had a standing invitation to his older sister Ingrid's enormous house in Onsala, but they had little contact. The main reason for this was the man Ingrid had married. In Tell's eyes he was an unpleasant boastful stockbroker who didn't always take a strictly legal approach to his share dealings. And then there was Ingrid herself. Tell didn't know what he feared most: whether she knew about her husband's underhand deals but didn't feel that she was in a position to get involved since he supported her, or whether she was just too gullible to notice what was going on.

Whatever the case, Tell felt sufficiently uncomfortable to avoid his sister's house except on Christmas Eve, when he and his father, an increasingly confused widower, were invited to sit on ridiculously expensive furniture as a symbol of the host couple's generosity

148

and goodwill. Tell couldn't stand it. He suddenly realised this was why he was glued to his desk as the lights in the station went out room by room.

He reached for the telephone, keyed in a number and waited for the high slightly strained voice.

"Krook."

"Hi sis, it's me. How are you coping?"

"Not too bad. But there's such a lot to do. Are you coming tomorrow? I rang you the other day, and Dad, but there was no reply."

"No, I should have called and let you know, but I'm right in the middle of a complicated murder investigation. I was waiting to see if there might be a window when I could get away, but . . ."

"It's not looking good?"

"No, I'm sorry. It looks as if I'm going to have to work right through Christmas. Unfortunately. I was looking forward to seeing you."

"Well, there's nothing you can do, I understand that. Duty comes first. But Dad will be disappointed. He says he only sees you at Christmas, more or less, even though you live so close to one another."

"Well, it's not that close," said Tell, the anger welling up inside him. Just like Ingrid to take the opportunity to make him feel guilty. No doubt she would mention Christmas presents soon; naturally he hadn't got around to buying any. "It's ten kilometres, not exactly next door."

"Oh well. Anyway, we'll meet up some other time. I'll put your present in the post. It's nothing special, just a few chocolates. And look after yourself, Christian. Don't go working yourself to death. Merry Christmas."

"Merry Christmas, Ingrid."

If he hadn't been convinced before, he was now absolutely sure he'd made the right decision. *Don't go working yourself to death*. There was certainly no risk of Ingrid doing that; she had never done a day's work in her life — if you didn't count housework, dinner parties for her husband's contacts and bringing up children. Still, it seemed petty for a person who had all the time in the world at their disposal — particularly since both her sons were grown up and didn't exactly need her to blow their noses or change their nappies — to place the entire responsibility for their father's social life on him.

He had sometimes wondered what the nervously animated Ingrid got up to all alone during the day in her big house. When there were no guests to look after. Were her features softer, was her smile less strained? Suddenly he could see her in his mind's eye at sixteen or seventeen, when they were both still living at home. He remembered how it used to bother him when his mates started sneaking off to the room next door, standing in the doorway and grinning inanely at his sister. She had been a pretty teenager. And cool.

A figure appeared on the other side of the fence surrounding the car park, and stood there gazing up at the building. Tell realised he couldn't be seen from outside as there were no lights on in his office apart from the electric Advent candles. When the boy started climbing the fence, Tell hammered on the window, almost frightening the life out of the poor kid. Because

150

you had to feel sorry for a lad who was trying to break into a police station on 23 December, instead of sitting at home with mulled wine and the television.

The feeling of relief at avoiding Christmas in the Krook household was beginning to ebb, and was replaced with a new sense of disquiet: the thought of an empty flat and the blue glow of the neon sign across the street. He wondered if there was anything left in the bottle of Jameson he'd opened just after the feast day of St Lucia, on 13 December. He looked at his watch again. Only ten minutes had passed.

The radio programme he'd been listening to was interrupted by the traffic news, informing listeners that the traditional holiday jam in the Tingstad tunnel had temporarily eased. And it was getting late. Most of those who had been going nowhere fast a few hours earlier up by Gasklockan, the huge gasometer, had presumably made it to their cottages in Bohuslän by now; perhaps they were already filling up the fridge with Christmas fare.

He decided to go for a little outing.

The examination of the crime scene had been completed but he still parked by the side of the road; old habits die hard.

Tell pulled down the garage door. He didn't want the cold fluorescent light flooding across the yard. Even if it was highly unlikely that the murderer would return to the scene of the crime so long after the murder, he still didn't want to advertise his presence. He hung his coat over the back of the chair in the makeshift office.

There was a computer containing a simple book-keeping program in which the company's income and expenditure had been entered. Tell couldn't see anything untoward in the services specified or the amounts involved, even if he wasn't exactly an expert when it came to cars. And it was obvious that the workshop hadn't made Waltz a rich man, unless he was doing work that didn't go through the books. Which of course he could easily have been doing, thought Tell.

He shut down the computer and sat there for a moment on the office chair, trying to decide what to do next.

The bottle of Jameson, hopefully still half-full, popped into his head. Perhaps it was time to go home and sit up late watching TV, like any normal Swede would be doing. Distractedly he took down two files from a shelf above the desk.

Apart from a list of telephone numbers, the files didn't contain anything that seemed unusual. He folded up the list and tucked it into his jacket pocket. He was just about to put on his coat when a noise made him jump. It seemed to come from outside, and sounded like the engine of a car being turned off a little way down the road. There were no other houses nearby. Could Lise-Lott have decided to come home after all, despite informing them that she would be staying with her sister over Christmas and New Year?

Instead of making a noise by opening the garage door, Tell decided to go out through a smaller doorway within the big barn doors. As quietly as he could he

152

moved across to the other part of the barn, where agricultural machinery in various stages of decay stood along the walls like the skeletons of prehistoric animals. Even though a full moon was shining on the cluttered cement floor, it was difficult to avoid stumbling over buckets, sacks and tools.

The doorway Tell was aiming for faced the road, which meant he would have a good chance of surprising any intruder from behind. He was filled with a mute sense of relief as he stepped out of the barn. It had stopped raining. A little way off on the gravel track he could definitely make out the silhouette of a car.

Tell crept around the corner of the barn, keeping his back against the flaking wall, and listened carefully. A sound in the bushes made his heart skip a beat. He wasn't carrying his service pistol, of course. He groped for something with which to defend himself and found a thick branch by his feet. The shadow of an animal, presumably a rat, darted from the bushes and disappeared under an outhouse.

He clutched the branch firmly. It was now pitch dark, except for a narrow strip of moonlight emerging from a gap in the clouds. Someone was moving towards the house with rapid, light footsteps. He didn't have time to think; he just took three long strides and wrapped his arm tightly around the intruder's throat.

The scream that shattered the silence took him completely by surprise. A moment's hesitation was all it took for his captive to gain the upper hand by elbowing him hard in the stomach then spinning around and

153

driving a knee into his crotch so that he doubled over in pain. Both the voice and the red wellingtons were familiar.

"Seja Lundström? It's Inspector Christian Tell," he gasped.

"Berg," she said, her voice trembling as she caught her breath. "Seja Lund*berg*."

He managed to straighten up, still furious as he looked into her terrified eyes.

"What the hell are you doing here? This is a crime scene, and you're a witness! Do you understand how serious this is, creeping around here in the dark? And how suspicious it looks?"

"No . . . well, yes. I do understand. But . . . it's not what you think." She took a step back as if her first instinct was to turn and run away.

"I don't think anything," Tell hissed, angrily wiping away a tear that had squeezed out of his eye as a result of the sudden pain. "The only thing I know is that you need to come up with a good explanation as to why you're here, and bloody quickly. I think the station is the best place for that conversation."

She backed away from him and shook her head so violently that the hat under which her hair had been tucked fell to the ground. Momentarily distracted from his rage, Tell noticed that her brown curly hair looked surprisingly coarse, like horsehair.

"No! I mean, there's no need. I know it seems odd, but I have absolutely nothing to do with all this, with the murder. I wasn't even with Åke when he found the body, you already know that. I will explain, but I'd

154

rather not do it at the police station. It's Christmas, after all . . . not that I'm that bothered about Christmas . . ."

Tell thought about the station, virtually in darkness. Right now it would be empty apart from a few duty officers and some poor sod on the desk who was probably doing the crossword and looking at the clock every ten minutes. He sighed and set off towards the car, taking Seja Lundberg's arm.

"Didn't you see my car?" he couldn't help asking.

She was almost running to keep up with his long strides.

"No. It's dark."

She hesitated as he opened the passenger door.

"Would you trust me to drive my own car? Otherwise I don't know how I'm going to get it home." She added, "Perhaps we could drive into Hjällbo and get a cup of coffee somewhere. I could really do with one. Then you can question me at the same time."

Tell wondered if she was teasing him. He was bothered by the lack of respect she was showing in the face of his attempt to exert authority. He thought about letting her go and booking an interview after the holiday. She was hardly a suspect, after all, and was highly unlikely to take off anywhere. But coffee sounded like a good idea, especially compared with the alternatives on offer — the whiskey, the TV and the glow of the neon sign. He made his decision.

"We'd better go into town. I shouldn't think there'll be anything open in Hjällbo by now."

"We could try the pub at the railway station," she said. Her smile seemed familiar, but he couldn't work out why.

He pulled himself together. She was a witness. He'd found her in an isolated location where a man had recently been murdered. If she wanted to even out the balance of power by pretending they were friends or flirting with him, he wasn't going to be stupid enough to fall for it. He pushed her firmly towards her own car.

As he drove behind her on to the empty main road, heading into town, he couldn't help wondering about the sudden awkwardness Seja Lundberg had aroused in him.

After they had abandoned the idea of the pub at the central station, since the clientele consisted largely of faces that were too well known to Tell, they walked around for half an hour searching for a café or restaurant that was still open on the night before Christmas Eve. The place they finally ended up in was crowded, mostly with young people packed around tables in a huge space covering three floors. The floor was painted pale grey, with a very high shine slightly reminiscent of dirty ice. The walls were a deep red and covered with photos inspired by the 1950s. He recognised the flicked up hair and big sunglasses of Jackie Kennedy. Somehow the sea of young people rubbing up against one another seemed even more alien since the smoking ban had made the picture clearer. In Tell's day veils of smoke had lain thickly over bars and pubs, smoothing rough edges and giving you

156

something to do with your hands, as well as a dreary but acceptable chat-up line.

Seja took the words out of his mouth.

"This isn't exactly the kind of place I usually go to."

"No."

The music was far too loud for Tell's taste. They took a window table from a couple who appeared to be on their way home so that they could concentrate on each other undisturbed. It made the conversation Tell had intended to conduct with Seja seem somewhat absurd.

She was rummaging in her rucksack, her head down. That hair again, covering her face in a great heavy swathe, like a separate entity in itself. She wasn't wearing a scrap of make-up, and was dressed in practical clothes: jeans and a warm sweater.

She emerged with a tin of snuff. Tell discovered two things: her upper lip was beaded with sweat, and although he was fighting against it, he couldn't help finding this extremely sexy. The second thing was that she had a piercing in her nose, which surprised him. It suggested a certain kind of self-awareness he had thought Seja Lundberg lacked. She wasn't wearing anything in it, and at first he had thought the black dot was a birthmark.

She leaned forward, her elbows on the table.

"I wasn't with Åke when he found the body," she said, taking a sip of her beer.

"No, I know that," said Tell. "Anyway, it was perfectly obvious you were lying." He put his cup down on the saucer. "The question is, why? That's what I want you to explain to me."

157

She sighed and chewed on a nail as she gazed out at the outdoor bar, which was closed.

"I can't explain it. I know it seems insane, but I . . . I wanted to see the dead man. Something drew me there, not just Åke. I'm a journalist — at least, I soon will be. Maybe I thought that . . . well, it doesn't matter what I thought. Åke was disturbed by the whole thing, and he didn't want to go back there on his own. Besides, he did actually need a lift. His wife isn't very well and I think he didn't want to worry her. I usually help them out. With all kinds of things." She kept her eyes fixed on Tell as she repeated, "I wanted to see the body. That's why I lied and said I was there when Åke found it. Otherwise I would never have been allowed past the gate."

"And what did you think?"

His expression was challenging as he held her gaze over his coffee cup, and he noticed her hesitation. Enough interviews, if not exactly along these lines, had taught him to see whenever a person was wondering just how truthful they should be. A range of possible versions flitting through their mind, like lines that had to be followed to their conclusion so that they could be dismissed. In the end lies wound themselves together into one big tangle that became impossible to sort out, under the implacable searching gaze of the professional. Some people broke down and told the truth. The difficulty lay in knowing whether the person in front of you was lying or simply concealing part of the truth.

"I was fascinated. And scared."

He nodded. A fascination for crime scenes was something they had in common.

"But what were you doing there today? In the dark."

Instead of adopting a veiled expression, which Tell would have found appropriate, a wry smile twitched at the corners of her mouth.

"And what about you? Haven't you got anything better to do than lurk about at the scene of a murder on a night like this? Shouldn't you be decorating the tree? Cooking the Christmas ham?"

"Answer the question," said Tell, feeling torn. In a different context he would have interpreted the smile as a definite sign she was flirting with him. And he couldn't help being turned on by her warmth; it seeped out of those grey-green eyes, from the corners of her mouth and through her voice, which was deep and sensual.

She leaned back in her chair.

"Christmas frightens me. I split up with my partner not long ago, and I get lonely sometimes. Not always, but today. Tonight. I got the heebie-jeebies and just took off. As I said before, I was scared. And fascinated. I'm often fascinated by fear and, for me, checking things out is a way of controlling it. Finding its roots. I drove to Björsared because somehow I already felt involved. I was thinking about the woman, his wife, and I wanted to see if she was there. Talk to her."

"As part of your research, I suppose?"

She ignored his cynical undertone.

"I just wanted to talk to her, that's all. But she wasn't there. And then you jumped on me."

159

A techno version of "Jingle Bells" was turned up to full volume, and a gang of boys and girls at the long vermilion bar began to sing along.

Tell looked at Seja and risked a smile.

"Let's go. I think I know a better place, if you can cope with a stronger drink. But Detective Inspector Tell won't be coming with us." He hesitated for a moment before throwing all reason overboard. "Christian will have to do."

She smiled back. As he thought about the fragile heart that had decorated the froth on top of his coffee, he suddenly remembered an evening in the pub at the central station. Seja had been sitting next to him on a bar stool, with her coat on. Tell had thought that this woman seemed to exude the same kind of loneliness as himself, a loneliness that was above all spiritual, and incurable. Being surrounded by other people somehow increased the sensation of standing all alone on a spiritual plane where everything else has been flattened by a strong wind. Carina, the person with whom he had come closest to creating a life together, had put it like this: *Christian, according to your view of the world, you are all on your own there in the middle. Everyone else is just a peripheral shadow. Unreliable. Unnecessary.*

"He'll do fine."

Seja Lundberg put on her anorak.

She could handle her beer better than he'd expected. This miscalculation cost him the remains of the sense he had left behind, and his sobriety. The hole in the

160

wall underneath the Hotel Europa had countless brands of lager, and at some point during the course of the evening they decided to try them all. When the jovial Irish owner turned off the artificial candelabra at around midnight and threw them out with a kindly word — "Don't forget Christmas, kids" — they had to lean on one another.

A sharp frost had followed the rain. The canal, its bridges adorned with sparkling ropes of light, was covered in a thin layer of ice, as were the broad stone steps leading down to the water and the iron chains that were meant to stop the public from falling in. As far as he could remember afterwards, they had no qualms about ignoring this safety barrier. They just sat there on the bottom step, the soles of their shoes resting lightly on the thin ice.

Gradually the frost found its way through their clothes. With numb frozen behinds and feet, it seemed obvious he should invite her up to his flat.

"I don't live far away," he said. "We're going to freeze to death."

And it was true. In any case, she wasn't exactly capable of driving.

Ending up in bed wasn't part of the plan. It was, he thought on the morning of Christmas Eve as the pale sun stabbed him in the eye, the result of poor judgement followed by severe intoxication. This could cost him dear and would be difficult to explain to his colleagues. And to Östergren, if the gossip got that far.

And it probably would, given that the police station was like one big coffee morning.

He reached out and traced the contours of her body, careful not to wake her. The bones of her spine lay defenceless beneath the thin skin, and the morning light revealed downy hair at the back of her neck. Her calm even breathing reminded him of a sleeping child.

Memories of the previous evening came back to him in disjointed chunks: he suddenly remembered her face beneath him, her mouth and eyes open, telling him about fear and trust.

When the breathing changed, he knew she was awake.

"Christian?"

"Yes."

"I daren't turn over. I'm so afraid of being confronted by your regrets."

Her voice was hoarse from the alcohol and out-pourings of the previous evening. It broke and became a whisper, more sensed than heard. He was filled with a warmth that began at his toes and spread like wildfire through his limbs until it reached his aching head and exploded in the form of a smile that he wanted to hide and show at the same time.

He had always found these unwritten rules difficult to understand: the game that had to be played at the beginning of a relationship. The precisely measured amount of give and take a man must master, in order to avoid being perceived as an arrogant bastard with intimacy problems, or a suffocating control freak.

162

She turned over, and he clumsily stroked her tousled hair.

"Merry Christmas," she said, pulling the duvet over her head with a muffled howl.

All day Seja kept saying that she would take a stroll over to the northern part of town to pick up her car and go home. First of all they were just going to have a traditional Christmas Eve breakfast. She rang Åke and asked if he could see to Lukas, while Tell went out shopping for rice pudding, spiced wort bread and Cheddar cheese; he also found some eau de toilette on the perfume counter, and wrapped it in flowery paper.

Then they collapsed together in front of the TV, watching Donald Duck, *Karl-Bertil Jonsson's Christmas Eve*, and an old film before finishing off the half-bottle of Jameson, which Tell had produced from the cupboard. And that was how she ended up staying until Christmas morning, after ringing Åke once again and pointing out that he still owed her a favour or two.

In the hallway they held hands for several minutes before Seja pulled away. Tell stood in the doorway until the sound of her footsteps died away and the outside door closed behind her. For the first time in almost two days he thought about work. It gave him a sinking feeling in the pit of his stomach.

CHAPTER
TWENTY

1994

Maya's teacher was talking about the "disturbing development in the level of her ambitions". He really wanted to discuss her relationship with Caroline, but it was clear that he was unable to formulate the words to describe what was really troubling him.

Maya didn't offer him any assistance. He would have to deal with his jealousy as best he could. In the end the conversation died away, after she had dodged the issue and promised to pull her socks up.

Oh yes, she knew she was young and had very good prospects, if only she would make the same effort she had made at the beginning, a year or so ago when nothing of any significance had happened in her life. Because that was the most terrifying thing of all: she didn't care about anything except Caroline. Why? Because Caroline made her happy. Because Maya was more than happy to fulfil her expectations.

She had returned to school after visiting Borås for a couple of weeks that seemed empty because of her longing to get back to Stensjö. Therefore she was bewildered when Caroline met her with angry accusations, saying she had lost her passion. That she was drifting away from her.

There were small but unmissable signs, Caroline insisted, blind to Maya's growing fear: *Maya was friendly, but not intimate. Her lover but not her twin soul. She couldn't bear it.*

However much Maya professed the sincerity of her love, it was never enough.

When the anger had worked itself out, Caroline turned her back on Maya, hurt. She suddenly began to hang out with one of the boys in Maya's class, a dark-eyed silent young man. They held hands behind the canteen, and Caroline's cheeks were red. At dawn Maya would stand behind the curtain in the school's guest room, where she now slept; she had found a refuge there in her anger. She saw him on the porch of the studio cottage, his shirt buttoned up all wrong and his hair standing on end.

She had no one to talk to. In her darkest hours Maya thought that Caroline seemed to be enjoying her despair.

Maya was lucky and managed to get another room; it wasn't her old one, but it did look out over the garden. It was fine. For two whole weeks she left her cases without unpacking them, like a tourist just passing through.

Then Caroline was standing there again, triumphant: *I love being the first one for you, not just the woman you go to bed with, but the first one who has touched your soul.* She had let the hair on the top of her head grow into a stubby coxcomb. "Now I know I mean something to you."

Maya forgave her and moved back into the studio. She handed in her room key, blushing with embarrassment as she gave it to Greta in the office. Greta tilted her head to one side and tried to look pleasant, despite the fact that her cryptic comments were poisonous.

"You're not the first one to get caught up with Caroline. I think a conscientious girl like you should be careful, Maya. You can't always be sure you know everything it's important to know about a person."

But who knows what is important and what is right in life, while it's still going on? Maya allowed herself to be swept away by a passion that held her in its grip for weeks, during which she and Caroline hardly let go of one another. Love was a roller coaster, the betrayals unspoken and barely touching the scope, the breadth and the depth of the emotion; betrayals that it was impossible to put into words, and therefore impossible to come to terms with. When Maya did not fulfil her expectations, Caroline would retreat, needing to be alone, silent and inaccessible, and Maya would weep once more.

And if Maya devoted only part of her attention to her studies when she and Caroline were passionately in love, she was barely capable of bothering with them at all when they weren't speaking. All her strength went into resisting the impulse to plead and pray, to beg on her knees to be loved again, the way she now knew it was possible to be loved. Sometimes she gave in to this impulse and detested the way Caroline closed her eyes and allowed herself to be filled up, apparently entranced by the fact that Maya was humiliating herself for her sake.

Caroline was smoking outside the door of the main building.

Maya thought once again how Caroline was capable of making her feel less lonely, how she could choose whether to love or not. She wanted to run up to her and take her to task for the careless way she handled other people's feelings, but the number of people around them stopped her.

Suddenly the situation seemed so constricting and stifling that she felt as if she couldn't move. The little group of houses on the edge of the forest aroused nothing but loathing in her, the charm of the old school building seemed musty and out of date. It was suddenly incomprehensible to her that Caroline should have stood this year after year, a world where nothing changed except the fresh cohorts of students, who stayed for a while and then moved on in life.

She pushed her hands down into her pockets. The clock struck ten, and dutiful students headed for their classes.

"We're going to move away from here," said Maya when they were alone on the steps. "We'll move out and get a place of our own, you and me. We can't stay here for ever."

Caroline's face was completely expressionless.

Maya went on: "I mean, I'll finish my exams soon, and there's nothing for me to do here after that. Maybe we could move to Gothenburg. Or get ourselves a little house."

The words released the emotion. It was too late for pointless power games, and she wasn't that kind of person. Maya was no strategist when it came to love.

"You and me?" A smile played around the corners of Caroline's mouth. "So you're sticking around then?" As she gazed at Maya, her eyes narrowed. "A lot of people are treacherous by nature, but not you. Do you understand? We're the same, you and I. You'll be there for me until the end."

Her pupils contracted, making the iris appear unnaturally blue. Maya dared to move closer.

"Yes, I'll be there."

"You won't let me down, will you?"

"No, I won't let you down."

CHAPTER
TWENTY-ONE

2006

Bärneflod let out his belt one more hole and sadly contemplated what Christmas had done to his already corpulent torso. He jumped as Karlberg rapped briskly on the desk.

"We've found a tyre model that matches the casts. What's more, one of the tyres shows specific damage from wear and tear, which could be very helpful indeed."

"When we've found the murderer, you mean? And his car."

"Spoilsport. Where's Tell, anyway?" asked Karlberg.

"Nobody knows. But I think he's on his way in. And I'm on my way out."

"OK. See you later."

"Hey!" He shouted back to Karlberg. "Why don't you come with me? I'm going to see Edell."

"Are they digging him up?"

"The younger brother, idiot."

They hadn't phoned in advance, and when they arrived at the farm it seemed as if they were out of luck. After all, it was between Christmas and New Year, and normal people were on holiday and had gone away. Bärneflod grunted discontentedly at the thought of all the holidays he'd worked through during his career.

There were no lights on, and there was no car on the driveway.

They swore at some length, and were about to turn away when a window on the ground floor opened and a cascade of water came flooding out, splashing on to the frozen flower bed and over Karlberg's shoes, much to his surprise.

"Oh, goodness, I'm so sorry. I didn't know anybody was there."

The apologetic voice belonged to a woman who would presumably turn out to be Gertrud Edell, Reino Edell's wife. She didn't seem to know what to do with herself, standing there at the window.

Bärneflod and Karlberg took control and invited themselves in, after wiping their feet on the fir branches by the steps. They were provided with coffee and something to dunk in it, along with a stream of apologies concerning both the involuntary shower and the inadequacy of the biscuits on offer.

Gertrud seemed nervous. Her husband was not at home, she said repeatedly, and it was clear from her reluctance to sit down that she found the situation uncomfortable. She kept flitting around the kitchen, finding pointless things to do. Bärneflod and Karlberg had seen this kind of behaviour before, usually from people who didn't want to talk to the police. An invisible mark was wiped off the draining board, a mat was moved a fraction to the left. *It would be good to find out the reason behind her nerves before Reino Edell got home*, Bärneflod thought. He had a feeling that this woman was accustomed to letting her husband do the talking.

He passed on his thoughts to Karlberg when Gertrud Edell left them alone for a moment to visit the bathroom. Karlberg nodded in agreement. Or, he whispered back, they could turn it around and highlight the husband's habit of speaking on behalf of his wife. You needed two people to form a destructive relationship, he said. Bärneflod leaned back and shrugged his shoulders, but Karlberg wouldn't give up.

"Can you say that an unequal relationship is destructive if neither party perceives it to be destructive?"

Bärneflod looked at him in exasperation. "For God's sake! Just forget it."

Gertrud Edell came in and was surprised to see the older police officer looking so annoyed. He increased her feeling of unease by smiling sweetly while pointing decisively at the chair opposite his own. It was an exhortation not to be ignored. She sat down on the very edge of the chair.

Bärneflod decided to stop pissing about.

"What sort of relationship did your husband have with Lise-Lotte Edell and Lars Waltz?"

Gertrud Edell looked down at her hands, which were bright red, as were her face and throat. She twisted her wedding ring round and around.

"Well?"

"Why are you asking if you already know the answer?"

She looked up defiantly. So there was a bit of spark in the old girl, Karlberg thought, pleasantly surprised.

"Waltz made a complaint against your husband alleging threats and harassment on three separate occasions. That's what we know. You can tell us the rest."

She carried on twisting the ring around her finger as she watched a fly making its way across the plate of biscuits. She was saved by the sound of a tractor outside.

Reino Edell crossed the yard, came up the steps in just a few strides and stood in the doorway. Tall and powerfully built, he was dressed in his work clothes, and most of his face was adorned by blue-black stubble. Karlberg, who couldn't exactly boast about his ability to grow a beard, noticed that Edell had missed a few long dark hairs just under one eye. He wondered quietly to himself what the man would look like with a full beard.

Edell took off his cap and nodded grimly at the visitors. He didn't come over and offer his hand, which suited Bärneflod perfectly. He preferred to keep things simple too.

"We're from the police, and as I just said to your wife, Lars Waltz made complaints about you on three occasions; would you like to tell us about that?"

The man looked at his wife as if he were trying to discern whether she had said anything inappropriate.

"Nothing to tell."

"I very much doubt that, particularly given the fact that Lars Waltz is dead."

172

"I don't know anything about that."

Bärneflod had had enough.

"OK, then we can continue this conversation at the station. We have access there to more detailed information about your quarrels with Waltz. And I think you won't find anybody there who's as well disposed as I am to give you the chance to tell your side of the story."

Edell twitched and decided to cooperate.

"All right, I can explain things!" He slammed his cap down on the worktop. "I admit I was furious with him. He was an arrogant bastard! He wouldn't listen, and he had no respect for other people's property! That's what I told him."

Bärneflod nodded thoughtfully.

"OK. This is what I think happened. You went to see him several times. On one occasion you shoved him up against a wall and threatened him. What was it you said? All that stuff about respect for other people's property?"

"Yes."

"And you also accused him of being gay."

"Maybe I was right," said Edell. "He was a queer. He had a bloke down in town, I even know his name, Zachariasson. I did a little bit of investigating too. He was being unfaithful to Lise-Lott, the cocky bastard." Edell cleared his throat. "But I didn't murder him because of that, if that's what you're thinking."

"I'm not thinking anything, I'm just saying that a man was murdered shortly after you threatened to kill him. I don't know. Perhaps you wanted to frighten Lise-Lott away?"

"Yes, but killing somebody is a bloody extreme way of doing that," Edell muttered. He wiped his hands on his trousers and picked up two large pieces of sponge cake.

"I've got to get going. I only came home to pick up my dinner."

A lunchbox was standing ready on the worktop; he grabbed it on his way out.

Bärneflod waved away Karlberg's move to stop him. "Forget it. We'll keep an eye on him. We can bring him in later if we need to."

Gertrud Edell gave a hollow cough and squeezed the dishcloth between her hands.

CHAPTER
TWENTY-TWO

I never want to live like this, thought Christian Tell, who had just found the address he was looking for.

The semi-detached houses were arranged in horseshoes around a grassy area, with swings and sandpits in the middle. It was a relatively attractive place, serviced by the tram, and only quarter of an hour into town by car.

Tell was standing in front of a mailbox with a Dalarna County motif on the flap and WALTZ in ornate writing. He turned around and waved to Gonzales, who was trying to bring to an end a conversation with God knows who.

A straight line of paving stones split the garden in two, and there was a set of garden chairs in dirty white plastic with puddles of rain on the seats. *Never like this*. He had lived in the city centre all his life, and was used to its roar and pace. Without the noise he felt oddly naked, as if he and the city were one and the same. In an odd moment of confusion he had thought about moving, like others who had stopped making use of the wealth of bars and cafés and whose only contribution to inner-city life was to cough up a ridiculous amount in rent each month for a tiny two-room apartment. He could use his ridiculously small savings to put a deposit on a little house somewhere on the coast, or perhaps in the mountains with a view, rather than feeding it to the greedy capitalist landlords. He might even be able to get a transfer to some little police station out in the country. Investigate one murder every ten years and have time to do other things.

The thought brought him some comfort, mainly because he knew it was never going to happen. He would remain in his little apartment in Vasastan, not far from the house where he was born. He would carry on renting instead of buying, because the world looked the way it did and because a police officer's salary was a joke. He would complain when the rent went up, but secretly he would be content with the way things were. He had never really seen himself in any other context, and definitely not in a place like this. Carina had called him elitist, teased him about his phobia of the middle class and his fear of living on some suburban estate — joking, but with a sting of pedagogical seriousness: *these people are happy, and they are not inferior to you.*

He would never contradict her, and yet he and Carina had never taken that step from going out to moving in together, from a rented apartment to a house. It was all down to him. And in the end Carina had packed the few belongings she had in his apartment, an embarrassingly small carrier bag that she held up in front of him, tears glistening in her eyes. *This, Christian, is why I'm moving out. This!* And that was down to him as well, what entrenched habits and an unwillingness to change had cost him.

The rusty framework of a hammock stood beneath the roof of the veranda. The blinds of the house were partially closed, but shadowy movement was perceptible between the slats. Just as Tell was about to knock, the door was pushed open so suddenly that he had to take a quick step back to avoid being hit in the face.

"Who are you looking for?"

Tell flipped his wallet open to show his ID.

"Detective Inspector Tell. My colleague Detective Constable Gonzales." He made a sweeping movement towards his colleague, who was striding up the garden path. "Maria Waltz? It's about your ex-husband."

If the woman's face had been expressionless before, it became even more rigid now.

"Lars? What about him?"

"May we come in?"

She looked as if she were considering the possibility of saying no, but then moved away from the door. She went ahead through the narrow hallway and into the kitchen. They were invited to sit on a sofa, with a clear view of a room where an oval dining table adorned with several showy Christmas ornaments was the main attraction. Large steamed-up windows with red and green curtains looked on to a conservatory.

Maria Waltz sat down opposite Tell, who cleared his throat.

"I'm very sorry to have to inform you that your ex-husband, Lars Waltz, has been found dead.

Unfortunately we are not talking about a death from natural causes."

Maria Waltz's lips stiffened into a grimace.

"You're not serious?" She shook her head as if trying to shake off the unpleasant information. For a long minute there was silence, then suddenly her body shuddered with a sob. "I didn't want him to die," she whispered.

"We know that," said Tell calmly.

She had begun to tremble. If she was putting on an act, she was very good at it. Suddenly she realised what Tell had said.

"Not from natural causes? You mean he was murdered?"

"I'm afraid so. That's why we're here."

"You can't think I had anything to do with it? That's just crazy!"

"But we were hoping you might be able to give us some information about your ex-husband. I believe it's been six or seven years since you split up?"

Just as she was about to reply, Tell's mobile rang. He apologised and dug it out of his pocket. *Seja Lundberg*. There was a stab of pain under his left eye as he cancelled the call and turned back to Maria Waltz.

"I mean, I have wished him dead, I'm not afraid to admit that, but . . ." She stared vacantly at the overripe pears in a red glass fruit bowl. "So I won't say that I can't understand how someone could have done this. Have you ever been really let down, Inspector?"

Tell met her gaze without speaking and waited for her to go on.

178

"On the other hand, I can't think of anyone else who had reason to feel that way about Lars. He was a peaceful person."

She gave a half-smile but her expression instantly became serious again.

"He was kind, responsible, all that sort of thing. A good father. Then everything was turned upside down. He met that woman and . . ."

The tears began to flow.

"You must think I'm being ridiculous. That was six years ago — I should have got over it by now."

"We're not here to make any judgement," said Tell and paused for a moment. "I get the impression you didn't part on good terms?"

She shook her head.

"He left me from one day to the next. One night he told me he was moving out the following day. He'd already booked a van to move his stuff. I got no explanation, apart from the fact that he didn't love me any more. He'd had someone else for a while. But what about the boys? I said. They were ten and twelve; they needed their dad. And the house? We were living in Hovås at the time, and the house was far too expensive for me to be able to afford on my own, to go on living there with the kids. He knew that."

She dashed away the tears from her cheeks, took a deep breath and slowly exhaled.

"He wrecked my life and the children's in an instant. It was as if I was suddenly seeing a darker side of him. As if all the suffering he was causing simply ran off him, like water off a duck's back. He was ice cold."

She fell silent. Tell nodded discreetly at his colleague to take over.

"I can understand how difficult it must have been for you." Gonzales edged a fraction closer to the table and sought eye contact. "There were some financial disputes after the divorce, according to what we've learned."

"Yes."

She tore off a piece of kitchen roll and blew her nose.

"I suppose I thought it should have been worth something — eighteen years of marriage and two sons. If not emotionally, then at least financially. It's a classic situation: my career took the back seat in favour of his. I stayed at home with our children and supported him in his professional life. Maybe you're too young to understand this, but in somewhere like the USA things never turn out the way they do here. Over there they value traditional woman's work, they value the family. Here you just get a divorce. Did you know that Sweden has the highest divorce rate in the world?"

Gonzales nodded despite the fact that he'd never heard any such thing.

Tell's mobile rang again. He checked the caller ID, excused himself and moved into the living room.

"Did you know," he heard Bärneflod's voice on the other end of the line, "who made complaints against Reino Edell for harassment on no fewer than three occasions over the past two and a half years? Lars Waltz, that's who. Karlberg and I have established that he's an ugly bastard."

"So did you get anything out of him?"

"Well, Edell claims that Waltz was having an affair with some queer who —"

"Is that worth looking into?" Tell smothered a yawn. "What are the others doing?"

"Beckman's going through Waltz's telephone records."

"Landline or mobile?"

"Both."

"Has she found anything?"

Bärneflod took the phone away from his ear and some ghastly music piped up as he put Tell on hold.

After a few seconds he was back.

"Bingo again. There's one number that comes up over and over again, both on the landline and on the mobile, apart from Lise-Lott's sister's number. It's a Kristoffer Zachariasson in Västra Frölunda."

"OK. But listen, Bengt."

"What?"

"Just take it easy."

Bärneflod was already gone.

Tell went back to the kitchen, where Maria Waltz had calmed down and was taking a packet of biscuits out of the cupboard.

"To begin with he did make an effort to keep his promise — I'll say that in his defence. He would ring the boys from time to time, wanting to see them and so on. But they . . . well. They were at a sensitive age. They both took it very badly, especially Jocke. He's our eldest. I suppose Lars just gave up after a while. But it can never be right to give up on your children, can it?"

The look she gave Gonzales was challenging, and obediently he shook his head.

"Children have the right to give up on their parents, but the reverse is never true. No, his greatest betrayal was of our boys."

"So you're saying that your sons have had no contact to speak of with their father since you divorced?" Gonzales asked.

"Not for the past four years, not really."

"When was the last time you saw your ex-husband?" asked Tell from the archway between the kitchen and dining room.

She jumped as if she'd forgotten he was there.

"It was . . . I don't remember. Quite a long time ago. Two or three years, maybe. We had a meeting at my solicitor's office, after selling the house."

Tell moved back to the table and sat down, trapping Maria Waltz in her seat by the wall. He ran a hand over his hair, his expression thoughtful.

"I hope you won't think I'm being insensitive, but I believe you were a little . . . unstable . . . for a period after the divorce. How are you feeling now?"

He met Maria's startled gaze. She got up abruptly and virtually shoved him aside so that she could get to the tap. She filled a glass and managed to spill half the water before taking a couple of gulps.

"I'm fine, thank you. And I've been fine for the majority of my adult life. Don't you understand? Everything was snatched away from me: my family, my home, my security. I was abandoned, betrayed, cast aside like a rag. So yes, I lost it for a while — does that surprise you, Inspector?"

Tell didn't reply.

"I'm fine now. I've been seeing a good doctor for many years. I didn't murder my ex-husband, Inspector."

"It wasn't our intention to make you feel we were accusing you of anything. If that is the case, then please accept our apologies. But if you don't mind, I would like the name of your doctor and your permission to speak to him."

She nodded, her face whitening around the jawline as she searched for the doctor's card in one of the kitchen cupboards. A muscle was working frenetically in her temple.

"I'd like you both to leave now," she said, positioning herself in the hallway.

"We're on our way. Once again our apologies for any distress we may have caused you, and our condolences on your loss," said Tell.

She double-locked the door behind them.

They didn't speak during the short trip back to the station. Just as they turned into Skånegatan, Tell's mobile buzzed with an incoming text message.

"You're popular today," said Gonzales. "Bärneflod again?"

Tell shook his head as he opened the message: "Last chance. Dinner at mine. 18.00."

His watch told him he had exactly forty-five minutes to get there. He had just put the handbrake on, but released it immediately and turned to Gonzales.

"Out you get, I have to be somewhere. When you go upstairs, could you check out Seja Lundberg's address

— she was one of the first two witnesses. Then give me a call on my mobile."

"OK."

When Gonzales rang twenty minutes later, Tell was just passing the turn-off to the scene of the murder. The fog from the river lay like candy floss in the hollows. He shook a cigarette out of the half-full packet he had found in the glove compartment, much to his delight, and wound down the window a little way to let the smoke out. It was almost completely dark. The mist quickly found its way into the car, covering the headrest like a damp film.

Tell flipped open the ashtray. He shouldn't have asked Gonzales to find out the address. Seja Lundberg was a witness, so there wasn't really anything odd about the fact that he was going to see her in her own home, but he should have called the information desk instead.

She had tried to get hold of him three times. Every time he had been too much of a coward to take the call. The first time he wasn't prepared but a warm happiness had flooded his body. However, the feeling was quickly replaced by unease when he remembered what he had done and what the consequences would be if someone like Östergren found out.

He quickly worked out that the most intelligent thing he could do at this stage was to break off the relationship and hope nobody found out it had existed. This would mean explaining the situation to Seja: he would need to get her to understand his position, why they couldn't see each other again.

184

He hated the thought of upsetting her, but the thought of never seeing her again was even worse. He didn't know what to do. Because every time she called the fear grew stronger. He convinced himself that the only humane thing to do was talk to her face to face. He simply had no other choice but to see her again.

After a steep tarmac slope and an even narrower gravel track he thought the road was petering out, and that he had taken a wrong turning. A NO THROUGH ROAD sign seemed to confirm his fears until he caught sight of a row of mailboxes on a wooden fence by the side of the road. At least this was a sign that there was some kind of life further up the hill. With the help of the miniature torch he carried on his key ring, he made out LUNDBERG on one of the boxes.

It took Tell twenty minutes of wandering around other people's property before he finally found his way over the bog via the footbridge. Where the forest opened out, he spotted the house; he had been able to smell the smoke all the way back on the road. He pulled his coat more tightly around his shoulders. It was colder this high up; the grass in the glade was already covered in frost, and crunched beneath his shoes.

He couldn't help peeping in as he passed the kitchen window. The table was laid, and Seja was inside, wearing a red and white checked apron over a long skirt. He was just about to knock on the door when he trod on a metal bowl he hadn't spotted in the darkness.

185

The clatter made her look up at the window. Tell raised a hand, somewhat embarrassed, and opened the door.

The hallway was tiny, and cluttered with shoes and jackets. And then she was standing there in front of him, taking his coat and nodding to him to come in.

"You found your way then."

"You don't exactly make it easy for admirers. Nobody but a top detective would have found his way out here."

Tell had to duck to avoid banging his head on the low door frame leading into the kitchen. Apart from two upholstered armchairs by the wood-burning stove, there was a sofa in front of the window, a folding table and two chairs. The walls were hung with wide shelves that held everything from books to pictures, kitchen equipment and china. On the worn wooden floor lay a long narrow rag rug.

"Take a seat," she said. "The food will be ready in five minutes."

A fire crackled in the stove. Tell sat down in front of it and took out a cigarette.

Seja came and stood in front of him with her arms folded and an unreadable expression on her face. He was getting ready to explain why he hadn't returned her calls, but then she handed him a glass of red wine. He couldn't help interpreting the gesture as an invitation to stay the night and did his best to suppress a broad smile. The purpose of his visit, to end the relationship face to face, suddenly seemed irrelevant.

"Is there an upstairs too?" he asked, mainly because he couldn't see a bed anywhere. She nodded, smiled, and he was embarrassed to realise that his thoughts were all too obvious.

"Come on, I'll show you."

She opened a narrow door hidden in the panelling. A ladder led up to a tiny loft, where a mattress covered in wine-red velvet bedspreads lay on the floor. She was right behind him and touched his hand. He had the sudden feeling that he had never been more vulnerable.

The walls and ceiling were covered with old film posters: the classic one from *Casablanca*, *Les Amants du Pont Neuf* with Juliette Binoche, *Time of the Gypsies*. A round window was adorned with an Advent star, and when the wind blew the branches of a tall birch tree scratched against it.

Tell sank down on the edge of the mattress. She took hold of his wrists and gently forced his body to lie back before unbuttoning his shirt, undoing his belt.

The bedclothes smelled faintly of woodsmoke and soap. The light from the hallway seeped through the opening in the floor, along with Tom Waits' rasping whisky voice. Tell thought distractedly that it was years since he had heard "I Hope That I Don't Fall in Love with You". He closed his eyes.

In the morning Tell was woken by the tapping of the tree on the window and realised at once that he had overslept for the first time in many years. It was already light outside, and there was an empty space beside him. He could hear the sound of running water in the kitchen. He climbed down the ladder and saw Seja with

187

her back to him, wearing a dressing gown and sheepskin slippers.

She realised he was there when he loudly inhaled the aroma of the coffee.

"Good morning. Are you hungry?" She gestured in the direction of the pans on the stove. "We could always have dinner now — we forgot about it last night. If you don't fancy stew I can offer you a simple cup of coffee."

She dried her hands and slipped self-consciously into his arms. "I'll just go and get dressed."

"Why don't you get undressed instead."

She laughed, her mouth level with the hollow at the base of his throat.

"Someone's very keen to get hold of you; your phone has rung several times."

Three messages from the office. Just as he was about to listen to them the phone rang again. It was Bärneflod's number. Tell left the room.

"Tell."

"Where the fuck are you? I've been calling since eight."

"Something new?"

"Yes, Strömberg has narrowed the time of death down to some point between seven and nine in the evening."

Tell went through the hallway and clambered up into the loft to find his clothes. "So he'd been lying there overnight."

"That's right. And presumably he could have ended up lying there for a lot longer, since nobody passing would have seen him from the road. But you remember that old gossip Beckman and Gonzales talked to, fru Rappe? She did say there was an open evening at a house nearby."

"I remember. Do you mean the open evening was between seven and nine?"

"Exactly."

"Find out which estate agent —"

"Beckman's already done that. A firm called Swedish Properties was showing the house. The agent's name is Helena Friman. And even better: apparently everyone who was interested in seeing the house registered on the net. She's already faxed us the list.

"You mean everybody who was at the open evening, and therefore passed the scene of the murder, is on this list?" It was almost too good to be true.

"With addresses and phone numbers."

"How many are we talking about?"

"Fifteen or so. Of course, people can just turn up, so the agent couldn't swear that absolutely everybody at the house was on the list. Apparently most came around seven, so there has to be a good chance that at least one of them saw or heard something significant."

"OK. We'll get the local force to go through the list. Anything else?"

There was a rattling sound on the other end of the line.

"Hello? Bad reception on the stairs. It's fine now. Well, speaking of the local boys, it turns out they've come up with a possible candidate among the missing psychos. Nothing from Lillhagen and St Jörgen — only one matched and he had an alibi for that evening —

however, someone did escape from a secure unit at the Långtuna youth remand centre a couple of days before the murder, and it's only about ten kilometres away as the crow flies. He's still on the run, but they're looking for him right now."

"Is that it?"

"For now, yes. Are you coming in?"

Tell ended the call and went down to the kitchen. Seja was holding up a coffee pot, and Tell nodded. She was wearing her jeans and a sweater, and had put up her hair.

"Are they wondering where you are?"

"Hmm. They just can't do without me. They're like kids without a babysitter as soon as I turn my back."

She watched him in silence as he helped himself to some breakfast.

"Is this going to be a problem for you, Christian?"

"Probably," he said, shrugging his shoulders. "We can talk about it some other time. I really have to go."

By way of illustration he quickly took a couple of gulps of coffee and burned his tongue. He caught sight of his unshaven face in the mirror.

"Bathroom?"

"Outside toilet."

He laughed. "You're just a woodland troll!"

Her expression became serious. "But you do want to see me again?"

"Of course," he heard himself saying as he stopped to kiss her. She took his face between her hands and gazed into his eyes as if trying to ascertain whether he

190

was telling the truth. She seemed to decide he was as she caressed his rough cheek.

"Good. I would have been very sad otherwise."

Honesty seemed to come naturally to her, and a disinclination to play the kind of games he was used to in his dealings with women. He found it liberating.

CHAPTER
TWENTY-THREE

Bärneflod shook his head. There was something going on with his colleague, even if he couldn't quite work out what it was. Tell wasn't the type to give anything away about his life outside work — if he actually had a life outside work. But oversleeping, not being available by phone during the most important phase of a murder investigation, it wasn't like him, Bärneflod thought, even if it was quite satisfying to see his team leader for once letting go of his wearying performance anxiety. And for some unfathomable reason Tell's dip in performance had a stimulating effect on Bärneflod. It was a long time since he had regarded the job as anything other than exhausting, but right now he was feeling extremely positive.

Was Tell in love? The thought was certainly amusing.

There was no doubt Reino Edell was a paranoid bastard, but he was right about one thing — Zachariasson definitely was gay. It wasn't just the pale pink shirt hanging loosely over his jeans, despite the fact that the man must have been getting on for fifty, or the fact that his jeans were skin tight. Nor was it the fact that Zachariasson's manner was effeminate. He had met Bärneflod's eye when they shook hands, but he hadn't tried anything. No, it was just a feeling. Bärneflod had a well-developed gaydar, which he liked to boast about. He could spot a gay man in a group of people from twenty metres away. There was something about the way they moved, he would have claimed if anyone had asked him to define this particular talent in more detail. Gentle movements, like those of a woman.

Bärneflod had been a copper for almost forty years. As he saw it, knowing about people was part of the job; it was just a shame the younger generation didn't have the sense to value experience. In terms of salary he was worse off than Beckman, for example, and he was well aware of it. It wasn't difficult to work out why Karin Beckman was shooting up the hierarchy with consummate ease, what with quotas and all this talk of equality.

No, they would soon be extinct, the coppers who valued good old honest police work. Nowadays it was all about who was best at brown-nosing. Who was a happy little soul, changing their methods every other year to fit in with some astonishing new computer program that would no doubt be scrapped a couple of years later. He could certainly teach the management a thing or two about cost-effectiveness. And what would last in the long term: the old, tried and tested methods.

In another situation Bärneflod would have assumed that a woman's hand was responsible for the kitchen in which he found himself. It was warm and cosy but tasteful, as his wife Ulla would say. He would never be able to create a pleasant home — not that anyone

193

would entrust him with such a task — the way Ulla had. He had to give her credit for that.

He was the first to admit that there were a number of areas in which women were superior to men. It was all about the details, something men generally missed. Ulla would sometimes accuse him of not appreciating such things, or not even noticing them, but she was wrong. He noticed the flowers at Easter. The butter dish and milk jug instead of the margarine tub and milk carton on the table. The children's birthdays. He could go on for ever. He even had a tear in his eye at the thought. And to think there were those who said he was an insensitive bastard.

Bärneflod wiped his eyes discreetly with his shirt sleeve as he became aware of Zachariasson's enquiring expression.

Pull yourself together.

In order to be sure that his voice would hold, he barked out somewhat more fiercely than necessary, "You know why I'm here?"

"Yes," said Zachariasson calmly. If he was surprised at Bärneflod's volatility, he chose to hide it.

"I imagine it has something to do with Lasse's death."

A pet name — just what you'd expect.

"Lise-Lott rang me not long after it happened. Lasse and I were quite close."

That was one way of putting it.

"It's just terrible. It really upset me."

Bärneflod raised his eyebrows and made a great performance of taking out his notebook in order to jot

194

down something. In fact he wrote *Ulla — flowers* on the top line because he was still thinking along the same lines as earlier.

"What was your relationship with Ulla like?"

"Ulla?"

"Waltz. I mean Lars Waltz. You said you were close?"

"Yes, we were. We grew up together. Went to the same school."

Bärneflod nodded, and this time he did actually write: *Check school.*

"In Majorna. Our mothers spent time together too, at least when we were little. We went to the same nursery — we used to go together. Then, when we specialised in different subjects at grammar school, we carried on meeting up in our spare time."

"Did your relationship ever change, for example when you were adults?"

Zachariasson wriggled out of the question by becoming philosophical.

"Isn't a meaningful relationship always in a state of flux? I mean, it's affected by the current situation of both parties, wouldn't you say?"

Bärneflod's expression was comment enough, and Zachariasson was quick to clarify his point.

"I mean, there was a time when we didn't see much of each other — that was during the 80s when our lives were very different. Lasse was working a lot, and when he got together with his friends it was in a way I didn't particularly enjoy: lots of drinking and . . . well . . . Then, a few years later, when he was going through his divorce, he got in touch and we found a way back to our friendship."

Bärneflod gave an inward sigh. This was proving more difficult than he'd expected.

"What did you do together, you and Lars Waltz?"

"The same as most people, I suppose. We'd meet up, have a chat. We spoke on the telephone when we were both busy. Sometimes we'd go for a beer, but I've never been all that keen on pubs. I think Lasse had grown tired of that kind of life as well, towards the end."

"I thought your sort loved the party lifestyle," Bärneflod spat out.

Zachariasson immediately became more reserved.

"I presume," he said, a noticeable chill in his voice, "that by 'your sort' you are referring to the fact that I am a homosexual. As indeed I am. However, it is rather simplistic to assume that homosexuality is restricted to a certain type of person. We are all very different from one another, Constable. Just like those of you who are straight. Some like the good life; others live in a terraced house and play bingo. Some like going for long walks in the forest; others like to have sex with strangers in public places. Some are absolute geniuses; others are as thick as two short planks."

The latter phrase was emphasised quite deliberately, knocking Bärneflod completely off balance.

"It's Inspector," he said feebly. For simplicity's sake he decided to allow the possible slur on his intelligence to pass. After all, it was nearly lunchtime and he certainly didn't want to spend any longer than necessary in this man's house. Particularly as he hadn't

196

even had the manners to offer him something to eat with his coffee.

That was one thing that definitely showed the lack of a woman's hand in this house. Ulla would never have let a guest sit there without the offer of a biscuit or a piece of cake.

The thought of lunch suddenly made him tire of games.

"Were you and Waltz having a relationship or not? I just want a yes or no."

"I wasn't aware you'd asked the question, Constable — forgive me — Inspector."

"I'm asking it now."

"Lasse lived with Lise-Lott, I thought you already knew that. He was married to a woman called Maria before that, but I presume you know that as well. I live alone, since I have yet to find a man to share my life with."

He smiled at Bärneflod, defiant rather than roguish. Bärneflod regarded him with distaste.

"As you yourself just said, you gays are no different from straight people, and straight people sometimes stray. So I'm asking you again, as you still haven't answered my question: were you and Lars Waltz having a relationship?"

"We were not having a relationship. And if we had been, what's that got to do with Lasse's murder?"

Bärneflod shrugged his shoulders. "Well, say he refuses to leave his wife, and you, the jealous lover, have had enough. If you can't have him, no one will."

197

Bärneflod was pleased with himself but Zachariasson shook his head as if he couldn't believe his ears.

"You're just being embarrassing now. You're also implying that a gay man can't be friends with a straight guy without trying to turn him. I don't even feel flattered that you're assuming I succeeded. One more time: we were not having a relationship."

"Someone else has a different view."

"A crazy farmer who wants to get his hands on Lise-Lott's land. Yes, I know. Lasse was pretty upset about it for a while. He even made a complaint when the whole thing started to get out of hand."

"Would you say Lars seemed frightened of Reino Edell?"

Zachariasson got up and poured himself a cup of coffee. He didn't offer Bärneflod a top-up.

Bärneflod pushed his empty cup away demonstratively. *Mean bastard.*

"I wouldn't say frightened, exactly," said Zachariasson. "Angry, more like. The farmer had evidently threatened him at some stage. He made the complaint mostly to show him that enough was enough. To get him to come to his senses." Zachariasson looked at his watch. "I really do have to go. I start work in twenty minutes."

"OK. I'd just like to know when you last saw Lars Waltz."

Zachariasson thought it over.

"It must have been a couple of days before Lucia. Lasse was doing some errand or other around Frölunda Torg. We bumped into one another and went for a coffee."

198

"Was there anything unusual about him? Anything you noticed? Anything he said?"

"No. He was the same as always. Talked about a trip Lise-Lott was going on. He was worried about his finances, as usual, but not enough to let it destroy his good mood. Look, I really do have to go; I'm already late for work."

"Where were you on Monday night?"

"Am I a suspect?"

"Just answer the question. I'm sure you've seen enough detective shows on TV to know that I have to ask."

"After work I went to Göta's Café Bar on Mariaplan, along with three colleagues. After the others left I stayed on with a friend I met there, until about ten thirty, then I took a taxi home."

"Alone?"

"Yes, alone."

"And these colleagues and this . . . *friend*?" He emphasised the last word meaningfully. "Can they confirm they spent the evening with you?"

"Of course. I'll give you their phone numbers. And the friend in question was actually a female friend, an old classmate from university." He stood up with an expression of ill-concealed contempt. "Right, I'm going to work now — if you want to talk to me again you can bring me in for questioning."

"So you're working between Christmas and New Year? Where?" asked Bärneflod, out of curiosity.

"Sheltered housing. I'm on the afternoon shift today."

CHAPTER
TWENTY-FOUR

1995

Her art tutor squinted into the sun as he packed his Volvo estate.

"Are you coming back after the summer, Maya?" he asked, lowering his sunglasses from his forehead.

Maya nodded.

"In that case, keep painting until I see you again."

He stopped what he was doing.

"You think I say that to everybody, but I don't."

Maya was balancing a piece of yellow mica on her bare foot, somewhat embarrassed. She'd handed her work in regularly, always leaving it in his pigeonhole in the staff room, since she was too shy to hand it to him in person. They were mostly small quick pencil sketches of people on the move. She had also tried painting in oils, the result pictures with thick layers of colour, the surface satisfyingly rough. She liked being able to feel all the other layers beneath the top one.

Caroline had posed for her, and would never know what was beneath the surface either. Maya had begun to take pleasure in that too. But the rapid sketching on her notepad was what gave her the most energy. Drawings done while she restlessly waited for something else, more focused on the movement and intentions of other people than on her own portrayal. This gave her the chance to be surprised by the final result, by what or who emerged from the mêlée of apparently insignificant events.

The tutor's car was the last to leave a cloud of dust behind as it headed for the bend in the road. The sound of the engine died away, leaving a compact silence. Maya had longed to be alone with Caroline, had thought that some time together would cure the growing silence between them. Instead she was terrified.

It was only a couple of days since most of the students had left for the summer, but the emptiness had already seeped into the walls. Maya was suddenly aware of how worn the wood panelling was. How the floor was covered with dirty ingrained marks, how the white paint in the window recesses had begun to flake. The emptiness was even in the smell of the place: dampness and old chalk.

She had grown used to the fact that with Caroline fidelity was tested; love was subject to certain conditions, was portioned out, compared, constant proof demanded. Even if she could see how destructive it was to turn love into a power struggle, the form of the relationship was strangely familiar to her. Her mother had always struggled with the proximity and distance of other people, on the one hand terrified of being consumed, on the other of being alone. And what is familiar feels safe.

CHAPTER
TWENTY-FIVE

2006

Tell felt the pang of a guilty conscience, painfully familiar. Seja hadn't said a word about him getting dressed up to go to the traditional police Christmas party, which covered several counties and was held every year in elegant and not particularly representative venues. This was the police showing its more generous, more positive side, and everyone's partner was supposed to be dragged around and introduced to colleagues. Food and drink, too much of both for some people — there was always someone who went too far, talking out of turn or kicking over the traces, always someone walking about the next day with their head down. It was just an ordinary office party, but on a grand scale.

Not that Seja could reasonably have expected to go along as his date. The times they had met could still be counted on the fingers of one hand. In spite of this, and for the first time in ages — perhaps for the first time ever — Tell felt the desire to force the issue. He *wanted* her at this ridiculous party. While he was shaving he fantasised about introducing her to Östergren. He wallowed in his martyrdom. She was like his secret mistress, even though neither of them was married. But this wasn't about taking Seja to a party; it was about the fact that he was acting contrary to his principles, that he had lost control, and as a consequence had lied to his employer. It was about a lack of self-discipline; he should have been able to control himself. He could have waited to embark on the relationship until they had finished with Seja and the enquiry had been concluded. Instead he had gone to bed with her while the investigation was ongoing.

In addition, for as long as he could remember his relationships with women, particularly the few he had managed to prolong, had been characterised by constant feelings of guilt. The sense of being inadequate was usually fed by accusations on the part of the woman that he was emotionally inaccessible, and the frustration aroused by these accusations made him even more closed in on himself, leading to a vicious circle which inevitably ended with the break-up of the relationship.

With hindsight he could see that in every one of his longer relationships (there had been three) he had been well aware of his skewed priorities — of his tendency to bury himself in his work, both mentally and in practical terms, in order to avoid having to open up and run the risk of becoming vulnerable. And yet, clearly, he had chosen not to change. Not once had he decided to give the whole thing a real chance and try to make different choices. Instead he had carried on doing more of the same, grimly observing the journey towards the demise of each relationship.

Carina had called him cold, lacking in empathy. Perhaps he was. But it was more likely he had simply never regarded himself as a man with a woman by his side. Managing to get a relationship to work was not part of the image he had of himself. He had never had any kind of counselling, although perhaps he should have done. So life just carried on as before, however many people he hurt along the way.

"I won't be too late, if you want to wait here. I'll give you the spare key, and you can push it through the letter box if you go home during the evening."

"If I don't go home, I'll be here."

She was leaning against the door jamb, wearing his white shirt.

"I'd really like you to be here when I get back," he said honestly, meeting her eyes in the bathroom mirror as he knotted his tie.

She slipped her arms around his waist and kissed the spot at the corner of his mouth where the razor blade had nicked the skin and a narrow strip of dried blood remained. For a moment she let the tip of her tongue rest just inside the corner of his mouth, and the heat electrified his body.

"I want to stay here," he mumbled, almost twisting his neck out of joint in an attempt to kiss her.

She laughed teasingly and skipped away.

"Oh no, Detective Inspector, you'll be late. You don't want to miss the speeches. Or the canapés."

The assumption that there would be canapés was a serious underestimation of the level of ambition among

204

the top brass. Instead they were presented with an ostentatiously expensive three-course dinner. Vidström, the commissioner, tapped ceremoniously on his glass when they were part way through the main course. As always he started his speech by emphasising that each and every one of them should regard their invitation as a heartfelt thank you for all their hard work over the past year. And as in previous years there were a certain number of stage whispers about pay, security issues and several other much better ways in which people would have preferred to be rewarded for their efforts; some of these developed into animated discussions between tables, which eventually had to be silenced by Vidström's secretary.

Tell didn't join in the discussion for two reasons: for one thing he thought it could well be interpreted as presumptuous by some people, since he was on quite a good salary these days in comparison to many of the other guests. The fact that he had started with nothing, or almost nothing, and had worked hard to achieve promotion was of no relevance in this particular context. And secondly, the fact that he risked his life on a daily basis — some crazed punter did pull a knife on him from time to time — for a salary that was approximately a third of the amount a twenty-two-year-old computer programmer earned wasn't something he wished to take up on this particular evening. As he saw it, it was better to be thanked with a three-course dinner than not be thanked at all.

After the last mouthful of dessert had been shovelled down, the partygoers were let loose to mingle with their brandy glasses and cocktails in another part of the venue. Coffee cups and dirty plates were whisked into the kitchen by skilfully invisible youngsters dressed in black and white. That was the end of the freebies, but they were informed that the bar could provide anything from extra-strength beer to twelve-year-old single malt whisky.

People gathered as usual in their normal work groups to carry on talking about the same topic they had discussed during dinner. For want of a better idea Tell went and stood by the bar, along with his former colleague Jonas Palmlöf, who had been replaced in the team by Gonzales. Karlberg, dressed in a suit for once, was also without female company, and soon came to join them.

Karlberg looked around the room. The chandeliers above their heads were exceptionally large and suspended from a vaulted roof adorned with paintings. Tall windows with recesses wide enough to lie down in were dressed with heavy dark-red velvet drapes. A silver candelabrum burned in each and every one.

"Gustavsberg Palace. Who's privileged enough to hang out here the rest of the time, do you think?"

Palmlöf wrinkled his nose.

"I believe it's very popular for parties and conferences. That's why they booked our work function between Christmas and New Year, when the rest of the country is on holiday; it was fully booked before Christmas. I don't know, I'm not all that keen on the Dracula style. It's all a bit dusty, somehow."

206

"What are you, a feng shui expert?" A blonde in a sparkly silver dress clinked her sherry glass against Palmlöf's beer glass and smiled.

"Cheers."

"Cheers."

He turned his back on his colleagues.

"I don't even know what that means, but you look fantastic in that dress, like a catwalk model."

Tell and Karlberg exchanged a meaningful look. Palmlöf was very popular with the ladies and never missed an opportunity to take advantage of the fact. With a teasing wave over his shoulder he allowed the blonde to draw him towards a group on the far side of the room.

"Oh well, there he goes, I suppose it was only to be expected," said Karlberg, taking a large gulp of his Heineken. "It certainly seems as if girls like his Casanova act. He just goes for it. I'd never have the nerve. I'd be scared of being laughed at, or that thing girls do when they roll their eyes at their friends. I hate that."

"And you probably would be laughed at, Andreas. Cheap compliments have to be delivered in the right way, or else they're just ridiculous. It has to be done by someone like Palmlöf, who's quite obviously immune to the idea that he might seem over the top. That's why it works. It would never even occur to him that he might be on the wrong track."

Tell spotted Johan Björkman, a former colleague from his days on patrol, and laughed at Karlberg's gloomy expression.

"Cheer up, my partner in misfortune."

They clinked glasses again, but deep inside Tell was suffused with a happiness that was growing in direct proportion to the amount of alcohol he consumed. He was a lucky man, and he gave Karlberg's shoulder a reassuring squeeze.

"Feeling a bit low?"

Karlberg nodded.

"She's decided, has she?"

"Marie, yes," Karlberg replied morosely. "It's not just that — she's met someone new. A mate of mine bumped into them outside some leisure centre. No doubt he's some kind of mountain-climbing market analyst."

"Yes, but it won't last. Relationships on the rebound never do. He's just a stopgap."

Tell amazed himself with his cheerfulness. However, Karlberg didn't seem inclined to be convinced. Tell decided to do what any decent man would do, follow his unfortunate friend down into a morass of alcohol. He ordered two double whiskies.

"We could just hope that he falls down a mountain and hurts himself."

Karlberg looked at Tell in surprise, as if he'd never seen him be so upbeat — which in fact he hadn't — but he followed his example and knocked back the Scotch. He shook his head, laughing.

"If I didn't know you better I might have believed Bärneflod the other day, when you overslept. He said you'd got yourself a woman."

Tell buried his nose in his glass, the fumes bringing tears to his eyes.

"That's what I've always said. It isn't a workplace at all, it's a bloody coffee morning."

It was getting on for two o'clock when Andreas Karlberg gave in to the alcohol and let his head fall back against the soft leather armchair. People were starting to make a move.

Tell tried to shake some life into his colleague, who opened one eye a fraction, only to decide a second later that nothing could possibly be worth the effort. Tell considered whether he should take Karlberg home with him — he could crash out on the sofa for a couple of hours until he was in a fit state to get home under his own steam. But then he thought about Seja, who might be waiting for him in the double bed, if he was lucky. That decided the matter. He called a taxi and propped Karlberg up in the street as they waited. The taxi driver shook his head anxiously when Tell gave him the address.

"This is my own car."

Presumably he was afraid that Karlberg might throw up, but Tell took no notice and manoeuvred Karlberg into the back seat. If the taxi driver refused to take everyone who was drunk, he would never manage to balance his books at the end of the month.

Tell lit a cigarette after the taxi had gone and started hunting for his cloakroom ticket. He heard voices nearby and spotted Palmlöf canoodling with the sparkly blonde under a balcony a little way off. The girl laughed again, her voice high-pitched and carefree. Tell went back inside to the stoic remains of humanity who were determined to stay till the bitter end. At the bar he met Beckman.

"Christian. I haven't seen you on the dance floor this evening. Or anywhere else, come to that."

She tapped him hard on the chest, unaware of her own strength in the way people who've had a bit too much to drink tend to be. He backed away and smiled patiently, suddenly glad he'd switched to mineral water a couple of hours earlier, when he thought about Seja, and had regained perspective.

"What's hiding in there, behind that . . . facade?"

"Somebody who's very tired and is about to go home. I just came over to say hello."

She laughed and put her arm around him. They went over to the table together to gather their things. Palmlöf and his blonde were right behind them, the night air still in their clothes.

"Are you leaving already? Not you, Karin, surely — the evening has only just started. We can manage a couple more beers before we call it a night. Come on, Tell. I won't take no for an answer."

When he came back he was balancing four tall glasses of Irish coffee on a tray.

Johan Björkman came over to join them.

They started chatting about old memories — not that there were many. Soon after completing his training, Björkman, a dyed-in-the-wool Borås man, had been stricken by homesickness, and when he was offered a post in his home town he had accepted

210

quicker than you could say patrol car. But it was possible to make a good career there too, he said.

He went on to talk about the wave of narcotics that had flooded the town, finding its way into places where they hadn't even heard of drugs twenty years ago.

"They picked up a guy in Svaneholm, no more than thirty, who'd been selling amphetamines to sixth-form students. It turned out he had a stash out in his old man's barn worth a couple of million." He shook his head. "The whole bloody country's being poisoned, no doubt about it."

Tell nodded in agreement, even if he had heard it all before and was far too tired for such a serious conversation. He tried not to stare at Palmlöf's hand, resting on the blonde's knee. Björkman had introduced her as one of his inspectors.

"At the moment the whole team is investigating a murder just outside Kinna," Björkman went on, undeterred. "Presumably it has something to do with drugs as well. Some guy up past the Frisjö area got shot the other day, way out in the forest. It was just like an execution, *bang bang*, like an American movie, then the cold bastard reversed over him in a car. Twice. There wasn't much left of the body. You have to wonder what things will be like in another twenty years. Particularly in view of the fact that they're now saying we shouldn't have any police officers in rural areas. I mean, an unmanned police station, what's the point of that? It takes a bloody hour before anybody turns up if someone raises the alarm."

Tell closed his eyes and tried sobering up through sheer willpower. "Hang on. What you just told me. Can you go over it again? Tell me about the Frisjö murder."

Björkman looked up in surprise.

"You want to talk about work?"

Tell nodded and reached for a half-full bottle of Vichy Nouveau.

"I do."

Ten minutes later — Beckman had also sobered up with impressive speed — Björkman had finished telling them about the murder, which clearly had sufficient in common with their own investigation to be worth looking into.

"I'll see you tomorrow morning, first thing. At the station in Borås." Tell's watch showed twenty past three. "Let's say nine o'clock."

"But . . ." Björkman looked at Tell in bewilderment. "But . . . it's New Year's Eve tomorrow. We're not at work."

"You appear to have missed the point," Tell replied. "Nine o'clock. And don't be late."

CHAPTER
TWENTY-SIX

Tell had found his way to the right floor in the police station in Borås and had managed to track down Johan Björkman's office. And there he sat behind his desk at precisely nine o'clock, still wearing his coat and more asleep than awake. Björkman got to his feet with some difficulty and shook Tell by the hand.

"Bloody hell, I feel a bit rough this morning," he greeted Tell. "Coffee?"

"A pot, please."

Björkman set off for the coffee machine, and Tell took the opportunity to look around. It was obvious that Björkman was still very tidy. The red and black files were arranged separately on the bookshelves, and not one sheet of paper sullied the empty surface of the desk.

Tell thought about his own desk. At least he knew where everything was. Besides, he was suspicious of people who were too tidy; any form of enthusiasm for work had to be combined with a certain amount of mess, he felt. A Freudian would no doubt have pointed to Tell's father, who had made it a question of honour to maintain an absurd level of order in every single aspect of his daily life. Only when he was an adult did

Tell realise that his father was something of a compulsive neurotic. This insight somehow made it easier to accept his mania.

It hadn't always been easy. As a teenager he couldn't stand his father's routines: everything in its place, packaged in countless plastic bags fastened with elastic bands. If something ended up in the wrong place, which of course it constantly did, thanks to other members of the family, his father had to sort it out. Indeed Tell would sometimes deliberately hang the scissors on the wrong hook in the larder or move the emulsion paint to the shelf for gloss, just so he could watch — with a mixture of sadistic pleasure and disgust — his father anxiously rearranging things. As if to demonstrate that the world would come to an end if you lost control of things for a single second.

Tell also sabotaged the orderliness that was so vital to his father because his parent made him so incredibly angry. The thought of those oceans of wasted time. All those hours he and his mother and sister had to wait. He had seen only the self-righteousness in his father's actions, his lack of awareness that there was something wrong with him, and his condescending attitude towards those who chose to organise their lives in a different way. It had been difficult to see that these habits were his father's way of handling fear and anxiety.

These days Tell's father was no longer able to maintain such a regime, since he no longer had a home of his own; he was completely in the hands of the staff at his care home and whatever routines they chose to follow. It was undeniable that he looked quite carefree these days, despite the aches and pains that inevitably came with age. Perhaps he was enjoying the fact that he no longer had any choice.

Björkman reappeared with a flask of coffee and two chipped mugs. Tell realised the depth of his addiction as the aroma drifted up towards his face. He was a serious caffeine junkie and had only managed to knock back half a cup that morning. He had drunk it standing up in the kitchen with the imprint of the buttons of Seja's nightshirt engraved on his cheek.

She had stayed. She'd been there when he got home at half past three in the morning. The thought filled him with happiness but also a sense of unease that the first thing he had done, and on New Year's Eve, was to head off to work yet again. But on the other hand, she might as well get used to it. If she couldn't cope with that kind of thing, then she couldn't cope with living with him, that's just the way things were. That's what the job was like. Sometimes, at least.

"Did you want me to come out with you?"

"Is it far?" asked Tell, despite the fact that they both knew this was irrelevant.

Björkman shrugged his shoulders. "No. A few kilometres." He leaned forward and sniffed Tell's breath. "Are you really in a fit state to drive?"

"No, but then neither are you. Shall we talk on the way?"

"OK."

They left the police station and drove through the town just as children were starting to arrive at the play

215

areas with their parents and the first retired couples of the day were feeding the ducks in Annelund Park. Shop owners were putting out signs advertising fireworks, and in a couple of hours the car park at Knalleland would fill up with people buying the essentials for their New Year parties. The town was getting ready to welcome in 2007.

"Idiot!" Björkman slammed on the brakes and sounded his horn at a lorry driver who had ignored his obligation to give way. When they were on the move again, he said, "So how will you be celebrating the New Year, Tell?"

"I . . ." He hadn't given it a thought. "I've been invited to a party by some former colleagues." This was actually true, although Tell had forgotten to let them know whether he was coming or not. "What about you?"

"I'm going over to some neighbours. A few of us take it in turns to have a party on New Year's Eve. It works really well — it's hard to get hold of a taxi after midnight."

The windows of the car were beginning to steam up, and Björkman leaned forward to clear the windscreen. He turned down the radio and glanced over at Tell.

"Who's going to start, you or me?"

Tell went over the facts about the murder of Lars Waltz as they gradually left the main roads behind. Soon they were travelling along the increasingly narrow gravel tracks in the forests around Viskafors, the larger brick-built houses being replaced by small wooden cottages. Eventually, the pine forest was the only thing they could see; the trees were windblown, and looked as if they had been badly affected by the storms of the past few years.

"Hurricane Gudrun wasn't exactly kind to this land," Björkman confirmed.

In certain places trees still lay on top of one another like pick-up sticks. They passed an area on the left-hand side where trees had been felled. Tell had stopped talking, and Björkman was thinking things over.

"Hmm. Most things seem to match. The method. The shooting — we've only had a preliminary report from forensics so far, but in all probability we're dealing with the same kind of weapon. Deliberately run over several times by a relatively heavy car with broader tyres than the average."

"And the victim?"

"Olof Bart. About the same age as your guy. Lived alone. A bit of an oddball, apparently. The neighbours didn't really have much of an impression of him — he kept himself to himself. Did a bit of everything work-wise, a lot of clearing up after the storm. He'd also done some casual work at a workshop in Svaneholm, repairing forestry machinery and so on. No family."

They drove down a hill to an opening in the forest and a grassy area covered in brushwood and moss in the middle of which sat a large square wooden house. It must have been impressive once, but now the red paint was flaking off, exposing strips of silvery-brown wood. Between the trees at the edge of the plot, they could just catch a glimpse of a lake.

Tell, who had not thought about suitable clothing, felt his shoes sink into the muddy moss.

A separate double garage lay behind the house, and the area between the house and garage was cordoned off with police tape. The lawn had been torn up where what was presumed to be a four-by-four had skidded, regained its grip and accelerated once more to run over the man. Rainwater had gathered in the tyre tracks, transforming large areas of the plot into a muddy morass. In front of the garage doors a separate area, a square measuring a couple of metres, had been cordoned off where Tell assumed the man had been found.

"We think he was shot there," Björkman confirmed. He made a sweeping movement with his arm. "After that he managed to stagger a short distance, or possibly he fell forward against the garage wall here, where he was run over for the first time." He pointed at a number of dents in the metal siding. "You can see where the vehicle rammed into the wall, but Bart's body was roughly here when it was found." He waved his arm again. "So he must have been dragged along by the car, or perhaps he got caught on the bumper. Or he crawled, calling on his last reserves of strength, but that's unlikely. It's more likely that he was already dead."

"Then he was run over one last time," said Tell, pointing to the area where the ground was most badly torn up.

Björkman nodded.

"That was Nilsson's hypothesis. He's one of our crime scene officers."

Tell moved as carefully as he could over the cordoned-off area, making sure he didn't destroy any evidence as he checked the whole plot, and ended up squatting in front of the damaged garage wall. He examined the dents closely, and could just about make out a darker shade in the buckled metal.

"Is that paint from the car?"

"Presumably," replied Björkman. "And Olof Bart's . . . well, you know. It's gone for analysis."

"We didn't find anything from the car apart from the tyre tracks," said Tell without turning around. "But I'm sure we'll be able to find out if it was the same one."

He stood up with a grimace, and both felt and heard his knees crack.

"Anything else? It looks a real mess here, what with the rain and everything."

Björkman agreed gloomily. "Yes, it was absolutely pouring down the day before he was found."

"Who found him?"

"A girl and a boy out for a walk. They thought they'd take a short cut. Their dog had run on ahead and must have picked up the scent . . ."

They set off slowly back to the car.

"We haven't found anything else," added Björkman. "Not so far, anyway. I'll fax everything over to you as it comes in, and you can do the same. Then we'll both get on with —"

"Door-to-door enquiries first and foremost."

"We'll leave the organisational stuff to our bosses, don't you reckon? If it's the same killer, that is."

Tell nodded absently. "Can I borrow an office to go through what you've found out so far?" he asked. "I just need to gather my thoughts."

Björkman gave a sigh. "You can borrow the entire place, Tell. Apart from the duty officer there's unlikely to be anybody there apart from you."

CHAPTER
TWENTY-SEVEN

1995

Solveig Granith had downsized from a four-bedroom apartment in Rydboholm to a three-bedroom place in the centre since her daughter had made it perfectly clear she had no intention of returning home. Now she was sitting at her desk pressing her cerise silk pyjamas to her breast as the smoke from a menthol cigarette curled up towards the ceiling. Maya's train was due at the central station at 15.35. Solveig was probably not going to be able to meet her on the platform. Not today.

Earlier, after Maya had moved out but before she changed apartments, Solveig had made a habit of spending some time each day in her daughter's old room. She would just sit there on the edge of the bed for a while, perhaps looking at the posters or smoking a cigarette by the open window.

She was finding it hard to get used to the new place. There was so much less space and nowhere to put anything, but also no trace of a teenage girl — she had had to put Maya's things up in the loft. She had just one drawer in the desk containing a few drawings, a couple of well-thumbed books her daughter had loved as a child, jewellery and clothes she didn't want any more. It was rare for Solveig to unlock the drawer and leaf through the sketch pad, sniff at the dress Maya had worn for the school leavers' celebration. But it did happen. Despite the fact that there were periods when she talked to Maya on the telephone almost every day, she would catch herself thinking of her daughter as someone much loved and much missed. As if she were dead rather than simply living elsewhere.

The first time Maya announced that she was moving out, she was no more than fifteen years old. Of course she'd had neither a place to live nor any income, but she was talking about moving in with an older friend who had just got an apartment in town. The friend had told Maya she could start paying when she got a job; it didn't really matter because social security was paying the rent anyway.

Solveig's whole being had tied itself in a knot. She had wanted to hurl herself at her rebellious child and hold her fast. Instead she had swallowed hard and sat in silence in her bedroom as Maya packed her things. The Winnie the Pooh suitcase left over from childhood was the only one big enough. That night it had stood in the dark hallway, surrounded by the evil which her daughter had drawn down over her skin like a suit of armour to protect herself from Solveig's pain.

She remembered how she got up in the middle of the night before the move. How she had found the key to her daughter's room; it was still in the same place where she had kept it hidden all through Maya's childhood, just in case the door jammed. The old lock was stiff and she was afraid the noise would wake Maya. She stood there for a long time with her ear pressed to the gap between the door and the frame, so close that she could hear her daughter's steady breathing, that characteristic little whistling sound that was due to narrow nasal passages, and a pleasant sense of calm had come over her.

She had tiptoed over to the sofa. Curled up in one corner she allowed the moon to shine in between the slats of the blind, creating diagonal stripes across her turquoise dressing gown. She had experienced a feeling of liberation. The moon disappeared behind the clouds and first of all it became dark, then gradually grew lighter as dawn broke. When she heard the sound of her neighbour's alarm clock through the living-room wall, she crept back to Maya's room and unlocked the door.

Despite the fact that the next day her head was almost exploding with the monotonous noise of her tinnitus, the memory of that moon-drenched night gave Solveig a sense of control that helped her through the few lonely weeks that followed. She had convinced herself that the only reason the girl had left home was because she, her mother, had chosen to release her for a short while, to allow her to try out her fragile wings. She would come back, and Solveig would be there, her arms open wide, ready to console her. She would let Maya know that she knew. She actually did know how terrible the world was out there. Solveig had experienced its cruelty at an early stage. The difference was that she had been completely alone.

Maya would never be alone. Solveig would never let her down, she would always be there for her child. She was as firm in her resolve now as she had been in that midnight hour when her daughter first lay in her arms, smeared with blood from inside Solveig herself. The girl had seized her heart in a grip that brought her warmth and caused her pain in equal measure. For the first time she had experienced fully her value as a human being, a sense of pride in actually being someone in life: being someone's mother, if nothing else. And when the midwife had placed Maya at her breast and Solveig, exhausted after a lengthy labour, had looked down at that little red screwed-up face, the overwhelming love and inexorable demands had broken her. A doctor had to be called to give her such strong tranquillisers that Maya had to be bottle-fed for several days. A couple of years later, when Sebastian came along, Solveig was better prepared.

Sebastian was small consolation for Maya's absence. Not that there was anything wrong with him or their relationship. They were very close. But it was different with a girl, her first-born. She had always been able to see herself in Maya's face. They were so alike. Ever since Maya had lain there in her cradle, everyone had mentioned it: like carbon copies of one another.

After that first time Maya tried moving out — she was back three weeks later, the Winnie the Pooh suitcase crammed with dirty washing — mother and daughter had lived through the trauma over and over again. Each time the agony became a little easier to endure. That was how it was supposed to be, no doubt.

Maya spent a few weeks living in some sort of commune, then she fell out with someone and moved back home again. She met a boy with a place of his own and lived with him until the relationship broke up and she came back to Solveig in tears. She always came back, and that was probably what made it possible for Solveig to endure the constant separations. She would grit her teeth and carry on with her life and her son's life while she waited for Maya to turn up on the doorstep once more.

The evening before Maya took the train to the folk high school, they had had one of those quarrels that made the neighbours hammer on the walls. Even if Maya had tried to put right some of her worst remarks in her letters, they were still etched on Solveig's mind. That depth of humiliation could never be erased.

To be honest, the change of apartment had been made not only for practical reasons. It was true that her sickness benefit was quite meagre, but the old apartment wasn't particularly expensive, and she could have afforded to stay there at least until her son was also ready to move out. Instead it was an irrational desire for revenge that had driven Solveig to make the change as quickly as possible. Hurt to the very marrow, she had thought that if the girl found it so unbearable to live with her egocentric, sick, suffocating parasite of a mother — *You're like a stinking wet blanket over my face; you stop me from breathing* — then Solveig would make sure it was impossible for her to change her mind in the future. And when she came back, full of apologies and with her tail between her legs, it would be too late. She would discover that her mother was a person with feelings and a life of her own. She would see what it was like to have to stand on her own two feet.

The anger gradually cooled and the pain of the harsh words closed in on itself.

But Maya never came back home with her dirty washing. This time she had moved out for good, and when she came to the little three-room apartment with the sofa bed in the living room, it was as a guest of Solveig and Sebastian.

It wasn't too bad. In many ways most things were different after they left Rydboholm for Norrby. The monotonous buzzing in her ears fell silent, at least for a while, and this brought with it the benefit that Solveig could cut down on the sleeping tablets and the other pills she took when she felt she couldn't cope.

Sebastian was at that outgoing age — he was thirteen years old — and was starting to bring friends home. The little hallway was filled with size 10 shoes. The boys played deafening music, which distracted Solveig's attention from her feelings of abandonment. Sebastian was a teenage boy to the very tips of his fingers, in the sense that he avoided her questions and all gestures of affection.

She consoled herself with the thought that at last he was starting to make friends. He had always been so lonely. And even if he no longer had as much time for her, she was still his mother, however much he fought against it. Perhaps the most important person in his life. As an adult he would have the sense — both children would — to appreciate everything she had done for them. All the effort she had made.

"Mum?"

Solveig turned towards the door in slow motion. The adjustment from thinking she was alone to interacting with another person took such a long time. And it seemed to be getting worse as the years went by.

"Mum?"

Sebastian had already assumed That Expression, the one she disliked so much. The one that made her feel small in front of her own child. Judged. As if he thought he was privy to some kind of secret information about his mother. What gave him the right to be worried?

Solveig loathed this false concern. She had encountered it in so many different contexts. As a child in the face of the social worker, in her foster-parents' expression. As an adult in the doctors' rapid movements as they leafed through her notes. Social security, staff at the nursery, the class teacher, the parents of her children's friends, all with their head tilted to one side, when it was really about one thing: condemnation. *We're worried about you, Solveig; we're wondering how you manage,* which meant, *We think you're completely worthless and hopeless.* But she'd shown them, hadn't she? That she could manage. She had coped and she was a brilliant mother to her children: loving, committed. Always there, unlike so many of today's parents, who were so focused on their career, so self-centred.

"Mum."

"What!"

Her tone was sharper than she had intended. *I must pull myself together*. Her thoughts drifted away so easily these days.

"What do you want?" she asked in a more gentle voice, but the boy's face had already shut down.

"I was just wondering if you'd bought me some cigarettes. You said you were going to, and I've promised Krille he can have some of mine."

Everything stopped inside her head.

"We can't get them from the Greek any more. He wants to see ID."

She examined how she felt. Couldn't go out today, no. Not today.

"I'll do it tomorrow. I'll go to the Co-op and buy a box. I need some too. And it'll be cheaper that way," she decided.

"No! For fuck's sake, you promised! And tomorrow's no good! Tomorrow's too late! I need them for the party!"

"Party? What party?"

He sighed and rolled his eyes and his voice became supercilious.

"I told you — you never remember anything. I told you I was going to Evil tonight, with Krille. His brother's a member, and there's a party."

"Evil?"

"Evil Riders, a bikers' club. There's a band I want to see. I told you. You just don't get it, you never listen. It's in Frufällan, that's why I told you to get petrol for the moped. Oh, let me guess — you didn't do that either?!"

228

"You're not going."

"What are you talking about?"

"You're not going. Your sister's coming today and we're going to have a nice time together. I think she's been looking forward to seeing us. I don't think she's having a very easy time of it at the moment. She's arriving on the train at 15.35, and I said you'd go and meet her. You're staying at home tonight, Sebastian."

He looked at her with a mixture of contempt and pity.

"Are you stupid, or what? It's too late now, it's all arranged."

He didn't wait for a reply, just walked into the hallway and yanked his jacket from the hook. The door slammed behind him.

She looked at her hands, carefully examining the ring on her right hand, a broad silver ring with a green stone. The children had given it to her on her thirty-third birthday.

"Besides which, you get bad people at parties like that," she mumbled. "Gang members, drunkenness and fighting. No, you're not going. Over my dead body."

CHAPTER
TWENTY-EIGHT

2006

It was that name, it triggered a confusion of unwelcome memories Seja didn't know she'd been harbouring. If anything surprised her, it was the fact that the memories hadn't chafed more over the years.

For a moment this very fact made her feel as if she were emotionally cold, and a wave of shame flooded over her at the thought of the article. Shame over those intimate hours with Christian Tell, suddenly tainted by deception. During the lonely nights when she lay half-awake it was established that the guilt was hers; she was guilty, and the jury was unanimous. Yet she carried on writing. She wrote to keep the anxiety in check and because her suppressed shame fuelled her writing.

When she woke up and considered her options in the cold light of day, she decided she couldn't have done anything. She didn't know anything, after all, couldn't put it down to anything other than a teenager's confused guilt over a tragic event. The evening at the bikers' club had probably shape-shifted thousands of times in her head. It was strange, because although it was many years since she had thought about that night, she realised that it had coloured her own transition to adulthood in many ways. Perhaps she hadn't understood that until now.

Christian had called her quarter of an hour before midnight, just as the kids down the hill started letting off fireworks. The living room was in darkness, apart from a faint red glow from the stove. She was relieved to hear his voice.

"I'll be there in ten minutes."

Seja had turned down her only party invitation by pretending she was already going elsewhere. The truth was that a party at which half the guests were strangers and the other half were couples she and Martin used to spend time with was not appealing. She was also fairly sure Martin himself would be there and she didn't feel at all ready to see him.

She went out into the garden to meet Christian. They missed midnight by a quarter of an hour, for which he apologised as he hugged her, out of breath after running across the footbridge in the dark. For a dizzying second Seja dared to hope she could just stay there, with the beat of his agitated heart against her throat.

"I was invited to a party, but I decided not to go," she said simply, assuaging his guilty conscience at having let her see in the New Year alone, waiting for him. "It's fine, I promise. We didn't arrange anything definite, after all. But I'm glad you're here."

He took her by the arm as she tried to move away and gazed at her with a serious expression.

"I've got it wrong so many times in the past, this business of getting a relationship to work. I mean, it's not my strong point. I know we haven't known each other very long, but . . ."

A tendency to feel guilty is something we have in common. When he fell silent, she didn't encourage him to go on.

She walked ahead of him into the house to switch on the lights. He outlined the reason why he had been working on New Year's Eve.

"A man has been found murdered outside Kinna. It's exactly the same pattern as the man at the car repair workshop. We suspect it's the same killer."

He carried on talking, still a little nervous but eager, as if he were seeking her approval. Or perhaps he thought she was already involved, in a way.

She silenced him with a kiss and said it was fine, but soon left him to make an unnecessary trip to the outside toilet. Out there she tried to regulate her breathing. A cold hand had grasped her stomach so tightly that she could hardly take in any air.

She suspected that Christian Tell was suffering because he felt that in going to bed with her he had overstepped the mark as far as his profession was concerned. But instead of suffering with him, his embarrassment made her own deception easier to bear. He would never dare to confront her or challenge her, she thought; he was far too caught up in his own transgression.

There was a reason why it felt impossible to tell him about the memories that had begun to chafe at her so unbearably, despite the fact that perhaps she ought to. That was where the guilt came in. Not just because she

232

was withholding information that might possibly be relevant to a murder enquiry. No, her guilt went much deeper.

CHAPTER
TWENTY-NINE

2007

The day's task — door-to-door enquiries — was a foretaste of future cross-district collaboration. Detective Inspector Sofia Frisk, the sparkly blonde from the Christmas party, had driven like a joyrider. Around every bend on two wheels, insane overtaking; it wasn't what you'd have expected when you first met her, slender and blonde with blue eyes, like an advert for coloured lenses. Now she put on a pair of sunglasses that covered half her face and made her look like an insect.

Gonzales couldn't help laughing.

"What?"

"You look funny in those glasses."

She smiled and stretched her legs beneath the fleece rug.

"Mmm, lovely. But my feet are cold."

Michael Gonzales didn't think it was lovely at all. He had decided to look good when he was detailed to spend the day out and about with Sofia Frisk from the Borås team. Therefore he was wearing his cool, but thin, leather jacket. His backside was well on the way to freezing firmly to the garden furniture, despite the fact that he had been given a blanket and a fluffy cushion. Not to mention how cold his feet were in his sodden trainers. At the moment there was actually no feeling in them at all.

"Just imagine living like this. What a luxury, waking up to this every morning."

She leaned back, allowing her gaze to sweep over the islands, apparently scattered at random in the lake down below the terrace.

Their hostess appeared, dressed in a warm padded coat. She was carrying a tray with three cups and a cake on it. "And you're not cold," she stated rhetorically, but Frisk shook her head anyway, the beetle shades bouncing up and down on her nose.

"Goodness no. I was just saying what a magnificent view you have. It's hard to believe when you're driving along these narrow roads that a place like this can suddenly appear."

Good God, she was laying it on with a trowel.

"Yes, it is lovely." Anette Persson smiled contentedly. "When we retired about ten years ago, we didn't want to stay in Borås. We wanted to live in the country, and so . . . We'd inherited this place from my father. It's in such a beautiful spot, although we were a bit anxious that first winter. It's quite inaccessible out here, after all."

"Are the houses around here mostly summer cottages?"

Gonzales made a start on the cake, since it seemed no one else was going to.

"Yes, more or less." Fru Persson nodded. "There's the Tranströms' that you passed at the top of the hill, the red house — they live here all the time. Then there's a young couple who moved in not very long ago if you carry on past Bart's place. It looks as if the road comes to an end there, but it doesn't. They've got a little shop in Borås. Berntsson, their name is. And then there was Bart, of course — he lived here all year round. It's just terrible. I still can't believe it."

"Did you know Olof Bart well?"

"Definitely not." She made a defensive gesture with her hand. "We didn't know him at all. I think we only spoke a couple of times. It's a bit odd when you live so close, but . . . He wasn't the kind to invite you in, if you know what I mean. Not that we have a great deal to do with our other neighbours. We keep ourselves to ourselves, but we help each other out if necessary. When we were doing some building we were down at his place a couple of times to fetch water, but he wasn't all that talkative."

"You never went inside each other's houses?" asked Gonzales.

Fru Persson looked surprised.

"Well yes, when we were fetching the water. Ernst went into his house — he said it was a real mess."

She appeared to be thinking.

"That's it, yes. Our boiler was playing up and he came to give Ernst a hand. It was a friend of ours, Anders, who told us that Olof could fix all kinds of equipment. Anders owns a heating and plumbing shop, and he also has a warehouse just outside the village.

Olof had done some casual work for him in the past . . ."

"Anders?" Frisk's pen was poised over her notebook.

"Franzén, with a z. Nyponvägen 13."

"Thank you. Can I ask whether you've been down to Bart's place since he was killed?"

Anette Persson flushed red.

"Well . . . Ernst did pop down. We wondered why the police were here, naturally, but the body was already gone by then."

Frisk made a big production of looking at Gonzales, who nodded thoughtfully.

"Can you think of anyone who might have done something like this to your neighbour?"

"No. As I said, we didn't really know him."

Gonzales stood up, partly to try to get the circulation going in his legs and partly to look over the hedge.

"Only you and Bart and the young couple use this road, is that right? It comes to an end after that?"

Anette Persson nodded, appearing to discover her coffee all of a sudden. It must have been cold as she took a tentative sip. She looked anxiously at Gonzales over her cup.

"It's important that you think very carefully about this, fru Persson. Did you see an unfamiliar car, a stranger, anything at all out of the ordinary before Bart was found dead?"

Fru Persson took a deep breath. "I'd just got up, and I was extremely tired. It was still dark, of course, but I did see a car I didn't recognise. And it was driving down towards Bart's place."

"When?"

"Well, the same morning the police turned up. It was just before four, I'm sure of that because I couldn't sleep and I'd been lying there, looking at the clock."

"Did you notice anything else? What colour was the car?"

She sighed. "I can't say because it was dark, and besides —" she frowned "— it just had on . . . what are they called? Fog lights, or hazard lights, I don't know. But it must have been really difficult to see the track ahead. I remember, because I thought it was peculiar."

"This business with the lights?"

"Everything. The time, above all. Bart doesn't usually have visitors. And it was so quiet as well. I think the car must have been moving down the hill with the engine switched off, because otherwise I'd have heard it. But it was almost completely silent, just a faint crunching on the gravel. It was a bit ghostly."

"And?"

There was an air of desperation about fru Persson as she shrugged her shoulders.

"Nothing. I went back to bed, put my earplugs in and managed to fall asleep. I have earplugs because Ernst snores," she explained, seemingly relieved that the conversation had moved on to safer ground. "We slept right through till nine, if I remember rightly."

The wind grabbed hold of an enormous parasol at one end of the veranda. It fell beside the fence, and Gonzales only just managed to avoid being hit by the pole.

"Good God!" Anette Persson leapt to her feet, but seemed happy about the interruption. "It's getting a bit cold to sit out here anyway."

She ushered the two officers into the living room. A distinct aroma of alcohol reached Frisk's nostrils as she stood next to Anette Persson. The woman's hands flew up to her face, as if she had only just realised that she had been just a few metres from the murderer.

"I had to . . . It's all so dreadful." She burst into tears. "How are we going to be able to live out here now, in the middle of the forest, after something like this has happened? I'll never be able to . . ."

It was no longer possible to make out what she was saying. Frisk placed a hand on her back.

"I realise it must have been a shock for you, but I think we can tell you that the murder was carried out in a way that leads us to believe that the murderer knew Bart and wanted him dead. This has nothing whatsoever to do with you, fru Persson. You have nothing to fear."

"You said dark, fru Persson," said Gonzales, ignoring the look Frisk gave him. "You said it was dark. Was the car dark in colour?"

Anette Persson looked up through her tears and appeared to consider the question.

"I think so," she said eventually. "As I said, it was dark outside, but I think I would have noticed if it had been white or a pale colour. I think it was black or maybe dark blue."

"And I don't suppose there's any chance you noticed what make it was?"

She looked surprised. "Well yes, of course. We used to have one, before we bought the Berlingo. It was a Jeep. A Grand Cherokee. It looked new."

Before they left the area and headed for more civilised parts, they called at the Tranströms' place at the top of the hill, even though they knew Inspector Björkman had already spoken to them. There was no harm checking whether the neighbours had remembered anything new. No one was home, however.

Gonzales took a stroll around the outside, putting his foot through the layer of ice on a puddle and soaking his trainers once again, just as they were beginning to dry out. There were no lights to be seen around them; the other buildings consisted of summer cottages closed up for the winter, their windows covered in frost.

Frisk pushed back her seat and put her feet up on the dashboard while Gonzales drove — calmly and carefully — towards Borås and the shop belonging to the Berntssons. This job was already dangerous enough, without needing to risk killing yourself on the road. *We've got plenty of time*, he thought as Detective Inspector Frisk pretended to snore beside him.

Maja Berntsson hung the CLOSED sign on the door just as her husband arrived.

Sigvard Berntsson's face and chest were covered by a huge reddish curly beard and he had to be twice as old as his wife. Gonzales thought he looked a little shaken, but that didn't necessarily mean a thing and his appearance didn't prevent him from offering a firm handshake. People were often scared when they talked to the police. Gonzales knew that better than most; a whole load of the friends he'd known as a teenager had chosen lives of crime.

Unfortunately, the Berntssons didn't think they had anything to contribute to the investigation, since their bedroom faced the forest and not Bart's place. They had been asleep on the night in question, with a couple of brief interruptions.

"I got up to go to the loo just after midnight," said Maja after thinking for a few moments. "I remember the time, because I turned off the video — I'd recorded a film during the evening. Then I woke up first thing in the morning as well. Olof Bart was definitely alive then, because he was making so much noise."

Her husband frowned.

"You never mentioned that."

She gave him an indulgent look. "Yes, I did. I even woke you up with all my complaining, but you just turned over and went back to sleep."

She turned to Gonzales.

"It wasn't unusual for Olof to be up early, revving the engines of those cars he fixed. It could be really annoying sometimes, particularly at the weekend when all you want is a bit of peace and quiet."

"What time was this?"

"Er . . . I don't really know. I'd guess five or six o'clock? He was nearly always up at first light."

Frisk looked meaningfully at Gonzales.

"Is there anything else you can tell us, Maja? Did you hear any voices? Think carefully."

She looked uncertainly at Frisk and shook her head. "No . . . I was really half-asleep."

Frisk placed her card on the table. "OK. It's important that you get in touch with me if you remember anything else. Anything at all. That applies to both of you."

Sigvard Berntsson still seemed confused.

"There was just one thing," he said thoughtfully as they were about to get up. "I was talking to Olof on Tuesday. It was an ordinary conversation, although we didn't talk all that often — he was a bit of a lone wolf. I didn't think anything of it at the time, but in the light of what's happened . . ."

"What did you talk about?" Frisk helped him out.

He linked his hands together on the table. "Olof came to see me while I was out chopping wood. He seemed keen to chat for once, as if he wanted something. He started talking about different kinds of burglar alarm and what you should and shouldn't get. I think I more or less dismissed the whole idea. To be honest, I'm not keen on that kind of false security — you know what I mean, capitalists making a profit out of people's fears. Anyway, he finished up by saying that we ought to keep an eye out for each other. I thought he meant burglaries, that sort of thing, but . . . I suppose he might have meant something else."

"You mean he seemed afraid of something in particular?"

"Yes, as if he had an idea of what was going to happen. As if he knew about the murderer."

242

CHAPTER
THIRTY

Analysis showed that the bullet in Olof Bart's head came from the same gun that had killed Lars Waltz. It therefore seemed reasonable to conclude that the perpetrator was one and the same.

Björkman and Frisk took their places in the conference room at police headquarters in Gothenburg for an initial joint briefing.

At first Tell had been surprised that Björkman hadn't sent someone from the lower ranks who had been involved in the investigation. By coming himself, he became yet another inspector in the new constellation. Tell wondered distractedly whether Björkman's mania for tidiness had now developed into a powerful need to remain in control, and in that case how effective he was as a team leader. On the other hand, the members of Björkman's team he had met appeared to think highly of their boss. And he had to admit that his own prejudice about small-town police officers and their little-brother complex had so far proved unfounded. If you could call Borås a small town.

Östergren had asked for a meeting with both detective inspectors to find out how they were planning to proceed. Two murder enquiries had suddenly taken a completely new turn, and new methods were required. Perhaps the top brass had a strategic plan.

"We need to make a decision on what we're going to do about talking to the press," she had said, among other things.

Tell sighed. He'd been waiting for that.

"The media already have some idea of what's happened — there was a fairly woolly piece in *Göteborgsposten* after the Olofstorp murder. The question is whether it might do us some good to go public with the whole thing, to avoid media speculation."

The team had gathered in full force in the conference room. Since they were on his territory, it seemed natural for Tell to take the lead.

"I assume you are all familiar with the background of these cases and why we're here, therefore I have no intention of going through it all again. I also assume that everyone," nodding mainly in the direction of the officers from Borås, "has had a look at the interview transcripts linked to the Olofstorp murder, along with the SOCO reports and the forensic pathologist's report."

Björkman and Frisk nodded.

"I would therefore suggest that you run through what you've got, then we can look at the information and make an initial comparison."

Björkman tapped the bundle of A4 paper in front of him into a neat rectangle.

"OK . . . let's see. Olof Bart was shot with the same gun as your victim, that has been confirmed. The bullet was found after a detailed examination of the crime scene, but nothing else. The killer does not appear to have got out of the vehicle. However, we did learn from the forensic pathologist's examination that the execution did not go exactly according to plan, as happened in your case. A mark just above Bart's left ear shows that the murderer first pressed the barrel of the gun against the victim's skull. However, the shot was fired from a distance of approximately half a metre. It seems likely that the perpetrator held on to Bart and pressed the gun to his head, but Bart managed to tear himself free. The murderer could have shot him while still sitting in his car."

"What's that all about?" groaned Gonzales. "Can't he even manage to get out of his car? Either he's bloody lazy, or he's got some kind of mobility problem."

"That is possible, of course," said Björkman thoughtfully. "But it's also possible, in both cases, that the murderer *did* get out of his car but didn't leave any traces behind. As we know, it poured with rain all that day."

Everyone around the table nodded gloomily: rain was every officer's worst nightmare when it came to examining the scene of a crime.

"Apart from blood and other material, there are traces of paint on the metal wall that was rammed. We will probably be able to establish what kind of paint we are dealing with. There were also tyre tracks. The place was ankle-deep in mud, but here and there we were able to make a decent cast. I'll come back to that."

He took a deep breath and blew the air out of the corner of his mouth.

"As I said, the perpetrator was unlucky, if I can put it like that. The shot was not fatal, at least not directly. It went through the nose and came out behind the ear without passing through the brain. Bart would probably have survived, looking like shit admittedly, if he hadn't died from loss of blood or frozen to death. However, as you know, the perpetrator decided to be on the safe side and ran over him as well."

Björkman leafed through his papers again.

"The perpetrator drove into the victim on the lawn, pushing him in front of the car towards the garage. Then the killer put his foot down, pinning Bart against the wall and . . . well, any of his internal organs that were still intact were crushed at that point. The driver then reversed and the victim was pulled, or dragged, a couple of metres along the grass, where his body was eventually found. We do have a time frame: our forensic pathologist has estimated death occurred between four and six in the morning, and according to an interview with a neighbour, Anette Persson, who evidently suffers from insomnia, it was quarter to five when an unknown Jeep rolled down towards Bart's place. I think we can safely assume that this was our murderer."

Sofia Frisk cleared her throat.

"The Berntssons, Bart's other neighbours, were also woken at an early hour by noise from Olof Bart's place — the roar of a car engine, among other things. Maja Berntsson assumed he was up early, working, which he often did, but again it seems likely that what she actually heard was the murder."

246

"Isn't it a bit strange that she didn't hear anything else — screaming, for example?" said Karlberg.

Björkman shrugged his shoulders. He looked up to check that no one had any further questions about the cause of death, then took a document out of a red plastic folder and carried on.

"As I said, he was found by two young people, David Jansson and Klara Päivärinta, who were out for a walk; their dog ran on ahead and started barking. The dog had evidently been up to the body and . . . well, I don't know. The boy said its nose was covered in blood. At first he thought it had been bitten by some animal." Björkman shuddered at the unpleasant picture that came into his mind. "They made the call straight away. The police from Kinna turned up after only a couple of hours."

A few of his colleagues laughed appreciatively at the aside.

"Were they questioned?" asked Tell, temporarily deaf to any kind of in-joke.

"They were very shocked, of course, but they were interviewed at the scene and didn't really have much to say. They hadn't seen or heard anything, but then that's hardly surprising. It was three or four o'clock in the afternoon when the call was made."

Björkman started rustling through his papers again, and Frisk took the opportunity to jump in.

"Michael and I spoke to Anette Persson. Apart from telling us the precise time when she saw the car, she was also able to tell us that it was a Jeep Grand Cherokee, fairly new —"

"A Grand Cherokee, yes," Tell interrupted.

Frisk cleared her throat.

"Apparently they used to have one themselves, that's why she was so certain. She was less sure about the colour, but she thought it was black or blue. Another thing: Sigvard Berntsson remembered that Bart had been anxious about something just before he was murdered. He'd been talking about burglar alarms and neighbourhood watch. As if he had a bad feeling about something."

Björkman nodded thoughtfully. "There's one more house that's occupied all year round, the Tranströms'. They were away on the day itself, but they did say that a sports car driven by an immigrant had been seen down in the village a week earlier. They thought it was odd."

Björkman's expression showed exactly what he thought of this, and a couple of his Gothenburg colleagues shook their heads incredulously.

"OK," said Tell, taking over once again. "We'll carry on interviewing those who live in the vicinity. We'll work our way outwards from the scene of the crime."

He stood up and made a note on the whiteboard.

"So, we're assuming that we have a murderer in a Grand Cherokee. They can't be all that common."

"Well no, bearing in mind how much you have to cough up to buy one," Karlberg agreed.

"So our murderer is upper class. A politician or a brat," said Beckman.

"Or a plumber," Bärneflod added.

248

"Focus," said Tell. "The vehicle registration office: all those who own a Grand Cherokee. Start with black and dark blue. In Gothenburg and Borås to begin with, then we'll work our way across the country."

"What limits are we setting?" asked Frisk.

"We don't know yet," said Tell.

Björkman raised one finger in the air. "There was one thing I wanted to come back to with regard to the tyre tracks. It's annoying, to say the least. The impressions show that the tracks from the two crime scenes were not made by the same vehicle. Or to be more accurate, they're not from the same wheel."

Everyone sat in silence for a moment, digesting this fact with some confusion.

"But according to our technical boys, the tracks were made by a heavy vehicle, something like a Jeep," Gonzales protested.

"Yes. We know that one tyre manufacturer recognised their specific model from the impressions we took in Olofstorp," said Tell. "Plus we have the exact distance between the wheels. A Grand Cherokee is a match for our case too."

"What does that mean — it's not the same murderer after all? Did the murderer swap cars, same model but a different vehicle? Or did he change the tyres?" said Karlberg.

"It is the same murderer — the gun matches," Beckman broke in.

"Shit," muttered Tell. "OK, we'll check the vehicle register anyway."

He thought for a moment.

"We should also look at car hire companies in the area who have a Grand Cherokee. Same method: start at the centre and work your way outwards. Check if they have CCTV cameras; if so, it would be useful to have the tapes."

Somewhat disheartened, Tell found it difficult to summon up enthusiasm for the investigation, yet they had actually managed to gather far more information than could reasonably be expected at such an early stage. They had an exact time; they had the make of the car. Even if the car wasn't the same one in both murders, they could link one car to one murder through the specific wear and tear on a tyre, and hopefully they would be able to link the car to the murderer through the registration office, a car hire firm or witness statements. And then the murderer could probably be linked to both murders, since it could be proved that the same weapon had been used. He pulled himself together.

"The method is the same, the murder weapon is the same. We need to think about common denominators between Lars Waltz and Olof Bart. In order to do this, we need to map each man's background. We've made a start on this with Waltz, as you can see from the reports, so we'll tackle Bart in the same way. The focus for this task is to try to find points of similarity between these two men. Can anyone think of anything now, just off the top of your head?"

"They're about the same age," said Beckman.

Karlberg nodded. "Waltz is two years older."

"Grew up in the same area, perhaps? Went to the same school?"

Björkman shook his head.

"Olof Bart has only been Olof Bart for about ten years. He changed his surname in 1997. Before that he was called Pilgren. Odd, don't you think? So far we haven't managed to track down any relatives. His parents are no longer alive. He's supposed to have an older sister — Susanne Pilgren — but she hasn't had a fixed address for years. Evidently she's a known user. But when Olof was young the family lived in Gothenburg, in Angered."

He scratched his head.

"They don't seem to have had an easy time of it as kids. The sister was taken into care by social services, but that's where the trail ends — it's all confidentiality crap. If we're going to get any information, we need a piece of paper to wave about."

"OK, Björkman, that's fine," said Tell. "Someone needs to look up Bart's social services file, if it still exists, and check out the family in general: mother, father, possible foster homes, care homes, time in prison, whatever. Actually, I can do that. I can go through Östergren if we hit red tape," he added to himself.

"Karlberg, you go and have a chat with the guy who worked with Bart. And Bärneflod, you can start setting up the search for the car. Check if there's any transport company that uses the killer's presumed route, and if there is, find out the drivers' schedules. Somebody might have seen our man, maybe at a petrol station or in a lay-by. The same applies to taxi firms that serve the area we're looking at. I know it was an ungodly hour so I'm sure there weren't many people about. Talk to the staff at petrol stations and places that serve food along the road; we know he was driving a dark-coloured Grand Cherokee. He might have stopped to fill up with petrol or got something to eat. The CCTV cameras could be of interest there too. As usual we need to work with the resources available, and we have one or two other cases going on as well. But we do need to strike while the iron's hot. The police in Angered, and I assume in Kinna too, are at our disposal within reason. But we should expect to work hard for the next few days. I'll talk to Östergren about how many people we can use."

Tell had added the last sentence hastily as Bärneflod was beginning to look more and more grim.

"We'll make a start along those lines. It's too early to begin talking about motive until we have a clearer picture of victim number two and what the link is between the victims. But let's assume that the perpetrator had some kind of relationship with both of them."

He reached for a glass of carbonated water from the Sodastream, the station's latest acquisition.

"Any questions?"

"Yes. Why?"

That came from Frisk.

"Why?" Tell repeated blankly.

"Yes, why are we assuming that the perpetrator had a relationship with the victims?"

252

Silence briefly fell around the table. Karlberg leaned forward and grabbed a tin of snuff somebody had left behind. He opened it and contented himself with inhaling the aroma. Sometimes it helped.

"Because the alternative is a maniac who kills at random. And we all know the statistics about how unusual it is for a victim and killer to have had no previous contact. Plus that scenario doesn't really fit in with the method and the evidence left behind — or rather the lack of evidence."

Beckman agreed. "A confused person would leave more clues behind. Besides which, the method is far too full of hatred to be an impulsive act. I mean, the victims were both shot and run over, not once but twice: one right across the body, the other crushed against a wall. It almost looks like . . ."

She fell silent, but Tell prompted her.

"Like what?"

She shrugged, suddenly embarrassed at the attention. She hadn't quite finished formulating her ideas.

"I don't quite know what I meant, but it looks like the kind of rage that could have been caused by some deep wrong. I actually thought of something sexual at first, but I don't know why."

"You mean the murders were committed by a woman?" said Gonzales.

"No, I didn't mean that at all. I just mean I think there was a great deal of anger behind the killings. That much rage builds up over a long period, and is directed at a person who has some significance for you. I think any profiler would agree with me on that," she said,

253

missing Bärneflod's meaningful glance at Karlberg, who thankfully failed to respond.

"I think you're right. That's what I meant when I said we should assume that the victims knew the killer." Tell turned to Frisk. "But you're right too. We can't exclude the alternatives. We can't tie ourselves down to one theory without any proof. That was a good reminder."

With those words, and with the feeling that he was an excellent team leader — clear, ready to listen, generous, constructive — Tell brought the briefing to an end.

CHAPTER
THIRTY-ONE

1995

The gastric pains kicked in as soon as she got off the train at Borås central. She had taken an earlier train than she'd said and didn't expect to see any familiar faces on the platform. Apart from an elderly man in a raincoat and sou'wester, it was deserted. She bought a couple of bananas and a bottle of mineral water from the kiosk in the hope of settling what her mother usually referred to as her "nervous tummy", which was protesting against several cups of coffee she'd drunk in the buffet. She'd been travelling all day.

Early that morning a classmate had offered her a lift to the station. Maya had agreed immediately, throwing a few clothes into her rucksack and scribbling a note to Caroline, who was still asleep: *Making my own way to the station — see you Sunday night. Love M!* Deep down she knew that this bright little message was a way of hiding the real reason why it felt so indescribably good to leave Stensjö in a hurry. She wanted to be free, even if it was just for a couple of days. Wanted to prove to herself that she could still cope on her own. To have the chance to miss Caroline, as she had done at the start of their relationship.

Talking to Caroline about her need for freedom was pointless, and every time ended in despair and long drawn-out punishment in the form of silence or a sophisticated nastiness. Up to now Maya had not thought that her longing for freedom had in any way matched the pain it caused Caroline; she had adapted, despite the fact that the empty feeling in her stomach had returned, and sometimes became actual pain.

Otherwise she might have thought that the gastric discomfort was associated with the town, with the lifeless greyness surrounding Borås station. Her "nervous tummy" — the snare inside her — characterised her relationship with her mother, Solveig. Poor Solveig.

The same pain had coloured her teenage years and was closely intertwined with guilt, the constant gnawing guilt that she could never rationally explain but which had nevertheless always been there. She had realised at an early age that her mother was a pathetic soul, but over the years the guilt had become interwoven with anger at the guilt, and love interwoven with the anger, all of it associated with this person who lived and breathed other people's guilt.

No behavioural therapy in the world would be able to remove the snare that had ceremonially been placed around her neck, tightening slowly now as she opened the door.

The smell of home struck her like a slap in the face. It pervaded the people who lived there and their dealings with each other, the hall furniture made of pine and the armchair upholstered in Laura Ashley fabric that her mother had won in a competition in a women's magazine. The vibes, her well-developed sixth sense, told her that she ought to call out to warn Solveig that she'd arrived. That she shouldn't surprise her by walking in unannounced. She tried to clear her throat, but the sound turned into an indistinct mumble.

Solveig was in the bedroom. Maya waited in the doorway until the shoulders stopped shaking and she knew that her mother was aware of her presence.

"Darling girl," said Solveig, turning her tear-drenched face to Maya. The wet cheek was pressed against Maya's hand, cold and soft like a lump of dough. "Mummy's just a bit upset."

Maya knew the words well from her childhood.

"But it's fine now you're here."

After dinner they left the washing up and moved into the living room. Solveig had bought soft drinks and crisps and made some popcorn in the microwave, and there was a romantic comedy on TV. In order to be able to watch it from the revolving armchair, which was covered in dust as Sebastian usually watched TV in his bedroom, they had to push a pedestal out of the way and lean a folding table up against the wall. The living room was much smaller than the one in Rydboholm, and Solveig had found it difficult to get rid of things. She had mentioned several times during the course of the move that it was hard to find room for everything.

Maya had reassured her patiently, time after time. "You've done the right thing, Mum, honestly. It's much better for you to be living in town."

"When Sebastian leaves home, you mean? Any day now? When I end up all on my own? I miss my things. I filled a whole attic with furniture, and I miss my parquet floor. This thing is just pretending to be a parquet floor. What am I going to do here in town, anyway? I spend all my time at home. If anybody ought to spend money on where they live, it's me — I should have thought about it that way."

"First of all, Sebbe is only fifteen; he's not moving out anytime soon. And you really ought to find something to do, now you haven't got anybody to look after any more. A hobby, something to get you out and about."

Her mother met her gaze with an expression of sheer contempt.

"Like what?"

"How should I know? Dancing lessons. Learning a new language."

Maya couldn't summon the energy to put her heart and soul into the all-too-familiar conversation; she knew it was a waste of time. Her mother snorted and took her cigarettes and lighter over to the chair by the window. She pushed it open and blew the smoke out through the gap, peering anxiously into the street.

"It's so dark here. They were talking about putting some lighting on this street," she mumbled. "So women would be safe from rapists and so on. As if that would help." She squinted. "Turn the light off so I can see."

Maya went and stood beside Solveig. Together they watched a lone dog-walker.

258

"Is it Sebbe you're worried about?" asked Maya in the end.

Solveig nodded, and the tears started to trickle down her cheeks.

Maya sighed. "Mum! It's only half past eight. He was going to a party, wasn't he?"

"I told him he couldn't go!" yelled Solveig, her face distorted by weeping once more. She sucked the smoke down into her lungs so sharply that she started to cough and had to bend over and take deep breaths. As she did so, Maya noticed that her hair reached right down to the floor. She had a lot of split ends. It was grey now, Solveig's hair. How long had it been so grey?

"You said it yourself, Maya." Her mother's voice sounded different as the words bounced off the floor. "He's only fifteen. These bikers' parties attract all kinds of rough people. I won't be able to sleep without tablets tonight. I don't think I can get through this." Solveig straightened up and slapped one ear with the palm of her hand. "Evil, that's what it was called. Evil."

"The bikers' party? Where is it?"

"I think it was Frufällan."

"The Evil Riders. Yes, they've got a place there. I know people who've been."

Maya knew what was coming. She sat down on the sofa and placed a cushion over her stomach.

Suddenly she found them utterly laughable. And she would have laughed, in fact, if it hadn't been so oppressive: she and her mother in this claustrophobic, insanely over-furnished little flat, each with her own psychosomatic cramp presumably exacerbated by their

259

being together. And now Solveig wanted her to go out to Frufällan, on those narrow roads in the rain and the wind.

Solveig pointed at the darkness outside the window as if it were argument enough — which she thought it was.

Solveig shook her head crossly. "He's your brother! He's only a child; it's your duty as his older sister to go and fetch him. Please, Maya, please, darling. My nerves can't cope with this. You can go on the bus, can't you, if you're worried about getting wet?"

By this point Maya deeply regretted coming home. If she had ever longed to get away from Stensjö and Caroline, that was nothing in comparison to how much she now longed to be anywhere other than with her mother.

"Solveig," she said, because she knew her mother hated it when she called her by her first name. "OK, I know where it is. It's a long way from a bus stop, so that would be pointless. I presume the bike's still here?"

Solveig nodded and her face immediately softened. She stubbed out her cigarette in the overflowing ashtray on the coffee table and wiped the tears from her cheeks.

"It's downstairs in the cellar, in the storeroom. You'll probably need to pump up the tyres; nobody's used it since you disappeared."

Maya nodded grimly. "I'm going to have a glass of that wine you've got in the cupboard while I get ready to go and embarrass Sebastian in front of his friends. And to freeze my backside off."

She couldn't even bring herself to look as Solveig hunted among her facial expressions for one that would show how hurt she was at the suggestion that she kept wine in the cupboard, since she had made a big thing in recent years of the fact that she didn't drink because of her "heart tablets". In the end she appeared to decide it wasn't worth the trouble. She'd already got Maya to do what she wanted, after all.

Her mother used to lie more quickly, if not more credibly, thought Maya as she struggled against the shards of icy rain a couple of hours later, following the dots of light illuminating the cycle track out of town.

She had stupidly thought that things would have changed when she came home, simply because external circumstances were so different. A strong wind had got up, and the rain lashed her face until her forehead ached with the cold. She started to swear out loud, the words muffled in her woollen scarf at first, but soon she was yelling her frustration at the top of her voice. Her curses seemed to be eaten by the wind, which had free rein now she had left the factories and the old warehouses behind and was cycling past open fields.

Things improved slightly when she turned off the cycle track, heading for the Evil Riders' club. There had been no need for her to worry about not finding it; the track was marked with a sign, and beneath it a burning torch had managed to stay alight in spite of the weather. Nor was there any risk of taking a wrong turning, since the narrow gravel track carried on into infinity, with no crossroads or any other buildings. It was pitch dark, the way ahead illuminated only by the feeble dynamo lamp on her bike. It felt like travelling into nothingness with neither a map nor compass to guide her.

It had been quite late by the time she had drunk her wine, put on suitable clothes and managed to find her old bike and pump up the tyres — she thought it must be getting on for midnight now. *Please let it not be much further.* She could leave the bike there and get Sebbe to give her a lift home on his moped. The thought cheered her up slightly.

Her energy held out and finally she spotted the lights of the club at the end of the winding black track. The sound of engines was getting louder; two cars and loud voices were coming towards her. She stopped and dragged the bike to the side of the road to let them pass. Music was pouring out of the club. The main door and several windows were wide open in spite of the cold. A dog ran out and relieved itself, lifting its leg against the plastered facade. It stared straight at Maya, before finding some scent on the ground to concentrate on.

Immediately after that a girl emerged; she had bleached blonde hair and was wearing a short skirt and boots. Maya felt as if she knew her from somewhere. The girl called to the dog and squatted down to scratch behind its ear before nodding briefly at Maya and going back inside. Maya took a deep breath and walked through the gate of the surrounding fence. She propped her bike against the wall next to an enormous motorbike with a sidecar.

The muscles in her face contracted before she stepped inside. She knew this meant that the familiar mask had settled into place, like a thin but strong film which would allow any insults simply to run off, or at least to give the appearance of not sticking.

A tall man in leathers with a long ponytail loomed up in front of her, blocking her view. When he moved she gazed across the smoky room. Apart from candles in bottles on rough tables and benches, a dozen glowing cigarettes and a small electric lamp above the long red-painted bar, there was no lighting. The corners were murky. The loud hum of voices, interspersed with the odd burst of laughter and the occasional shriek, revealed that the room was full of people doing their best to shout over the top of the music coming from upstairs. When her eyes got used to the darkness, she noticed figures sitting on the floor along the walls.

She couldn't see Sebastian anywhere. Most people were older — in their thirties — and many were wearing the bikers' club emblem on their backs. The man with the ponytail had stepped outside and was lighting a cigarette. He looked friendly. Maya leaned out.

"Excuse me! I was wondering if you've seen a boy called Sebastian. He's only fifteen, and he's with a friend who must be about the same age. I think his friend's name is Krister."

Ponytail smiled and blew a puff of smoke into the air.

"There must be two hundred people in there — I haven't a clue what anybody's called or how old they are. There's a gig tonight, a band from the USA. Some

263

kind of monster rock, not really my thing, but they pull in the crowds. So it's open house — anybody can come as long as they pay. We don't check everybody's ID, if you see what I mean. You're not a cop, are you?"

Raised voices broke through the general hubbub behind them. Maya wasn't ready for the sudden blow to her back which made her lose her balance and fall against Ponytail. He caught her adroitly and aimed a kick at the man behind her, who was somewhat over-refreshed.

"Watch it, dickhead."

Ponytail didn't appear to take any notice of Dickhead's unrepentant response as he staggered back inside; he merely shook his head and pointed at Maya's jacket at breast level. "You've got some beer on you." He seemed to be wondering whether to help her wipe it off, but possibly decided that the gesture could be misinterpreted.

She waved away the mishap.

"No, I'm not with the police; I'm looking for my brother. I just thought you might know."

He nodded and looked as if he were making an effort to think.

"Well, if he's only fifteen, I suppose maybe I should have spotted him. Go up and have a look — he's bound to be upstairs if he's here, that's where the band is playing. Have you tried the bar? He could be drinking himself senseless — that's what I did when I was fifteen." He grinned, revealing a substantial plug of tobacco. "Still do, in fact. But tonight I'm working, right through till daylight."

He pulled a watch with a broken strap out of his pocket.

"I'm on the bar in a couple of hours. I'll treat you to a beer then," he added. Maya didn't reply. She had no intention of staying that long.

On the steps leading to the upper floor sat a group of kids not much older than Sebastian. One of them nodded cheerfully when she finally managed to make her voice heard above the wall of sound coming from the heavy metal band. He pointed at the mêlée of headbangers jumping up and down in front of the stage. There was an ominous creaking underfoot; the floor seemed to be threatening to give way.

And there was Sebastian right at the front, absorbed by the band in their black robes, their faces painted white, emitting guttural cries through the feedback into the microphones. He was sitting at one corner of the stage, in front of a loudspeaker. Judging from the volume he ought to have been blown away, and would be at least half-deaf for the rest of the weekend.

Maya pushed her way forward. Just as she was about to grab her brother's sleeve, she stopped, seized by an impulse to look at him. It was months since she'd seen him. She thought he'd lost weight.

He gave a start, as if he really had been in another world. For a moment he looked at her, his expression unreadable. She yelled his name and more or less dragged him across the floor. The group on the stairs shuffled to one side to make room as she pushed her brother towards the exit, suddenly filled with righteous indignation at having to endure this trial.

He tore himself free, but not before she managed to push him outside in one last moment of superiority. The rain and wind had died down, and snowflakes were hesitantly drifting from the sky.

"What the fuck are you doing?" he yelled.

Maya calmed herself and tried to put herself in his situation.

"Mum made me come to fetch you. She's out of her head with worry, apparently she'd said you couldn't go."

"Yeah, and? If I took any notice of what *she* said I'd be as crazy as her."

He had lost weight. With those dark rings under his eyes, he looked older than his fifteen years. She was filled with an unexpectedly powerful feeling of tenderness. She had always felt indifferent to her brother — when he wasn't irritating her with his chubby cheeks and tear-filled eyes, he was competing for her mother's affections.

She reached out and touched his denim-clad arm.

"Anyway, hello. I haven't seen you for ages. Is this all you're wearing?"

He nodded defiantly, crossing his arms tightly over his chest. She placed her hand on his, slightly embarrassed, but suddenly she couldn't get enough of touching him. Things must have been so difficult for him since she moved out. Her cheeks burned at the thought. She drew his hand towards her. Sebastian lowered his eyes as if he were considering going home with her, or as if he were about to say something important, but then he seemed to change his mind.

She was shivering in spite of her coat.

"You need to come home now, Sebbe."

Any hint of a concession was wiped out in an instant as he looked at her.

"Forget it. I've come to listen to the band. I'm not going home."

He turned to go back inside, but she stopped him by moving in front of him. A couple of boys and a girl of Maya's age were standing chatting to the driver of some beaten-up passion wagon. They laughed raucously and shouted to Sebastian that it was long past his bedtime.

Maya tried to keep calm as something wild came into Sebastian's eyes. She couldn't bear the thought of going back to Solveig without her brother.

"Come on, for fuck's sake," she hissed between clenched teeth. "Besides, I can't get home if you don't give me a lift on the moped. I can't cycle back all that way," she added in a slightly louder voice.

"That's your problem," he said.

For a moment they weighed each other up. Maya felt exhausted after her long journey and then the bike ride. The tension of spending time with Solveig hit her like a blow to the back of the knees, and she was the first to look away. Sebastian roughly tore himself free of her grip, and pushed her away. She hadn't the strength to protest.

The band was taking a break. Applause and loud whistling could be heard from the upper floor now the music had stopped. People came pouring down the stairs to the bar. Sebastian pushed against the crowd as he made his way back up. Maya stood there at a loss, hoping he would change his mind.

Sweaty, out-of-breath rockers moved outside to cool down in the chilly night air. Deafened by the decibel count of the band, they were shouting at each other rather than talking.

The blonde girl came out, wrapping a wine-red scarf several times around her neck. This time Maya was sure she recognised her. She made eye contact and raised a hand in greeting. "I think I've seen you at the station café."

The girl smiled again and took a packet of cigarettes from her inside pocket. As former regulars at the Northern Station café — those who arrived when it opened and sat there until it closed, writing in their diaries, on napkins or in the visitors' books — they had a better idea of each others' innermost thoughts than of what other people looked like. As with all of those who wrote in the visitors' books, they had revealed their secrets and desires for others to applaud or mercilessly denigrate; everything was done in writing and under an alias, like a hidden world. It had been so important at the time.

"I thought you were from Gothenburg," said Maya to the girl, who nodded.

"I am. I came here with a guy to see the band. And I've just found him snogging another girl. That's life." She shrugged her shoulders. "So you're from Borås, then. Tingeling."

She had remembered Maya's alias, which was impressive after such a long time. Maya was warmed by the fact that she had made an impression.

"And you're Girl," she replied, recognising her companion. They stood there for a while, considering the official exchange of letters that had taken place a couple of years earlier.

"You draw very well," the girl said suddenly. "Really well. You should do something with that."

Maya squirmed in embarrassment. She could feel the colour rising in her cheeks. "Thanks," was all she could manage.

Raised voices could be heard from inside the club. A man in his thirties came tumbling out; it was Dickhead. He landed a couple of centimetres from Maya's shoes.

She rolled her eyes. "And who are *they*?"

The girl watched Dickhead as he staggered back and forth.

"I don't know. They're from somewhere around Gothenburg, I think, but I don't know them. They seem to be completely rat-arsed already. Fucking pissheads."

She turned back to Maya.

"Anyway, forget about them. Come and have a beer and we can chat about old times. I hardly know anybody. And on the way in we can accidentally knee that bloke in the groin, the one over in the corner who's practically sitting on that girl with a face like a monkey!"

Maya laughed and shook her head.

"I don't think I have the energy, to be honest. I've got to cycle back home to my mother — she'll go crazy otherwise. I was supposed to fetch my brother, but he's refused to leave, and if neither of us turns up, she'll ring the police — guaranteed."

The girl looked at Maya, her expression inscrutable, and Maya almost changed her mind. She didn't know why she should suddenly take Solveig's feelings into account. The thought of a beer with Girl was far more appealing than the long lonely pitch-dark ride home, but still she felt she couldn't cope with the scene that would inevitably be waiting for her if she didn't hurry home. Solveig seemed more brittle than usual.

"If you like we can go to the bus stop together. I can give you a lift on my bike," she offered.

Girl thought for a moment, but then shook her head.

"No, I'll stay. I'll try and get a lift to the station with somebody, it's so bloody cold. And then of course I don't want to miss the chance of telling Mårten exactly what I think of him. I'm just waiting for the right moment."

Maya nodded. She acknowledged that she was beaten as she wheeled her bicycle through the gate, ignoring a suggestive male voice calling her back. She definitely wasn't in the mood for flirting or witticisms.

She clenched her teeth until her jaws ached, concentrating on avoiding the icy patches on the track.

It was the same distance back to the club as it was up to the main road when the tyre burst. Only then did she begin to cry, from a combination of tiredness and anger. She tried to carry on cycling, despite the fact that the old, dried-out inner tube was flat against the ground. Soon the lactic acid was burning in her legs and she gave up. There was no alternative but to walk through the dense darkness and silence as the tears froze on her cheeks.

CHAPTER
THIRTY-TWO

As usual he bitterly regretted having agreed to drive home, and after a long wait that definitely tried his patience he'd had enough. Even if it annoyed him to have to go back inside yet again — at the risk of provoking Wolf he had called him by both his first name and surname, nagging like some old woman — that was exactly what he did.

"Will you shift your fucking arse."

Not that it helped. Wolf had just bought yet another strong beer, and was slurping it at his leisure, half-sprawled across the table talking a load of bollocks to Pilen. And they were both happy to leave their mate standing out in the snow, waiting for them. *Fucking bastards*.

"If you're coming with me, you need to come now, otherwise you can find your own fucking way home."

Målle had good reason to be in a bad mood: he'd been slumped over the wheel of his rusty pickup for over half an hour. Wolf had had his licence taken away, and it wasn't the first time this year that Målle had ended up waiting outside like some kind of fucking chauffeur, jumping up and down to keep warm as dawn broke, before finally seizing his pissed-up mate and dragging him into the truck so that he could get away. And no doubt he would have to help Wolf into the house when they got back, bearing in mind that he couldn't walk, stand or sit.

Fuck. The idea of simply opening the door and shoving his friend out was tempting. Just to teach him a lesson. Although he'd end up lying exactly where he was dumped, and on a night like this he would freeze to death. Perhaps it was a bit harsh. But how that wife of his coped was a mystery.

Wolf was the only one of the three who had a wife, which proved that women always fall for a bastard with a pretty face, rather than a decent bloke with a face like an arse. Not that he was quite in that category, but looks had never been his strong point.

When it came to Pilen, the third comrade-in-arms, the arse theory was definitely no exaggeration. For most people, acne disappears along with their teens but Pilen had been unlucky. Not only did countless craters from old zits make his face resemble a moonscape, it was also covered with painful new eruptions that from time to time made his face look like a piece of raw steak. Stress, he would always claim — and he must have been seriously stressed.

In a way, perhaps it was a good thing that Pilen was able to blame his zits. It was probably much more difficult to handle the realisation that you were just too stupid to score; indeed most women ran a mile as soon as he opened his mouth. And bearing in mind the calibre of those around him — Wolf for example — it

272

was obvious how incredibly stupid a person had to be in order for that particular quality to stand out.

The ladies hadn't exactly been falling over themselves to pull Målle either, although the odd one had made her interest known. But to tell the truth, he preferred to stay single rather than have some nagging whining old bag at home to provide for, poking her nose into everything and getting fatter with every year that went by. That's what had happened to most of his mates who had made the mistake of acquiring a wife, not to mention kids. They really did fuck things up completely.

Wolf's wife might be a bit different — she still looked good and didn't seem to be completely losing it, which made it all the more incomprehensible that she had chosen such a tosser.

He brought the truck up to the door and Pilen helped him bundle Wolf inside despite the fact that he was demanding one more beer.

Målle was annoyed with Pilen as well — he always went along with Wolf. If he hadn't been given an ultimatum, he would probably have sat there all night listening to Wolf talking bollocks, knowing perfectly well that they had agreed to leave by midnight at the latest. He was like a girl: scared of conflict, always taking the easy way out.

As he drove through the gate Målle realised with a slight feeling of unease that he wasn't quite as sober as he'd thought. The odd beer had slipped down. He didn't usually worry too much on the gravel tracks around where he lived — he'd never even seen a police car out there — but they were going on the motorway tonight.

Anxiety made him even more annoyed. Fucking Wolf. If he hadn't been so bloody awkward, Målle wouldn't have drunk so much. Throwing all reason out of the window, his anger made him grab the bottle Wolf and Pilen were passing between them. He took a couple of gulps. *Fuck it*. If he got caught he would lose his licence anyway. He was possibly the most sober of them, but the police wouldn't care about that.

On top of everything else, it was snowing heavily by now. The pickup's useless windscreen wipers made it difficult to see, and the effort of driving in a straight line was making his head hurt; he didn't want to end the night in a ditch. Wolf had just fallen asleep, dribbling against the seat belt, when Målle heard himself cry out and for a second he lost control. The wheels had skidded on a patch of ice, and the truck slid alarmingly close to the ditch before stopping with a jolt. Wolf had woken up and was staring at him, his eyes wild.

"What the fuck are you doing?"

"There was something there. I nearly hit . . ."

With his heart in his mouth he frantically wiped the condensation from the inside of the windscreen and caught sight of a dark figure to the side of the car. He flung open the door.

"What the fuck! You need to look where you're going!"

The man slams his fist against the bonnet of his truck and yells at her.

274

"What the fuck!"

Maya is dazzled by the headlights and holds her arm up to shield her eyes. She has seen enough drunks in her time to be able to determine straight away what kind he is: he's the kind who gets angry.

"Look where you're going," he says again, but with less force behind the words. For some reason this wavering makes her angry. She drops the bike and takes a couple of steps towards him.

"Look where *I'm* going? What about the way you were driving, you fucking lunatic! You nearly hit me, even though I was standing on the verge!"

"You've got a flat."

"You think I don't know that?"

For a few seconds they can hear the dying sound of the wheel, spinning around in the air where she threw the bike down. When it finally stops, the noises of the forest are very clear. A steady quiet drip. A creak, a rustle. And silence.

She can only see the man's silhouette, his hair, a broad-shouldered jacket. His face is in darkness. She takes a step back, out of the circle of light.

There is movement inside the pickup: someone is coming to life and groaning. At the same moment the passenger door opens and another man practically falls out. *He's huge and he's completely pissed.*

"What the fuck! Are you coming or . . . Oh, a girl. You can sit on my knee."

He slurs his words and pats his crotch with a whinnying laugh, then places one foot on the ground and heaves himself unsteadily out of the truck. His bearded face is sweaty and his eyes are bloodshot.

There's a third one, in the back seat.

Maya's heart is thumping unevenly, but there is no turning back. *Don't let them see you're afraid.* She leans forward slightly towards the man who was driving. The unmistakable smell of alcohol meets her halfway.

"You're drunk, for fuck's sake. You were lucky. If you'd hit me you'd have been arrested." She moves back towards her bike. "Arsehole," she mutters.

"OK, I'm sorry, just stop going on about it!" His voice has acquired a whining undertone; he seems unsure about his anger. "Shall I put your bike on the back? You don't look too good."

Don't let them see you're afraid. *I just want to get home. Just get through this.*

"I wouldn't get in a car with a drunk like you even if I was dead."

The girl was standing in the full beam of the headlights once again. This time she wasn't shielding her eyes, she was just standing there like an idiot, waiting to see what would happen next. She couldn't really see him from where she was standing, not the way he could see her.

Her face was ridiculously sweet and girlish, juxtaposed with those old man's clothes that were too big for her, and her cheeks were red from the cold, like a small child. *A fucking furious child.* Målle somehow found this both attractive and exciting. He'd apologised, for fuck's sake. He'd offered her a lift up to the road, where she could have caught the night bus or taken a taxi or whatever. What else could he do? The party was an all-nighter, and it would be many hours before the narrow forest track was illuminated by cars and motorbikes on their way home. It wasn't a good idea for a girl to be wandering about out here in the forest on her own in the middle of the night. Anything could happen. And nobody would see or hear a thing.

Wolf let go of the door and approached the girl.

"Come on, come for a little ride with us. We've got booze and other stuff I'm sure you'd like . . . Or maybe you swing the other way? Maybe you don't like cock?" he went on, his voice low and challenging, sounding almost sober now.

Målle was on the point of telling Wolf to pack it in, but he couldn't quite bring himself to do it. The girl's insult still lay there, like a thorn in his eye. He discovered that he was enjoying seeing the mouthy little cow suddenly looking so scared. Not quite so full of herself now.

She seemed to have decided it was best to keep quiet. Good decision. She was intending to pick up her crappy bike and get the hell out of there, but Wolf had reached out and grabbed her arm. Then she screamed, *Leave me alone, you bastard! You're fucking disgusting!* She screamed for help too. She was welcome to try, nobody would hear her.

At the same moment he realised she didn't have a chance. They had the power to do whatever they wanted, and there was nothing she could say or do to stop them. The thought turned him on, as did the sight of Wolf, an expression on his hairy face that Målle had never seen before, pushing the screaming, struggling girl ahead of him towards the truck.

Wolf had pinned her arms behind her back with one of his huge fists, while with the other hand was fiddling with his flies. The drunken babbling idiot had completely disappeared.

Pilen had opened the door of the truck to make it easy for Wolf to push the girl head first on to the seats, then he stood there turned to stone, looking as if he hadn't the faintest idea what might be expected of him.

Maya leaves her body and contemplates the scene from above, from the tops of the trees. This is a relief in itself, the fact that there is no need to offer any more resistance. The details become razor-sharp: a piece of chewing gum in the shape of a horse's head stuck to the seat. The remains of a burger meal and countless empty beer cans on the floor. Homer Simpson looped around the rear-view mirror. The smell of sweat and cow dung from the fur hat beneath her cheek.

Come on, urges the Big One.

The one who seems scared pulls her coat up above her waist with an expression that would be comical in a different context: disgusted, as if he were dissecting a rat. From her perspective high up above them, Maya can see that he is indeed afraid. Her short brown skirt over black trousers is exposed. He pulls a face and breathes quickly and heavily as if he were having an asthma attack, then tugs at the skirt as if trying to rip the seams apart.

278

In the end the Big One has had enough and pushes his useless pal out of the way, but before he has time to pin Maya to the seat with his body, she sees her chance. In a fraction of a second she returns to her body, manages to shift backwards and drives her heel into her attacker's crotch. The Big One loses his balance and falls back into the Scared One, who seems to have been waiting for the opportunity to pass out. He slips and tumbles down into the ditch.

Maya seizes her chance and runs, straight out into the black nothingness. A protruding branch tears at the skin on her face. She runs and clamps her jaws shut; she will cry about this, but not yet — with tear-filled eyes she would be lost in the darkness. She is terrified of tripping and falling, but pushes away the pictures crowding her brain: Maya lying there with her face close to the frozen ground, her pursuers catching up with her in seconds. Focusing on the moment is the only thing to do. The blood trickling down into the corner of her mouth has the bitter taste of iron. She will scream about this, but not now; she must run with the piercing scream unborn inside her body. The sound of a snapping twig makes her glance back over her shoulder. The headlights of the pickup seem alarmingly close.

She can hear nothing but the pounding of her heart.

Before his brain even had time to register what was happening, Målle had run around the truck and set off after the girl. He couldn't bear the idea of her getting away and winning. Not now, when they were going to show her who was in charge.

Off into the forest she ran, pathetic, her clothes in disarray. They caught up with her after just a few dozen metres, in among the fir trees. He couldn't speak for Wolf, but he had given up any idea of actually fucking her, she was too pitiful, but for that very reason she had to learn some manners. Then they would drive her up to the road and she would feel a deep sense of gratitude that they had chosen not to harm her, even though they had the power to do so.

Take it easy, he yelled, as much to her as to Wolf, who had flecks of foam at the corners of his mouth.

And suddenly she fell. Afterwards he couldn't be sure whether she had slipped on a root or whether she just fainted, but she certainly fell, head first, and she didn't move.

All he could hear then was his own heartbeat, and then Wolf's heavy breathing on the periphery, louder and louder, until he yelled at him to shut the fuck up.

It was so dark, too bloody dark to see anything, but he thought again that the body on the ground was too still. With trembling hands he took out his torch, but he couldn't bring himself to switch it on. Wolf snatched it from him and shone it on to the snow, and afterwards, during that insane drive home, it was Pilen who wept like a child, with his fingers in his ears. And he was the one who hadn't even seen how the snow was stained red by the blood around her head, or the blind staring eyes.

CHAPTER
THIRTY-THREE

2007

Karlberg arrived at the heating and plumbing shop just in time for Anders Franzén's break, at least that was the impression he got from the owner, who was sitting in a little office behind the showroom with his feet up on the desk. With his earphones firmly in place and his eyes closed, Franzén seemed completely deaf to the world around him, including Karlberg's discreet tapping on the door frame.

Karlberg tried gruff throat-clearing, but this didn't penetrate the wall of sound behind which the shop owner was hiding either. When he finally took two steps forward, he almost frightened the life out of Franzén. The earphones and the iPod clattered to the floor, and for a fraction of a second Karlberg was afraid he was heading for a punch. He backed away and groped for his ID card.

"Police, I didn't mean to startle you. I did knock."

He pointed at the earphones now lying under the chair. Bearing in mind how loud the music was from a distance of two metres, it was hardly surprising that Franzén hadn't heard him knock.

"I usually hear when a customer comes in," Franzén apologised. "I must have turned the volume up too high. I've got Lucinda Williams's latest on here. Brilliant. Have you heard it?"

He held out the earphones to Karlberg, who declined.

"I'd like to ask you some questions about a man you supposedly shared these premises with some time ago. Olof Bart."

The corner of Franzén's mouth twitched.

"These premises, is that what he said? Is he in trouble, then?"

"You could say that," said Karlberg tersely. "He's dead."

The colour drained out of Franzén's face in an instant.

"Dead? But what the hell! If you're here that must mean he was —"

"Murdered, yes. That's why I'd like your help with some information. You worked with Bart, is that correct? Did you see him on a daily basis?"

"Well . . ." Anders Franzén looked at Karlberg, his expression hesitant. "I don't really know what I can tell you. For a start we didn't share these premises. He rented a small area in my warehouse for a couple of years. I can't tell you what he did there, except that he took on all kinds of repairs. Agricultural machinery mainly, the odd car or motorbike. I assume he wasn't exactly keeping accounts and paying his taxes, but surely that can't be relevant now?"

Karlberg shook his head.

"No. So you had no real idea of who you were renting this space to?"

"Oh yes," Franzén protested. "I did know him personally, but I don't know how far my obligation to check on someone's business dealings goes, just because he pays me rent. He was a jack of all trades — did all kinds of things to earn a bit extra. Bought stuff and did it up then resold it, so of course he needed a place to store everything. I had a big warehouse and I was only using half of it and . . . well, I needed the money."

He looked at Karlberg defiantly.

"How did you get to know Olof Bart?"

"Through friends, Ernst and Anette Persson. Bart was a neighbour of theirs. They knew he needed storage space and I needed a tenant, so they put us in touch."

That was rather strange, thought Karlberg. According to Persson, he had only spoken to Bart on a few occasions. It would seem a little odd, although not impossible, if Bart's need for storage space had come up on one of these rare occasions. Of course it was also odd to live next door to someone for ten years and never speak, although no doubt it wasn't unique. If the Perssons had, in fact, had a closer relationship with Bart than they had let on, they must have had a reason to lie.

Anders Franzén's tone was now quite defensive.

"I use the place for storage myself, but obviously I'm not there every day. I don't think he was there every day either, because he did other work as well. In the forest, among other things, I think. I didn't really ask him much about what he wanted the space for, or go poking about his stuff when he wasn't there. Besides, his section was locked and —"

"I understand. You don't know anything about his business affairs," Karlberg interrupted, "but do you know anything about his character, his background?"

Franzén firmly shook his head.

"You said you knew him personally?"

"Well yes . . . I thought he seemed a bit dodgy, to be perfectly honest. I don't have any real evidence for that, but I wasn't keen on the bloke." He shrugged.

"Go on."

"He was very difficult to talk to. Didn't look you in the eye, if you know what I mean. Didn't give a proper answer to anything. A bit evasive. But I did only see him occasionally after we'd signed the contract."

"I understand that."

Karlberg decided to try a different approach.

"I heard that you cancelled the contract with Bart because of a disagreement."

Judging from the colour of Franzén's face, the tactic worked.

"I did tell him he had to go, yes. If I'm honest, I'm not completely sure I had the right to do it but I'll tell you anyway."

He crossed his legs.

"It was 2003, I think. I'd been on my guard for a while because I'd had a nasty break-in at my summer cottage. It was horrible. They hadn't just stolen my stuff, they'd wrecked the place as well. They'd even crapped on the floor. Kids, maybe, drug addicts . . .

how should I know. Anyway, it might have affected my judgement and made me overly suspicious. But I had been thinking that Bart seemed a shady character. I didn't know where I was with him, and that bothered me. One evening I went out to the warehouse after I'd closed the shop — it was November, so it was bloody dark. I don't know if you've checked out the area, but it's remote and deserted, just old warehouses nearby. Anyway, I didn't have time to react when a man crept up on me from behind and slammed me against the wall. I felt something sharp in my side and got the idea that he had a knife. You don't take chances in a situation like that, so I gave him my wallet and my watch. I actually had a Rolex at the time; my sister works in advertising and she'd been able to buy one cheap."

Franzén's forehead was glistening, but it was rather warm in the little office. His gaze wandered vaguely towards the door, almost as if he was expecting his assailant to march in, demanding to be allowed to give his side of the story. He seemed to have lost the thread.

"So he got your wallet and your watch," prompted Karlberg.

"That's right. I was really shaken up afterwards. It was all a bit much, and I think that even then, totally illogically, I somehow linked the incident to Bart. Then a couple of weeks later I spotted him, Bart that is, in town. It was from a distance, on the other side of the street, and he didn't see me, but he had someone with him. I'm not one hundred per cent certain, since it was dark that night out by the warehouse, but I was sure it was the man who robbed me."

"Who was with Bart in town."

"Exactly. And I just felt that everything was so bloody unpleasant that I took the first chance I could find to chuck Bart out, which happened to be a month later. He was a bit late with the rent, just a few days — he often was and it didn't usually bother me — but that was the reason I gave for cancelling the contract with immediate effect."

He exhaled.

"How did Bart react to being kicked out like that?"

Franzén looked thoughtful.

"Well, that's what was so peculiar. He hardly reacted at all. He just nodded and agreed to be out in two weeks. Then, the following day, he turned up here in the shop." He pointed at the floor in front of him. "Absolutely livid, but in a really nasty way. Quietly menacing is how I'd put it. I remember he really gave me the creeps."

"Do you remember what he said?"

Franzén shook his head.

"Not exactly. As I said, it was several years ago. But he hinted at a few things about my business, and I think, if I remember rightly, he talked about how you need to be insured because anything could happen . . . At any rate, I interpreted it as a threat."

"Did you report it?"

"No," Franzén admitted. "I was just glad to get rid of him. I didn't see him after that. By the way, I didn't tell Ernst and Anette about the incident, so I'd be grateful if you didn't mention it to them." When Franzén saw Karlberg's raised eyebrows, he went on, "The thing is, I didn't want to worry them unnecessarily, as they were neighbours of his. And if they find out I've kept it from them . . ."

Karlberg nodded. He looked around the office as he fished his card out of his wallet. While they had been talking the door to a big cupboard behind Franzén had swung open, revealing shelves of CDs — an impressive amount for a heating and plumbing shop. Franzén noticed the direction of Karlberg's gaze, and beamed like a proud father on a maternity ward.

"I spend almost as much time here as I do at home. And at home — well, you know how it is — there's never any time, what with the kids and such, so one day I brought the whole lot over here. My wife isn't all that interested in music anyway."

He got up and ran his hand lovingly over the cases.

"My older brother ran the business before he moved abroad," he explained. "So I thought, why not? A job is a job, and I needed a job at the time. Not that business is exactly booming these days. Big DIY superstores have popped up all over the place, and I can't match their prices."

He looked gloomy, but only for a moment.

"I've always dreamed of running a record shop, ever since I was a little boy. It was vinyl then, of course. Do you like country?"

"Er, not particularly," said Karlberg honestly, and a light went out in Franzén's eyes; evidently there was more to him than at first appeared.

"Only there's a new wave of singer-songwriters coming along. They've got the heritage of country culture in their bones, but they've developed it and made it a bit easier to digest."

He searched the shelves eagerly for something that might appeal to a sceptic.

Karlberg moved politely but firmly towards the door. "I'm not much of an expert," he said apologetically. He was saved by a customer who had walked into the shop looking as if he wanted a guided tour.

Franzén sighed heavily as if he regarded customers as nothing more than an interruption to his musical experience. "I don't usually get anybody in at this time of day."

Karlberg seized the opportunity to take his leave.

CHAPTER
THIRTY-FOUR

As he had arrived two hours later than agreed, he could hardly complain about being shunted around like a hypochondriac at A & E.

Tell was in the dirty yellow brick building that housed the family care section of social services. On the telephone he had been promised a morning meeting with a member of the management team. However, it had taken him longer than expected to get the necessary permission for access to confidential notes. When he turned up late, the person he was supposed to see had gone off to a meeting.

After Tell had painstakingly explained the order of priority when it came to a murder enquiry and a management meeting, a secretary offered to try to find the leader of the children's and young people's section instead.

"I'm sure she'll be able to help, given that the information you're looking for relates to a childcare issue. But I think she was supposed to be in court this morning."

Sitting there with nothing to do in the section leader's waiting area, Tell's thoughts drifted to Seja and the New Year they had welcomed in together, a perfect night and morning in many ways. At the same time they had both silently wished everything were more straightforward.

He had sensed in Seja a hesitation, just for a while, then it was gone again. But he couldn't work out what it was all about.

When it emerged that the section leader in question wouldn't be back until after lunch, Tell left the building grinding his teeth and set off to walk around the square in the centre of Angered.

The usual gang of alkies were shouting to each other outside the door of the off-licence. A face from the past suddenly registered.

Lisa Jönsson. He had known her since he'd started on the beat, when she was a skinny stroppy hollow-eyed teenager hanging around Femmanstorg. Later he had come across her via the vice squad; she'd ended up on the streets to finance her heroin habit. It was many years since he'd last seen her, and on that occasion she'd been beaten black and blue. She had wanted to report her boyfriend for abuse. Whether she'd gone through with it or not he didn't know, as it had no longer been his job to deal with that sort of thing. He'd left the dog days as a beat officer behind.

I'd have put money on her being dead. They didn't usually get to be very old, these girls. Because Lisa was in no way unique. Girls swarmed around bad boys like Ronny, Lisa's boyfriend and pimp, who had become vicious and emotionless from the constant need to survive, dodging and weaving to satisfy the constant

290

craving for drugs. Boys with only a couple of teeth left who hit their girlfriends because that was the only way they could feel they were in control, at least for a little while. And then there were the boys who played in a higher league, boys who bought and sold and delegated responsibility to underlings who had to learn to hit first and think later. Who lived by the motto *Rule by fear*. They were also surrounded by girls living a dangerous life in a world where nothing but your latest proof of loyalty counted and a single mistake could cost you your life. Boys like that wouldn't touch Lisa with a bargepole.

She had acquired long red plaits made of wool that hung down past her slender boyish hips. When you saw her like that, from behind, you could easily have taken her for a girl of thirteen.

It was a real shock when she turned around. Tell was surprised, both at how the past can suddenly catch up with you when you least expect it, and also at the fact that a man who has been a policeman for over twenty years can still be shaken when he is confronted with a reminder of how vulnerable human beings can be.

He thought about going over to her, but decided against it. Perhaps because she was holding on to a vicious-looking dog tugging at its lead, or because the drunks around her were so numerous and noisy. Besides which, Tell was not sentimental enough to think she would recognise him. She had met hundreds of coppers over the years. He'd met hundreds of girls addicted to heroin, but for some reason she had made an impression on him, perhaps because he had been so young at the time and still imagined that he could help. As time went by the bloody bruised faces of the women he met through his job had melted into one. Perhaps to him Lisa's face was representative of . . . of what, exactly? The dark side of society? Women's vulnerability?

"What are you looking at?" bawled one of the drunks, taking a couple of unsteady steps towards Tell and shaking his fist.

Lisa Jönsson looked Tell in the eye for a moment. He thought he saw the muscles in her face twitch before she lowered her gaze. She probably didn't recognise him at all; it was just that she could recognise a cop, any cop, from a mile away. He knew that people who live outside the framework of the law can do that, even though the police don't really understand what it is that gives them away.

Or else Lisa Jönsson simply looked away because old habits die hard.

Finally, after being delayed by a further half an hour, section leader Birgitta Sundin marched into her office. Tell was already sitting in a red armchair next to the table.

Sundin was an older woman with glasses, her grey hair cut in a bob. A brightly coloured shawl was draped around her shoulders, in stark contrast to her otherwise severe clothing.

"I've been told why you're here, but I don't know enough about the situation to be able to give you anything at this point," she said, her voice tense.

Tell could feel the rage bubbling up inside him.

She quickly added, "But as soon as I've spoken to Eva Andersson, our manager, I will personally ensure that all the relevant material is sent over to you by courier. If it's here, that is. There is a risk that the material you're looking for has been destroyed as we're talking about papers that are almost forty years old."

Her mobile phone started to vibrate. She linked her hands firmly in front of her as if to ensure they wouldn't reach for the phone against her will.

"I'm sorry you've had a wasted journey," she added.

"That's not good enough," said Tell. "I have been informed that the notes I'm looking for were included in the percentage saved for research purposes, so I know they haven't been destroyed. They do exist, either here or in some archive. I have all the necessary papers in order and I'm not leaving here until I have received what I need for my murder investigation."

Sundin's telephone vibrated once again, and this time, to Tell's surprise, she had the nerve to answer it. She spun her chair round so that she was facing away from him, but quickly concluded the monosyllabic conversation.

"Actually that was Eva. She'd already got the notes out. She put them away in her filing cabinet when you didn't arrive at the agreed time."

A pause to ensure that Tell had grasped the point.

"Yes, yes, carry on."

"Her secretary will unlock the cabinet for you."

Tell stood up and noted that the conversation with Birgitta Sundin had taken exactly five minutes.

"So is that it then? Thank you so much for your assistance," he couldn't help saying sarcastically.

Sundin pushed her hair behind her ears, irritated at first. Then the air suddenly went out of her. Or, as Tell would later say to Karlberg, *She managed to pull the poker out of her arse.*

She sighed and leaned forward slightly. "I'm sorry, I didn't get your name."

"Detective Inspector Christian Tell."

She passed him one of his gloves, which had fallen to the floor.

"Detective Inspector Tell. It's not that I don't realise how important it is for you to have these notes, but I was put in a difficult situation here. You must also realise that I would be guilty of serious professional misconduct if I didn't check that everything was in order."

Without replying he extended a hand across the desk.

She didn't take it.

"Sit down for a moment," she said. "I think I might be able to help you with something. I realise we may have got off on the wrong foot."

Tell was readying himself to go upstairs to do battle with the manager's equally diligent secretary.

"And what might that be?"

"I heard the notes you were interested in concern the Pilgren family and their children, Susanne and Olof."

Tell became interested again.

"I'm retiring next year, but I've worked here for ever — at least that's what it feels like," Birgitta Sundin went on. "I've been a social worker, dealing with financial support, then I worked with adults, young people, families with children, employment initiatives ... Anyway, for the last few years I've been a section leader. What I'm coming to is the fact that I actually know this family fairly well, or at least I used to know them. It is a long time ago but I was their social worker in those days."

She stopped speaking and looked out of the window.

"You certainly don't remember all the children or families you work with," she said eventually. "But I do remember this family very well. I don't know why. Perhaps because they were one of my first cases."

Tell nodded, and the picture of Lisa Jönsson's red woollen plaits came into his mind. He understood perfectly.

"The first time I visited the family, Olof was on the way and Susie was three or four," Birgitta Sundin continued, after they had collected the notes from Eva Andersson's filing cabinet.

"They'd only just moved in. They came from somewhere up north originally, but had moved around in the Stockholm area. They ended up in Gothenburg after leaving Stockholm in a hurry right in the middle of an investigation —"

"What kind of investigation?"

"Social services has an obligation to ensure that children and young people grow up in a secure environment. If it comes to the attention of social services, for example through a complaint, that this is not the case, we have to start an investigation."

She glanced at Tell

"It's not really my area," he said. "Can you tell me a bit about Olof's parents?"

She glanced through the notes in the file where all major interventions by social services were documented, then placed a thick bundle of follow-up notes next to it. Together they made up a kind of chronological diary detailing all contact with the family.

"As I recall . . ." she said, and started flicking through the notes with no apparent purpose in mind. Many of them were signed with her own initials. She placed the pages together and rubbed frantically at her cheek just underneath the frame of her glasses. The skin beneath her eyes was red and irritated.

"How can I put this . . . Two weak individuals, each with their own form of addiction, meet and have children together."

She gave a crooked smile but immediately became serious again.

"In fact, Cecilia Pilgren was really easy to like. I think she had a potential that was never realised because of her own difficult childhood. But that's the way things are. After a while I came to realise that she simply had no good role models. She always ended up with men who had problems. Magnus had a serious addiction. He was violent and abused both Cecilia and the children when he flew into a rage. Deep down I'm sure he wanted the best for his children — everybody does after all — and during those periods when he was clean it was actually possible to reason with him. You could see that he had a broken soul beneath that tough surface."

She looked as if she were lost in thought for a moment, before shaking her head.

"As I said, there'd been a couple of complaints about the family where they were living before, and after a couple of unsuccessful interventions from social services, they moved. To Solna, if I remember rightly."

"Unsuccessful interventions?"

Tell contemplated the two stacks of notes gloomily. They were as thick as telephone directories, crammed with pronouncements from all kinds of professionals: social workers, people within the judicial system, doctors, teachers, nursery staff. It was a long list, but what the reports had in common was that they all expressed a deep concern for the situation of the Pilgren children.

"The thing is, before we go so far as to take children into care, which means placing them in a foster home, we must try other possible means of support."

"For example?"

"For example, support within the home. Magnus started a course of treatment for his addiction but didn't complete it. Cecilia was offered different types of help too."

"But nothing came of that."

"No, exactly. The main reason was that Cecilia didn't go, but then that isn't unusual for mothers in her situation. It's strange, but at the same time it's understandable."

"What do you mean?"

"You have to realise that even if these measures are meant to support parents by showing them an alternative to the life they've lived so far, that support frequently comes with a knife to the throat. If they don't accept the support and at least turn up and show willing, they can end up having their child taken into care anyway."

"So even though accepting help is supposed to be voluntary, they don't have any choice?"

"Exactly. That's why these parents rarely have a positive attitude towards activities arranged by social services, and Cecilia certainly didn't. She distanced herself, her life was chaotic, and this meant that she constantly failed to fulfil her side of the contract. As you know, the children were eventually moved to foster homes, and that was presumably what would have happened in Solna too, if they hadn't moved away."

"So how come social services here didn't follow through what had been planned there? They had already made an assessment, I presume?"

Sundin's smile was slightly indulgent.

"You might think so, and in principle that is the case. However, it isn't unusual for this type of . . . let's call it a problem family to make a habit of moving on as soon as things get a bit tough. And I'm sure they often do believe they're going to make a fresh start in the new place, that everything will be better if they can just get away from all the rubbish of their former life. And maybe that's what happens, for a while, until the family

298

structure once again starts creaking at the seams, and a new social services team has them in their sights."

"Or else things really *are* different in the new place," Tell broke in, surprising himself with his new-found and somewhat desperate optimism.

"Hmm, well. It would be nice to think so," replied Sundin.

"So you're saying that information about problem families isn't automatically passed on to a new authority."

"Quite."

"In other words, children of these families can go through hell time after time without anybody doing anything about it, because the family moves and the case is signed off."

"Yes."

They contemplated this in silence for a moment.

"And there's no kind of premise behind all this?" said Tell eventually. "I mean, the idea that a person is capable of changing his life, or that he has the *right* to do so, without being judged in advance because of past failures?" He was thinking of Lisa Jönsson again. "Protecting a person's integrity, that sort of thing."

Birgitta Sundin shook her head.

"The premise is that we should work primarily from the perspective of the child, but as with all large organisations sometimes people fall between the cracks. Anyway, I came into the picture when they'd been living here for a few months. We'd had a complaint from a neighbour of the Pilgrens about what was going on next door, and how much bloody noise there was, if you'll pardon the expression. Shortly after that Magnus beat Cecilia so badly she ended up in hospital. She stayed in a women's hostel with Susie for a while and made a formal complaint against Magnus. Then she changed her mind."

Tell nodded. He was familiar with this pattern.

"To cut a long story short, we did what we could to motivate Cecilia to accept some help. The couple separated just before Olof was born. I remember I regarded it as a step in the right direction. She had cut down drastically on her amphetamine use during the pregnancy. This is quite a positive report from the assessment home." She showed Tell a yellowing typewritten report subheaded "Hästeviken Assessment Home." "If there's one time when a woman using drugs is likely to pull herself together, it's when she's pregnant, and when Magnus disappeared I saw it as a real chance for Cecilia."

She took a box of throat sweets from the top drawer of her desk.

"Unfortunately, we often discount the father at an early stage in families such as this," she said. "We tried various tactics, but after Olof was born Cecilia started using heavily again, and she also lost her grip when it came to looking after Susie — you can see here I've made a note about the fact that she'd stopped taking her to nursery. She broke off all contact with both social services and the childcare authority. If I remember rightly, Olof was about six months old when Susie was taken into care."

"So the girl was taken into care but not the boy," said Tell in surprise.

"Yes, the judgement we made at the time was that the girl was suffering the most. It isn't uncommon for weak mothers to be able to cope with a small baby reasonably well, but then lose control as the child gets older. When it begins to defy her and make demands. That's exactly how it was with Cecilia. In spite of everything, we were prepared to give her a chance with Olof. I'm sure you can understand how easy it is to be wise after the event."

Her expression became defensive.

"I must stress that in contrast to what people think, we don't take children into care unnecessarily. I don't think we do it often enough, if you ask me. Anyway, through a combination of promises and threats we managed to get Cecilia to accept a place in a home for mothers and children. It was somewhere north of here — Dalarna, I think. Cecilia and Olof lived there for a year."

"What are they like, these places?" asked Tell.

Sundin didn't have time to answer the question because a knock on the door was followed by a corpulent man in his thirties. He informed her that the youth team was sitting in the conference room awaiting their briefing.

"Just a moment, Peter," said Sundin brusquely. "I'll be finished with the inspector shortly."

She glanced at her watch, but remembered Tell's question.

"The staff at the home observe the mother and child and report continuously on the mother's parenting ability, the bond between them, or whatever the client has asked the home to focus on. These days most homes tailor their services according to the client's wishes. And of course the market is getting tougher for them too, partly because they charge a fortune."

She cleared her throat and leafed further through Olof's file, before closing it with an apologetic expression.

"To summarise, everything went well for a while. They had faith in her in Dalarna. She was given a rented flat of her own when she moved back to town. And she did stay off the drugs for a couple of years, even if it was with frequent intervention and a great deal of support from social services. However, when Olof was about five she met a new man, who was already well known to us — a complete bastard, if you want my opinion. He dragged her straight back down again, and it happened very quickly. When Olof ended up in A & E the following year, badly beaten and with a broken arm, he was immediately taken into care. It was impossible to find out whether it was Cecilia or Marko who had hurt him, since they blamed each other."

"Where did Olof go then?"

"First of all to an emergency placement, then to a permanent foster home. The family lived in Öckerö, and they had many years' experience of fostering children. Olof lived there until he was just ten, when the husband unexpectedly died of a heart attack. His wife couldn't cope with the job on her own."

302

"The job?"

"Yes, she couldn't cope with the foster-children any more. She was grieving and . . . Olof was moved to a family in Bergum, Olofstorp."

Christian Tell brightened up.

"Olofstorp?"

"Yes, somewhere around there. The family's name began with J. Jid . . . Jidbrandt perhaps. They were very experienced too. When Olof arrived they already had a girl staying with them who'd been placed there some time before."

Tell leaned forward.

"Can you tell me any more about these two families? The foster-families, I mean."

She shook her head. "No, it's such a long time ago. There could have been more than two foster-families, and I think there might also have been a short stay in some kind of institution for Olof, but I wouldn't put money on it."

Tell pointed to Olof Bart's notes.

"But all the information should be in here?"

Birgitta Sundin nodded.

"It should, or at least all the information the social services board takes into consideration will be there — a family care home investigation of each family, a report on why the social worker and the family care home worker are recommending that a particular child be placed with a particular family. You'll be able to find out more if you read through these."

She got up and quickly picked up a notepad and her Filofax.

"I have to dash. I hope I've been of some help."

Tell nodded and shook her outstretched hand.

"Thank you for your time. Just one more thing: who can I contact with regard to Susanne Pilgren? Is there someone who might know where she is?"

"Do you know if she lives here in Angered?"

"Here? No, I don't know. Her last recorded address was in Högsbo, I think."

"Then she's not in our area; you'll need to contact Högsbo. I really do have to go."

She was just about to close the door of her office when she paused.

"What's happened to Olof, anyway? Has he been murdered, or has he murdered somebody else?"

CHAPTER
THIRTY-FIVE

1995

His room was his own private space. Despite the fact that Solveig had abandoned all sense and reason, she seemed to understand that there was only room in the apartment for one person who had completely lost their mind. And he would lose his mind too if he wasn't able to withdraw to his room without the risk of her following him, churning out her bitter accusations.

He had been ashamed of his room for a long time: the grubby posters of racing cars, the bedspread from Åhlén's department store with pictures of Tintin and Snowy — he had loved Tintin when he was little — the embarrassing rug in the shape of a fish, which had been embarrassing right from the start, when Solveig gave it to him on his thirteenth birthday. The only reason he had kept it next to his bed in Rydboholm was because there was a pale stain on the floor underneath the fish. Then again, the stain was better when his friends came over — the fish went in the wardrobe until he was alone again.

Right now he was grateful that when they'd moved, in spite of everything, he had more or less copied the childish decor of the old room: the ugly fish rug expressed a pure childish innocence he now found calming rather than offensive. Anyone who came into this room without knowing who he was or what he had done would see straight away that a child lived here. And a child could never be guilty of anything. Not really.

The social worker who came to talk to his mother after Maya's disappearance clearly shared this view. His voice was impossibly monotonous, like a robot or the pre-recorded message on the speaking clock.

"It isn't your fault, Sebastian," over and over again, and, "It doesn't necessarily mean that anything has happened to her, Solveig."

Sebastian, who knew his mother better, was waiting for the explosion. It came, and as a result the social worker ended up with a cut on his hand from the smashed vase. Solveig didn't actually throw it at him; he cut himself when he was trying to pick up the pieces from the floor. She did, however, attack him verbally, her voice as quiet and monotonous as his had been earlier, but seething with rage. The social worker, who was presumably trained to deal with individuals in crisis, said in the same calm, monotonous tone that *He could see Solveig was upset. He could hear that Solveig was upset.*

At that point Solveig threw him out, incandescent with rage. As if it were the social worker's fault that Maya hadn't come home after the party. His fault that she had set off home several hours before her younger brother but that there was still no sign of her when Sebastian — slightly the worse for wear — crept into the hallway at four o'clock in the morning, and was faced with the same fury that hit the receptionist and the person on the telephone exchange at the police station the following morning.

The police officers who finally took the time to listen to Solveig also managed to remain calm when they felt the full force of her rage.

"She's nineteen years old, fru Granith. You have to understand that she could have gone off of her own free will. That's what they're like at that age. Grown up enough to take care of themselves, but not mature enough to think about others who might be worried. She'll turn up soon, fru Granith, you'll see."

Sebastian realised that the police officers probably regarded his mother as a hysterical old woman. He was used to that. On one occasion he had accidentally overheard their landlord refer to Solveig as "the psycho on the eighth floor". That was the time Solveig had got it into her head that there were rats living under the floorboards. She had made Sebastian ring up because she suspected that the secretary wasn't passing her calls on to her boss.

It didn't particularly bother Sebastian when people spoke disparagingly of his mother.

They didn't acknowledge the extent to which Solveig's conviction influenced their actions, but the police did decide to start a search. They spoke to the people who had arranged the party at the bikers' club, who were required to give the names of all those who had attended the event, as far as they could recall. There was no official list, of course, so the police ended up with just a fraction of those who had actually attended. Only a few of those named were contacted and asked if they had seen the young woman at the party, or if they had seen or heard what her plans might have been after leaving the club. If she had been seen talking to anyone. That was as far as they got.

The search in the nearby forest ended the same day it began, since Maya was found just over a mile from the club. She was lying out in the open, about thirty metres from the track, and the dogs found her almost at once. Her bike was in the ditch, with a puncture.

This time different police officers came to see Solveig and Sebastian, an older man and a younger woman. The female officer wore an expression of sympathy that seemed to have been glued on.

Solveig was certain that Maya was dead.

"She isn't dead, fru Granith," said the male officer. "But she has severe hypothermia, and she's unconscious. You need to prepare yourself for the worst."

Sebastian tiptoed into the apartment just as Solveig closed the bathroom door behind her, releasing the drawn-out howl he had loathed since he was a child.

The older officer jumped when Sebastian suddenly appeared at the living-room door. He cleared his throat. "She's hit her head and she's unconscious. She . . . There's no guarantee she'll regain consciousness."

The police officers had refused to leave Sebastian alone in the apartment, despite the fact that he had clung silently to the door frame of his childish room. Now he was sitting in a consulting room with muted green lights. He could feel the doctor's hands resting heavily on his shoulders, as if he were intending to hold on to Sebastian in case he made a run for it.

"She fell and struck her head on a stone," explained the woman who was holding Solveig's hand.

Two police officers, now two doctors: the female was the older of the two, but the male was some years away from middle age. Sebastian hadn't heard his name.

"Her body temperature is very low because she was lying out in the cold for such a long time, and she's lost a great deal of blood from the wound in her head."

The doctor wanted to let the words sink in before she went on, but the woman opposite her was completely broken. There was hardly even a blink, and her face was ash-grey.

"She's still alive in the sense that her heart is beating, but her brain is no longer able to function."

She pushed her chair closer to Solveig, so that their knees were touching. Solveig jumped. The screech of the chair's metal legs across the floor made everything in front of Sebastian's eyes go black.

"Her brain will never be able to function again."

Behind him the male doctor still gripped Sebastian's shoulders, pressing Sebastian's head and body against his stomach and chest, which smelled of aftershave with a hint of disinfectant.

"There now. There there," he said, turning Sebastian's head so that his cheek was lying flat against his green scrubs, his nose close to the armpit. The smell was suffocating.

Sebastian tore himself free and threw up over Solveig's trouser leg. He didn't bother looking to see whether he had caught the female doctor as well. He was out of the room in a flash.

"I said I wanted to stay at home," he mumbled as he hurtled down the corridor. "I said I didn't want to come."

He managed to find some peace and quiet in an anonymous waiting area somewhere deep inside the vast hospital. The thing he found consoling about this particular waiting room was the fading daylight. No one had yet thought of switching on the lights to illuminate the gloomy corners. He couldn't cope with looking anyone in the eye.

Sebastian sank down on a shabby green sofa and waited for the tears that didn't come. His eyes were dry and sore and hot, as if he had a temperature. With his heart galloping irregularly he picked up a magazine and opened it, placing it on his knee as if it were some kind of protection, something to fix his eyes on to stop them wandering.

Someone dressed in white stepped into the tunnel that was his field of vision; it was a young woman with a ponytail. She tilted her head to one side and spoke to him, her expression conveying unease. The roaring in his ears rose and fell. Despite the fact that he was making an effort to understand — not because he cared, he just didn't want to look crazy — he was unable to grasp anything beyond the fact that she

310

was uttering words. Combinations of words, but words didn't change a thing.

He got up and left her stunned face behind him. Walked quickly along the corridor towards the hiss of the swing doors, out to the lifts that could take him to a different part of the hospital. He could choose the floor where his mother presumably lay sedated and probably also strapped down by now, at least until the injection took effect. By this stage she had doubtless attempted to strangle one of the doctors, and Sebastian thought that even in a situation where any normal person would be well within their rights to scream and yell and carry on, she would be incapable of containing herself within the accepted framework. No ceiling could be high enough. In the end they would have to take her to the secure unit for crazies.

Or he could choose the floor where Maya lay, looking as if she were sleeping or dead, when in fact she was neither.

He thought about a comic he had once read. It must have been a long time ago because he remembered spelling his way from one picture to the next with some difficulty, and sometimes, when he couldn't manage the words, he had had to make do with looking at the pictures. The cartoon was about a man who had been stabbed but survived and ended up in a coma. As he lay unconscious he hovered between life and death, in a special land: *the land of transition*. Most people who die instantly from a heart attack or from the *splat* when they land on the concrete below their block of flats only get a glimpse of it, so brief that afterwards they might think they had imagined it — if there was an afterwards, that is.

The ghost people who populated the land of transition had a particular character: they were restless, rootless. Transient. Maya was like that now, in exile.

Set them free was the thought that came into his head. Free the ghosts from their fear, that's the most humane thing to do. Something told him that was the real meaning of the story, if there was a meaning in comics.

Another white coat approached seeking eye contact.

"I'm waiting for my gran," he said in a voice that sounded unfamiliar.

Why was it so fucking difficult to be left in peace? He could feel the panic lurking just beneath the surface once again. Whitecoat nodded but didn't seem completely satisfied. Just as he was about to say something, the pager in his belt went off and he hurried away.

Sebastian suddenly felt afraid: perhaps his mother's doctors had put out a call for him all over the hospital? Perhaps his description had been e-mailed to all staff: *If you see a nervous fairly ugly fifteen-year-old in a denim jacket, jeans and a red sweatshirt, with his face covered in zits, please send him back to his mum and her two sickly-sweet doctors on the psychiatric ward.*

He was filled with rage at the false concern that only partly masked the accusations still visible in the eyes of the Samaritans. It was true of them all. The old bags from social services, the doctors, the counsellors, the teachers. Their contempt for Solveig because she constantly failed to cope with her own children and the crap in her life, because she kept on cracking under the pressure, always ended up washing her dirty linen in public — none of this was any guarantee that they wouldn't despise him at the same time. Sebastian, the boy who lacked any normal protective instinct towards his sister.

He forced himself to think about it now.

He had known it was dark, that they were miles from anywhere that night. That the place was full of drunken idiots. If it hadn't been for the band he would never have gone there, mixing with all those farm boys who shared a single brain cell.

If only Krister hadn't gone on about it so much. Krister, who thought death metal was a joke, just like all the others he hung out with. Nobody they knew dressed like that or hung out with other death metal freaks. Nor did Sebastian, and Krister had only wanted to go to the party because they sold strong beer to fifteen-year-olds without checking their ID.

He always gave in to Krister, to everybody. He had no backbone, no clear will of his own. He blew this way and that, following the path of least resistance.

So it was his fault that Maya was lying in that bed, regardless of his protests that he hadn't asked to be saved, that he was perfectly capable of taking care of himself and that he could do without Solveig's cloying oppressive anxiety, which was nothing but egotism when it came down to it. The logic was simple.

But the thought had crossed his mind. As Maya set off on her bike and rode out through the gates, he had heard one of the Neanderthals — the one whose mate had had a go at him earlier — shout something nasty, something filthy after her.

Sebastian had hidden on the dark staircase leading up to the first floor and watched through a small window as she pedalled away. That was why he had to take the blame this time: because he had just sat there with the feeling that she might never make it to the main road. He hadn't stopped her despite the fact that she had been raped and killed over and over again on the cinema screen in his mind.

But she hadn't been raped. The doctors had said this several times, as if it might make Mum and Sebastian feel better. She had no physical injuries apart from the wound to her head, which she had sustained through falling on to a sharp stone which had crushed her skull. The police investigation had proved this.

Maya had scratches on her face and hands from running through the trees.

Nobody could yet explain what had made Maya run like that, straight into the dark forest. However, Sebastian thought he knew what she had felt as she ran. If he didn't put every ounce of strength he had left into keeping it at bay, he could easily allow his own body to be filled by her panic until it imploded.

He kept this insight into Maya's panic during her final minutes locked deep inside his body. He stored a lot of things in that locked room. Sometimes he thought about what would happen on the day he chose to take out the key, open the door a fraction and wait for the great flood. Woe betide anyone who was standing in the way; he could only hope that he or she deserved to be there. Because evil people did exist, that much was certain. Whatever the doctors and the police said, he was convinced that Maya was lying there as a result of evil.

Why would she have thrown down the bike and run into the forest if she hadn't feared for her life? No, it was pure fear that had made Maya tear her hands and cheeks on the frozen branches. He was quite sure of that. Once again he had to drive the fear out of his own body. It must not take over. He crept back to the dark waiting area and sank down on to the sofa.

In general, accusations and guilt ran off him like water off a duck's back; he had acquired a thick covering of waterproof feathers in order to survive life with Solveig. In order to avoid becoming like Maya, who got into arguments with her all the time, and who had been ready to kill Solveig more than once. He had decided at an early stage that he was not going to join in. He had had to live with the fact that his punishment had been a withdrawal of love and a permanent place as silver medallist when it came to his mother's favours.

A nurse with clattering clogs and rattling keys came into the waiting area and switched on a floor lamp. Its soft glow reached Sebastian's shoes.

He couldn't sleep here at the hospital, of course. That would attract attention, even if he could easily imagine sitting here on this shabby sofa for the rest of the evening, staring into space. The only thing he really missed was his Walkman. To be able to hide behind a wall of death metal would be a release right now;

nothing else could make him tear himself away from the indefinably meaningless failure that was Sebastian himself.

Solveig reacted nervously to outfits inspired by horror, black and white make-up and other things that reinforced the association with violence and blood and death. That was the whole point. That just for a little while you didn't have to think about the fact that even the creators of extreme music were just a gang of ordinary lads.

He couldn't go home, that much was certain. Maya's bag was still in the hallway. Maya was lying in a room somewhere like a cabbage. The doctors were already one hundred per cent certain that she would never be anything but a cabbage. And nothing he said to himself about his responsibility or guilt would ever change the fact that Solveig thought it was his fault.

It was his fault, therefore he couldn't go home. He would have liked to go to Maya, except she was surrounded by a whole troop of healthcare staff. He would have liked to explain to her, to tell her why he had reacted as he did when she came to fetch him that evening. And how important the music had become to him: it was the thing that made him forget. There were to be no bridges between the two lives, no links between his refuge and school, his mother, the pointlessness of it all. She ought to have understood, if anyone could. If there was a risk you might be found, then it was no longer a refuge. If only he could talk to her.

It was likely that Solveig would not be sleeping at home tonight; experience told him that the hospital staff were unlikely to let her out in her current state. She would end up in the unit for crazy people, and she would probably stay there for a while. In other words, the apartment would be empty.

He decided to go home, have a sleep and pack his most important possessions tomorrow morning. To be on the safe side he would leave as soon as he woke up, so he wouldn't be caught unawares if Solveig came home earlier than expected. He just couldn't cope with seeing her.

When everything had settled down he would come up to the hospital at night, when there was only one nurse on duty. He would ask if he could sit with Maya for a while. She was his sister after all; what could they say? And it wasn't as if Maya would notice any difference between night and day.

It would all sort itself out, as long as he kept out of Solveig's way.

CHAPTER
THIRTY-SIX

2007

"I'll have to ask you for the surname as well, Inspector," said the man with a voice that suggested he had a terrible cold, or perhaps it was the result of many years' smoking or even the phone line. Tell thought about Marlon Brando in *The Godfather*, but he concluded that any similarities between Brando and Knut Jidsten, one of Olof's foster-fathers, ended there. After dogged detective work he had managed to track Jidsten down to a little village north of Östersund.

"I think we must have had about thirty placements here over a period of twenty-five years. And that's not counting the ones who were only here for a few days. We were the local emergency foster home for a few years at the beginning of the 90s," he explained. "But it all got too much. Our own kids just couldn't cope with all the coming and going."

Tell stretched and tried to recline his desk chair even further, which turned out to be impossible as he was already virtually lying with his feet on the desk.

They had spent a depressing morning on the telephone and computer without achieving any significant results. Together with Sofia Frisk, Gonzales had set up a system to list all the proud owners of Jeep Grand Cherokees in the area. The details were then passed on to two constables from Kinna, who had been given the uninspiring job of contacting the owners for an initial check and to establish if they had an alibi. It was a time-consuming task. So far nothing of value had turned up, apart from the news that Kasper Jonasson, who was well known to both the drugs squad and the violent crimes unit, was driving a Jeep these days. He had spent the relevant evening, night and morning at the Radisson Hotel. It was his younger brother's twenty-fifth birthday, and fortunately for Jonasson lots of people were able to confirm his presence.

They also checked car rentals within a hundred-kilometre radius of Gothenburg and Borås. Tell was more inclined to believe that the murderer had hired or borrowed cars — judging by the forensic report, it seemed likely that two different vehicles of the same make and model had been used in the murders. No Grand Cherokee had been reported stolen in the weeks leading up to the murders, and the search had been extended to the whole of western Sweden.

Their work was made easier by the fact that comparatively few rental firms offered a Grand Cherokee, but they still had to ring up and ask. This consisted mainly of listening to themselves asking the same question over and over again, speaking to bored assistants who never turned out to have been on duty at the time in question, who had no access to details of previous rentals, or who had to wait for permission from their boss before revealing anything at all.

They also contacted petrol stations within the same area. That was even worse. Partly because they got the impression that at least ten people covered a single day. And partly because every single employee appeared to have an average age of seventeen. Tell's experience told him that teenagers were aware of nothing apart from the displays on their mobiles and the music on their iPods. Most of the larger petrol stations had CCTV cameras, and they would no doubt end up going through every single tape. Östergren had promised Tell that if the tapes were brought to the station, she would try to find people to carry out this deathly dull task.

"Get Bärneflod to go through them," Beckman had said. "He's too idle to lift his arse off the chair anyway."

Well yes, but there was a considerable risk that he would simply fall asleep.

"Pilgren," said Tell, attempting to scratch his ankle without tipping over backwards. "Olof Pilgren. He came to you in 1975. He was eleven then and —"

"Olof, yes, of course," Jidsten broke in. "Olof lived here for several years, until . . . 80 or 81, I should think."

"So you think he would have been . . . sixteen or seventeen when he moved out?"

"I think he ended up in some kind of institution, when he made a complete mess of things."

"You mean Villa Björkudden?"

Tell underlined the name in the photocopied notes from social services.

320

"That might have been the name, yes. The whole thing was a bit odd, actually," said Jidsten thoughtfully. "It was odd that he messed things up, I mean. Don't misunderstand me, I've seen most things; foster-children are rarely little angels." He allowed himself a humourless laugh. "Then again, angels probably don't have to go through half the crap our foster-kids have been through before they come to us. But I still remember I thought that what happened to Olof was strange."

"Why strange? I see from his notes that he tried to rob a petrol station. And there was a stolen car as well."

Jidsten exhaled. "No, I just mean that Olof always gave the impression of being so . . . cautious. He was a bit peculiar, really. Slightly submissive, almost scared. Couldn't look people in the eye, as I remember. So it seemed strange that this boy, who seemed incapable of action, should suddenly get the idea of shoving a gun in somebody's face and demanding money. I remember I almost thought that it was some kind of perverted progress. That he'd actually done something on his own initiative for once. I know the police would see this as a strange way of reasoning, but I think you understand what I mean."

"So Villa Björkudden was some kind of sanction following this crime?"

"Exactly. It was an educational facility or something like that. He was only there for a year, but I'm sure that's in your notes. We carried on being his contact family, so he came home at weekends for the first six months."

"And then?"

"Social services changed his support so that it no longer included a contact family."

"And when he'd served his time?"

"You probably know that better than me. We lost contact with Olof." He gave a rueful chuckle. "I presume things turned out badly for him, otherwise you wouldn't have come looking for us. I'm impressed that you managed to track us down."

Tell brought the conversation to an end, then stood up and rubbed the base of his spine. It was hard to get used to the idea that his body no longer served him without complaint. That age was beginning to take its toll. He realised he ought to take some exercise.

In years gone by he had played regularly with an indoor ice hockey team on Thursday evenings, ending up with a sauna and sometimes a beer in town. It had been good fun. But those evenings had been conspicuous by their absence over the last few years. He sat down at the computer again and sent an e-mail to Kenth Stridh, who had been team captain at the time. Good habits should be preserved.

As far as Tell was able to interpret from the notes, Olof Pilgren had moved to a place of his own after Villa Björkudden. He couldn't find the address, other than it was an apartment in Hjällbo. The name Thorbjörn Persson was written in the margin, along with a telephone number. Naturally, when he tried calling, the subscriber had not been available on that number for a long time. Instead he called Birgitta Sundin, and she explained that Pilgren had been offered a place in a block of apartments for young people that was overseen by a contact person.

Tell spent the next half-hour ringing up people called Thorbjörn Persson in the Gothenburg area, asking if they had worked as a contact person in the 80s. Finally he struck lucky. Fortunately Persson was still living in the city, at an address in Hisingen, and had time to meet him.

"I'll be there," said Tell, just as Gonzales appeared in the doorway with a phone to his ear.

"Bingo. A girl at a petrol station in Hedvigsborg outside Borås apparently served a customer filling up a Grand Cherokee. The time matches, and they're going to give us the tape from the CCTV camera. And two car rental firms have come back to us after the appeal we made the other day: one on Mölndalsvägen, but apparently their camera is broken, and one just outside Ulricehamn — they haven't got any surveillance. But in both places they remember very clearly the client who hired the Jeep."

"What did you say?"

"That we're on our way."

"OK."

Tell arranged a time with Thorbjörn Persson after lunch in two days' time. If his back hadn't been so bloody painful, he would have leapt out of his chair with joy.

He had planned to call Lise-Lott Edell's neighbours, Bertil and Dagny Molin, to find out if they were familiar with the name Olof Pilgren-Bart, but he could do that later.

"Let's go," he said, punching Gonzales on the shoulder.

CHAPTER
THIRTY-SEVEN

Gonzales walked into the petrol station as Tell took a stroll around outside. A woman in a fur coat was filling up her vintage Mercedes. She reached into her pocket and for a second Tell thought she was going to light a cigarette, but instead she extracted a small make-up bag and applied her lipstick with a practised hand.

The door crashed open and a couple of lads came in. "Forget it, I paid last time!" They started grabbing cans of beer and packets of crisps, making plenty of noise. Gonzales glanced at the headlines in the evening papers while he waited to speak to the assistant; her name badge said ANN-CATHRINE HÖGBERG. She didn't ask the lad for ID when he came to pay, although she was no doubt under strict instructions to do so. Maybe she just couldn't cope with the same old routine: *I've left my driving licence at home. Anyway I always shop here. There was no problem last Friday* — and so on.

The woman in the fur coat came in and paid for her petrol. On the way out she bumped into a scruffy man in his thirties. He picked up an evening paper, then went over to the till and started fiddling with a packet of condoms.

"Are these any good?" he asked, exposing yellow teeth in a grin. Ann-Cathrine Högberg gave him a dirty look.

"I think you need two people to use that particular brand," she said coldly, rapidly keying in the cost of the newspaper. "Will there be anything else?"

The man shook his head sulkily. Gonzales watched him cut across past the petrol pumps, his head down between his shoulders, his footsteps unsteady. There were no customers left in the shop.

Gonzales went over to the till and showed his ID. "We spoke on the telephone."

The girl laughed nervously and slammed the drawer of the till shut. "Oops! I was expecting someone in uniform." She had gone bright red, possibly because she had just sold alcohol to someone who might be under age.

"I only have a vague memory of the man with the Jeep." She ran her fingertips under her eyes to hide her embarrassment. "I might not be much help."

Gonzales shook his head and said that any information could potentially be important. The girl relaxed and seemed to be thinking.

"He wasn't threatening in any way, I'm sure of that — if he'd behaved oddly I would have remembered."

She told him that when she heard that the police were looking for anyone who might have seen a dark-coloured Grand Cherokee, she had phoned straight away, even if the times didn't quite match. She had finished work at midnight, and she was sure she had served the driver of the Cherokee at least a couple of hours before the end of her shift. Yes, it *could* have been a similar car but a different make; she wasn't all that brilliant at identifying cars. And she'd only seen it from a distance. But she was reasonably sure it was a Grand Cherokee. At any rate, the tapes from the CCTV camera would show the exact time, and would also provide a more precise description of the man in question.

"Kurt, my boss, he's just sorting out the tape," she said, nodding to Tell, who had just come in.

As she mentioned her boss they heard an impatient voice from the depths of the shop. They followed Ann-Cathrine into the staff room. The voice turned out to belong to a middle-aged man with a comb-over and yellow-tinted glasses. He was in a room where a fridge, two hotplates and a sink gave a vague impression of a kitchen, sharing the space with a two-seater sofa and a small television.

Without bothering to say hello the man pressed the remote. He pointed helplessly at the black and white grainy mess on the screen, the CCTV recording from the day in question. You could see the four pumps and the entrance to the shop, with blurred figures moving between the two. However, it was impossible to make out any details.

"Look at that," he said eventually, sounding disappointed. "This is no use to the police. In fact it's no bloody use at all." He gave his assistant an encouraging look. "I'm sure you can fill in the details, Anki?"

But that was the problem. For the next half-hour Tell and Gonzales sat there in the shabby little room asking the same questions over and over again. *What did he look like — can you remember any details, anything at all? Clothes, accent, voice, wallet, age. How did he pay? Cash, of course. Did he buy anything apart from petrol? Did he seem nervous? Hair colour, height?*

In the end Ann-Cathrine Högberg put her head in her hands. The more they asked, the less she seemed to remember. Tell and Gonzales exchanged a crestfallen glance; if they carried on behaving as if they would walk over burning coals for even the smallest scrap of information, the girl would soon be making up a description to satisfy them.

They backed off, dissatisfied in spite of the fact they had assured the owner that the video technicians could often work wonders with the most unpromising material.

Ann-Cathrine too seemed very disappointed at her inability to remember much. Back out in the shop she leaned absent-mindedly against the snack display, causing a minor avalanche of crisps, cheese puffs, chilli nuts and nachos. Kurt rolled his eyes at Tell, who was putting the tape into his bag.

"We'll take care of this," he said idiotically, as if he thought the police were going to clear up the mess before they left.

Ann-Cathrine smiled bravely, her eyes shining with unshed tears. Gonzales placed his card in front of her on the counter.

"Get in touch if you think of anything, if you remember anything else, I mean. You might be called in to describe the man to one of our forensic artists. Thanks for getting in touch."

She nodded, her eyes fixed on the sweet display in front of her.

They were just on their way out when she called, "He bought Läkerol."

They stopped in the doorway and turned back.

"He bought a box of Läkerol sweets," she said. "And a sandwich."

She was still staring at the throat sweets in front of her, as if they might conjure up the picture of the man who had bought them.

She closed her eyes and seemed to be visualising that evening. *Her striped uniform shirt and that slightly tired smile. Her hands on the till. And there he was: blonde hair and a baseball cap.*

"I don't remember if the cap had any kind of logo on it, but I think it was black. His eyes were quite deep-set, and he had dark shadows underneath, as if he hadn't slept for a long time. His lips seemed too red, as if he was wearing make-up. I think he was quite short, or maybe medium height. Some kind of padded jacket, or maybe a windcheater. Although it was really cold that night."

Tell and Gonzales drove along in silence, both thinking the same thing. There was absolutely no guarantee that the man Ann-Cathrine had just described was the murderer, but it was definitely the nearest thing they had to a clue.

Although it was rush hour, the main road between Borås and Ulricehamn wasn't particularly busy. Tell was driving well over the speed limit, and it struck Gonzales, as it had done so many times since he joined the force, that police officers were the worst offenders when it came to traffic regulations.

He switched on the radio and caught the latest news bulletin. So far the media hadn't paid any attention to the murder of Olof Bart. As long as they didn't get wind of the connection between Bart and Waltz, they were unlikely to make a fuss. And that was probably for the best: as long as the murderer didn't know that they had linked the two deaths, they had an advantage.

It was dusk, and as always during the Swedish winter the darkness came quickly. By the time they drove into Ulricehamn, it had settled over the town.

"I don't know about you," said Tell as he pulled into the car park of the first pizzeria he spotted, "but I'm bloody starving."

Gonzales nodded gratefully. His stomach had been grumbling for quite some time about the ridiculously low-calorie canteen lunch he had bolted down before they left.

Just as they were about to take the four steps in two strides, the door was opened from the inside by a stout man in his forties.

"I'm just closing," he said, rattling his bunch of keys. "Excuse me."

He stood patiently on the top step as Tell blocked his way.

"What do you mean?" He was unable to hide his agitation. "When do you think people actually eat pizza — for breakfast? What kind of bloody pizzeria closes before six o'clock in the evening?"

"A lunch pizzeria," said the man tersely. He moved Tell firmly to one side and marched down the steps.

Tell was therefore in a particularly bad mood when they eventually found Johansson & Johansson. The car rental company was located on a small industrial estate on the way out of town, directly opposite a paint shop and a locked warehouse. Light from the sparse street lamps was reflected in puddles of petrol and melted snow. They parked outside the entrance and Tell took a quick drag on his cigarette, sniffing the air like a tracker dog. A smell like burnt plastic pervaded the whole area.

Berit Johansson had obviously been waiting for them: there was a pot of coffee and a plate of cakes and biscuits on the desk.

"I'll close up," she said. She locked the door then went and sat opposite Tell and Gonzales, who had already helped themselves to cakes.

"Help yourselves," she said ironically.

"You rented out a Grand Cherokee during the period we're interested in," said Tell, his mouth full of Swiss roll. He was far too tired and hungry to bother with small talk.

"Yes," said the woman, opening out a sheet of paper she had been keeping in the breast pocket of her shirt. She put on her glasses and began to read.

"He was here between five thirty and six on the Wednesday. I stay open until seven on Wednesdays. And I open between Christmas and New Year — that's always a good time for us. Lots of people hire a car to visit friends and relatives over the holiday."

Tell nodded pensively. If this was their man, it meant he had hired the car the day before he went to see Olof Bart. He thought about what this might mean. That he lived in the Ulricehamn area? On the other hand, would he have been so stupid as to hire a car from a local firm? Tell wouldn't have done that if he was about to go and murder somebody.

"Go on."

"He was medium height and he had blue eyes. Light-coloured hair, I think. He kept his hat on. Indoors as well."

She looked up from the sheet of paper.

"I made a note of all the details I could remember after I spoke to you on the telephone, herr Gonzales."

Gonzales nodded to her to continue.

"He was quite untidily dressed. I think he was wearing some kind of dark tracksuit."

"How did he get here?" asked Tell.

"Er . . . I don't know. On foot, I think. Sometimes clients leave their own vehicle in our car park, for example if they're hiring a bigger car, but I know the car park was empty at the time. So he must have come on foot."

"Is there a bus that comes out this way?" asked Gonzales.

She nodded. "There's a bus stop about a kilometre from here, Majgatan, the number 12. It doesn't run all that often though."

Bus/driver no. 12 wrote Gonzales on his pad, followed by *Door to door in area.* But first they needed to find out the name used to hire the car.

"I assume you keep a record of rentals," Tell went on, biting into another ginger biscuit despite the fact that he was beginning to feel quite ill.

Berit Johansson had obviously been waiting for this question, because she produced the receipt showing that a certain Mark Sjödin, born 18 July 1972, had hired a Jeep Grand Cherokee between Christmas and New Year.

"He had ID of course. We always insist on that. And I did try to contact him afterwards with regard to the insurance, because there was some damage to the front of the car when it was returned. He just left it in the car park with the keys in the ignition, but I never managed to get hold of him."

She passed the A4 sheet to Tell. The receipt was signed by both Berit Johansson and the man who claimed to be Mark Sjödin. Unless of course this was a perfectly genuine Mark Sjödin who had nothing whatsoever to do with the murders.

The signature was printed in small, disjointed letters. *Written by someone who wasn't used to that name?* But of course that was just speculation; Mark Sjödin could easily be dyslexic.

"Is the car here? Good. We'd like to take a look at it, if you don't mind."

Berit Johansson looked unsure of herself.

"It's been hired out since, I mean . . . We didn't know . . . It's been cleaned, several times. And it had been thoroughly washed when the client returned it — it was shining, in fact."

"We'd still like to see it," said Tell.

He stood up and dusted the crumbs off his jacket.

"No problem. This way, gentlemen."

As radio station P3 played "Have I Told You Lately That I Love You" by Van Morrison just outside Bollebygd, Gonzales fell asleep. He didn't even wake up when Bärneflod called Tell's mobile to report on his visit to the car hire firm on Mölndalsvägen. He informed Tell that a Ralf Stenmark had rented a Jeep from them between Christmas and New Year. The description provided by the staff was in direct contrast to those given by Berit Johansson and Ann-Cathrine Högberg, since everyone who had been working on the afternoon in question had stated that Stenmark was tall and slim, dark, and wearing a suit.

Tell ended the conversation and thought about what it all meant.

The Jeep Berit Johansson showed them had certainly been thoroughly cleaned. Two clients had had it after Sjödin, so it had been vacuumed inside three times, which had probably reduced their chances of finding decent fingerprints to zero. And of course any murderer would have wiped the steering wheel and instrument panel before returning the car. According to Berit Johansson, the car had never been so clean.

They had walked around the vehicle several times and made a note of the damage Berit Johansson had mentioned, a dent in the side of the bonnet. Berit was sure the dent had not been there before the car was signed over to Sjödin.

They told her the car had to remain where it was until they decided whether to have it brought in for forensic examination. Tell reassured her that if Mark Sjödin did exist and could give a reasonable explanation as to why he had hired the Jeep, along with a valid alibi for the night of the murder, then Johansson & Johansson would immediately be given the go-ahead to start renting out the car once again. It was clear that from a financial point of view the company needed to have all its vehicles available. However, if Sjödin did not exist, that was another matter altogether. The car would then be regarded as a probable source of evidence, and would be examined meticulously, along with the area around Johansson & Johansson.

Tell tried Karlberg's extension in the hope that he would be in the office, which he was.

"Will you be there for a while?"

"I should think so."

"Mark Sjödin and Ralf Stenmark. See what you can find."

"Is this from the car hire companies?"

"Yes, Ulricehamn and Mölndalsvägen."

Beside him, Gonzales shifted position, allowing his chin to fall heavily on to his chest. He started to snore.

It was late by the time Tell pulled in behind the Co-op in Hammarkulletorget and parked across two spaces. Gonzales jumped at the sound of Tell's hands clapping rapidly.

"Time to wake up, Sleeping Beauty. Bloody good job I didn't let you drive."

He winked at Gonzales' bewildered expression.

"This is where you live, isn't it?"

Gonzales nodded in some confusion, rubbing his eyes. He couldn't believe he'd fallen asleep — it must have been lack of food that had made him so tired.

"I'm not used to skipping meals," he apologised, and started gathering his things from the back seat.

Tell stretched awkwardly and rubbed his aching back. Gonzales felt guilty that he hadn't offered to drive back, particularly since Tell had been kind enough to drive him to his door. Tell seemed to know what he was thinking.

"It's OK. As a punishment I'll come in with you for a couple of minutes. I've been needing a pee ever since Borås."

In the darkness the huge buildings seemed to lean over the square, as if the windows and satellite dishes were eyes and ears, watching and listening. Gonzales said hello to a group of young lads who, despite the late hour, were hanging around outside Maria's Café in the community centre. In accordance with the dictates of fashion, they were all displaying the brand name of their underpants in the gap between their short jackets and their jeans, the crotch of the jeans hanging somewhere down by their knees. The café was closed,

336

but the kids were taking advantage of the lights inside, which were left on around the clock. The roof extending out over the main entrance provided shelter if it rained. Unfortunately there wasn't much they could do about the cold, thought Tell, other than go home to their bedrooms and play with their train sets. That's what he'd done at their age.

Every one of them had a cigarette dangling from his lips.

"What makes young lads hang about in the cold at this time of night? Are they planning to mug a few pensioners?" Tell mumbled. A series of muggings had recently been carried out by a gang of small boys, and because of the brutality involved, the attacks had attracted a certain amount of media attention. He glanced at the gang, now ambling across the square towards a hot-dog stand. "Haven't they got anywhere to go?"

Gonzales laughed.

"That lot? They wouldn't dare mug a squirrel. Sweet as lambs, every last one of them. It's the kids over in Biskopsgården who are mugging old ladies. There are only well-behaved blacks here."

"For God's sake, that's not what I meant," said Tell, put out.

Gonzales chortled again.

"I know."

When they met a group of noisy young men on their way out of the Somali club, which was in a small cellar bar on Bredfjällsgatan, Gonzales couldn't help whispering, "Hold on to your wallet, Grandad."

There was a smell of food and a hint of dampness on the landing outside the Gonzales family apartment on the eighth floor. The hallway was cluttered with furniture. On a battered pink corduroy sofa a note from the landlord threatened dire consequences if the furniture wasn't removed within a week. The bass beat of Latino pop poured out through the letter box, filling the stairwell when Gonzales opened the door.

He stepped through a rattling beaded curtain.

"Mum! You promised to move all the crap from the landing today!"

A woman in a long dress appeared, her frizzy chocolate-brown hair like a cloud around her shining face.

"Michael."

She examined Tell from head to toe without a hint of embarrassment, making him feel like a ten-year-old visiting a classmate for the first time, although he didn't think this woman was much older than him.

"And you've brought a friend with you."

Gonzales rolled his eyes.

"This is my mother, Francesca. This is a colleague, Mum. Christian. He just needs to pop to the toilet."

After this elegant introduction, Tell felt it was time to take command of the situation. With his hand outstretched he took a couple of steps towards Francesca Gonzales, who backed away in horror, pointing at his feet.

"Shoes, please."

Tell stopped short.

"But I just wanted to pop to the toilet."

338

"Bathroom there." She tapped on a door with a ceramic heart on it. "Then dinner. Been ready since six."

"Mum," pleaded Gonzales in embarrassment. "Christian's got other things to do."

She vanished into the kitchen without listening to a word he said.

"Perhaps I should ... you know." Tell gestured towards the front door. He couldn't remember when he'd last visited someone's mother.

Gonzales grinned.

"Do a runner? You try telling her that."

His mother's generous frame once again filled the kitchen doorway. She wiped the sweat off her forehead and slapped Gonzales on the backside.

"Michael, what is the matter with you? Show your friend round. *Pastel de choclo* ready in three minutes."

Tell opened his arms in a vague gesture. He was hungry, after all.

Apart from Michael and his mother, the Gonzales family consisted of his father José — a skinny taciturn man who smiled and shook his head when Tell spoke to him — and Eva, who at twenty-four was the oldest girl, and so beautiful that Tell dropped his fork on his plate when she directed her dark brown eyes at him. She explained politely that her father wasn't very talkative.

"Isn't that right, Dad?"

Gabriella, the middle sister, was a typical sulky seventeen-year-old. When she had finished eating she shut herself in her room and turned the volume on

MTV up so high that Francesca had to hammer on the door and yell at her to turn it down.

The youngest was Maria, an eleven-year-old whirlwind whose idol was Elena Paparizou. When the table was cleared and Tell once again started to mutter about making a move, she made him sit on the sofa and put on a performance, miming into a can of hairspray and practising her dance moves.

Francesca, who was drying the dishes with Eva, shook her head and said something in Spanish, but José Gonzales just laughed at his youngest daughter's antics, lit his pipe, and after inhaling the cherry-scented smoke got up and went over to a dark brown cupboard with a pattern of frosted flowers on its glass door. He took out a bottle of brandy and poured measures into three red and green glasses. When he had silently served Tell, his son and himself, he nodded seriously and knocked back his drink. Then he put the glass to one side and closed his eyes. After a while he started snoring.

The heat spread through Tell's spine. Gonzales picked up the bottle with an enquiring expression, but Tell shook his head.

"No, I've got to get home." Tell could feel how tired he was. "It's getting late. We ought to get some sleep. It was a good day's work."

"So what do you make of it?"

"Of what? The day's work? We'll have to see. But there's one thing about this whole case that I really don't like."

"Which is?"

"These two guys. They were obviously shot by the same killer, but that's the only thing about them that matches. I mean, we've got Lars Waltz, a photographer with artistic ambitions. Divorced suburbanite with two well-behaved teenage children. A bitter ex-wife, that's true, but not bitter enough to kill him. Grew up in a normal family, no hint of anything criminal. Fairly well balanced, has friends, is popular, has a relationship. And then we have Olof Bart, a complete oddball. Troubled childhood, criminal activity from an early age. Never had a long-term relationship with a woman, as far as we know. Socially inept. Unbalanced. Makes a living doing this and that, not all of which is strictly legal. Lives alone in the forest; nobody wants to let on that they know him."

"You're wondering what these two men have in common."

"Exactly. Why would you go on a killing spree, taking out Mr Average and then Mr Weirdo, in a very similar way, as if it were some kind of ritual? I mean, it would have been enough to shoot them, but to run over them as well?"

Gonzales followed Tell into the hallway.

"We have to assume that their paths crossed somewhere, however unlikely it seems."

Tell nodded mournfully.

"And the worst of it is, the more we look into it, the more unlikely it seems."

CHAPTER
THIRTY-EIGHT

"We have to assume that both of them crossed the murderer's path at some point," said Gonzales, repeating Tell's words from the previous evening.

Tell was fifteen minutes late for morning briefing, and was fully aware of how annoyed he was whenever anyone else turned up late. His head was aching from too little sleep. Or perhaps it was the large whiskey he had knocked back just before he fell into bed, exhausted, at three o'clock in the morning.

He poured himself a coffee and glanced at Gonzales. Evidently he was still enjoying the privilege of youth, the ability to look fresh even when you ought to resemble a withered apple.

"I think we can come back to that point after we've run through the new information. We'll spend the final part of the meeting thinking about what fresh conclusions we can draw. I can start with my report on the meeting with social services."

An agenda was quickly agreed, with Bärneflod volunteering to take notes, which took Tell by surprise.

"We've learned that Bart was placed in a foster home in Olofstorp, with a family called Jidsten, from the age of eleven to seventeen."

"Have you spoken to them?" asked Beckman.

"Only on the phone. They live up in Jämtland these days."

"But Waltz wasn't living in Olofstorp at that time," Beckman pointed out. "When Bart was a teenager living there, Waltz was in Majorna."

"I know," sighed Tell. "But perhaps we're getting closer."

"I've been going after Susanne Pilgren."

Bärneflod leaned over and gave Karlberg a slap on his bare arm. "Bloody hell. Did you get anywhere?"

"Very funny. I have been trying to find her, if I can rephrase things so that even Bärneflod can understand. She seems to be a frequent guest at a hostel for homeless women; the place is called Klara. The supervisor at the mission hostel also knew who she was, but she doesn't go there as often. She's registered with social services in Högsbo, but she hasn't turned up to a meeting with her social worker in over a year. They found her a place in a boarding house in the eastern part of the town. Linden's B & B."

"A boarding house?" said Tell suspiciously.

"That's what they call it. Apparently, social services pay for a certain number of places for homeless people at Linden's. And it's not cheap."

"OK," said Tell. "But you don't know where she is now?"

Karlberg ignored the impatient undertone.

"No, but I've asked the staff in all three places to get in touch as soon as they see her. I can also tell you that she is no longer known to anyone as Susanne Pilgren, but as Susanne Jensen. She got married ten years ago, and carried on using her married name even though they got divorced the following year. So she's registered as Pilgren, but uses the name Jensen."

He shook his head as if she had changed her name purely to make life difficult for him.

"We'll wait to hear from them, then," said Tell. "I've had a closer look at the crime Bart committed when he was sixteen," he went on. "Armed robbery, but the pistol turned out to be a replica. He was alone, but a friend was outside keeping the engine running. The assistant was too shaken up to remember anything but Bart's appearance, and they never found out who his accomplice was."

"Couldn't they get it out of him?"

"Not a word, apparently. He seems to have been good at keeping quiet even then. When it came to sentencing, they took into account the fact that he had already been done for nicking a car — no, two cars. His foster-father's car and another one. Both when he was fourteen."

"So his foster-father reported him for stealing the car?" said Beckman.

"Indeed he did," said Tell. "The secure unit, Villa Björkudden, is still there today, although it has a slightly different brief. These days it specialises in dealing with young men with schizophrenia or some kind of psychosis. Anyway, a couple of people who worked there in the old days are still on the staff. One of them is the supervisor now: Titti Moberg-Stark. She might able to help us and is going to look in the old registers to see who was there at the same time as Bart. We might get something out of that."

Tell pushed a route map over to Bärneflod.

"The place is outside Uddevalla. They've set aside some time for us tomorrow morning. I thought you might deal with that, Bärneflod." He moved on quickly. "What else have we got? Beckman?"

Karin Beckman cleared her throat. She was hoarse and looked as if a few hours' sleep would make her feel a lot better.

"Yes, what else have we got?" she muttered. She straightened her back and carried on, her voice stronger. "I've been going through the list of calls from Lars Waltz and Lise-Lott Edell's landline, but I didn't get anywhere. Lars also had a third phone, a mobile. There were very few incoming and outgoing calls on that over recent weeks. Zachariasson, Lars's childhood friend, came up a few times." She shrugged. "It's hard with such a wide search area. Hard to know where to start digging."

"Zachariasson's in the clear, isn't he?" said Tell, turning to Bärneflod.

"Yes and no. He has an alibi for the Tuesday evening — he was out with three colleagues and a former classmate. He went home alone that night, but he remembered he'd travelled up in the lift with a neighbour. The neighbour confirmed this. And another neighbour banged on the wall when he was playing loud music in the living room a couple of hours later. The neighbours' statements show that he was at home until at least three o'clock in the morning. Of course he could have gone out first thing —"

"Yes, but we know that Waltz was murdered earlier than that. And he doesn't have a motive," Tell interrupted. "We'll concentrate on those who have some kind of motive."

"Reino Edell," said Bärneflod. "He claims he was at home watching TV until half past nine, then he went to bed with the crossword. His wife confirms that he was home all night, but she did give away the fact that they have separate bedrooms, so he could easily have crept out. I'm also convinced that she would lie for him if he told her to."

"A pretty worthless alibi, in other words."

Bärneflod nodded.

When Tell looked up he met Ann-Christine Östergren's searching eyes. He wondered how long she had been standing by the door watching him, and immediately felt uncomfortable.

They had always worked well together in the past. He cursed himself for getting into a situation where he felt like a criminal in his own workplace. In fact, he felt as if he lacked control at every level. The enquiry was at a standstill; they were gathering material that led nowhere, and the only thing he could concentrate on at the moment was his own internal conflict. He was sufficiently in love to risk letting the cat out of the bag with regard to Seja, but he was far from ready to sacrifice his job or even his reputation for love. He just didn't have that kind of spontaneity in him. And, as

Carina had once put it, if he didn't have his job, what did he have?

Östergren sought eye contact again and indicated that he should come to her office after the meeting. He nodded silently. A chill spread through his abdomen. Did she know anything? But how could she?

He would have to stop seeing Seja. She was mixed up in an investigation he was leading, and no amount of explanation would convince Östergren.

He became aware that his colleagues were waiting for him to speak and pulled himself together.

"The ex-wife's alibi, on the other hand, is watertight," he said. "Maria Waltz was staying over at her parents' house in Kungsbacka, along with her younger son. Her mother confirms that Maria had stomach cramps during the night, and that she filled a hot water bottle for her a couple of times."

"So we can cross her out."

"What about the sons?" asked Beckman.

"What about them?" said Karlberg.

"You mean you don't think children are capable of murdering their parents, or that teenagers don't commit murder? Take a look at the crime statistics."

"We were intending to speak to the boys," Tell defended himself, looking over at Karlberg. "Can you call them in? The younger one can have his mother with him, then we won't get a load of earache about bringing in social services. He'll probably say there's no need anyway."

He saw Beckman stiffen. Presumably it annoyed her that Tell evidently felt it was more likely that Karlberg would get the boys to talk.

The age issue had been at the forefront of Tell's mind in making his decision. The younger officer's lack of experience was often noticeable in a certain inflexibility when it came to interview technique, and this could be counter-productive when questioning youngsters. But in this case he had faith in Karlberg, who perhaps had a better idea of how a seventeen-year-old boy thinks. Tell realised he still thought of Andreas Karlberg as green, despite the fact that he had a fair number of years in the job behind him now. He was also a quiet pleasant individual who often made people feel they wanted to confide in him, which wasn't something Tell could always say about himself.

He ran his hand irritably through his hair. He couldn't shake off the feeling that he had lost his focus in this investigation. The thought from the previous night came back to him: there was no logical explanation as to why the same person should want to kill two men from such completely different backgrounds and with such different lives. The discovery of the rented Grand Cherokee in Ulricehamn was certainly a step forward, but Mark Sjödin had had the car for only two days, and therefore could have run over only one of the victims in it.

Before the meeting Tell had been informed that the Mark Sjödin whose ID had been shown to Berit Johansson did in fact exist, and was registered at an address in Dalsjöfors. Initially he had had no hesitation in ringing Sjödin to ask him to come to the station so that he could be eliminated from their enquiries. He totally discounted the idea that Sjödin might be the murderer and had hired the murder weapon in his own name. Unfortunately Tell had been unable to get hold of him before the meeting, which gave him a little time to consider whether he ought to treat Mark Sjödin as a suspect.

Having decided to send a patrol car out into the sticks to pick up Sjödin, he didn't want to waste any more time. He excused himself and went to ask Renée to take care of the matter.

When he came back into the conference room, he felt a little more cheerful.

After Beckman and Bärneflod had summarised what they had found out by going through old reports of similar violent crimes, the team went through the other cases that were crying out for attention.

Tell was well aware that the extra resources they had been granted were now hanging by a thread. If he was unable to demonstrate concrete progress soon, they would lose the additional help. When Beckman brought up the fact that Lise-Lott Edell had moved back home and was asking for protection, the tiny fragment of desperately won pleasure in his work disappeared.

Lise-Lott was obviously afraid that the murderer would come after her, given that no one yet knew who he was or why he had murdered her husband.

"Out of the question," Tell said, not bothering to hide his irritation. "There are no indications of any such threat. And we just don't have the staff for that kind of thing."

CHAPTER
THIRTY-NINE

The man on the opposite side of the desk in the interview room had an unpleasant habit of picking at his cuticles. Tell tried not to look at the sores that Mark Sjödin couldn't leave alone, which didn't really fit with the overall picture. Otherwise, Sjödin was impeccably dressed, and looked exactly like the expert in debit and credit that he was; he had informed Tell of this important fact right from the start. Sjödin Audit was based in Borås.

A drop of blood coloured Mark Sjödin's thumbnail red. It made Tell think of an example Beckman had once mentioned from her psychology training. A man, doubtless as apparently ordinary as Sjödin, had collected his own excrement in a box under his bed. Tell didn't have the expertise to give a sensible explanation as to what caused this kind of bizarre behaviour, but he assumed it arose from the very human need to find an outlet for one's frustration. If you didn't allow yourself to be less than perfect elsewhere, perhaps the thing you didn't want to reveal ended up under the bed in the form of a box of shit.

In his work Tell had a theory that perfection always masked something else. A person who displays an impeccable facade and the patience of a saint has something to hide. An anger so fierce that it has to be kept under strict control. A box of shit under the bed. Or a body buried in the garden.

Therefore he quite liked Mark Sjödin's inflamed cuticles. They made him human.

"So you're saying that I hired a black Jeep in Ulricehamn between Christmas and New Year?"

"I'm saying that the hire of a Jeep was registered in your name on 27 December at Johansson & Johansson in Ulricehamn. Are you claiming that you didn't hire a car at that time?"

"I wasn't even anywhere near Ulricehamn at that time."

The sore next to Sjödin's thumbnail started to bleed again, and he staunched the flow by pressing the top of his index finger against it.

The auditor's forehead was dry despite the heat from the powerful fluorescent lights, and his eyes were still firmly fixed on Tell. He certainly didn't seem nervous. Tell got up and fetched a packet of tissues from the handbasin. By handing over the tissues and gesturing in the direction of Sjödin's hand, Tell let him know that he had seen through the facade.

Sjödin muttered something and wrapped a piece of tissue around his thumb. He cleared his throat a few times, finally seeming to lose his cool. Then, just as quickly, the penny dropped. It was impossible not to notice how relieved he was.

"Now I know what happened! My wallet was stolen on Boxing Day, that must be it. Somebody pretended to be me and used my ID to steal the car."

"We're not talking about a car theft here; this is a murder investigation."

Sjödin became very still, breathing jerkily through his mouth. He didn't even bother to wipe the condensation off his glasses.

"You mean the person who pretended to be me murdered someone?"

Tell didn't reply; he simply watched as Sjödin absorbed the information.

"Why didn't you report the theft of your wallet?" he asked eventually.

"But I did!" Sjödin exclaimed indignantly. "If my daughter's cat hadn't been run over I would have reported it as soon as I got home from the Co-op — that's where it was stolen. I'd been shopping in Borås and I paid for my stuff; the thief must have taken the wallet while I was packing everything into bags. I must have put it down for a few seconds."

"When did you report it?"

"Two days later, on 28 December."

"Can you remember anything about the person in front of you or behind you in the queue at the checkout? Or anyone who stood unnecessarily close to you?"

Sjödin shook his head firmly. "I've been thinking about it, because I wondered who would have had the nerve virtually to steal my wallet out of my hand, but . . . I can't remember anything in particular."

"Do you perhaps remember which checkout you were at?"

"I do, it was the one furthest away from the entrance. I went back to speak to the cashier to see if she'd picked it up, but of course she hadn't."

"OK." Tell stood up and held out his hand.

"I'll have a look at your report. Otherwise we're done."

Mark Sjödin stayed where he was for a moment. He took off his glasses and polished them before finally leaving the interview room with Tell.

"What about the chances of getting my wallet back?" he asked.

"What do you think?" Tell replied, leaving the auditor to his fate, or rather to the receptionist, who helpfully showed him out.

It was as he'd thought: the ID was stolen. This increased the likelihood that it was their murderer who had hired the Cherokee in Ulricehamn.

He stuck his head around Gonzales' door.

"Get the Jeep from Ulricehamn brought in straight away."

Gonzales was just keying in the number for Johansson & Johansson when Tell heard the phone ringing in his own office.

The caller display showed Seja Lundberg's number. This immediately made him think of Östergren's searching gaze that morning. He swore as he realised he'd forgotten his promise to go and see her straight after the meeting, and now Östergren would be wondering more than ever whether he was avoiding her. Which he was, of course. The phone stopped ringing.

"One missed call".

Sometimes you have to make choices in life, he told himself. The only reasonable choice in a situation like this was to end the relationship with Seja, even though it had only just started. It wasn't even a choice, really; it was the only possibility. Because as Carina had said, if he didn't have his job, what did he have?

With a heavy heart Tell walked over to Östergren's office, only to be informed by her secretary that she had gone home for the day. He felt an enormous sense of relief, although he knew it was childish; the problem would still be there tomorrow. Since he didn't have to face a difficult conversation with Östergren, he felt ready to listen to the message from Seja.

"I'm trying to revise for an exam but I can't stop thinking about you," she said. "So I'm giving up and calling you, since you never seem to call me. I've decided I'm too old to play hard to get, when I'm not hard to get at all."

The message broke off, leaving a painful emptiness where her voice had been. Tell deleted it.

CHAPTER
FORTY

1995

Until the moment he saw her standing there on the stairs, without a scrap of make-up, her hair on end and looking as ugly as a troll, the thought of Solveig had made him want to stick pins in his brain.

He imagined staying away for years: they would meet by chance on the street one day in twenty years' time. That was the only way she could be allowed to exist in his consciousness. In the daydream he was twenty-five, dressed in a beige summer suit which made him radiate the confidence he imagined came automatically with age. For some reason the scene always took place in Villastaden outside one of the gates to Annelund Park. He took her grey hands, distorted with pain, and she would whisper, *Because of my stupidity I lost you, Sebastian. I never want to lose you again.*

He would forgive her, of course. In one version she said, *I have searched for you all over the world*, but that was just too far from reality. In the first place, Solveig would never manage to travel the world looking for him, and secondly, the only hiding place he could come up with when he ran away was Brasse's flat. Brasse was the only person he knew who had his own flat.

If he'd gone to Krister's, his mum would have phoned Solveig the very first day. Krister's mum would never allow him to turn up with his rucksack and announce that he was staying — nor would any mum he could imagine. But given that Brasse's flat wasn't exactly a secret, that would be the first place Solveig would look. If she did decide to look for him, that is, which in the daydream she did.

Which she had done. She had found him. However heavy the burden of his guilt, she had still found him. A strange warm energy flooded his body and he realised that he had been frozen until now. For how long he didn't know, but when the tired troll looked at him it felt like stepping into a hot bath after being out skiing in a snowstorm.

"What are you doing here?" he said, just to make sure she hadn't come to accuse him of murder or to throw a bomb into Brasse's crappy little one-room flat.

"They wanted me to think before I made a decision," she said in a thin voice. She looked like a child, so skinny in those grubby wrinkled tights and the long pale yellow cable-knit sweater. On her feet she had nothing but her trainers, which had once been white; the rubber soles were so worn they were virtually splitting. Her toes were pointing inwards. Not even the lines on her face beneath the hair peppered with grey could make her look like a middle-aged woman.

"You must be half-frozen to death," he said, pointing at her windcheater and the shoes.

"They wanted me to think," she said again, "about whether to switch Maya off or not."

356

Her voice gained a little strength, echoed through the stairwell. He heard the outside door below open, and someone began to walk up the stairs.

"Are you coming in or what?" he said, relieved that Brasse was out. Solveig took a surprisingly decisive stride into the little hallway. She was standing so close that he could smell her breath: the throat sweets she always sucked, and something else, something chemical. She was gripping his arm so tightly that a bruise would later appear in the shape of her thumbprint.

"They think I would kill my own daughter. They don't know anything. Not about me. Not about Maya. I said I didn't need to think about it. But they wanted me to go home and think it over. I'm the only one who can decide, they said."

"But Mum, she's already dead. Her brain is dead," said Sebastian.

He didn't have time to react before the grip on his arm relaxed and a slap across the face left his cheek burning. Solveig burst into tears and threw her arms around his neck. She was sobbing.

He closed his eyes and tears squeezed on to his eyelashes.

"We're the ones who have to fight now, Sebastian," she said.

Her hair was in his mouth. Suddenly he remembered what the comic book was called: *The Living Dead*.

He moved back home.

During the night Solveig came into his room. She'd never done that before.

Although he had been deep in a dreamless sleep, he woke in a panic with the feeling that a hand was on his throat, compressing his windpipe. It couldn't be Solveig's hand, because she was standing in the doorway on the other side of the room. The light was on in the hallway, and from the bed Solveig was no more than a silhouette, long hair lying over her narrow shoulders.

He tried to slow his breathing and promised himself that he would sleep with the light on from now on. He still didn't know where he was with Solveig, whether she blamed him. If she was on medication. If she had fully understood the situation.

"What are you doing?" he asked her.

She didn't reply; she simply stood there. She looked as if she were swaying, as if a wind were blowing through the room and she lacked the strength to fight it. For a moment he thought she was drunk.

"Mum," he said, and he could hear the pleading note in his voice. He hated that voice. He wanted to get up, stand beside her and feel that he was no longer a defenceless child. Remind himself that he was a good ten centimetres taller than her now, that he wanted to be less vulnerable.

"Mum."

"You should know how afraid you look when I look at you," she said in a voice like cracked porcelain. "You're so scared of me, Sebastian. Because you think it was your fault that Maya went out that night. Because you know that I know you refused to come home with her, and that was why she died alone in the forest. You think that you might as well have raped and killed her yourself. It doesn't matter who struck the final blow. What matters is who set the ball in motion. That's what you think. That's why you're afraid."

He stared at the silhouette. It appeared to have stopped swaying. The words seemed to bolster the feeble figure.

"She wasn't raped," he said quietly. "She fell and hit her head on a stone."

"You don't need to be afraid, but I'll say what I used to say when you were little, Sebastian," the silhouette continued, turning slowly towards the hallway so that, for a moment, he could see his mother's profile, her weak chin. "You have to confess, not deny everything. It's when you deny everything that I get angry. You don't want me to be angry, do you? Remember, you're all I have now. We have to stick together, you and me."

The voice died away as she closed the door of her bedroom. Sebastian switched on the bedside lamp and concentrated hard on the fish-shaped rug, trying to breathe evenly. An indefinite amount of time passed before he became aware of the ticking of the alarm clock.

A realisation of what the choking hand around his throat had wanted from him began to take shape. He welcomed the feeling of strength as the idea came closer and grew in power.

The fish rug had slipped to one side to reveal the stain on the lino, just the same size as the one by the bed in Rydboholm. It struck him that this was very strange, and it was probably the sign he had been waiting for.

What came first, the rug or the stain? he chanted to himself until his heart stopped pounding in his chest. *What came first, the chicken or the egg, the rug or the stain?*

When he could see clearly once again he had decided to open himself up to other signs. In order to do this he must get to the hospital.

He dressed as quickly as possible, crept out into the hallway and pulled on his shoes and jacket. The door to Solveig's room was closed, but a strip of light was showing underneath. He listened intently, but couldn't decide whether his mother was fast asleep or whether the ragged breathing was his own; he had no control over his body in this apartment.

As soon as he got outside his heart slowed to its regular beat. When he was surrounded by the neon lights of the empty city streets, he stopped running and spat the taste of blood out of his mouth.

Nobody keeps watch over a person who is brain dead; it was as he had thought.

Nothing anyone could do would make any difference, he chanted, *so why keep watch?*

Maya was lying alone in her room, surrounded by all the apparatus keeping her alive. A yellowing nightlight was burning for the benefit of relatives, or perhaps for the nurse on night duty, who would presumably do her rounds sooner or later, measuring the rhythm of the respirator and checking the monitors that provided

360

information on how things were going for the living dead. *The Living Dead.*

There was very little chance that the night nurse would turn up during the next half-hour. And in half an hour he would be out of there.

Sebastian lifted the limp hand from the blanket and was surprised at how warm it was, at the fact that medical science was so successful at keeping the body alive by artificial means. No doubt they were proud of themselves, the doctors who had run all these tubes through his sister's body.

They knew nothing.

Nothing of the borderland between life and death, nothing of restless fear and rootlessness. Nothing of never coming in to land, of having lost your right to this world without being able to enter the next, because others had arbitrarily bound your hands and feet to prevent you from letting go, from being set free.

According to the comic, there was one particularly agonising aspect of being in this borderland, which was to do with the fact that the land of transition was integrated with the normal world.

He thought Maya was whispering the words to him.

The people in the borderland, the unfortunates, are invisible but they surround us all the time — they can see us, but we do not see them. Since there is no way to see the difference between a normal mortal and the living dead, not even for the living dead themselves, they live in constant fear of each other. Rootlessness brings fear. Fear

361

brings angst. Angst brings powerlessness. Powerlessness brings anger, and the living dead seethe with rage but have nowhere to direct this rage. They have no one to take out their anger on except each other, and no fear can be worse than not knowing if, or when, something terrible is going to happen.

What came first, the rug or the stain? Nothing could be worse than this restless deprivation of a world.

He would never be more sure that he was doing the right thing. He wouldn't be able to live with himself if he allowed his pathetic fear to stand in his way.

And his limited preparations turned out to be more than adequate: the whole thing went much more smoothly than he could have imagined. When the respirator fell silent and its final sigh sounded like a farewell, he replied, "Goodbye, Maya." Suddenly he found it easier to breathe.

Maya had left the land of transition and entered into the kingdom of the dead.

CHAPTER
FORTY-ONE

2007

The cordless phone lay next to her on the bench by the stable wall. She didn't know how long she'd been listening to the constant beeping that told her the line was open. She switched it off.

By this stage she knew the messages on Christian Tell's answerphone by heart, both at work and at home. She could, if she wished, by imitating his dark melodic Gothenburg dialect, produce a pretty good impression. *You have reached Christian Tell's answerphone. Unfortunately I am not able to take your call* . . . But it would be just too pathetic to develop that particular talent.

The hands holding the telephone — this instrument of torture that had filled her days of late, emanating malice — had become red and dry from the cold. She pulled on her gloves, trying to sum up the energy to get up and make a start on the stable. The box needed mucking out. Lukas needed grooming. The harness needed oiling.

Here I am again, she thought. Tears of anger forced their way through her. She had promised herself that she would never again end up humiliating and belittling herself like this. When Martin left her she had refused to let the cottage become a symbol of the fact that they had tried to achieve something together and failed. Instead she had clung to the idea that this place symbolised her new life as a strong independent individual.

The cottage, the horse, the cat and all the projects that were part of life in the country placed demands on her, were sufficiently taxing to distract her from being paralysed by the fear of finding herself alone and unloved, were sufficiently manageable to enable her to maintain her new-found calm and save her from going under due to stress and a sense of inadequacy. Even if she had her low points at regular intervals — often triggered by anxiety over the increasingly rapid deterioration of the cottage — she was generally happy with her life.

And that was why she cursed Christian Tell. Not only had he brought her old demons to the surface, he had also rejected her as a woman. Because she had to accept that that was how it was. He hadn't answered his phone for two days, nor had he called her back, even though she had left several messages.

The desire to key in his number came back, although it was only five minutes since her last attempt. She sighed. This really wouldn't do. She was an adult now: she knew perfectly well that nobody dies because of an unhappy love affair, not really. It was time she started behaving accordingly.

The case on which the unreliable rat was working was constantly in the back of her mind, the reason why she had got involved with him in the first place.

In the locked drawer of the desk she had inherited from old man Gren lay the folder containing the photographs from Björsared. During those first days, when she had still been in a state of shock, she had asked herself over and over again what she should do with the memories that had suddenly started clamouring for her attention.

Then the love affair with the inspector had got in the way. In his presence she had felt safe enough to put her thoughts to one side. Only then was she able to start writing. It was a contradiction she accepted: she needed a certain amount of distance from the experience. A reasonable space between herself and the dead man.

The empty space Christian Tell had left behind after such a short time made her realise how much she needed love, a man in her life, to feel completely contented. This terrified her, and once again made her prey to unwelcome thoughts.

She was hurled back helplessly to that period in the mid-90s when she had bleached blonde hair and a ring through her lower lip, and had clung to one boy after another out of a thirst for love which, despite the change in strategy, was not so different from her behaviour to this day. The thought was painful and she pushed it away; there were no other similarities. It was only ten years ago, but it was a different life. None of the friends she knew then were still around.

Unless Hanna . . . perhaps Hanna was still around? She had been the last "best friend" before the phrase became alien and embarrassing. A few years ago they had tried to re-establish contact, meeting for coffee a couple of times, a few beers, chatting about the old days. There had been something forced about Hanna at the time, a false familiarity that Seja didn't recognise from their teenage years.

But she herself had chosen to present selected highlights of her life, embroidering and enhancing both past and present. Yet she had felt disappointed afterwards. So much was left unsaid and still remained between them, because neither of them was ready to talk. The last time Seja had tried to ring her, Hanna had moved — with no forwarding address.

Now that Hanna Aronsson's face, plastered with too much makeup, had appeared in her mind's eye once again, Seja was unable to shake off the image. She felt ready to talk to Hanna now.

She would be lying to herself if she pretended she could free herself of the sense of unease. On New Year's Eve Christian had mentioned the other murder, and it had hit her like a body blow.

She would never be free unless she took action. Starting right now.

Directory Enquiries was able to offer the numbers of six Hanna Aronssons in the Gothenburg area. The first was in Engelbrektsgatan in Vasastan, and the woman put the phone down on Seja as soon as she realised it was a wrong number. There was a Hanna Aronsson in Gåsmossen in Askim and one on Danska vägen, but neither of them was home.

At the fourth attempt, on Paradisgatan in Masthugget, she struck lucky. She recognised Hanna's voice straight away. Dark and slightly tense, she had had an adult's voice even when she was a teenager with green and pink striped hair dyed at home in the bath and Doc Martens scuffed to precisely the right degree.

Hanna had been Seja's best friend from year 9 onwards, crossing all boundaries and with a certain semi-erotic charge. As teenage friendships so often were. They had found each other in the self-evident way people do when they need each other. For a few tempestuous years they had shared clothes and confidences, top to toe in Hanna's bed. They had even shared a boyfriend for a few days: it turned out the boy they had both been referring to as The One was in fact the same boy — a discovery that temporarily made them bitter enemies, before they came to their senses and ganged up on him instead.

Seja was overcome with nostalgia: Hanna's narrow bed on Landsvägsgatan with a pot of tea on a tray at the foot and a fantastic mixture of music on the stereo: Cindy Lauper, Doom, Asta Kask, Kate Bush. Barricaded in Hanna's room, safe from her mother, who would be drinking wine in the living room and listening to Ulf Lundell through her headphones, in a bad mood as usual. A few years later she would tragically take her own life. Seja had read about it in the paper, a small item stating that one of Gothenburg's cultural figures had been found dead in her apartment, no suspicion of foul play.

They were in the same class, and even if Hanna's mother and Seja's parents were not particularly keen on the fact that Seja stayed over on week nights, they obviously weren't sufficiently annoyed to put a stop to it. On Landsvägsgatan, sitting in a fog created by the cigarettes they rolled themselves, Hanna and Seja knew nothing of the future. Seja in her semi-transparent and, as she thought at the time, wonderfully kitsch nightdress from the 60s; it was so big over her almost imperceptible bust that the décolletage was practically down to her waist. Towards midnight they would turn down the music and start whispering; they didn't want to risk Hanna's half-cut mother banging on the door and yelling at them to be quiet. Luckily the location of Hanna's room meant that they could sneak into the kitchen — to make another pot of herbal tea with honey — and go to the toilet, a trip they made countless times during the night as a direct consequence of all that tea, without passing her mother's bedroom.

In the mornings Hanna's bedroom floor was sticky with spilt tea and honey. Empty record sleeves lay all over the place, interspersed with books from which they had been reading aloud to each other: poetry anthologies written by young adults, containing great pronouncements about love at the time of life when it is stronger than it will ever be again.

She no longer remembered what it was that had split them up. *Oh yes, grammar school* — they had chosen different schools. Hanna had started commuting to a school that was particularly strong in craft. She had dropped out the following year, but by then it was already too late. The contact was broken. That was the end of those nights at Landsvägsgatan. It isn't only love that is stronger and more fragile when we are young. Friendship is the same.

It was difficult to grasp that it had only been a couple of years. She had thought that Hanna knew her better than anyone else, certainly better than her parents, better than her childhood friends, who were denied friendship with this more grown-up Seja, the Seja who slept with boys and had to have an abortion the summer after she finished year 11.

It was as if their friendship culminated that very night. She had collapsed on Hanna's bed after being released from hospital on the strict understanding that she would go straight home to her parents. It was as if they had never been closer. Hanna's mother, talkative after too much red wine, circled suspiciously around Seja, asking over and over again if she shouldn't perhaps ring her mother after all. In the end Hanna had screamed at her to stay out of it.

It was also after that night that their friendship diluted. More and more, they spent time with other friends. Suddenly their contact was limited to bumping into each other at parties organised by other people.

Now Hanna was laughing in embarrassment on the other end of the line.

"It must be at least six years ago. Or more. What are you up to these days?"

"What about you?" countered Seja, as she heard a child's voice in the background. "Are you a mum?"

"Yes." The pride in Hanna's voice was unmistakable. "His name's Markus and he's four."

"Heavens. I had no idea you'd had a baby."

"No, but that's hardly surprising. I don't think we've spoken for . . ."

"Six years, as you said. Or more. I . . ." She hesitated. "I read about your mum. I'm really sorry."

There was silence on the other end of the line, and for a moment Seja thought she had jumped in too quickly. She heard Hanna take a deep breath.

"Thank you. It happened just after we last saw each other. It's terrible that you can feel so fucking angry with someone because they didn't want to live any more, but it felt like a betrayal . . . no, not a betrayal. It was like a fucking punch in the face. There you go, because you thought I'd always be there for you, just because I happen to be your mother . . . I suppose she never felt all that great, really. She cut her wrists in the bath, you know, like we wrote in our adolescent poems. That's what she did."

"I saw it in the paper, but not how . . . I mean, I didn't know she . . ."

"I know. One of 'Gothenburg's cultural figures', yeah right. That was diplomatic, I thought. For the last ten years she wasn't even a former anything, given that she had never actually been anything in the first place. Apart from a nasty old alcoholic with an inferiority complex which she hid beneath delusions of grandeur. God, aren't I terrible? You can hear how angry I still am. But you remember what she was like."

Seja didn't say anything. She had always felt uncomfortable around Hanna's mother, and not in the usual way when a friend's parent is giving you the third degree. She had never worked out what the problem was.

Hanna seemed to understand.

"I mean, I thought she was a pain at the time, but what teenager doesn't think her mother is a pain? It was only later that I realised she was actually sick in the head. An old woman on a permanent ego trip who would rather rob her child of its mother than pull herself together and get an ordinary job, like everybody else. Oh no, she had to be misunderstood, a maladjusted failed actress. Better to die than to work on the checkout at the local supermarket."

A silence followed Hanna's harsh laugh.

"Sorry. I feel just about as crazy as her right now. You ring me up after all these years and I come out with all that . . . It's just that all the memories came flooding back when I heard your voice. Getting pissed when we were teenagers, and our first . . . first everything."

"I suppose that was when we did everything for the first time," Seja agreed, regretting the fact that she hadn't got in touch with Hanna before now, hadn't been more persistent.

She told her.

"I've thought about getting in touch lots of times too, but you know . . . the last few times we saw each other I wasn't feeling so good . . ." Hanna hesitated. "It really started after I dropped out of school. I had anorexia for a while, and it all got a bit much. All the boys, all the crap . . ."

Seja nodded cautiously, even though they were on the phone. She thought she understood, having experienced herself how life had suddenly spun faster and faster in the punk circle of which they were on the periphery, ridiculous teenagers in leather jackets covered in rivets, padlocks around their necks. After that first, fumbling sexual experience, Seja had believed this was the key to love and approval, despite the fact that over and over again it only led to humiliation and a broken heart.

She remembered the two of them sitting side by side at Hanna's dressing table, examining their appearance in the mirror.

"We certainly are two filthy fucking tarts," Hanna had said, and Seja had nodded seriously before they both burst out laughing, and Hanna threw a wet towel at Seja's face.

Seja had held on to her reputation better than Hanna, because she had met a boy outside their circle of friends and had stayed with him for six months towards the end of year 11, while Hanna had carried on bed-hopping. The fact that Hanna's language was coarse with frequent references to sex, effectively hiding her insecurity, didn't improve the situation. Nor did her appearance: she was usually squeezed into tight tops and jeans that didn't look half as provocative on Seja's skinny flat-chested body. The combination of these and Hanna's well-developed curves was just too much for those around them, who were quick to judge. Hanna became known as the local bike.

The first time Seja heard the nickname Herpes Hanna was at a table by the window at the Northern Station. She hadn't gone so far as to agree with the claim; everyone knew that Hanna was her friend. But she had taken pleasure in it. As time went by the name became well established, and Seja would take every opportunity to protest: *Hey, she doesn't sleep around any more, she's actually grown up . . .* But even in retrospect she was aware that her own self-confidence was built on the fact that she had been compared, to her advantage, with someone she used to think played in a higher league: Hanna, with her big tits and her interesting voice and the parties that people actually came to.

No doubt all teenage girls have a capacity for taking pleasure in the misfortune of others and for constantly comparing themselves with their peers, but this didn't make Seja feel any less guilty as Hanna talked about how difficult things had been in the years after they lost contact.

"I moved to Strömstad and finished my education there — a friend of Mum's took pity on me. It did me good to get away from everything and start afresh. Like a clean page, a place where nobody knows anything about you. It can be like a drug, that feeling. You want to do it all over again, just up sticks and start again somewhere else."

Seja thought about her cottage. "I wanted to invite you to my place," she said. "Bring Markus and come over. But I won't lie to you: one of the reasons I rang was because I'd like your help with something."

"Help? What on earth could I help you with?" said Hanna in surprise.

"I need your help to dig into the past."

Hanna laughed. "Bloody hell, Seja. But I'm very good at digging into the past."

"And it will be brilliant to see you," Seja added quickly. "I'm in the middle of a love affair that's not going very well, and I've got several bottles of wine here. You'd be doing me a really big favour if you came over and helped me drink them."

This time Hanna's laughter was lighter.

"When? Now?"

"Now would be good. I'll pick you up at the bus stop."

"Junkie."

"She probably was, but I think she pulled herself together towards the end, before she . . . disappeared."

"Disappeared?" Hanna looked at Seja, deliberately opening her eyes wide in marked contrast to the drooping eyelids of a moment ago, a consequence of the quantity of wine they had consumed.

They had carried the TV and video up to the loft so that Markus could fall asleep watching the films his mother had cleverly brought with her. Downstairs Norah Jones was whispering from the speakers, and the remains of a Thai chicken curry stood on the draining board. An almost empty wine box was balanced on the edge of the worktop.

Seja pushed open the kitchen window to let in the midnight air as Hanna lit a cigarette.

She recoiled as the high flame singed her eyelashes. "Shit! Just like the old days!"

"Anyway . . . she did disappear, but never mind that. I just need to know who she was."

"Look, I'd really like to help you, Seja, but I don't remember her. There were so many people who drifted in and out of the gang. Lots of young girls and lots of friends of friends, people you didn't really know. People you just recognised, you know . . . but she had black hair, you said?"

"Yes, at least later on. I think she had red hair at first, pinkish red. I often saw her at the café — we talked about it that last time we met. She used to write in the visitors' books. Her alias was . . . Shit, I can't remember it."

Hanna smiled at the memory of the visitors' books. "My alias was Hannami."

Seja became animated. "I wonder what happened to the books."

"Later on, you mean?"

"Yes, when the café closed down."

"Let's hope they were burned. Bearing in mind all the embarrassing crap we wrote in them. I remember writing about my suicidal thoughts once; I just didn't think about the fact that my alias gave me away. The next time I turned up there were three complete strangers sitting there, three girls, waiting to convince me that life was worth living."

She splashed some wine on her trousers. Seja got up to fetch some salt, but Hanna waved it aside.

"Leave it. I can hardly do up the button on these old jeans. It's time to accept they're too small and chuck them away."

"I've a feeling she was friends with Kåre . . . I used to see them together. Not that they were a couple or anything. I haven't seen Kåre for ages either."

Hanna seemed to be thinking. The column of ash from her cigarette landed on her knee as the penny dropped.

"Hang on. I think I know who you mean. A little girl — short, I mean. She always used to wear a white leather jacket, do you remember that?"

"That's it! A white leather jacket with *Alice Under* on the back."

Now it was Seja's turn to spill her wine. The liquid was soaked up by the pale green tablecloth, making batik swirls around the saucers containing the flickering candles. Muted sounds came from the loft.

Hanna stood up on wobbly legs and went out into the hallway.

Seja stared at the stain for a moment before tipping salt over it, turning it into a pink sludgy mess.

The stairs creaked and Hanna padded back into the kitchen.

"She hung out with Magnus for a while. You know, Magnus with the plaited beard. He used to play the fiddle. I spent a whole evening talking to them at Solsidan. Not that I remember what she was called or what we talked about."

She sat down heavily and placed a hand over Seja's.

"Now tell me what this is all about!"

Seja looked at Hanna's hand. The nails were long and painted dark purple. Beneath her own short unpainted nails she could see a line of horse shit.

376

She hoped her expression conveyed her feelings.

"I promise I will, Hanna. In time. But right now I just want to know her name and . . . what happened to her."

"So you think something happened to her?"

"I heard a rumour that something happened to her, then I heard she was dead. I just need to find out, otherwise I won't get any peace, and the only thing I have to go on are my mixed-up memories and you."

"And the visitors' books from the café, of course. The alias," Hanna added.

"Yes, but I hadn't actually thought about those until now."

Hanna looked at her suspiciously. "Seja. What has all this got to do with you? Are you sure I don't need to worry about you?"

Seja put her hands together.

"You don't need to worry. At least not much. But right now I'm going to make myself a bed on the sofa, and you can squeeze into my bed with your son."

Hanna didn't seem to have the energy to protest. She nodded gratefully at Seja. "I'm absolutely worn out. And pissed." She turned back just as she was about to climb up to the loft. "You said it yourself."

"What?"

"The visitors' books. I know a guy who knows one of the people who used to run the station café. He has a restaurant on one of the streets off Kungsgatan."

After Hanna had gone to bed Seja took a last walk over to the stable. The old door creaked. *Must remember to oil the hinges.* She didn't bother putting on the light; she stood in the darkness listening to the restful sound of Lukas snuffling around in his oats. Her exhaustion disappeared and was replaced by a strange almost electric energy.

She went back inside, switched on the computer and wrote for the rest of the night in a kind of fever.

CHAPTER
FORTY-TWO

It had fallen to Beckman to go over to the Klara hostel at seven thirty that evening. She had just been on the point of calling it a day, having already phoned Göran and the kids twice to say she was going to be home late, when the supervisor at the hostel for homeless women had called just after seven and passed on the information that Susanne Jensen had booked in ten minutes earlier for an overnight stay. As usual when it came to interviewing children or vulnerable women, the inspector wasted no time in delegating the job to Karin Beckman. She liked Tell, but he was so predictable.

She accepted the job in silence, knowing perfectly well that this would enable Göran to debit her account with yet another night spent working late, which he would expect to cash in for a night at the pub with the lads.

She was getting over her cold but still felt exhausted to the very depths of her soul. If it hadn't been a matter of pride she would have asked Tell to send another member of the team, somebody who hadn't spent virtually all of Christmas away from their children. But she'd been in this game long enough to know that that would be like volunteering to eat the crap the conservative old guard happily slung as soon as the opportunity arose. It was difficult to credit, but there were still coppers who believed that the profession of a police*man* demanded greater commitment than a normal responsible mother with small children could reasonably demonstrate. It drove her mad. Then again, there were some days when she was tempted to agree with them.

When she called home for the third time she got the answering machine. Usually she would hang up and call back if she knew they were home, but this time she didn't bother; she wanted to avoid Göran's voice, at best teasing and at worst disappointed, when she told him that she wouldn't be home in time to say goodnight to the children this evening either. She left a short message with three kisses, and set off.

She was just navigating around Brunnsparken, through the conglomeration of trams, cyclists and people who stepped straight out into the road without looking, when Karlberg rang to pass on another message from the hostel. Susanne Jensen was no longer there. The supervisor didn't know what this meant. Either she had gone out to buy something and would be back soon, or she had got wind of the fact that the police were looking for her.

Beckman decided to carry on anyway. The court building was looming up ahead of her, and the hostel was supposed to be just behind it. If she had missed Jensen, at least she would be able to talk to the staff.

At this time of day there was plenty of activity in the long narrow hallway. Two women arrived at the same time as Beckman and heaved their shoes, jackets and handbags into lockers with practised ease. The keys were on an elastic band, like the ones you get at swimming baths. A signing-in book lay open on a desk, and beside it stood a young woman with her hair in thin bunches. She greeted the overnight guests briefly. Several seemed to be regulars as she called them by name.

Beckman tried not to regard those signing in as tragic, but told herself the same thing she usually did when she came into contact with vulnerable outsiders: they were just ordinary girls and boys who had been unlucky in life and were at rock bottom, on their way back up. Nothing was for ever, after all.

It could just as easily have been me. Right now she didn't have the strength to follow the thought through — for example, what would happen if Göran threw her out during their next excoriating row; the house actually belonged to him. *But it isn't me.*

An older woman with dark hair drawn back into a knot seemed familiar as she pulled off a bright green scarf. At first Beckman couldn't place her. Then she remembered a television debate on the new prostitution laws. The woman had introduced herself as a spokeswoman for prostitutes, homeless and abused women. She had furiously maintained that the new law did street girls a disservice by making their work something shameful and driving them underground. The old arguments for and against had been trotted out, and Beckman's abiding memory of the debate was surprise that this impressive woman should belong to what were usually regarded as the dregs of society.

Not that Beckman was prepared to go along with the myth of the happy whore. There was all the proof in the world that the opposite was true here in this airless narrow hallway. An overwhelming smell of unwashed bodies and stale alcohol. She noticed that no one seemed willing to meet her eye, and at first she thought it must be obvious that she was a police officer, although she couldn't for the life of her work out why. The girl with the bunches said, "You need to sign in," just as Beckman was about to introduce herself.

For a moment she didn't know what to say. She felt a childish urge to protest at having been taken for a homeless person, but realised this would be ridiculous, not to mention offensive to those around her. Instead she discreetly showed her ID, as she had planned to do from the start. The tips of the girl's ears went bright red, but she quickly pulled herself together.

"Margareta said you were coming. If you follow me, I'll show you where she is."

She went ahead of Beckman along a corridor which, judging by its fitted cupboards, had once been a service passageway. The girl was clearly upset by her mistake.

"This is a lovely building," said Beckman, smoothing things over and breaking the embarrassing silence.

"It used to be two huge apartments, but they were knocked into one. We've made some alterations, but we've tried to keep the old charm."

We, thought Beckman — she didn't look a day over twenty-five.

"Have you worked here long?"

The girl, who according to her name badge was called Sandra, stopped outside a door. A red light showed that the occupant was engaged.

"I've been here for eighteen months, since I graduated." She made an apologetic gesture. "So many people come here, it's impossible to recognise them all. Of course I could see straight away that you're not —"

"It's fine," Beckman broke in. "Have you come across Susie — Susanne Pilgren, or Jensen, while you've been here?"

"We've got a Susanne Jensen. She comes here one or two nights a week for a while, then she disappears. Then she comes back."

"What's your impression of her?"

"As a person, you mean? Well . . . often we don't know much about the women who stay here, it's not our job to find out. That's why they choose this place — they're left in peace and nobody pries. Susie isn't much of a talker anyway: she signs in, goes to bed, then leaves early in the morning. She's never caused any trouble."

"Is she always on her own? What's she like when she arrives?" asked Beckman.

Behind the closed door they could hear Margareta Skåner's voice increasing in volume, then falling silent, as if she was ending a call after letting the person on the other end of the line know exactly what she thought.

"Yes, she's always on her own. Are you asking if she takes something? Most of the women who stay here are users. Some places won't let them in if they're under the influence, but we don't have that rule. It wouldn't be much help to them — the most vulnerable women would be left to their own devices. So yes, she's often in a bad way, but she doesn't kick off like some of them do. Not here, anyway."

Beckman nodded. There was still silence on the other side of the door. In spite of the red light she rapped hard with her knuckles and pushed it open.

Margareta Skåner looked up in surprise from her polished desk.

"Excuse me?"

"Karin Beckman from the police. We spoke on the telephone."

Sandra mumbled something about going back to reception. Margareta Skåner nodded briefly in her direction.

"Of course, it was about Susanne Jensen. You've heard that she's gone off again. Sometimes the women who stay here have a kind of sixth sense when it comes to the guardians of the law. Perhaps I can be of some help?"

Just as Beckman sat down, there was a discreet knock, and Sandra's face reappeared in the doorway.

"Sorry, I just wanted to say that Susie's back. She's in the kitchen."

"I'm going to be busy in a little while," Margareta said quickly when she saw that Karin Beckman was getting up. "Perhaps we could have a chat before you go to see Susanne?"

Beckman hesitated. "I'll come back to you another day if necessary," she decided in the end. "I think it might be best to have a chat with Susanne straight away. As you said, the smell of the police spreads fast."

Through the glass panel in the upper half of the door Beckman could see that the kitchen was as big as that of a restaurant. The smell of food being cooked on the hob seeped out through the door, along with the aroma of several large dishes of lasagne. A note attached to a piggy bank said that the lasagne cost ten kronor per portion. Three women were already sitting at the table, eating in silence. One of them was reading a newspaper and talking to herself in an agitated way.

"Susie's the one with short hair and the red jumper."

Sandra took hold of Beckman's arm. "Do you think you could be a bit . . . gentle? It's just that one of the good things about this place is that the women feel safe here. I don't think there are many places in town where they feel safe."

Beckman smiled.

"I promise to be as gentle as I can."

As soon as she introduced herself, she realised that Susanne Jensen probably didn't even know her brother was dead. She had yanked her arm away when Beckman touched her and asked her to come to another room where they could talk in private. However, Jensen had obviously wanted to avoid a scene and had accompanied Beckman to the room where she would be sleeping later.

It was a small room, furnished only with two bunk beds and a desk, but the white-painted walls and tall

385

windows made it feel pleasant and airy. The beds were made up with starched white sheets. When Beckman saw them she felt an overwhelming desire to lie down on the bottom bunk and just sleep, without a husband or children demanding her attention. Then she was struck by her inability to feel grateful for her privileged existence, in spite of its problems. Exhaustion really did blind you to the important things in life.

Susanne Jensen sat cross-legged on the bed, staring at her socks. She didn't resemble her brother at all. At least she didn't look anything like the photograph of Olof Bart on the whiteboard in the conference room. He was dark and she was fair, although perhaps they shared the same slim build. Susanne Jensen's face was almost transparent and she had purple rings beneath her eyes, as if she'd slept badly her whole life.

"First of all I have to tell you that your brother Olof is dead," said Beckman quietly. Instinctively, she tried to place her hand on Jensen's knee. Susanne pushed it away, then sat completely motionless, giving no indication whatsoever that she had understood what Beckman had said. "I'm very sorry."

For a second Beckman detected the hint of a scornful smile on the face of the woman sitting opposite.

"I imagine you might have had some bad experiences with the police in the past," she continued, "and you don't want to talk to me, but I just want to say that anything you choose to tell me could be important in helping us catch the person who killed your brother. I don't know how much contact you had with each other after you were placed in foster homes, but I know almost nothing about Olof's life. Perhaps you could tell me whether he had any enemies, anyone who might have wished him ill."

She stopped speaking and waited for a reaction. It didn't come.

"Susanne?"

Jensen really did look as if she was frozen: her shoulders were hunched up by her ears, her jaws were clamped together, and her hands were clenched into fists.

Beckman pulled back. She had to respect the fact that this woman did not want to be touched.

"If I sit here for a while, perhaps you'll decide to say something," she ventured. "And if you can't think of anything you want to say while I'm here, then maybe you could ring me, or write to me. I'll give you my number. I'd also like you to think about whether you've ever heard the name Lars Waltz mentioned in connection with your brother. But don't worry about that too much. It's just one line of enquiry we're following."

Karin Beckman sat opposite a silent Susanne Jensen for almost three quarters of an hour before she got up and stretched her legs as one of them had gone to sleep.

"I'm going now."

She gently placed her card next to Susanne Jensen. The woman turned her head and met Beckman's eyes briefly before returning her attention to her hands, which were now tightly locked around her shins. She was sitting in a kind of foetal position, and if you screwed up your eyes she looked no more than twelve years old.

Beckman wasn't screwing up her eyes, and she felt as if she was seeing Susanne Jensen more clearly than she could cope with.

"Please get in touch," she said eventually. "Even if you don't want to talk about your brother."

When Beckman went through the entrance hall it was empty, and the ten lines in the signing-in book were full. She felt a weight on her chest as she let herself out on to the cobbled street winding down towards the northern part of town. A narrow strip of blue-grey sky was just visible between the silhouettes of the hundred-year-old stone buildings. At the end of the alleyway the sale signs on Femmanstorg shone out.

CHAPTER
FORTY-THREE

Ann-Christine Östergren was standing by the window of her office. Some building work was going on down around Ullevi, but he guessed that was not what was occupying her attention. It struck him that lately he had often seen her like this, deep in her own thoughts. She was twirling a strand of hair between her thumb and index finger and looked more tired than she had ever done.

She only had a couple of years to go before retirement, but this was a fact that few of her subordinates could take seriously. Östergren as anything other than a police officer, as a pensioner, embroidering cushions in her holiday cottage? It was impossible to visualise.

"You wanted to talk to me," he said.

She didn't seem in the least surprised when his voice broke the silence.

"Christian, thank you for coming." She gestured to him to sit down. "You look like a schoolboy standing outside the head teacher's office."

Tell smiled stiffly. He felt as if he had lost every scrap of social competence. Perhaps this pretence would end here and now, if the meeting was about the issue he feared. In a way it would be good to get it all over and done with.

He sat down in one of the two easy chairs and crossed his legs. For appearance's sake he had brought with him material concerning the Jeep murders and the arson attacks on which they had been working intensively before the murder in Olofstorp took priority.

When Östergren didn't say anything, he made a stumbling attempt to update her on the situation, but she waved his efforts away.

She took a packet of cigarettes out of a drawer in her desk, her expression a mixture of a question and pure defiance.

"Absolutely," said Tell.

Smoking inside the building was strictly forbidden since the smoking rooms had been replaced by the healthier so-called relaxation rooms — although of course the smokers didn't find them relaxing — so the balcony was often a refuge for nicotine addicts hell-bent on breaking the rules.

Östergren opened the balcony door a little way and pulled her chair closer to the fresh air before taking a drag with immense pleasure.

"I know I shouldn't but it's so bloody difficult to give up!"

Tell nodded. He knew all about that particular scenario. The room quickly filled up with cold air and smoke, and he thought back to the days when he would try desperately to get fresh air into his room when his mother or father knocked on the door.

390

He looked around discreetly. The office had been the same for as long as he could remember: the only furnishings were the desk, the easy chairs and a small round table, apart from the obligatory wall covered in bookshelves packed with files and books relating to the law. No pot plants, no personal items such as photographs of children or grandchildren. He realised he didn't even know whether Östergren had children or grandchildren. What she would be going home to in a couple of years.

For some reason he got the idea that she too stayed at work until late in the evening, postponing the moment when she opened the door to an empty apartment which the occupant had tried to make at least habitable, if not cosy, all alone. It struck him with powerful clarity that this was exactly how he perceived his existence since he had made sure that Seja had disappeared out of his life just as quickly as she had come into it. The keenness of her absence was just as intense as his former enjoyment of the single life: the opportunity to do what he wanted whenever he wanted, the option to choose company when he felt like it and to avoid all kinds of forced social contact.

It was possible that he had felt the same way about Carina. When their relationship was still at the stage when the words lay unspoken between them and he was, typically, struggling with his fear of commitment, Carina had waited patiently. He *had* been in love with her — he couldn't deny that — enough to throw his fears and his cynicism overboard in the end, and to have the courage to go all the way, with an engagement ring and promises of eternal fidelity. And still it hadn't lasted. So what was to say that this relationship wouldn't end the same way, with hurt feelings and bitter accusations?

When Östergren half-heartedly turned her head towards the open door to blow the smoke outside, he took the chance to look at her properly. She had never seemed so distant before. In fact, he had always appreciated her clarity, her presence, the energy that spread to everyone around her. Today the black polo neck that usually contrasted so elegantly with her pale skin and white hair merely highlighted the greyness of her face and the dark rings beneath her eyes. Her pale blue eyes were red-rimmed and surrounded by a network of deep wrinkles.

Tell suddenly got the strong feeling that what she wanted to tell him had nothing to do with the fact that his love life had briefly coincided with his professional life. *Such self-obsession.* Why had he never asked Östergren if she was married? Why had he never even wondered about it?

He was desperate for a cigarette and regretted not bringing his own. On cue, Östergren pushed the cigarettes over to him. "Sorry. I was in a world of my own." She stubbed out the cigarette even though she had smoked only half of it, and pulled a face.

Tell wondered if he ought to stub out the cigarette he had just lit.

"My doctor's name is Björnberg," she said, leaning back in her chair. "He's the same age as me, and both my husband and I have been seeing him for years. He said the other day that these things are killing me. Which I knew, of course. Just not that it was so close, or so literal."

She pointed at the cigarettes.

"The fact that I've changed to these low-tar ones won't make much difference. My first thought was to change to a different doctor."

She took off her glasses and rubbed the skin below her eyes.

"Do you understand? He's always given me nothing but good news, so I thought he was a good doctor. I've hardly even had so much as a cold. It's been nice to have a chat in his surgery now and again. My children go to him too, so he always asks how they are. Remembers the grandchildren's names and so on. And then he comes up with this! I was furious."

Her voice gave way and she cleared her throat.

"I thought you ought to know."

Slowly Tell grasped what his boss was trying to tell him. Without her glasses Östergren seemed strangely defenceless, and for a second he thought he could see fear in her eyes. It was so unaccustomed that he was glad he was sitting down. He wanted to say something to ease the situation — ask lots of questions or say there was always hope — but he thought he knew Östergren well enough to know it was best to remain silent and wait for her to carry on. *She would never mention this unless she was certain.* He felt he could read between the lines: she knew when it was worth fighting, and when it was time to accept the situation.

She pointed at the glowing cigarette in his hand.

"On the subject of smoking. For the first ten years both my husband and I smoked. Then he gave up, and for the next decade he lectured me in that irritating born-again way only ex-smokers do. For the last twenty years he's just given me a resigned look every time I've gone to stand by the extractor fan, with just a little dig every now and again: 'You know this will be the death of you one fine day, Anki.' God, he's so bloody annoying. And now, on top of everything else, he's right."

She smiled sadly.

"All the way home from the doctor's I could hear him saying, 'I told you so.' It was four days before I could bring myself to tell him."

"And what did he say?" Tell was relieved to be able to shift the focus to someone else's inadequacy.

"He cried and got very angry. With me, for not telling him straight away. And because I'd had the nerve to think he would have a go at me. But above all, I think, because he had spent so much time planning what we would do when we retired at long last. At long last — that's his view, anyway."

"And what about you?"

She shrugged her shoulders, then shook her head.

"I don't know. In one way it seems ironic. Or obvious. I've never really been able to relate to all the plans Gustav has been making for us: those trips to all the places in the world we've never visited, the interests we were going to develop. All those courses we were going to do, all that time we would suddenly have for one another. You know . . . Somehow I've always felt

394

. . . that I wasn't really a part of it all. As if I always knew I wasn't going to get there. As if I were only pretending to be involved in order to avoid upsetting him."

She got up and closed the balcony door without taking her eyes off Tell.

"As if I owed it to him to pretend, after making him wait all these years. My job always came first, you see. Before him. Before the children. He reached a point many years ago when he realised it wasn't worth shouting and complaining, and since then it has always been about the future. *Then* we'll have time. Then we'll have peace and quiet. Then we'll have a normal life. And now he finds out that *then* no longer exists. Only now exists. Then nothing."

"Is it cancer?" Tell asked quietly.

Östergren nodded. "It's very advanced. Björnberg did talk about chemotherapy but was honest enough to admit that the chances of success are minimal."

Tell was painfully aware of his breathing.

"I'm so sorry."

She nodded almost imperceptibly. He could feel the empty phrases in his throat and hated himself because nothing he could say would change anything.

"If there's anything I can do . . ." came out involuntarily. However much he wished that he could actually do something, Tell couldn't bear the banality of the phrase.

"It's strange."

She turned to look out of the window. Dark clouds hovered over the roofs, as if they were just waiting for the opportunity to burst and spill their entrails over the town.

"For all these years I've . . . not ignored Gustav's feelings, perhaps, but certainly I haven't bothered about them enough to change my priorities. I have been incredibly selfish. And now his feelings are the only thing I can think about, now I . . . And yet I still can't behave any differently from the way I've always behaved. Somehow I still have to follow my old patterns."

She was silent for so long that Tell got the feeling she'd forgotten he was there, until she took a deep breath and went on: "I feel as if I've let him down. How could it turn out this way, Christian? With love, I mean. That you choose to live your life with someone — someone you love — but their perceptions always seem to be the direct opposite of your own?"

Her cheeks were flushed.

"Maybe it's just what you said," mumbled Tell, even if he had realised the question was rhetorical. "Love." *Not that I know much more about it.*

She shook her head.

"Now, of course, he thinks it's obvious — well, I suppose it *is* obvious — that I should give up work on the grounds of ill health and spend my . . . my remaining time at home. Gustav and Björnberg have ganged up on me, and it hasn't even occurred to them that I would choose to do anything different. And the worst thing is that I can't do it. Do you understand? I ought to be taking the chance to pay him back, to show Gustav that I really do want to get to know him all over again, and that I do value him and everything we've somehow managed to build together over the years, but now more than ever I feel I have to be selfish. I'm finding it harder than ever to imagine giving up my job and just sitting at home waiting for death. I think I have to hang on here until they cart me off."

They jumped at the sound of a knock on the door. Karin Beckman poked her head around. She was clearly sensitive enough to pick up on the muted atmosphere because she apologised and was about to close the door when Östergren waved her in.

"It's fine. I've got time."

"It was actually Tell I wanted a word with." She took a step into the room. "We've heard from forensics on the Jeep from Ulricehamn. The wear on the tyre corresponds to the tracks at the scene of the murder, and there are six different fingerprints inside the car which are pretty clear. They've also found traces of blood."

With a supreme effort of will, Tell forced himself back to rational thought.

"OK. Check the database to see if the fingerprints belong to anyone we know. And contact the rental company for the names of the other people who've hired the car so that we can eliminate them. Bring them in and take their fingerprints."

Beckman nodded impatiently. Tell guessed that she didn't appreciate being instructed in basic police work in front of Östergren but it couldn't be helped. Tell needed to hear his own voice regaining some measure of control.

"Try to put a face to every print, or at least those who hopefully reserved in their own name," he droned on. "And don't forget that one of the prints probably belongs to Berit Johansson herself — she cleaned the cars, after all. Check her husband too, or whoever the other Johansson is."

Beckman gave an irritated snort. She disappeared when the mobile phone on Östergren's belt rang, and she indicated that she had to take the call. Tell nodded and got up to leave. His legs were so heavy he could barely lift them.

It was exactly four steps to the door.

CHAPTER
FORTY-FOUR

1955

The carefully maintained facade stood him in good stead with the pretty girl who had been detailed to help him. According to the social worker, he was entitled to support in the home as long as his mother was in the funny farm, which was where she had been ever since Maya's inexplicable death. Of course, it was inexplicable only to an imbecile. The doctor with the well-practised expression of empathy ought to have got an Oscar for his performance when it turned out that the equipment keeping Maya alive had for some reason been turned off for a period of time — after the nurse on the night shift had done her final rounds, and before the morning shift came on duty.

Deep in those eyes Sebastian could see that Dr Snell knew exactly what had caused the "temporary and extremely regrettable, inexplicable and totally unacceptable failure of the technical equipment". He almost felt sorry for the doctor, who had muttered something about how technology can never be one hundred per cent reliable, and how Maya's body had made its own decision to put an end to its artificial existence. As if he really believed that Maya was in any condition to make

399

a choice. It was stupid, particularly in view of the fact that had been Dr Snell's main argument for letting Maya die: she would never be able to think, feel or know anything again. He had said the decision rested with the relatives, but all the time it had been obvious where he stood on the issue.

Sebastian was grateful that Dr Snell had decided to avoid any accusations, but he was also upset on his mother's behalf because the doctors were treating her like someone who was a bit simple. As if she really believed they would allow the technology used to keep someone alive to be knocked out by some bloody power cut.

It was also perfectly clear that Solveig knew it was Sebastian who had nudged Maya across the threshold into the kingdom of the dead. He still hadn't found the courage to meet her eyes.

In the company of other people — for example during the laboured conversations with the family counsellor — she chose to lower her eyelids when she was forced to turn to her son. Sebastian was well aware of the rage burning beneath the smooth surface. He only had to glance at her for the exposed skin on his face to be seared as if by a flame. They had both chosen not to be alone together since Maya had stopped living.

Now he was taking things one day at a time. Amina, with her doelike eyes, came for two hours a day to help him "structure his everyday life", as she had put it when they sat at the kitchen table to plan their "joint project". What she actually did was take care of his laundry, clean up the messes he made, do the shopping and cook for him. It was as if he had gone from being a teenager to being an old man in one enormous stride.

He also noticed that the aim was for her to try to establish some kind of rapport with him. He had been there before — often enough to recognise the tentative questions from an anxious adult with a sense of responsibility. He could live with that; he was whatever he chose to show them. That applied to both Amina and the social worker. As usual he navigated through their statements and questions with playful ease. They could come into his home and do whatever they had to do to make themselves feel better, ask their questions and believe his answers, but the person he was deep inside had nothing to do with them. It never had done. He wasn't like Maya. Or Solveig. They opened themselves up time after time.

Still, Amina was very pleasant to look at. And the mask he wore was impressive, as usual. It was enough to be calm and collected, and to throw in a few episodes of teenage angst from time to time, with tear-filled eyes. That satisfied their inflated egos.

Amina tried to give the impression that she knew how teenagers thought and felt. She must have been a teenager herself not that long ago, but she spoke using her professional experience as her starting point — not that she could have had much of that. It didn't particularly bother Sebastian. He couldn't help innocently asking her how long she had been working, just to see her ears go red when she confessed that she wasn't yet qualified.

In order to ease her discomfort he confided in her that he was dreading the day Solveig came home from hospital. He didn't want to be alone on that day. Amina immediately promised to keep in touch with Solveig's doctor and agreed to be there to hold his hand when his mother was discharged. He could see her making a note in her internal diary: *Established rapport*. If there was one thing Sebastian had learned, it was that people, in general, were entirely predictable.

"You're a strong person, Sebastian," she had said in the embarrassed tone of someone who wasn't used to making such pronouncements about strangers. But they got used to it, social workers. Soon she too would have no problem poking her nose into everything. So it was Amina who told Sebastian that his mother was emerging from the mists. Suddenly Solveig had sat bolt upright in bed — as if she had temporarily broken free from the chains of her medication — and stated that she was no longer in touch with either her sorrow or her joy. For some time her mind had been dulled by strong tranquillisers, but no more.

Of course the main aim of the medication had been to spare her the experience of a grief that was clearly too much to bear. The medical team felt it was still early days, but she maintained she was ready to confront her demons. That was how she put it.

Amina sounded as if she thought this was a good thing.

Sebastian did his best to look relieved, which of course was the normal thing to do. Relieved that his mother was leaving her apparent insanity behind.

"She wants to come home straight away," said Amina. "To you, Sebastian. I think it was the thought of you that made her decide to fight, instead of giving up. And of course I'm here during the period of transition. You know that. If you want to talk, I'm here for you."

The first thing Solveig did when she got home was change the locks, as if she wanted to shut out the creature with the glassy eyes and the grey hair in a messy clump at the back of her head. That same morning she went to the hairdresser for a subtle ash-blonde tint, her hair cut into a pageboy style which was much more appropriate to her age. When she arrived home she was wearing a green corduroy dress he had never seen before, and glasses, which meant that the characteristic peering was gone. She really did look much better.

"Well, look at this," she said, casting a critical eye over the spotless hallway. "Thank you, you can go now."

Amina, feeling slightly confused, was politely but firmly ushered out on to the landing, and the door was shut in her face.

Once her hesitant footsteps had died away down the stairs, the atmosphere in the hallway was so thick you could have cut it with a knife. Solveig dusted off her hands.

"Dear me, Sebastian. Right, now I'm going to start on the housework. Then you can go shopping. And I'll make dinner. Then we can settle down in front of the TV."

"Mum . . ."

She immediately started frenetically cleaning the kitchen.

"Mum's home again. I'm not going to say a word about how quickly I was replaced, and by a younger model too — much easier on the eye."

She was still avoiding direct eye contact. She laughed, a brief, introverted laugh, then started emptying the kitchen cupboards and wiping her absence out of every single corner.

"It isn't your fault, Sebastian. You're getting to that age now. You're cast in the same mould as every other man: more banal with every passing day. Disloyal. Faithless. Fixated on superficial things . . . physical desires."

"Mum, this business with Maya —" Sebastian began, but stopped dead as she spun around and exposed him to her burning eyes.

"Not one word, Sebastian. We are not going to say one single word about that."

A couple of weeks later, with Dr Snell's encouragement, they reported the hospital and the doctors for the professional negligence that had allowed life to slip through Maya's fingers.

CHAPTER
FORTY-FIVE

2007

Fifteen years ago he had been thirty, and they had thought he was ancient. Seja hadn't expected him to have an insight into the secret world of the visitors' books and their coded chronicles. And even if the man now sitting opposite her had flicked through the books from time to time, it was likely that he had dismissed the love poems as rubbish, the implied suicide threats as an exaggeration on the part of narcissistic adolescents desperate for attention, and the overblown political discussions as being copied straight out of a basic course in sociology for year 11 students.

It was possible that he and his companions might have appreciated the skilfully executed drawings in ink or pencil; they might even have been able to guess which of the perpetrators would later apply to the various art colleges in the city. They were usually pictures of other customers in the café: a young woman with dreadlocks hunched over a glass of tea, a gang of boys all wearing the same uniform — a black suit bought at Myrorna, a long black coat and a hat just like the one Tom Waits always wore.

The owners of the café at the Northern Station had presumably had no idea what a cult they were starting when they bought the first A4 hardcover notebook on an impulse and placed it in one of the deep window recesses. And indeed the man opposite expressed both suspicion and surprise when he heard what they wanted.

"I thought you were looking for a job," he explained, running a hand through his hair, which appeared to be rigid with wax. "We've got an advert out — for a waitress. I don't suppose you'd be interested?"

Seja and Hanna shook their heads politely.

"Have you still got the books? Or does anyone else who was working here at that time?"

He leaned back in the leather armchair.

"You all went through a hell of a lot of those books. I think we ended up having to buy a new one every other week for several years. I'm sure you must realise we haven't kept them all; in fact I don't know why we ever kept any of them, but . . ."

He beamed and looked at Seja as if she had won the lottery.

"You're in luck. I happen to know that Cirka saved a pile of them, for sentimental reasons. It was a part of what we did in those days. They were kind of in tune with the people who came in, all those kids with their artistic ambitions. I mean, I'm no psychologist or any-thing, but it has to be a good thing for kids to be able to express themselves, doesn't it? And some of them had real talent, you could see that."

406

He gazed intently at Seja for a few seconds, then made his decision.

"I knew it. I definitely recognise you. How old were you back then?"

"Sixteen, seventeen."

Seja squirmed. It was many years since she had stopped feeling comfortable about spilling her innermost thoughts in front of people she hardly knew. She searched her memory in vain for some idea of the contributions she might have left in those books. But she had used an alias, and she doubted if the man opposite her was sufficiently well informed to know what it was.

To her relief he turned to Hanna.

"What was your name? Hanna? Not Hanna Andersson?"

"Aronsson."

"That's it. I definitely remember you — you were . . . I think you were at some of the gigs I put on. Velvet? Magasin 12? And you were with my mate Mange for a while, if I remember rightly."

Hanna looked as if she didn't quite know whether to feel positive or uncomfortable. "I don't really remember. You know how it was — there was all kinds of stuff going on. The memories are a bit vague."

He sniggered and rubbed his hand over his stubble.

"Too right. And you kids were pretty wild, as far as I remember."

"Cirka," Seja reminded him; she'd had just about enough of this. She folded her arms to show that he could skip the small talk.

"You can go over to her place if you want, she lives quite close. I can give her a ring and tell her you're coming. Or I can ask her to bring the books when she comes over in a couple of hours — if she's still got them, that is."

While they had been talking to the bar owner the sun had found its way through the clouds. Its rays were reflected in the chrome tables out on the pavement, and shimmered against the window of the café opposite. Outside a group of girls sat stoically sipping hot drinks in tall glasses wrapped in paper napkins. They were shivering in spite of the woollen blankets around their shoulders.

Seja and Hanna toyed with the idea of having a quick coffee — indoors — but decided instead to have something to eat once they had picked up the notebooks from Cirka.

The map the bar owner quickly scrawled on a napkin led them to an address on Kungshöjd, just a stone's throw from the bar, as he had said. They followed narrow alleyways and flights of steps from Kungsgatan to a stone building high above the sea that looked as though it had been built some time around 1900. They admired the view of the city and the harbour before ringing the doorbell.

"I've turned the whole room upside down."

At first sight Cirka Nemo hadn't changed. As teenagers they had admired her and the fact that she occupied her own space with confidence, despite her small stature. She was still just as small, slender and angular, but her dyed black hair now formed a cloud around her face. The clothes clinging to her thin body could have been the same ones she had worn back then; the style was just as timeless as the decor in her tiny one-room apartment.

"I just found the granny boots I bought in London when I was nineteen. How cool are they?"

She held up a pair of shabby button boots in bright orange. Seja nodded obediently, quietly amazed at how life turned out. Here she stood in Cirka Nemo's apartment, being treated as an equal. And Cirka didn't seem at all surprised at their strange errand; perhaps that was because strange things were just a part of her everyday life?

As a teenager Seja had admired this woman simply for her unambiguous air of authority, although most people had seemed worldly-wise compared with her contemporaries — girls still nervously dabbing Clearasil on those stubborn spots on their forehead. Confidence was sexy — she still thought so — but after blinking the teenage dust from her eyes she couldn't help noticing the hard lines around Cirka Nemo's mouth. Or the unpleasant smell from the overflowing rubbish bin in the tiny kitchen area — just like the one Seja had in her first student apartment when she was twenty.

She would guess Cirka's age as at least double that. When she wasn't smiling, those lines drew the corners of her mouth down towards her chin, and the skin beneath it was starting to slacken. The roots of her hair were peppered with grey. Seja couldn't help inspecting this woman as if she were under a magnifying glass. The passing of the years was never so tangible as when you examined a fragment of your own past face to face: in one way unchanged, in another bearing no resemblance to how it used to be. This encounter made Seja realise that she was also someone else now: no longer the insecure teenager who had sweated buckets every time she was spoken to by someone who, in the twisted hierarchy of a teenage girl's world, was worth more than her.

"They were right at the back, and that's where the notebooks from the café were as well, otherwise they would have been chucked out long ago. You can't afford to be nostalgic when you live in an apartment that only measures thirty metres square."

They took her point. The little flat was full from floor to ceiling, mainly with vinyl records. But it seemed not much had changed since the late 80s, the golden age of artificial silk and crushed velvet. One wall was painted black and strewn with luminous stars, and the space that remained around the record collection was taken up by framed posters of the Clash, Nina Hagen, the Cure, Sisters of Mercy, Nick Cave. An unmade mattress lay directly on the floor, and on top of it was a pile of battered notebooks with black covers.

Seja recognised them at once.

"I was absolutely crazy about Woody."

Hanna's expression was so veiled that Seja couldn't help laughing. They had moved from the Hungarian

410

restaurant, where they had had pea soup and sausage casserole with green chilli and jambalaya, and had settled down in the espresso bar next door.

"You don't have to be a genius to work that out, reading between the lines." Seja was referring to a number of comments written below Woody's drawings, for which Hanna was responsible. "Hannami. Where does the *mi* come from, anyway?"

Hanna rolled her eyes.

"Hannami, God how stupid. Maria is my middle name. I remember introducing myself that way for a while — Hanna Maria. Hannami was a kind of abbreviation. I even tried to change it legally, but to do that you need the signature of your guardian. Mum refused, of course, and it's probably just as well."

"Yes, but honestly. Listen to this: *Your drawings touch my soul, Woody. If you think everything is meaningless, then you are WRONG! . . . In the darkest hour, when you feel there is no one to comfort you, just remember I am there for you. Hannami.*"

Hanna shuddered. "How embarrassing! I thought I was being so discreet. And deep. But he was brilliant at drawing, you have to admit that."

They had spent a couple of hours ploughing through the material. From behind the counter the café owner was beginning to stare at their empty coffee cups so they bought a second round to appease her. Unfortunately they had failed to find the list of aliases they both thought they remembered at the back of each book.

The first book was from 1991, before their time. *Girl* and *Hannami* didn't appear until the following year, first sporadically and tentatively, as if they were waiting to check the response before throwing themselves to the wolves. Gradually their contributions became more personal. In some places there were sections that resembled an official exchange of letters or a political debate between Seja and *Crab*, who claimed to be an anarchist, while Seja chose to describe herself as a socialist. She read with fascination. Even if many of the arguments were naive, others were well thought through and interesting to follow.

At least we thought about the world. She couldn't help comparing this with the young today, obsessed with reality TV and interested in nothing but what people looked like and the functions on their mobile phones. For the time being Seja allowed herself to disregard the fact that she and her friends had been at least as self-obsessed, their political involvement as much of a fashion statement as the music and the interest in art.

"She used to draw too," Seja suddenly remembered. "The girl in the white leather jacket. I remember mentioning it to her, that time I talked to her at the party. I said she drew really well. Let's check all the drawings."

They flicked back and forth through the books, somewhat disheartened that what they had in front of them was just a fraction of the hoard the staff must have had when they closed the café. It was perfectly possible that what they were looking for wasn't even in these books, that the work of the girl in the white leather jacket had been thrown away many years ago. In which case Hanna and Seja's efforts would be in vain.

"This one ought to be on display in a museum or the city library," said Hanna, reading out a short poem about unrequited love. "Don't you think so? An exhibition about the thoughts and feelings of teenagers. About first love, unrequited love, sex. The meaning of life, angst, happiness and togetherness. Teen culture uncensored. Isn't it fascinating?"

"Yes . . . but hang on . . ."

Seja was holding a picture that folded out from a page in the notebook. It showed a curvaceous naked woman standing in front of a mirror. However, it was not the woman's reflection that appeared, but a wolf standing on its hind legs, its slavering jaws wide open. The drawing was on a loose sheet of paper that had been stuck in the book with something that looked like chewing gum.

"You see?" Seja said eagerly, pointing to a squiggle in one corner of the mirror. She had almost missed the signature because it was in the middle of the picture rather than in the corner. "I think it says *Tingeling*. Hanna, I'm absolutely certain that was her alias, the girl in the white leather jacket. Tingeling. I remember now. She signed all her pictures that way, right in the middle of the picture."

They studied the drawing in silence.

"Excuse me!" The café owner's voice brooked no contradiction. "I'm going to have to ask you to leave if you're not going to order anything else. You have to make way for other customers."

Seja and Hanna looked meaningfully at the row of empty bar stools but didn't feel like starting an argument.

"We're just going," said Seja, smiling as sweetly as she could. Unfortunately *just going* didn't appear to cut it, judging by the death stare she got in return. She glanced at her watch and realised they had been sitting there for several hours. The small of her back ached as they gathered their things together.

Outside Hanna looked at her own watch. "God, I promised the babysitter I'd be back over an hour ago!" She raced across Grönsakstorget with her jacket flapping open. Seja stood there for a while with the heavy bag of books. It was slowly getting dark. She ought to go over to Nils Erikssonsplats before the buses started running less frequently as the evening timetable took over but it went against the grain to stop now when she felt so close to finding the answer to the questions that had been swirling around in her head.

Now she knew the alias of the girl in the white leather jacket: Tingeling. As she spoke the name out loud the picture in her memory became much clearer. A finely chiselled face with a small mouth, the upper lip a little too thin in relation to the lower to be aesthetically pleasing. Tousled multicoloured hair. Skinny legs in torn stockings, layer upon layer with fishnets on top. Heavy shoes. Attitude, but who had the courage to drop the prickliness and be themselves at sixteen? The last time they met, however, she had

414

seemed noticeably less keen to make a statement and she had been wearing a man's black coat.

Seja walked slowly down to the canal and perched on the edge of a wet bench. The sound of music poured out of the Bärså bar on Kungsportsavenyn as the door opened and new customers arrived or left.

Only one of the notebooks had been completed after the fateful year: on the spine it said *NORTHERN STATION 1996–7*. That ought to have been too late. And yet it was in this book that Tingeling's name came up from time to time. The letters seemed to stumble over one another as Seja read, frantically flicking back and forth with frozen fingers. *Where did she go? What happened to her — was it true that something terrible had happened? Was it rape?* Many had wanted to pay tribute to her name with a poem or a verse from some song. Fear, grief and the desire for sensationalism burned between the lines. Even if the writers had known each other more through their writing than personally, it was clear that they felt a strong bond with each other. That was also how Seja remembered it.

Most seemed to believe that Tingeling had taken her own life, some that she had died of an overdose. Others expressed themselves more cryptically, hinting that a crime might lie behind her disappearance; someone had started this rumour and the ripples had spread. But no one seemed to know for sure. No one seemed to have been with her that evening when she disappeared.

Seja carried on reading until the dampness penetrated through her jeans and her hands were stiffened with cold from a sudden icy blast of wind. The restaurant boat *Åtta Glas* moved almost imperceptibly on the water. That was when she found what she was looking for.

There it was, the list she had kept seeing in her mind's eye, conscientiously written out by someone who clearly liked order and neatness. Her heart began to beat faster as she searched feverishly among the names for something that sounded familiar. Many had not filled in their details on the blank line following their alias, wanting to preserve their anonymity, refusing to accept that their given name was any more real than the one they had chosen for themselves, or perhaps they simply hadn't seen the list. Others, in contrast, had filled in their addresses and telephone numbers, perhaps hoping to create an extended network of like-minded souls.

She had filled hers in: *Girl: Seja Lundberg.* That was why she had been so sure of the list's existence. With her heart pounding she searched among the names, and there it was. *Tingeling: Maya Granith.* There was a Borås address, which definitely decided the matter. It was her.

Seja took out her mobile to ring Christian Tell. Her frozen fingers slipped on the keys and she dropped the phone on the ground between her feet. The interruption left space for reflection. She sat there with the phone on her knee listening to the misdial tone, before slowly sliding it back into her pocket.

There would be time enough to talk to him, face to face.

CHAPTER
FORTY-SIX

Under normal circumstances stress turned him into a miraculous organiser. He was like his father in that respect: he hated doing nothing. During periods when he was feeling more contented he could compromise on orderliness — he sometimes even made a point of it — while his father had remained the very personification of a pedant. However, when the mountain of commitments and unfulfilled promises rose above his head, that was when he turned into his father in every respect. At that point order and neatness became restful, and was the only strategy that enabled him to cope.

On the one hand he loathed it all — the diligence, the conceit, the smugness — and had done so ever since he realised this was a psychological defence mechanism for his father, who had used it as a point of honour and a reason to criticise those around them. On the other hand, like most men approaching middle age, Tell noticed that he was becoming more like his father with every passing day, and despite the fact that he loathed the lack of spontaneity and creativity caused by such pedantry, he was also starting to notice that people who lacked the ability to plan really annoyed him. As a young adult he had convinced himself that the quality he valued most, and the one he wanted to strive towards, was tolerance. He hadn't got there yet, and often felt he was moving further away from his goal.

When a murder enquiry wasn't going anywhere it stressed him out; it was always the same. As time passed, he felt a personal sense of responsibility that the crime hadn't been cleared up. Responsibility to the relatives, of course. But also to his colleagues and superiors. He slept without dreaming. He noticed that he was thinking differently. He made an effort to think in wide circles around the investigation, and often did so at the expense of other mental activity. He became more brusque in his dealings with people. Rational. Emotionally muted, in order to use his energy where it was needed most. What was left was a fairly isolated individual; he was well aware of that. After all, nobody said that being aware of your faults meant that you could change them. And he wasn't even sure he wanted to change. Like his father he had found a strategy for survival that seemed to work. He had solved a large number of cases. After many years in the job he knew his own patterns of behaviour very well, and on one level he accepted them.

Therefore he couldn't help noticing that he was now diverging from his routines. Despite being at a critical stage of the investigation he had acted not only spontaneously but completely irrationally. He was sitting in a shabby pizzeria in Olofstorp. It was the best place he could find for thinking things over, or to put it more accurately, it was the only place that served coffee on the way out to Stenared and Seja Lundberg. Because of course that was where the car seemed to be steering itself.

He had called in to the police station only briefly that morning. He had made his apologies for missing the morning briefing on the grounds that he had an urgent errand, and had got in the car with the vague idea of paying a visit to Maria Karlsson. Along with her husband Gösta, she had been the first to take in Olof Bart, or Pilgren, when he was taken into care by social services at the age of six. According to the information he had been given, Gösta Karlsson had died unexpectedly four years later, and Maria had decided to give up being a foster-parent. She was still registered at an address in Öckerö, but Tell had not phoned in advance to prepare her for his arrival. In certain cases it felt better to turn up unannounced, thus depriving the person to be interviewed of the opportunity to sift through and pick over their memories in a way that was often detrimental to a police enquiry.

Before deciding to make this unannounced visit to Maria Karlsson, Tell had checked out the chances of getting hold of Marko Jaakonen, the man with whom Olof's mother had had a relationship. It turned out that Jaakonen had hanged himself in prison seven years after Olof was taken into care. Not that Tell imagined these events were in any way related: Jaakonen had gone down for the premeditated murder of a known drug pusher, and was clearly unable to live with the guilt. Or something like that. Anyway, that was a dead end.

On top of everything else, Östergren had taken Tell to one side and questioned the wisdom of undertaking such a detailed investigation of the background of one of the murder victims. The only answer Tell could give her was that it was down to intuition.

The interview with Thorbjörn Persson, the contact person involved in finding homes for young people, had told them that Bart had returned to Olofstorp after serving twelve months in Villa Björkudden and spending three years under a supervision order in a one-room flat in Hjällbo. Persson remembered it all very clearly. Since Bart had been a model tenant he was in line for a first lease in his own name, but he had informed his social worker he had managed to rent a small cottage somewhere out in the sticks around Olofstorp. The social worker had tried to persuade him to reconsider, because even in those days it was difficult to secure a lease if you were an unemployed person with a criminal record. But Bart had stood firm. He didn't want to live in an apartment. He wanted to live on his own in the forest. This had made Thorbjörn Persson uneasy, and despite the fact that his job was officially over as soon as Bart was signed off, he had kept in touch with him for a couple of years. Given him a call now and again. Taken a drive over to Olofstorp to see how things were going.

Persson had shrugged his shoulders when Tell asked what life had really been like for twenty-year-old Olof Pilgren, as he was still called at the time.

"Well . . . he was a bit different, was Olof. It seemed a bit lonely out there in the middle of nowhere, but it

420

was OK. He made a couple of friends, I think, a couple of lads that he used to hang out with all the time. Sven and Magnus, Thomas and Magnus. Or was it Niclas?"

He had also forgotten the surnames, if he had ever known them. He didn't know what had happened after that. After a couple of years Bart had broken off contact for no real reason; he just thought they didn't need to discuss things any more. He was doing fine on his own. And it was true, he was. He had worked his way out of the social care system and Thorbjörn Persson had allowed him his newly earned freedom.

Tell had sent Karlberg to take Persson for a drive around the Olofstorp area to see if he could find the house Bart had rented when he was twenty. Something told him they would find the answer to the mystery in Olof Bart's past, which was colourful to say the least; that there was more chance of coming across something useful in his history than by putting Waltz under the microscope. Not that they had forgotten the photographer, but having turned both his team's brains and their resources inside out, Tell had almost given up hope of finding a link between the two murder victims.

But when it came down to it he hadn't actually driven out to Öckerö. He hadn't even driven in the right direction. Instead he took the Marieholm road out towards Gråbo. However, when he caught sight of the turning for Olofstorp and the road that carried on out to Stenared, he had got cold feet, and had kept on going until the speedometer was showing 120 kilometres per hour and he reached Sjövik.

He sat in the car for a good hour, gazing out across Lake Mjörn from a parking area close to the water. Cracked ice floes lay along the shoreline. In the end his breath had produced so much condensation on the car windows he could no longer see the lake. He took this as a sign that it was time to make a move.

Slowly he set off in the direction of the city once more. The pizzeria had looked reassuringly safe, and he convinced himself that he wasn't committing to anything by driving into the village. The place had just opened; he would sit down and think through the alternatives, weighing the pluses against the minuses.

Drive over to Seja's place and try to explain. Tell her about the chaos she had aroused within him and about Östergren's cancer and his father's agonies, which seemed well on the way to becoming his own. Or drive back to work and say sod the lot of it, including the fact that Östergren was dying.

Was it the fear of death that had struck him like a blow to the back of the knees?

He had heard that a certain amount of stress sharpened the senses and made it easier to concentrate. However, too much stress had the opposite effect: you lost focus and made errors of judgement. Acted without thinking things through. This terrified him: the idea that he might suddenly find he couldn't rely on his own judgement.

He felt the urge to order a beer instead of the coffee that had stopped steaming in front of him, but he fought the craving. It was still morning. He was on duty. He called the station to check on the latest news.

Nobody answered on Karlberg's extension, so he tried Beckman instead. She picked up just as he was about to ring off.

"I'm in the middle of something right now, Christian; I'll call you back," she said, and rang off.

He took a couple of sips of the ghastly coffee. A small pallid square of chocolate lay on the saucer, and he ate it out of sheer restlessness.

A few minutes later his mobile vibrated on the blotchy mock-marble table. The sound reverberated off the walls of the empty café.

"Yes?"

"Beckman here. I was interviewing one of the people whose fingerprints were in the Cherokee from Ulricehamn when you called."

"Have you spoken to all of them?"

"Two of them. I can't get hold of someone called Bengt Falk. A couple of prints came from Berit Johansson, the owner. A Sigrid Magnusson and a Lennart Christiansson have given us prints that match the ones in the car. So we still haven't identified two of the sets."

"They could belong to Bengt Falk, the false Mark Sjödin, or someone else altogether. So with a bit of luck we've got the killer's fingerprints. All we have to do now is find the killer."

"Yes . . ." Beckman sighed. "If only we could get together everyone who had featured in the victims' lives and take their fingerprints. Then we might find the answer."

"We'll find it in time," said Tell, impressing himself with the reassurance he was suddenly able to summon up in the face of Beckman's doubts.

All at once he was overcome by the almost irresistible urge to talk to Beckman about his conversation with Östergren, but he realised he would be breaking a confidence.

"What about Waltz's sons, then?" he said. "Is Karlberg there?"

"No. But I think he's got them coming in this afternoon. Apparently Maria Waltz started shouting about lawyers."

Tell whistled. "Interesting. Well, we'll see what that's about. I presume she's going to sit in when Karlberg talks to the one who's still a minor then?"

"No idea. I can ask Karlberg to ring you if you're not coming back today."

"No, no," Tell said quickly. "There's no need. I'll be in a bit later, I just . . . I had a few things to sort out . . ."

His voice gave way.

"No problem. See you later."

He made his decision on the spot. It was now or never.

He passed the entrance to the crime scene. It only took ten minutes to drive from there to Seja's house. Once he had finally summoned up the courage to go down into the hollow, over the footbridge and up the slope to the cottage, it was an anticlimax to see there were no lights on. He stood there on the lawn, trying to decide what to do next. Just to be sure, he knocked on the door. It annoyed him that she wasn't there now, now he was finally ready, especially as he could see her car parked up the road. At the same time he was relieved that circumstances had postponed the conversation.

He pulled open the stable door and the silence explained everything: she was out riding. That meant there was still a chance of seeing her.

He was gloomily conscious of the fact that he had ignored her messages and kept her on tenterhooks by making himself unavailable in every way. This was entirely due to his own cowardice and lack of backbone. He was bright enough to realise that she was probably furious, or disappointed. And disappointed was worse, without any doubt.

When he discovered that the cottage door wasn't locked, it settled the matter. He went in and sat down in the kitchen to wait, grateful for the initial warmth but pondering the casual negligence that made a person leave their home without taking even the most basic security measures. Perhaps she was the kind of person who thought nothing unpleasant could ever happen in her neighbourhood. As a police officer he was definitely not prone to that kind of naivety. In fact, he had reached the point where few examples of people's inventiveness when it came to damaging and stealing one another's property could surprise him.

The wall clock ticked away. Once he became aware of it, it became impossible to think of anything else. He tried taking off his coat in order to avoid giving the impression that he was temporarily visiting her life in more than one respect, but as the fire was not lit, the house was unpleasantly cold. It was difficult for him to understand how someone could choose to live like this: far from the comforts of modern life, entertainment and other people.

The waiting soon became unbearable. If he lit a fire, made some coffee, put on a CD to drown out the ticking of the clock, it would look as if he were making himself at home, which might annoy her — as if he were overstepping the mark, as if he thought he had rights but not obligations.

An enormous amount of time seemed to have passed. Looking at the clock wasn't a great deal of help, since he hadn't the faintest idea when he had sat down at the table and fixed his eyes on the path leading into the forest.

He moved into the other room in the hope that the chill from the hallway would be less noticeable there. As he was about to sit down on the sofa something caught his eye, drawing his attention to the desk. A world atlas lay open with a picture on top of it. He stared at the picture. It was printed on shiny photographic paper and was slightly out of focus, but there was no doubting the subject matter: Lars Waltz, his head shot to pieces, lying on the gravel at his farm. Underneath the picture were some hastily scrawled comments which he couldn't make out, and the back was covered with fine, elegant but barely legible script. On closer inspection he thought it was written in Finnish.

A sound made him stiffen. What if Seja was back from her ride? He would be forced to confront her with the incomprehensible object in his hand. His thoughts were spinning far too quickly; he was shocked at seeing his two worlds come together so inexorably without understanding how or why. He discovered that his hand was shaking. Was Seja involved in some other way, apart from having driven Åke Melkersson to the scene of the crime? Had she actually been there at the farm already that morning?

A shadow passed across the windowsill, making him jump. It was only the cat. He still had a little time.

Only now did he recall the hesitation he had felt on the morning of the murder. He had found it difficult to put his finger on what it was, but something about Seja Lundberg and Åke Melkersson's account of what had happened when they found the body had seemed wrong. Tell had found holes in their story, and it had turned out that they were lying. He had intended to question them both again at a later stage, to see if there were any further lies embedded in their statements, to break them down and see what was hiding underneath. But it wasn't unusual for people to lie during questioning; they often withheld information for the most banal and vain of reasons.

He hadn't followed up his plan, and he knew exactly why: bad judgement. Now he would have to suffer for his mistake, and in quite a different way from the one he had imagined.

Tell took two long strides across the floor and gazed out into the garden. The stable door was still closed. He thought fast. Somewhere in the house there had to be something, anything, that would provide further

427

explanation. Wherever it was, he intended to find it, even if he had to turn the entire house upside down. He opened the window so that he would be able to hear her coming.

Tell rummaged among the papers on the bookcase and on the desk and found several articles that she had started writing and in some cases finished, but nothing that explained the picture from the scene of the crime. One drawer in the desk was locked; it took him a couple of minutes to find the key in the bottom of a pot on the windowsill. The drawer contained a thin folder. He was so agitated that he had to read the two pages twice before he understood what he was looking at. The document appeared to be a synopsis of a longer text. Even if the brief sentences were more like questions, and even if he couldn't quite work out what it was that Seja Lundberg had withheld from him, there was enough information for a new idea to form in his head. It was obvious that she was involved in a way he didn't yet understand. But he was certainly going to find out.

He found the laptop pushed down between two coffee tables — she clearly had some idea of security after all. An eternity went by as the computer started up, only to deny him access. It was password protected. He glanced at the clock and wondered what time Lise-Lott Edell closed her shop. If he put his foot down he could be in Gråbo in fifteen minutes.

CHAPTER
FORTY-SEVEN

1997

She allowed herself to take the plastic cover off the bed twice a day, morning and afternoon. Without the cover, the smell of Maya would disappear within just a few months. Even now Solveig could tell that it was growing fainter each time she reverently folded back the shabby rose-patterned quilt which Maya had had since she was a child. Solveig laid her cheek against the sheet and took deep breaths — slowly and carefully, so that she wouldn't start coughing. She had even cut down on the cigarettes, because she wanted to preserve her sense of smell. Losing the ability to experience the smell of things would be like losing another part of Maya.

It would happen one day, inevitably. The particles from a human body did not remain for all eternity, and when that day came she would have to turn to something else. Maya's diary from when she was a little girl. Maya's clothes, which Solveig had hauled down from the attic, where they had been stored in bin bags. She had always had difficulty in throwing things away. She had always saved things, as if she had known all her life that there would come a day when she would be forced to cling to worldly objects in order to survive.

She had crammed her own clothes into the smaller wardrobes in the bedroom so that she could hang up Maya's in the dressing room. One item per coat hanger. The baby clothes were placed carefully in the blue-painted chest of drawers, the ripped punk gear in the middle of the rails and the outdoor clothes at the back next to the wall. She papered the walls with a ridiculously expensive dark purple wallpaper, then hung scarves on ornate gold hooks, along with the hats, berets and other accessories Maya had worn over the years, as if it were an exhibition in which every work of art symbolised an epoch in her daughter's all-too-short life.

Solveig spent most of her time in the dressing room. There was always plenty more to do. She was particularly pleased with the fitted carpet, which had also made a big hole in her savings. However, nothing was too good for Maya. It was important that everything was just right. Maya's colours. Her favourite materials. As long as Solveig was working, she could keep the tinnitus at bay and the panic at arm's length, well aware that the day the memory room was finished, she would be driven into the fire. But that day was far away, because there was still a great deal to do.

She had albums of photos to be sorted, enlarged and framed. She had boxes of Maya's music up in the attic; she would have to listen to it all to see what might be important. Every single lyric might contain those words Maya never had time to say. In her early teens music had been everything to Maya. She lived through her music, wallpapered her room with her idols, dressed like them, quoted them over and over again.

Solveig didn't know anything about music, and she definitely didn't know anything about the kind of music Maya listened to. But she realised that the words were at least as important as the melodies. Maya had written on her mirror with a black kohl pencil, and on the walls she had pinned up quotations written in red ink on rice paper, making the words into works of art. Solveig had never bothered to read them; her English wasn't as good as it had been. Nor had she realised before that it was important for her to understand them, those words, that they were potential routes into her daughter's innermost being. That they could provide answers to the questions she had never managed to ask.

There was no room for the crates of vinyl records in the dressing room so they had to go in the bedroom.

If in the past Solveig had regretted leaving the larger apartment in Rydboholm, she was now almost torturing herself to death. Maya's room was there, the room she grew up in — Maya was in every little detail. The marks on the wallpaper from the toothpaste she had decided to use to put up her posters. Inside the fitted wardrobe, where Maya had painted a landscape in tempera. Solveig had gone mad at the time, afraid she would have to pay the landlord to have the wall repainted when they moved out. The scratch marks at the bottom of the door made by that disgusting cat Maya had dragged home, the one that had caught ringworm and managed to infect them all before they got rid of the wretched animal.

Maya had only ever stayed in the new apartment on a temporary basis, so Solveig was trying to recreate something that had never existed. And there were new tenants living in Rydboholm these days. Maybe some other teenage girl in Maya's old room who played her music so loud that the walls bellied outwards and the neighbours complained. A girl who wasn't dead.

Eventually Solveig received Maya's possessions from the school, in a wooden crate with the address on a sticky label. It felt like receiving a coffin, and just as she was opening the lid she got the idea that it was Maya she would find inside. Lifeless, of course, but still a body to hold on to. Because she was terrified of forgetting.

She put the record player with the crates of albums. Only when she was so tired that her arms were aching, did she climb up on to her bed and start from the very beginning of the collection.

She tried to allow herself to be rocked into restfulness by the strange discordant music she had always loathed, telling herself that this was Maya's music, that it represented Maya's world and must be appreciated at all costs. Because Maya was irreproachable now. Perfect. Complete. Her death had ensured that this fact would never change.

While Solveig worked on her memorial, Sebastian gave his mother a wide berth. He rarely spoke directly to her, perhaps because he suspected that she only had ears for his sister's voice. Perhaps because his burden of guilt remained a silent agreement between them.

Sometimes he would sit a little way off, just watching. Occasionally he would be able to help in some way: holding a shelf while she screwed it into place, making coffee when she needed a break.

It wasn't only the physical things that had changed in the Granith household. For example, Sebastian had never seen his mother with so much energy; normally exhaustion was her signature, along with her infectious apathy and listlessness. He had often felt tired as soon as he walked in through the door. He and Maya had talked about it once: the way their home *sucked the strength* out of them both. It wasn't the only time they had discussed Solveig, but those were the words he remembered most clearly. Maya had said that Solveig sucked all the strength out of her. From time to time Sebastian was tempted to hurl her words in his mother's face, straight into that pale puffy face, the eyes bloodshot from the dust, the cheeks burning feverishly.

Maya hated you, you old cow. Got it? She hated you. You're remembering things that were never true. You remember that she loved you. That you were close. You think you were alike, you and Maya, but you were nothing like each other. Maya was strong, she was for real. You're nothing but crap, Mum. You're crap, and everybody knows it.

Of course he never said that. He had forfeited his right to have an opinion and he was well aware of that fact. Solveig now had the upper hand.

433

★ ★ ★

One morning she woke up as usual with a scream in her throat. The tablets produced such a heavy dreamless sleep that the arm she had been lying on was numb and useless. *Dead meat*, she thought as her numbed hand banged into the chest of drawers.

As soon as she hauled herself into a sitting position the scream began to work its way determinedly up her throat to await her decision: out through the mouth or stuck fast in the auditory canals like the cry of an animal in torment? There was nothing to be done about the tinnitus, according to one of the doctors she saw regularly. Avoid noisy environments. Which she did, of course. And he prescribed tranquillisers, either to reduce the noise level or for some other reason. She didn't really know. She took them anyway, but they didn't help much.

Her breathing was jagged, making her gasp for air. *Up you get, Solveig. Open the door. Walk through the hallway. Open the door of the dressing room just a little bit. Switch on the light.*

At the sight of her work she felt a temporary sense of calm spread through her body. The scream faded away. Her arm was slowly coming back to life, giving her pins and needles. She buried her nose in Maya's shabby white leather jacket. In some places the red lining had split and started to fray, so she decided to mend it. With slow movements she lifted down the hanger and pressed the jacket against her chest. She had no breathing problems now; she had found her project for the day.

434

Just as she was about to close the door, she saw it. She pushed aside the clothes to expose what she had glimpsed behind them.

The wall was covered in pictures, from the floor almost all the way up to the ceiling. She hadn't seen the collage for many years. It was battered at the edges, and had obviously been rolled up for some time.

Solveig ran her hand over the rough surface. She knew exactly how old the collage was. Maya had been eleven when she found a bag full of monthly magazines that someone had put out with the rubbish. Not the kind Solveig sometimes read, the cheaper ones, but thick glossy women's magazines with names like *Clic* and *Elle*, filled with reports on the latest fashions from Paris and interviews with film stars, artists and designers.

Maya had sat there for weeks with her nose buried in the magazines, reverently examining them as if they contained some kind of secret code. She had chosen pictures of slender women with pale skin and dark eyes, dressed in black and leaning against ancient trees; perfume adverts consisting of naked bodies in artistic poses; black men with bare torsos and gleaming white teeth with gold fillings; men in women's clothes; women in men's suits. Women with cheekbones to die for. She had snipped and glued for months before the collage was finally pronounced complete: an explosion of faces and bodies and colours. She had painted straight on to the pictures with pastel colours, capriciously altering them. She had stuck many pictures on top of one another with thick layers of fabric glue,

435

then torn away strips of the faces and bodies before the glue dried so that the picture underneath was partly exposed: a pair of eyes with a piercing gaze. A breast. A foot in the sand. A snake.

Solveig had not been pleased when Maya put up the collage in her room. She didn't appreciate the many pairs of eyes that seemed to be staring at her wherever she went. She knew this was because all the models had been looking straight into the camera when they were photographed. And that's why it didn't help when she pressed herself right against the wall next to the collage to avoid their scorn: they were still looking her straight in the eye. She also thought it was a little advanced for an eleven-year-old, all that bare skin.

She said so to Maya. *What's the matter with you? There's plenty of time for you to break your heart over all that kind of thing.*

Sebastian must have secretly kept it all these years and put it up during the night. He had chosen to contribute his treasure to the memory room. A lump of gratitude formed in her throat, and she had to clear it several times so that she wouldn't start crying. This was an acknowledgement on Sebastian's part. A small step along the road to reconciliation.

She padded across the floor and pushed open the door to his room.

That same afternoon, as Solveig was putting the finishing touches to the memory room, *she* knocked on the door. Solveig, who for a long time had found it difficult to distinguish clearly between daydream and

436

reality, thought at first that the tall woman in the long black coat was a product of her imagination. She simply didn't match the shabby stairwell, with her red-painted lips and the broad-brimmed hat that concealed a choppy, boyish haircut.

"At first I thought you were some kind of artist," Solveig said much later, and she meant it. Not that she thought the woman was particularly attractive — quite the opposite. According to the ideals with which she had grown up, girls were supposed to be sweet and slender and as transparent as elves. There was nothing elfin about this woman, with her wide full mouth and strong square jawline.

She had introduced herself as a friend of Maya, stepping inside with total confidence as if she already knew that she would be moving in. As if it didn't even occur to her that anyone would refuse.

In the hallway Solveig quickly became aware of the smell emanating from the woman's body, a faint but unmistakable aroma of cinnamon and woodsmoke. The woman unbuttoned her coat to take it off, and Solveig was enveloped in the sweet warmth that had been held within the fabric. It was almost intoxicating. She felt something that could be confused with a fleeting erotic attraction, swayed slightly and took a step back.

The stranger stopped dead, as if she had just become aware of the unexpected effect she was having on Solveig.

"Don't be frightened," she said quietly. "I just want to talk about Maya. I know something's happened to her, and I think I'll go under if I can't talk to someone about her."

Solveig grasped the woman's hand as a person in distress grasps the hand of their saviour, and led her into the dressing room without saying a word. Afterwards Solveig would regard her as being sent from heaven.

CHAPTER
FORTY-EIGHT

2007

Tell wanted to hit himself on the head with something hard, and would have done so if he had thought it would do any good.

How had he managed to lead a murder enquiry along such a narrow track that they had missed the simplest thing of all? If he hadn't illegally entered the home of one of the witnesses involved in the investigation, a witness he had also slept with and then neglected, since he was just as scared of her as he was of his boss, he would have let the team carry on digging deeper and deeper without realising that they were digging in completely the wrong place.

His confidence was at rock bottom. It took an enormous effort for him to go back to the station to start trying to put things right, to win back just a fraction of the time his thoughtlessness had cost them.

Karlberg was at the end of the corridor talking to a woman wearing a blue suit, and as Tell drew closer he could see that it was Maria Waltz. A couple of metres away stood two gangling creatures both wearing sullen looks as if they had the word "teenager" stamped on their foreheads. Although what else could you expect?

Their father had just been murdered and they had been brought in for questioning. Tell only hoped that Karlberg had had the presence of mind to formulate a plausible and inoffensive reason for the interview. If Maria Waltz had not been making such angry gestures he would no doubt have had the same confidence in his colleague as always, but her attitude made him wonder if Karlberg might have gone in too hard.

"They've only just lost their father . . ." he heard Lars Waltz's ex-wife say angrily, but she fell silent as Tell walked past and went over to her sons. Their expressions became even more blank, if that was possible, as he placed one hand on the shoulder of the older boy. At least he looked as if he were the older. The brothers were very alike, both in beige chinos and tight-fitting checked shirts.

Tell introduced himself and quietly expressed his condolences. The boy pushed his hair behind his ear. More than anything he seemed confused at being spoken to as an adult.

"It was a mistake to bring you here today," said Tell, speaking loudly enough for Maria Waltz to hear. "You can go home."

Karlberg was dumbfounded. Tell left without any further explanation. As he headed towards his office he could hear his colleague saying something lame about the police being in touch when they knew more or if they needed the boys' help. Dragging her bewildered sons behind her, Maria Waltz marched out of the station.

440

The sound of Karlberg's boots drew closer, and he appeared in the doorway.

"What the hell was all that about? I thought you told me to bring them in?"

"I did. But now I've changed my mind."

He slammed a bundle of A4 sheets on the desk and ripped them demonstratively in half in front of an increasingly bewildered Karlberg.

"Are you intending to explain, or are you just going to carry on ripping up paper? We do have a shredder, in case you didn't know."

Tell realised he might be trying Karlberg's patience a little too far.

"Bring the rest of the team to the conference room. I'll be there when I've gathered my thoughts."

Ten minutes later they were all waiting there. Since they had been forced to drop whatever they were doing without any explanation, they were both irritated and curious in equal measure. Tell couldn't resist making a Poirot entrance. Several people rolled their eyes at one another.

"I've gathered you all together because earlier today an idea struck me. I was — well, the how or why doesn't matter, but anyway it struck me that . . . I *think* we've been on the wrong track. No, not the wrong track, but we've been thinking about the wrong person all the way through this investigation. And it's not all that strange. We focused on one of the victims and his background and those around him. But we've been digging in the wrong bloody place. That's why we kept getting stuck or finding yet another dead end."

He looked triumphantly at the team but realised he was facing utter confusion.

"I may be wrong, but I think Lars Waltz was murdered by mistake. I also think there may be a link to a case that's already closed, but I'm not sure enough about that to say any more at this stage. I suspect the plan was to murder Lise-Lott's first husband, Thomas Edell. For some reason the murderer didn't know he was already dead, so instead he murdered the man he found in the car workshop . . ."

He waved his hand meaningfully in the air, and ended up pointing at Beckman.

"THOMAS EDELL — VEHICLE REPAIRS AND SCRAPYARD," she supplied. "The sign."

"Exactly, in the belief that he was in fact Thomas Edell."

A thoughtful silence descended over the room. Tell could feel his confidence returning.

"Why do I think this? Well, as you know, we've searched high and low for a link between the first and second victims. We've asked Lise-Lott if her husband Lars Waltz knew an Olof Bart, but not if her ex-husband Thomas Edell knew an Olof Pilgren. Are you with me? From '83 to '86 Olof Bart had a supervisor linked to his temporary accommodation. This was Thorbjörn Persson, who remembers that Olof had a friend called Thomas. I also talked to Lise-Lott on my way in, and she confirms that her ex-husband used to hang out

442

with someone called Pilen — which could easily be Pilgren."

Gonzales' eyebrows were firmly knitted in a scowl, but after a short silence Karlberg allowed himself to nod in agreement.

"OK, Tell, even if it does seem a bit off the wall. If we buy into the idea that the murderer was after Edell, we're still left with one important question — why? Motive and perpetrator. We're no further forward even if you are right. And if you hate somebody enough to want to kill them, it surely suggests some kind of obsession. Isn't it likely then that you'd be keeping an eye on the person, at least enough to know if they've been dead for . . . how long? Seven, eight years?"

"Yes," Tell conceded, "that's true. You're thinking it could be some kind of revenge attack on these two men."

"Yes. Are you thinking along a different line?"

"It's a little difficult for the rest of us to come up with something when the information you're giving us is so vague," Beckman interjected.

Tell seemed lost in thought. He nodded and stared at the door as if he were longing to escape from the room. He opened his mouth but closed it a second later without answering Karlberg's question. Suddenly he felt as if the looks his colleagues were giving him were much too challenging. He had things to do: he had to see Seja before he tackled anything else. He now regretted not staying in the house to wait for her. The sudden urge to act had misled him.

"What are you talking about, Tell?" came Bärneflod's irritated voice. He had sat in the corner in silence until now. "'The how or why doesn't matter . . .' Fuck that! Are we all in the same boat, or are you paddling your own fucking canoe here? Conducting a little enquiry of your own on the side? I mean, what the hell is going on here? Are you trying to solve the case all on your own? How the fuck can we work if we're not a team?"

He looked around the room seeking agreement but was met by total silence.

"Could we try to raise the level a little?" Karlberg tried to mediate, but Tell couldn't avoid noticing his hesitant expression.

Beckman clapped her hands together.

"We can't afford to sit here squabbling. Nor can we afford to ignore any possible leads. As Tell says, we haven't found a motive or any connection between Waltz and Bart. If we can prove that Edell and Bart's paths crossed, then of course we need to see where that takes us. And of course Tell will pass on his thoughts to us as soon as they're clear."

Tell stood up with a grateful look at Beckman, who rewarded him with an ambiguous grimace.

"Thank you. OK, so we change tack. We'll leave Lars Waltz in peace for the time being and concentrate on Thomas Edell: background, family, friends, job . . . I assume everybody knows what to drop and what to focus on. I suggest we regard this as a natural break and use the evening to go home and think about this new direction. We'll meet back here tomorrow, eight o'clock sharp."

444

"To start from the beginning all over again," added Bärneflod.

During the drive to Stenared Tell worked himself into a rage that had more to do with disappointment than anything else, a feeling that Seja had cheated in order to gain access to an area which was his alone. And, which was worse, there must have been a reason. She had failed to pass on to him information she had somehow acquired, even though she knew better than anyone how he had been tearing his hair out, trying to fit the pieces of the jigsaw together. That meant she didn't trust him.

He would have been even more angry if she had pretended she didn't know what he was talking about. At least she didn't do that, didn't shake her head and say she didn't know what he meant. Instead her reaction was unexpected in a completely different way: she was absolutely furious that he had gone into her house, that he had been prying among her things,.

"I can't believe you just walked in! Helped yourself! Opened drawers. SWITCHED ON MY COMPUTER!!! What were you looking for? Are you a detective inspector in my home as well? Am I a criminal?" Did he make a habit of going to bed with criminals, she asked him, to gain access to evidence? And he replied, without really thinking it through, that she didn't know what she was talking about, that she was bloody hysterical — she *was* actually hysterical, and for a fraction of a second he thought she was going to slap him.

Instead she went and sat down on the armchair by the fire, and put her head in her hands.

"You've searched my house. *You*. You even went through my underwear drawer. It's fucking sick."

"What's this *you*? Why do you have to keep saying *you* all the time?" he asked crossly, hating the whining undertone in his voice. "As if I were the last person who should be allowed to see your secrets."

"I just didn't think you'd do that," she said simply. "I hoped we were for real."

Silence fell over the room. A bird let out a harsh screech and took off from the top of a fir tree.

Tell felt a great tiredness descend over the whole situation, linked to the vast tiredness underlying every single quarrel he had ever had with women over the years. How many times had he said *Stop being so bloody hysterical*? He didn't know, but he was quite sure his words had never fallen on fertile ground.

He sank down in the armchair opposite Seja and tried to gather his thoughts, suppressing his natural impulse to get in the car and drive straight back to work. She had managed to make him feel slightly ashamed of himself, hysterical or not.

He *had*, in his manic state, gone through the drawer where she kept her underwear. Not that the underwear had interested him one iota at the time. At that moment the folder containing the photograph of Lars Waltz with his brains blown out had been the only thing on his mind, along with the text in Finnish and the document on the computer containing the name of Thomas Edell.

446

Part of him understood that she felt violated. But just as he accepted her indignation was partly justified, he also realised that she had cleverly made him forget his real reason for coming to see her.

He had been upset, *he* had been kept in the dark, and *he* was still furious, but he forced himself to calm down, because in spite of everything he realised he would never be able to get her to talk if he carried on in the same accusatory tone.

"Do you speak Finnish?"

She closed her eyes and shook her head as if she couldn't believe her ears.

"Do you?" he repeated.

"Yes," she said tersely and louder than necessary. "My mother was born in Finland."

She refused to look at him, clearly uncomfortable. Tell thought there was just a chance she was slightly embarrassed over her mendacity after all, and suddenly he felt sorry for her. He cursed the spontaneous satisfaction he had felt at her collapsing defences, as if she were the object of an interrogation and not the woman in whose hair he had buried his face just a few days ago, thinking *This is it.*

"Was it so that other people couldn't read it?" he asked, more gently this time. She shrugged her shoulders almost imperceptibly.

"I always used to write in Finnish when I was little, when I didn't want the other kids to understand." She was speaking quietly. "It was like my own secret language."

He quelled the impulse to place his hand over hers; she looked so vulnerable, lost in the secrets of her childhood.

"Were you going to tell me?" he asked eventually.

The illusion of defencelessness was instantly transformed into irritation once more. She threw her arms wide open.

"I don't even know if there's anything to tell, Christian. I didn't know — I still don't — if what I know has anything to do with your investigation. I mean it wasn't Thomas Edell lying there! *It wasn't him!* And that's exactly why I didn't say anything. How . . . how can you know if the memories from a difficult period in your life are true? You must know what I mean? Memory is like a bloody sieve — you decide for yourself what you want to remember, depending on your self-image at the time."

She stared at him, her shoulders hunched up by her ears, before she breathed out heavily and lowered them, allowing the images from the past to come pouring in.

Over the next hour darkness fell over the room; they didn't bother switching on the lights. Once she started talking he found he was holding his breath, as if the least movement on his part might cause a sudden break in her story, in her fragile trust. She kept on drifting off the point and he was itching to ask concrete questions — *Why have you got several enlarged photographs of a murder victim? How is this connected to the fact that you were first on the scene of the crime and then started a relationship with the officer leading the investigation?* — but he was sensitive enough to realise that too much pressure would just make her retreat.

He buried his fingernails deep in the palms of his hands in order to remain patient as she attempted to put the pictures in her memory into words and to formulate the conclusions drawn by her subconscious over the past ten years.

He should have contented himself with simply listening. Should have been patient and actually enjoyed getting to know her, but he couldn't. He was trapped inside the framework of his job. He couldn't split himself in two, and evidently neither could Seja. Sometimes the story became incomprehensible. Sometimes the words were not right, and she had to start again.

Gradually a picture began to emerge of two young women, each one at a fork in the road. Seja was one of them; the other had been a passing acquaintance. Seja talked about a bitterly cold December night at a bikers' club in the middle of nowhere. She had met the other woman briefly around midnight. They talked about travelling back into town together, but Seja decided to stay on. Deep inside she had had a bad feeling — at least that was how she remembered it now.

She stopped as if she were gathering strength.

Later there had been talk among her circle of acquaintances that a woman had been found dead in the forest around the club. It was in the paper. There were suspicious circumstances, but no one was ever caught. Some people said the woman had been raped; others that she was drunk and had passed out and hit her head on a rock. No one knew for sure.

"I pretended I wasn't really bothered. I remember saying to the boy who first told me — it was at a party — that I didn't know the woman who had died out there in the forest. And it was true. I convinced myself it had nothing to do with me."

The police had contacted a number of people who had been at the club and issued an appeal for all those who were not on the list supplied by the organisers to get in touch. Seja had never come forward.

Why not? Tell wanted to ask, but she pre-empted him. For the same reason she hadn't been able to tell him earlier about what she had heard and seen that night: she just wasn't sure. As long as she wasn't backed into a corner and forced to give an answer, she could avoid making a decision about her own reliability, or about the fact that she had done nothing to intervene.

Before she knew it the drama was over. The investigation had probably been put to one side due to lack of evidence, and life went on.

"I saw the way he looked at her, his expression. Like a mixture of rage and desire. I saw him watch her leave. And for some reason I noticed him and his friends leave just after she did. I noticed that she was on her own, that it was so bloody dark, and that gang of lads left just after her. I stood there in the yard for a long time, on my own. I couldn't bring myself to go back inside."

The tears began to pour down her cheeks, and she made no effort to wipe them away.

"I know it sounds ridiculous, but I could feel evil in the air, Christian. I sensed something, but I didn't

450

know what it was or what I could do to prevent it. So I just stood there, and I remember it started to snow and I was absolutely frozen. I could hear the band playing upstairs, song after song, and nobody else came out while I was standing there, nobody apart from those three. She should have made it up to the main road during that time. Do you understand what I'm saying?"

He nodded. He understood. Tentatively he reached out and wiped the tears from her cheek. She jerked back as he touched her, gazing at him with her tear-drenched eyes. He thought she was looking at him with an air of surprise. As if she had suddenly returned to reality and was wondering what he was doing there, with part of her life story on his knee. It was obvious she wasn't proud of it.

"Whatever happened that night, you couldn't have prevented it," he said gently. "Even if you believe now that you felt something, you have to realise that's just the way it seems after the event. How *could* you have known? And even if you had known, what could you have done? You said it yourself — you were seventeen, eighteen years old, barely an adult. When a crime is committed it isn't unusual for feelings of guilt to spill over on to people who just happened to be nearby, but it's wrong. You have nothing to feel guilty about. All the blame lies with those three men. You did say there were three of them, didn't you?"

As he spoke he was feverishly trying to link everything together. Even if he suspected he knew the answer, he had to ask the questions.

"That's just it: I remember everything, down to the last detail. One of them was furious. He wanted to get going and was moaning at the others to get a move on."

She let her hands drop to her knees, as she finally told him what had been torturing her over the past few days.

"At one point, just before they finally left, the angry one called one of the others by his full name, the way you do when you want to make a point. He called him Thomas Edell — *Thomas Edell, will you shift your fucking arse* — and several people must have heard, but as far as I know nobody mentioned it to the police. Earlier on he had just called him Fox . . . or maybe it was Wolf. I don't know why I remember that. In the end they had to more or less carry Edell into the truck, him and his mate."

Tell suddenly realised he had been holding his breath.

"Seja, listen to me. Would you recognise this mate, if you saw him now?"

She stared at him in surprise. Only then did it dawn on her that her confession could have more direct consequences than the relief she felt at unburdening herself.

She thought for a little while, then said, "I think so. I mean, it's a long time ago, but I knew straight away it wasn't Thomas Edell lying there on the gravel, even though there was so much blood and . . . I don't think I could have got it wrong. Even if I haven't been conscious of it, his face has been imprinted in my memory for over ten years."

CHAPTER
FORTY-NINE

The subscriber is not available. It was almost eighteen months since they had received the telephone number, written on the back of a photograph of that woman's two children. Dagny had insisted on displaying it on the piano as if they were Sven's kids, something to be proud of.

He had transferred the number into his black book, which was now lying in front of him on the telephone table. The only phone in the house was in the downstairs hallway. He therefore had to wait until Dagny had gone for a nap or retired for the night before he could call. But every time he was greeted by that impersonal female voice claiming that his son, or rather the subscriber, was not available.

It was of course possible that his son had given them a false number to avoid having to choose between the devil and the deep blue sea. The risk of being called by his mother and father when he was least expecting it had to be set against the alternative: being totally honest and refusing to give it to them at all.

Bertil Molin was a realist, far more so than his wife. He would never lower himself to pretend he had a good relationship with his son — unlike Dagny, who clung desperately to half-truths in order not to feel like such a bloody failure. But women were different. They were cut from a different cloth.

It was also a family trait. There was, according to Bertil Molin's way of seeing things, a strength in having the courage to look the truth in the eye. To recognise that you have lived a life that has not completely fulfilled expectations. It was good to pre-empt the wave of grief that could otherwise overwhelm you when you were least expecting it. It was different with Dagny: she always made a big thing of their son. As soon as anyone walked through the door she was boasting about that Chinese woman, or Thai, or whatever she was.

He snorted at the thought. They had never met the woman their son had married five years ago; they didn't even know her name. Sven had presumably mentioned it at some point in one of his telephone calls, which were few and far between. Or maybe he hadn't. Bertil Molin was smart enough to realise that, when it came to his son, the disappointment he felt was mutual. If Sven *had* mentioned his wife's name, it had disappeared from Bertil's memory.

What he did know was that his son had flown to one of the world's less developed countries with a grubby picture from a catalogue in his suitcase, in order to buy a wife in a place where people were so poor that everything was for sale. That was all he needed to know about her. He knew she had nothing to offer Sven apart from a lack of pride, which must have come in handy when she allowed herself to be dragged halfway around the world like an animal, along with her two bastards, to become a kept woman in the small community of Mölnebo, where Sven lived. No doubt everybody stared at her. And she had destroyed a man's reputation into the bargain. Not that he knew much about Sven's reputation.

The subscriber was still not available. He replaced the receiver carefully so the sound would not wake Dagny. She had turned her face towards the back of the sofa, and her heavy breathing had turned into snores. She would sleep for a while longer. This meant he could wait a quarter of an hour then try again.

Deep down he sensed that if he didn't get hold of Sven very soon, there would come a day when he would bitterly regret the fact that he hadn't done more. That he hadn't ignored his unreliable heart and the flickering before his eyes and driven up to Mölnebo to talk to his son face to face. To tell him about the article in the newspaper and the goings-on at the farm next door. To warn him.

He padded over to the window and moved the lace curtain a fraction to one side, gazing over the roof of the old Renault and across the meadow towards the Edell place. There was a light on upstairs. Lise-Lott had come home.

CHAPTER
FIFTY

1999

Afterwards it would be difficult to give an account of the course of events. If someone had asked Solveig six months after Sebastian had started sleeping on the sofa and Caroline had moved into his room, she would have answered evasively, something along the lines of *She was just standing there on the landing one day, with her hat and coat on, and she stayed.* Planted herself in the dark three-room apartment with its dusty corners with the intention of staying around. In fact this corresponded with Caroline's own words that first evening in the dressing room, which had become the memory room: *I'll stay around. I'm not the kind of person who just walks away.* This was after Solveig had presumably said something like *Don't go. Don't leave us here with nothing to think about but this crippling grief.* She had allowed this stranger to lick her wounds.

The fact that she had stayed felt like a blessing. First of all it was a kind of break, a period when Solveig and Sebastian no longer had to try to find a way to relate to one another in the shadow of the crime. Later she realised that Caroline was helping to save Maya's life from the oblivion Solveig most feared. She already felt the danger was imminent: she would forget Maya's precise expressions and features, replacing them with her own, and in the end she wouldn't know what belonged to whom.

Caroline had also loved Maya with the kind of love that Maya deserved — pure, elevated and irreproachable — just as her own love for her daughter had emerged after her death. It made Solveig feel noble in a way. Earlier in her life she had often been prey to devastating attacks of jealousy when her children's love was directed at someone else. She also managed to explain away the sexual relationship Caroline had presumably had with her daughter, just as she had become an expert at suppressing other unpleasant truths over the years. There was a hardness about Caroline, and in her eyes Solveig sensed a cold concentrated rage. The tip of an iceberg. She would never go against Caroline. In times of need you had to choose your battles, she reasoned; you had to prioritise what would bring the greatest gain. Right now Caroline was helping her to survive by filtering her grief. She talked about Maya and listened to Solveig when she talked about Maya.

Caroline was aware of every one of Maya's characteristics that up to now Solveig had thought only a mother would notice. How she put the tips of her fingers over her lips when she laughed. How she often tilted her head to one side when she was nervous. How she seemed to know a whole raft of stupid expressions that didn't match her personality at all and looked slightly embarrassed when one of these expressions slipped out by accident.

Maya was the hub of their relationship, the memory room, the central point from which all forms of looking back or forward had their origin. Particularly since the counsellors, psychologists and doctors had begun to close their ears to Solveig's grief, saying, *Now, Solveig, it's been nearly three years. You really have to try to move on, bury your daughter and start looking to the future.* By that stage the common platform she had found with Caroline had become so stable that Solveig was more indifferent than ever to the advice of the professionals.

She and Caroline withdrew from the world, became self-reliant. Out of the blame that Solveig had at first placed firmly around Sebastian's neck grew a conviction that something terrible must have happened to Maya. That her final moments in life had consisted of sheer terror. And however much Sebastian still bore responsibility for the fact that she had faced her murderer alone, it wasn't actually Sebastian who had driven that sharp stone into her head. But someone had done it, and that person had yet to receive his punishment.

"I'm going to find out who did it," said Caroline, holding Solveig's head between her palms. "Trust me. But I need Sebastian's help."

"Sebastian?" asked Solveig in confusion.

At that moment she would have agreed to anything at all. A faint current of electricity was running from Caroline's hands into Solveig's face, which had been frozen but was now slowly beginning to thaw. In the dark irises of Caroline's eyes she had caught sight of Maya, Maya moving inside Caroline's eyes.

"I need him for his local knowledge."

The same evening Solveig blessed Caroline's project to find out what had really happened that December night, they found Sebastian on the bathroom floor. Both of his wrists were slashed.

He was unconscious, and even though it turned out a few hours later at the hospital in Borås that the wounds were not particularly deep, they decided to keep him in for observation.

Evidently an interview with a counsellor was compulsory in cases of attempted suicide.

"Sebastian? Your girlfriend is here."

The nurse who stuck her head around the door gave him an exaggerated wink.

"My girlfriend?" said Sebastian in a voice that wasn't quite steady yet.

"Yes! She's . . ." The irritatingly cheerful girl searched for the right expression. She settled on "awe-inspiring".

Sebastian realised it must be Caroline waiting for permission to enter the secure unit. His stomach turned over. As it had so many times before, it struck him that he knew nothing about her. She only ever talked about herself in short often contradictory bursts; that way she had no life story, no contours. When he tried to visualise her face in his mind's eye he often saw only a diffuse image that could be just about anybody, like a face from a dream that has already begun to fade. At those times he doubted whether she actually existed. Was she perhaps merely the product of his own imagination and that of his mother?

In a Bruce Willis film he had seen the room grew cold when a ghost made its entrance. Before she made herself known, Sebastian could always sense Caroline's presence by the chill wind on the back of his neck. He told himself he was being ridiculous, and yet he still tried to avoid being alone with her.

She was constantly changing her appearance, and not in the usual ways, with a new haircut or a change of clothes. No, the most confusing thing about Caroline was her ability to slough off her skin and take on a completely new guise. From one day to the next he would meet a different person in the kitchen; even the pitch of her voice, her accent, the shape of the face changed. She could be as tender as the mother Solveig had never been. She could be bleached blonde and stooping, anxiously sorry for herself in contrast to the dominance she usually displayed. But Sebastian was not fooled: he never doubted for a second that Caroline could kill him with a glance.

Solveig never seemed to question Caroline's changeable personality; perhaps she didn't even notice it. He had never thought he would miss the old Solveig. But he was missing her now. She was moving further and further away from him, deeper into Caroline's web. Trapped in its centre, she seemed to have been robbed of the ability to see, and he was convinced that she would never be able to free herself while she lived. He mourned Solveig, just as he mourned himself and the fact that he was an outsider. He had rarely felt so lonely in all his life.

460

No visits were permitted without the patient's agreement, but he had never dared deny Caroline anything.

"It's OK," he said, waving vaguely in the direction of the door. Like another Godfather, even if a patriarch was the last thing he felt like, lying there in his bed. He didn't even understand why he was still in bed, as if a washed-out sheet stamped with the county logo could take the sting out of the sordid reason why he had been brought in.

What he remembered after cutting himself was the crap between the floor tiles, the yellow layers of shed skin smeared right next to his face as he lay in the corner thinking about the expression *The life seeped out of him*. It was like falling asleep: your body grows heavier and lighter at the same time. He was sucked into a vortex of vivid colours, spinning faster and faster until he lost all sense of time and space and it became fascinating and solemn before everything went black and he just had time to think, *I'm dying now*.

According to the doctor, the association with sleep was likely to have been correct: he had presumably fallen asleep there on the floor. Since the blood in the wounds had coagulated, his life had never been in any danger.

He wished there was a way to stop Solveig and Caroline finding out that he hadn't even managed to create the tiniest risk of dying, despite the fact that that had been the whole point of the project. Instead he had woken up in an ambulance with its siren wailing, a male nurse on one side of him and Solveig on the other.

Oddly enough, he couldn't remember what he had been thinking beforehand, whether he had really wanted to die or not. Therefore he felt neither relief nor disappointment, just a comprehensive indifference. In order to avoid showing any form of reaction, he had kept his eyes closed and allowed his hand to be squeezed by his mother's cold, damp one.

He heard a sound from the corridor before the door opened with a sigh.

"Hi there."

He had subconsciously focused on the door ever since the nurse told him he had a visitor, so it wasn't the sound of her voice that surprised him. Nor was it the way she looked, even though Caroline's appearance had transformed once more over the past few days. It was the *way* she was looking at him. He noticed that she was wearing a lot of eye make-up — blue and green and sparkly. Her lipstick smelled of fat and stickiness, like sweets.

"I hardly recognised you," he said, pointing at her hair, which tumbled over her shoulders in chocolate-brown ringlets. "Is it a wig?"

"No." She smiled and bent her head so that he could see the half-centimetre plastic solders fixing the mass of extensions to her own short hair. "It's still cheating, but it looks better."

It was as if the smile had got stuck on her face. It made him feel embarrassed. Caroline was his mother's ally. Even if she had been a natural, if not necessarily pleasant, part of his everyday life for some time now, there was no affinity between them. On the contrary: he

462

had clearly felt himself to be outside the little group with his dead sister at its centre. None of them mentioned the reason for this, despite the fact that it was living and breathing under their roof. Solveig had always believed he could have prevented Maya's death. The only reason she chose not to articulate her accusations was because she knew it was unnecessary. He had not been slow to accuse himself.

He didn't respond to Caroline's smile — the rules of adolescence still applied as far as he was concerned, and sullenness was the expression he adopted when nothing else came naturally.

She moved her chair closer to the bed and leaned forward. He caught a glimpse of her breasts beneath the low neckline of her blouse. To his surprise he felt the same mixture of excitement, distaste and embarrassment he had felt on the few occasions he had caught sight of Maya's naked body. He didn't need to think for too long before he recognised the scent: she was wearing Maya's perfume.

Caroline frightened him, but he couldn't stop the rage that came bubbling up inside him.

"You're wearing Maya's perfume."

He stared at her, even though the look she gave him in return made the room spin. Instead of replying she spread her arms over the bedcover with a slight but unmistakable pressure that made his thighs tingle. He gasped for breath but refused to look away.

Slowly, emphasising every syllable, Caroline spoke his name.

"Did you know that on the other side of the world there's an extremely religious tribe who live in complete isolation. Their teenage boys undergo a special ritual in order to become men: they cut their arms and legs and smear themselves with the blood. It has something to do with confessing their sins, like the Christian martyrs. Then the boy has to lie in a cave, which the older women have prepared by burning a particular kind of wood. I can't remember what it's called but I think it's like our juniper and it has a powerful smell. The boy has to lie on a bed of leaves for three days and three nights. Sometimes the boy has cut too deep, and he bleeds to death. This means that the gods have seen his courage and called him to them — they want him straight away. But usually the boy survives and returns to his village after the three days, and the wounds become scars — long dark snakes on his body. The more striking the network of scars, the higher the status the man will have. They are proof of his bravery. And of the fact that he has gained insight into something important. That he has understood and shouldered the burden of his guilt and is ready to devote the rest of his life to atoning for it."

She leaned towards his face. Sweat broke out on his brow and under his arms. His nostrils caught a whiff of her breath. It smelled sweet and acrid and made him want to pull back and lean closer.

"There's no such tribe, is there?" he said in a thin voice, and her moist lower lip glistened as a smile passed over her face.

464

He wanted to stand up for himself and tell her what his social studies teacher had said — that revelling in guilt and martyrdom is exclusive to Western religions — but he was unable to get enough air into his lungs; she was too heavy, leaning on his body, and her gaze was too much like fire burning into his eyes, frightening him into silence. Just when he thought he was going to pass out from lack of oxygen, she pulled back, but only after allowing her hands to roam across the sheet. She leaned in again. Her moist lips closed over his thin dry ones, and she sucked his lower lip into her mouth. The pain shot along his spine like a bolt of lightning as she bit him. He exploded in convulsions, his knees drawn up, forming a protective wall around himself and his body with his hands and arms.

Caroline took a step back, her face expressing sympathy and contempt, a kind of tenderness that his tears of embarrassment had evidently aroused within her.

She caressed his wet cheek with her fingertips.

"When you come home you can move back into your own room."

CHAPTER
FIFTY-ONE

2007

The dog had been winding itself around his legs, making a high-pitched whimpering sound that didn't seem appropriate for the huge Newfoundland. After Sven had fallen over him several times, a well-aimed kick saw to it that the dog quickly put some distance between himself and his irritable master. Sven pushed a pang of guilt to one side. He had other things on his mind.

Under normal circumstances they both enjoyed the slow ritual of feeding the mink. Albert was his third Newfoundland. They didn't usually live into old age, which was the disadvantage of large dogs: their hip joints gave way. Twice he had had to take his dog and his gun round the back of the house. It wasn't much fun, but it was more humane than letting the dog suffer.

Through the window slits he could see from the tops of the fir trees that the wind had died down.

Two figures in identical red padded jackets, both too large, with matching red and blue backpacks, appeared in front of the house. They were waving at something over by the road. Eriksson's ageing Saab pulled up beside them. The next moment they were gone.

Every third day Sven picked up Eriksson's and Kajsa's kids in the morning. He dropped the whole shower of them at the school gate, and picked them up at the same place at three o'clock. Car pooling, it was called. He was rarely in a good mood when it was his turn to play school bus. Usually he just grunted briefly when the kids jumped in the back of the car. The kids were also strangely silent during the journey. Sven's only experience of children was the two he had been landed with as a result of his marriage to Lee, but he still had the idea that kids usually made a racket. Anyway, it didn't matter. He was just glad they were quiet.

It annoyed him that Lee hadn't managed to learn to drive. He had explained to her many, many times, with varying degrees of irritation, that you needed a driving licence when you lived as far from town and the public transport system as they did.

Lee. Food and housework had been the main things on his mind when he realised a few years ago that he needed a woman in his life. Love, of course — he wasn't made of wood, after all — but above all he wanted to be spared the worry about all those jobs at home that were not a man's responsibility. The alternative — employing some kind of home help — cost money he didn't have. And the house had never been so clean. He couldn't take that away from her. She was never difficult about her duties the way Swedish women sometimes were, particularly those who turned to feminism to find the answer to why they were unhappy with themselves and their lives. He'd met their sort. The fact that he had previously chosen to live alone didn't mean he lacked experience of the opposite sex.

No, it wasn't because of social ineptitude that he had contacted the organisation that had found him Lee — after all the forms had been filled in and matched up — nor because he couldn't manage to get himself a Swedish woman. He was not unsavoury in any way. In fact, as the owner of a working business, he was attractive — even if the mink farm mostly ran on subsidies these days, thanks to the bloody animal rights fanatics. It wouldn't have been all that difficult to get some woman from town to paint herself a romantic picture of a country kitchen and a herb garden, working herself up until she would have married the devil himself. But to get hold of a woman who would roll up her sleeves and throw herself into her work without going on about equality and self-fulfilment, that was tricky.

The idea had been maturing for a couple of years, after he had made a fresh start and bought the farm. He had gone for a Thai mostly by chance. And he also went for Lee mostly by chance, if he was completely truthful. The catalogues contained thousands of hopeful women of all ages. He had concentrated on the younger ones, but not the youngest of all: he suspected their eyes were still full of dreams. The slightly older ones, he reasoned, had hopefully already realised in the hard school of life that reality rarely lives up to those dreams. Because what he wanted was a helping hand in the everyday running of the place, not constant

468

discussion from someone who felt sorry for herself or told him what he ought to be doing.

So, in many ways, he was happy with Lee. This was despite the fact that she had kept her children hidden from him right up to the moment the wedding was booked, and they had arranged passports and the trip home. Then, once she had him in her grasp, she had dropped the bombshell about the two fatherless children out in the country, living with her old grandmother.

"Well, they can stay there," he had said at first, seething with rage, "or we forget the whole bloody thing." If there was one thing he couldn't stand it was being deceived or exploited.

She had wept, there in the hotel room. Hurled herself on the thread-bare carpet, clung to his legs like a madwoman, screaming so loudly that the hotel owner had come knocking on the door, afraid that someone was being murdered.

He had spent a whole afternoon and evening wandering around in the disgusting tumult and stench of Bangkok. Up and down the streets until the black cloud in front of his eyes slowly faded and was replaced by sober reasoning. He had put a lot of money into this project. Under no circumstances was he going home empty-handed. To start again from the beginning would mean spending another fortune. There was no guarantee he would find another woman who matched his requirements as well in every other respect. Nor could he stand the thought of another round of artificial parties and eternal dates in slightly seedy restaurants. Particularly as one woman was bewilderingly like another in his eyes and the language barrier precluded any form of real communication.

He had returned to the hotel room towards morning, expecting Lee to have packed her bags and left. Admitted her mistake and gone home to Grandma, the kids and the village he didn't know the name of. Or she might have gone back to the agency to see if she could trick some other Westerner into providing her with happiness and financial security. When he slipped his pass card into the door he was prepared for the sight of the far too soft hotel bed, neatly made up with its light brown throw and empty.

Instead, in the light seeping through the tasteless curtains, he saw the contours of her body beneath the sheet. Something that could only be described as gratitude came over him unexpectedly, bringing a lump to his throat. Not love, it was too soon for that. *Loyalty* was the word that came into his mind as he stood there in the doorway. And a working marriage was built on loyalty.

They hired a car and drove out to pick up the two children. A boy and a girl, both as quiet as mice, with skinny brown bodies and hair like shining helmets. As he had expected, the house was tiny, poor and damp, and the old woman who was Lee's grandmother served him tea but refused to look him in the eye. When they were finally ready to leave, she took his hands between her wrinkled shaking ones and let the tears flow.

Incomprehensible words came pouring out of her toothless mouth, and he would have liked the woman he had just married to step in and spare his embarrassment. But she stood there, unwilling to save him. He had pulled his hands away uncomfortably, and went to sit in the car while Lee and the children took their leave of the old woman. A gang of nameless individuals had gathered outside the hut. He had felt a strong aversion to them, not because he was so clearly excluded from their circle, but because he was aware of the reproach emanating from their eyes. Sometimes he imagined he could see that same reproach in Lee's eyes.

It annoyed him, the fact that she hadn't learned to drive.

"I'll pay," he'd said, time and again, "I pay the car school," in broken English. For the first few months he had driven her and the kids around as if he had nothing else to do. "But you have to practise. I'll teach you."

The resistance when he jokingly nudged her into the driver's seat and took the handbrake off, that had annoyed him. He could see the fear that passed over her face when the engine started, but decided she'd soon get over it. As soon as she learned to manoeuvre the car.

It didn't happen. She really was hopeless when it came to driving. She lacked the ability to do things simultaneously, as if she was completely ignorant of the relationship between cause and effect. As if the car were a creature acting entirely on its own impulses, completely independent of what she did with her hands and feet. Above all she was afraid, and it didn't improve matters when she went into the ditch outside

Carlsson's garage. She just let go of the wheel, put her arm over her eyes and screamed.

Carlsson had to pull them out with his tractor. Laughing, of course, but Sven didn't find the situation remotely amusing.

"Everybody can learn to drive," he had said. It was meant as encouragement, but he could hear the acid in his own voice. "Sixteen-year-old kids can learn, why can't you?"

That was the only time Lee had ever raised her voice. She had glared at him and said, "No more drive, understan'?" When he had opened his mouth to respond, her expression grew fierce. She clamped her teeth together then firmly said once more, "Understan'?" And that was the end of the matter.

From then on nothing was said when she took the children on the long trek to the nearest bus stop. She hauled bags of shopping along the dusty gravel track, or pushed them on a little cart she had found in the barn. It really had been a miserable sight, the three skinny strangers with their glossy hair, their little red cart bumping over the frost-damaged track, their expressions stoical. He had had to grit his teeth to avoid exploding.

In order to avoid pointed remarks from the neighbours, he had resumed driving Lee to the supermarket twice a week. Even if it did annoy him.

Albert stretched out his curly-haired body and spotty tummy for general admiration on the slope. Sven crouched down to scratch him. The dog gave himself up to pleasure and when Lee opened the back door of the house and walked across the grass to the stand for beating the rugs, he paid her as little attention as he would a fly on the kitchen floor. She was stooping beneath the weight of the big rug from the living room, not much taller than the two children she had just waved off.

Sven was always pleased when he and Lee were alone at home. Not that they talked to each other much, or had sex in the living room or kitchen. Mostly they moved around in parallel, silently engaged in their own activities — Lee indoors and Sven outdoors. But it felt good. They were two adults who knew exactly what had to be done. When they woke up in the morning, they already knew how the day would look.

By this stage he should have grown used to the children. And yet they still made him slightly nervous. Not that they were particularly unpredictable — they were far too well brought up for that, and he had done up the attic for them so that they could go up there to play and keep out of his way. It was more that there was something about their self-control that made him uncomfortable. As if there were thoughts and impulses they had to conceal behind those timid masks. Sometimes he could hear them giggling behind the closed door of their bedroom late at night. At those times he was sure they were laughing at him. On one occasion he had flung the door open with such force that the strong draught had made their fringes fly up in the air, exposing two high brown foreheads. He had just stood there in the doorway, embarrassed. They had met his gaze with their calm, questioning eyes. Diminishing him.

He put the pails on the floor in front of him and forced himself to breathe more slowly. He was a wreck. The only strategy he could employ to tackle his nerves was to convince himself that nothing mattered. And in a way it was true. There was a six-pack of beer right at the bottom of the fridge in the house. He seriously considered not bothering to feed the mink and simply crashing out on the sofa — because it was all going to come out, and if the worst came to the worst, he was going to have to pay.

In the silence a fly banged repeatedly against a filthy windowpane. He felt as if his shoes were stuck fast in the cement, and sweat broke out beneath the brim of his cap. With an enormous effort he lifted the pails. There was another way of looking at it: on the brink of catastrophe, routine was the only thing left to cling to.

The impacts of the carpet beater on the rug echoed off the metal walls like the sound of gunshots. An unpleasant shiver ran down his spine. The noise died away as Lee lowered her arm. She was so short that the beater reached the ground. All at once she looked old, crippled with pain, like the toothless woman she had introduced as her grandmother.

Since he had spoken to his father for the first time in months, the fear had become a constant presence, a gnawing anxiety chewing its way through his nervous system, sometimes turning into ice-cold terror. At the sight of Lee with the carpet beater it leapt up to his

Adam's apple, and for a bewildering moment he thought he was going to burst into tears.

She was standing there looking at him, equally lost.

Please God, don't let anything happen to her, he thought suddenly, and his throat constricted even more. And it was only then that he made his decision. There was no turning back. Not if his life was dear to him.

Strangely enough, he had just realised that it was.

CHAPTER
FIFTY-TWO

The offices of his colleagues were empty. However, every single door was open wide and their computers were still on. They would be on overtime by now. Tell followed the sound of voices. An area just off the kitchen served as a staff room for those who didn't enjoy sitting in the canteen. The doorway was filled by Bärneflod's broad shoulders.

"Nice to see you," said Beckman, who was perched on the draining board stirring a cup of hot chocolate. Someone had opened a packet of biscuits and put it on the table. Tell suddenly felt the hunger tearing at his stomach; he couldn't remember eating anything since breakfast.

Karlberg cleared his throat. "I tried to call you a while ago."

Tell nodded, his mouth full. "I think my mobile needs charging."

Or it might have been turned off, he could have added, but he had no wish to damage his reputation any more than he had done already. He poured himself a cup of coffee.

"I thought maybe my colleagues wouldn't be here so late in the day," said Tell with forced lightness, "but obviously I've underestimated your diligence. How about going over where we're up to, since we're all here?"

He opened the window with the special movement that had been necessary ever since all the windows and doors had been replaced by soundproof ones with a child safety feature. Bärneflod said they weren't just child-proof, they were people-proof.

"You criticised me earlier today, with good reason, because I didn't share with you my thoughts on our Jeep case. So perhaps I can take the opportunity to do so now. I've done a little more research into the unsolved case I mentioned before, and —"

"I've just reported back on an interview with Susanne Jensen, Olof Bart's older sister," Beckman interrupted. "That's why we were trying to get hold of you, and Gonzales, but he's sitting on the Fredrikshamn ferry, so if he can't persuade the captain to turn around, he probably won't get here."

"Fredrikshamn?" exclaimed Bärneflod in mock horror. "Didn't I say I wanted to know if anyone was planning a booze cruise? I could have placed an order."

"There's no point these days," interjected Karlberg.

"Enough! Beckman?"

"OK. Susanne Jensen was sitting in reception earlier today," Beckman went on. "I was just about to leave, but she'd asked for me. You remember, I met her at the Klara hostel the other day. At the time she didn't say a word, but today she had evidently decided to talk. She told me that a few years ago she and Olof had got very drunk together, and in the early hours he'd broken down and told her about some incident he'd been involved in where a young girl had been killed at some Hell's Angels hangout. In Borås. It was an accident, he said. Susanne didn't know if it was a rape or a mugging that had gone wrong, because he was fairly incoherent and she didn't like the idea of digging any deeper. I presume that's the unsolved case you were talking about?"

Tell nodded eagerly. "Go on."

"She didn't say much more. Except that she'd thought about the incident when I asked her if she knew anyone who might have wanted to murder her brother. She felt she wanted to help, and it wouldn't matter now he was dead. Grassing him up."

"A junkie with the unusual ability to think clearly," commented Bärneflod.

"She didn't remember if he'd said anything about when this crime was supposed to have taken place. She also didn't remember when exactly Olof had told her about it, but they hadn't had any contact for five or six years. She said that since Olof had moved to Kinna, she had only been to see him once, and that was when he had opened up to her." Beckman pushed her fringe out of her eyes, her expression thoughtful.

"She says the same as everyone else: that Olof was hard work. Taciturn, a bit sullen. And you could say the same about her. It's obvious she's seen a lot of violence in her life . . . but I liked her."

"But we know that already," said Bärneflod with a peculiarly broad grin that exposed his fillings. "We know you like most users and whores and whatever else

478

the cat drags in. I mean, we have to feel sorry for them, don't we?"

"Shut it." Tell was leaning over the table, both palms flat on the surface. He couldn't conceal his excitement. "So the question is —"

"A, was he alone? No, Bart was not alone," Beckman interrupted once again. "Susanne had the impression there were three men involved. B, did he tell his sister the names of the others? And C, does she remember them? The answer is again no, of course. But I think as soon as we're done here I'm going to sit down and go through every single unsolved murder or suspected murder of a young girl in the Borås area between 1990 and 2000."

"There's no need."

Tell straightened up so quickly that his spine cracked ominously.

"Check 1995. A bikers' club called the Evil Riders. The girl was Maya Granith. We also have an address."

Karlberg, Bärneflod and Beckman stared at Tell.

"You have an address?" said Beckman eventually.

"We know where Maya Granith was living in '92. The chance that some relative might still be living there isn't great, but it's possible. Beckman, look for relatives and go through the old investigation. And talk to Björkman, it's his territory after all. The important thing is to see if we can link Edell to this party at the bikers' club, and above all if we can get hold of some kind of membership list to see if we can work out who the third person was. I don't have to tell you he could be in danger too."

"But what the hell were they doing in Borås?" wondered Bärneflod with genuine puzzlement.

Tell realised he was incredibly hot, and shrugged off his coat with some difficulty in the cramped kitchen. He barely registered Karlberg's grunt as his elbow made contact with the man's stomach. "Beckman, I came across something in your transcript of the interview with the neighbours — was their name Mollberg?"

"Molin," said Beckman, siting bolt upright. "Bloody hell! The son! Edell was his best mate!"

"Exactly. That's why I thought somebody should check. Actually, just ring Björkman at home. Karlberg, could you take care of that? And look for Molin's son. Call me or Beckman as soon as you get in touch with him."

Karlberg was still rubbing his stomach and could only manage a nod in the direction of his boss.

"Beckman and I will go and see Mummy and Daddy."

The last time they visited the Molins' farm, a wine-red somewhat rusty Renault had been parked in front of the outhouse. Now only an enormous branch lay on the gravelled parking area — it must have been blown down by the strong winds during the night. Since the windows were dark rectangles in the dirty grey facade of the house, it would have been easy for Tell and Beckman to assume that nobody was at home, particularly as there was no answer when they repeatedly rang the doorbell.

Blessed with the scepticism that came with the job, they took a walk around the house. They found the Renault straight away. It had been driven up on to the grass behind an annex, its wheels gouging deep wounds in the lawn which had already filled with water.

With fresh determination Tell ignored the doorbell and hammered so hard on the flimsy front door that the glass pane rattled. For a moment he thought it was going to give way.

"Open up. We know you're in there."

He was just about to park himself on the porch to wait it out when there were footsteps inside the house accompanied by the muted sound of someone clearing their throat. The key rattled in the lock and the door opened. Bertil Molin was wearing cotton trousers and a blue and white check shirt. There was no mistaking that he wasn't all that pleased to see them. When the throat-clearing — which seemed to stem mainly from a desperate desire to avoid a challenging silence — turned into a coughing fit, Tell thought the man had had sufficient respite.

"Are you going to let us in?"

"It depends what you want," replied Molin sourly, still red in the face from the exertion.

"Shall we call it reliving old memories?"

Tell pushed past Molin. He walked through the hallway and into the small kitchen. A table and two chairs were the only furnishings. He sat down heavily on one of the wooden chairs without bothering to take off his coat.

Beckman followed him in and leaned against the draining board, below the collection of blue and white plates covering most of the wall. On top of the wood-burning stove stood a mug made of plainer china. Bertil Molin had been drinking tea when he was disturbed. The aroma of lemon filled the room.

While they were waiting for Molin to join them, Tell rang Karlberg, who answered straight away.

"Is he answering his home number?"

"Sven Molin? No, and he's not answering his mobile."

"OK. Keep trying."

It was worryingly quiet out in the hallway. Tell caught Beckman's eye, and she pulled a face. *Has Molin done a runner?* However, the next moment Molin and his camouflaged anxiety appeared in the doorway.

He looked first of all at Tell sitting at the table, then at Beckman, and seemed to find his options limited. He rubbed the palm of his hand frantically against his trouser leg as if he had a particularly troublesome itch.

"We can go to the dining room. My wife's asleep upstairs. If we go in there she won't —"

"No need," Tell broke in. "In fact, I think if you wake up your wife, we'll find that she can contribute to our discussion. I have a number of questions about your son."

Molin twitched involuntarily. Then he seemed to resign himself, placed his palms flat on his thighs and looked down at his hands as if he had never seen them before.

"I can't see why you would have any reason to speak about Sven," he said eventually. "He can't possibly be involved in any of the bad stuff going on here. He hasn't set foot in this place for years."

"And what exactly do you mean by 'bad stuff'?"

Bertil Molin raised his eyes slowly, as if trying to assess Tell's intentions, then he let his gaze drift past the police officers towards the darkness outside the window.

"Well . . . a man was murdered on the other side of the meadow, wasn't he? That's why you're here, unless I'm wrong? I can't see that you would have any reason to come here asking me questions unless it had something to do with the murder. And if you're asking questions about my son Sven, I presume you think he has something to do with it. Which is insane, given that he hasn't exchanged a single word with Lise-Lott in over ten years."

Tell and Beckman had to take a moment to recover from Molin's unexpected bout of talkativeness. On the way from the station they had discussed how best to confront the Molins with their hypothesis. The only thing they had to offer so far was the fact that their son, according to hearsay, used to hang out with two men who, also according to hearsay, might possibly have attacked a young woman about twelve years ago. A crime that had never been proved.

If they had ever doubted whether Molin had any dark secrets, these were now blown away like leaves on an October day. There was definitely a skeleton in the cupboard here.

"Why are you so worked up?" Beckman looked searchingly at Molin as she dug a nasal spray out of her handbag. She sprayed into each nostril and tipped her head back. A packet of chewing gum fell out of an inside pocket and landed on the floor by her feet. She bent down to pick it up. "You've moved your car round the back of the house."

"So?" said Molin, but couldn't quite manage the insolent expression to match the tone.

Beckman shrugged. "I thought it might be the kind of thing a person would do to make it look as if they weren't at home."

They heard a thud from upstairs, followed by a faint creaking, as if someone had padded to the top of the stairs in their stocking feet. Perhaps this someone wanted to get an idea of what was going on without joining in.

"Stay there, Dagny!"

Tell raised his eyebrows as Molin called out to his wife.

"Stay where you are."

They heard an indistinct mumbling in response.

"She has to think about her heart," he explained to Tell and Beckman. His tone was unexpectedly confiding all of a sudden. "She mustn't get upset."

"Which brings us back to my question," said Beckman. "What is there to get upset about?"

Molin sighed heavily and shook his head. He excused himself and went out into the hallway. They heard him take the staircase in a few powerful strides, an achievement for anyone, let alone a pensioner. Then everything went quiet. No muffled whispers penetrated the silence. Nobody seemed to be shinning down the outside of the house with the help of sheets knotted together.

Tell shushed crossly at the splash of the tap as Beckman took the opportunity to get a drink of water.

"But it's so bloody hot in here," she hissed, pushing the window open.

"Are you going to bring them downstairs?" she asked after they had waited a while. "Or shall we just go straight for Sven Molin?"

"Hang on. It won't take long. You can see how wound up he is. I just want to make sure it's for the reason we think."

A door closed upstairs, and Bertil Molin came down the stairs with heavy footsteps. He made a vague gesture in the direction of Tell and Beckman, slipped on a pair of shabby slippers and went outside ahead of them. At the corner of the house he burrowed deep in his breast pocket for a box of matches and a small pipe held together with an elastic band.

Bertil Molin seemed to gain strength once the pipe was glowing and he had taken a couple of deep pulls. He turned to Tell; he was of the age when a female police officer could be ignored once things got serious. Beckman knew the type. Early on in her career, when she had also been discounted because of her age, it used to drive her mad. These days she was happy to leave the interviews with the whingeing old sods to her male colleagues, since she was perfectly confident in her own abilities and didn't need their approval.

"Let's have it — what is it you think you know?" Bertil said.

Tell nodded, happy to cooperate.

"We think your son Sven was involved in an attack on a girl at a bikers' club just outside Borås twelve years ago. We think the two other lads who were there and who knocked the girl down were Olof Pilgren and Thomas Edell."

Bertil Molin opened his mouth. The frustration on his face was transformed into exhaustion and he gave a quivering sigh. Tell took a step towards Molin, and noticed the yellowing line around his shirt collar.

"Listen to me. We don't actually need anything from you. While we're standing here our colleague back at the station is checking up on your son, everything from where he went to nursery to how many unpaid parking fines he has piled up at home."

He dug out his mobile and held it out to Molin.

"As soon as I hit speed dial I'll find out if that nineteen-year-old girl died as a result of injuries sustained that night. If she was raped. If there were any suspects."

Molin stubbornly refused to look Tell in the eye. Instead his gaze was fixed on the attic window just below the roof, the moss-covered slates and the collection of clouds above it.

"The only reason my colleague and I are standing here," Tell went on, "is that Sven's life could be in danger, and something tells me you've already worked that out. So, either you help us get in touch with him as quickly as possible, or there's a chance the murderer will get hold of him first. Your choice."

Molin started to breathe heavily, wheezing and clutching at his chest.

"Calm down."

Tell took a step back to give the older man some space. Molin cupped his hands over his mouth and his breathing soon eased.

"Do you know of any hiding places Sven might have had?" Tell persisted. "And what about Sven's involvement back in 1995?"

"He was beside himself."

The voice came from behind them. Tell turned and met Dagny Molin's tear-filled eyes. She was dressed in a faded ankle-length skirt and had thrown a flowery dressing gown over her shoulders. She was trembling and had to lean against the wall of the house to remain upright.

"Dagny . . ." Bertil Molin warned, but his wife shook her head.

"No. Let me tell them."

She pulled the dressing gown more tightly around her shoulders and clasped her hands against her chest to stop them shaking.

"He was beside himself when he got home that night. I didn't usually wait up for him — I mean he'd been an adult for a long time; he had a flat of his own down in the basement — but that night he went into the living room. I was having a sleepless night and was sitting in the kitchen, and when I went to see how he was, he'd thrown up on the floor."

She wiped the tears from beneath her eyes with her thumb.

"When he saw me he ran towards the basement steps, but he slipped on the mat in the hallway and fell. Then he just started crying, there on the floor, and the noise woke Bertil and he came downstairs . . ."

Her voice was shaking and she had to catch her breath before she could go on.

"Sven was all muddy and wet and he might have had blood on his clothes as well, or perhaps that's just the way I'm remembering it . . . I tried to get him to talk to us, but he just kept crying. Eventually he fell asleep on the sofa."

"And the next morning?"

"He closed up like a clam. He refused to talk about what had happened. But it was a long time before he was himself again. I would almost say that in a way he was never himself again. It was like a yoke that weighed him down, stopped him laughing."

"But you must have wondered," said Beckman.

Dagny Molin nodded sadly.

"Even if I convinced myself that it was down to the drink — he stank of alcohol when he got home that night — I didn't really succeed in calming my fears, because . . . well, it was just so . . . primitive."

"It?"

"Yes, the fear. The grief. He was screaming like a child."

Beckman found a packet of tissues in her bag, which Dagny Molin, with an anxious glance at her husband, gratefully accepted.

"How did you find out?" said Tell.

She nodded, after noisily blowing her nose.

"Somebody got in touch with us, much later. Several years after the event we got a letter. It was addressed to Sven, but I opened it because . . . well, Sven didn't live here any more. Anyway, the letter said that . . . Sven, along with Thomas Edell and Olof Pilgren, had . . ."

She sniffled into the tissue for a while before continuing.

"The writing was strange, I remember. Childish, with capital letters and small letters all mixed up, and spelling mistakes. I might not have taken any notice of it, I might have thought it was just a tasteless joke, if I hadn't seen Sven's eyes that night. The fear in them. I realised it was true."

"Why do you think someone sent the letter?"

"To force him to go to the police, I think. That's what it said in the letter, that he ought to take his punishment, otherwise he would have to . . . pay. Perhaps the person who sent it was after money."

"Have you still got the letter?"

This time it was Bertil Molin who responded, shaking his head.

"No. We threw it away."

He looked down at his slippers; their frayed edges had absorbed moisture from the grass, and they had turned dark grey.

"It was such a long time ago. We thought . . . we got the impression that the person who wrote it wasn't quite . . ."

"Who wrote the letter?" said Beckman.

489

Dagny Molin met her eyes. "I have no idea. We have no idea." She straightened her back and looked at Beckman with an expression of defiance. "Unfortunately we know next to nothing about Sven's life these days. We really don't have any contact with him at all."

Her defiance collapsed as the sobs welled up from her stomach. Beckman placed a hand on her back and felt the knobbly spine trembling beneath her fingers.

CHAPTER
FIFTY-THREE

Seja allowed her upper body to slump back as she sat on the sofa. A broad crack running across the ceiling had branched out into thinner cracks, forming the shape of a spindly tree. She followed the crack steadily with her eyes. Yellowish-brown patches bulged between the ceiling and the edge of the window, caused by a leak she hadn't noticed before. It was easy to follow the progress of the water underneath the wallpaper.

She realised the ceiling would have to be redone. Maybe it would need to be taken down and replaced? What if there was mould up there in the loft? What if the dampness from years of melting snow had run down the walls and damaged the wood? An icy chill passed through her body at the thought that the entire house might be rotten.

"The cottage smells exactly like my aunt's summer cottage on Gotland," she had whispered to Martin with starry-eyed enthusiasm as they went on the brief tour of the house with old man Gren just before they jumped in and bought the place. At that time nobody had lit a fire in the grate for months and it looked as if the most obvious common denominator between her aunt's rarely visited summer cottage and this charming but

491

oh-so-neglected little house was that the chill of the outdoors had eaten its way into the walls, or as Tove Jansson wrote, "the rain and storms had moved into the rooms". The whole place was probably on the point of falling down, she realised. And there she was: a lonely town mouse, and a girl into the bargain — no reason to insist on equality when there was no one to be equal with.

She sniffed the air tentatively, hating the idea that the smell of Christian Tell still lingered in the curtains and covers, that mixture of cigarette smoke and some unfashionable aftershave like Old Spice or Palmolive. And sometimes, at close quarters, a sweetish hint of fresh sweat beneath his jacket. Tears of self-pity welled up and threatened to spill over at the thought of the betrayal, the loneliness, the cottage and the stable and the many, many hours of time and money it would take to make a decent home for herself and Lukas — far more than she could afford with her student loan. Perhaps you could borrow books on doing up houses from the library? *Home Improvement for Dummies.*

She needed to get herself off the sofa, sit at her desk and start writing; go out to the stable and give Lukas his evening feed; go across to the shed and fetch more wood so that she could build up the fire, which was slowly going out. Bring some warmth to these little rooms, and into her soul. Get up off the sofa and open the windows wide to let in the evening air, ridding the place both of the smell of damp and of Christian Tell and his old-fashioned scent and unfulfilled promises.

Since he had left she had felt hollowed out, caught up in her own life story. Admittedly his bitterness had been replaced by a desire to understand during the course of the evening. For a moment she had also imagined he was groping for the closeness they had lost, until she realised it was the case he wanted to understand, not her. When he finally left, the distance between them was tangible.

There was a slight draught coming up between the floorboards. The fingers of her hand dangling over the arm of the sofa were gradually going numb, and that finally decided the matter: she had definitely made a fool of herself once more. Fallen in love and allowed herself to hope for a future that would never happen. But this was her home, mouldy or not, and there was no reason to freeze.

Before she went out on to the steps she turned off the light above the porch and stood there with only the light from the kitchen behind her, until her eyes grew accustomed to the dark.

For some reason, when she had to go to the stable or the shed after dark, she often found the limited pool of light from the outside lamp more frightening. Having to step over that border between what was illuminated and what was hidden, out into the blue-black unknown and its brooding dangers, just waiting for her to take that step.

CHAPTER
FIFTY-FOUR

He had thought about opening the cage doors wide and letting the revolting little animals run away. That way he could fool the local police into thinking that Molin's death was the result of a raid by the Committed Militant Vegans, or whatever they were called, those rabid fanatics dressed in black. It would give him a head start of a day or two. Not that the forests of Dalsland were home to any murder investigation teams worthy of the name, of course — it was more Keystone Kops than CSI.

Since before Christmas Caroline had bought and read every single newspaper that was available. Sebastian knew perfectly well she was looking for something about the murders. He didn't know how she had realised it was him. It was strange, both of them knowing something they could not mention. She gave him her support, her silent collusion. He interpreted her looks: *We're in this together. We have to keep going to the end of the road.*

He established later, shut in the memory room with burning cheeks, that there had been only a couple of brief articles, a short unemotional item on the local television news, but nothing else. He felt a certain disappointment, despite the fact that he was intelligent enough to realise that the ignorance of the media served their purpose.

It was an unfamiliar feeling, but he was proud of the fact that everything had gone according to plan. That he had succeeded in something that demanded greater courage than most people would be required to summon during their lives: he had killed two men, no, two miserable bastards, whose very existence was an insult to the surface of the earth and the air they breathed. The fact that he had succeeded gave him the sense that he was slowly approaching the point at which he would receive Caroline's love, and in the long term his mother's love, and he would actually deserve that love. Because that was what this was all about, after all — being worthy of love.

This time he was driving a different make of car, hired down in the Varberg area to be on the safe side. He had wanted to stay for a while on the shore at Skrea, resting in the sand dunes and listening to the wind blowing through the tall dry grass, and the sound of the sea rolling in. Instead he had allowed himself to drive slowly along the promenade. For a few minutes he switched off the engine and gazed out along the blue-grey horizon, just visible between the beach huts and the luxurious houses with their burglar alarms.

Closely linked to this seascape was his only clear memory from childhood; the rest remained only as blurred fragments of things he was at best indifferent to, or in many cases had chosen to forget.

He hadn't been very old when he and Maya were sent to stay with a family in Falkenberg for the summer. He ought not to be able to remember anything at all, yet the pictures were surprisingly sharp, with a clear band of colour around them, like in a catalogue. In Skrea the water was clear blue, the beach blissfully sunny, the sand the colour of hot chocolate with cream. The swimming trunks bought before the trip were bright red.

They were meant to go back the following summer and the one after that, perhaps during the Christmas holiday too; instead Solveig had withdrawn her application for support after only a week. Presumably being without the children hadn't been as pleasant as she had expected, so there were no more trips to Skrea for Sebastian. No more azure sea until now, when he had finally decided to take his life into his own hands.

He decided to leave the mink in their cages. There was no reason to cause mayhem and put the isolated farm on the police radar before it was necessary.

At the distant sound of an engine, he raised his binoculars. A cloud of dust surrounded the dirty grey truck coming round the bend in the track. Molin was on his way back; it was exactly two hours since he had moved the Asian woman and the children out, his expression grim. Sebastian realised this meant that Molin had found out about the fate of his former friends and smelled a rat. Now it seemed as if he was planning to go to ground as well. Earlier in the day he had thrown a sleeping bag and a bulging supermarket carrier bag into the truck. His gaze had roamed over the field in front of the house and in among the trees behind it.

The fact that Molin was preparing his escape didn't make Sebastian nervous; he was actually enjoying almost being able to smell the fear. He realised this was the reward. Molin had put two and two together: he understood why he had to die. And the fact that he was planning to run away was irrelevant — he wouldn't get very far. However, Sebastian did feel obliged to change his plans. Presumably Molin knew that the previous two victims had been shot from inside a car and he was clearly on his guard. He would have the hunting rifle he doubtless owned at the ready. It other words, it would be difficult to get close enough to execute him, even on an ostensibly innocent errand. In addition, Sebastian's shooting skills were limited, to say the least.

The gun had been laughably easy to get hold of, thanks to a friend's father who had criminal connections and swallowed hook, line and sinker Sebastian's woolly explanation involving gambling debts and that he only needed the gun to gain the respect of the people who were threatening him. Once he had the pistol he had practised out in the forest a couple of times.

Shooting Edell and Pilgren and running over them had given him adrenalin-fuelled pleasure, hearing their bones splinter and their bodies being torn asunder beneath the weight of the car. But this was nothing compared with the enjoyment of observing Molin's twelve-year-old shame and terror from his hiding place.

Sebastian moved further in behind the dilapidated old outhouse. There was no reason to reveal his presence to Molin yet. For one dangerous moment Sebastian was almost overcome by an urge to walk up to the house and knock on the door. Ask the way to the nearest garage or something, just to watch Molin weighing him up. He grabbed hold of the rotting corner of the outhouse with an iron grip until the urge passed, talking to himself all the while: just a recce today. He had positioned his camouflaged one-man tent in the densest part of the forest, at a safe distance from the farm.

All in good time. All in good time he would see Molin's mortal terror close up, even if it wouldn't be for nearly long enough.

CHAPTER
FIFTY-FIVE

Driven on by his misgivings, Tell floored the accelerator. It was after eight in the evening, and as expected once they had passed Kungälv there was nothing, just an empty carriageway, the forest growing thicker and thicker on both sides. His breathing was rapid and shallow. Going to see Sven Molin had been a snap decision, and if they hadn't been in such a sparsely populated area, his speed would definitely have attracted flashing blue lights and sirens.

He really wanted a cigarette. Instead he wound down the window and replaced the stuffiness with the aroma of the pine forest and a starry sky that was just too beautiful for the occasion. Irritatingly, this made his mind wander. He fixed his eyes firmly on the road ahead and tried to deny Seja a place in his thoughts. Mainly because during their brief acquaintance she had managed to erode his normal decisiveness.

Her betrayal seared his chest and throat like heartburn. The feeling of reconciliation he had had as she sat in front of him had disappeared completely.

It was quite simple really. As he saw it, she had played fast and loose with his job, which in the final analysis meant she had put people's lives at risk. How could he ever trust her again? Not only had she deliberately kept from him facts that would have helped solve a murder case, but she had also carried out her own private research. And at the same time she had exploited him, listening to him as he put forward his hypotheses in good faith, hypotheses that turned out to be completely wrong. She had deceived him. The more he went over it, the more embarrassed he felt. The knowledge that he had also committed a serious professional error by allowing himself to be seduced and misled by a witness made him feel even more unbalanced.

When he remembered his most recent conversation with Östergren he just had to have that cigarette. He gave Beckman an apologetic look.

"You look as if you need it," she responded.

The cross-draught whirled the smoke up towards the roof and out through the window.

"I'm thinking about that letter," said Tell after a while.

"Me too."

"It's reasonable to assume that Edell and Bart received one as well."

"But Edell was dead."

"What do you mean?"

"He was dead by that time, I assume. The Molins said they got the letter some years after the attack, which happened in 1995. Edell died in 98 or 99, if I remember rightly?"

"He might have been alive. Or if he'd just died there's a chance that Lise-Lott might have ended up with the letter."

"But wouldn't she have mentioned it, in that case?" Beckman rummaged in her handbag. "No point in speculating."

She keyed in Lise-Lott's number. After a short conversation she flipped her mobile shut.

"She doesn't know anything about any letter. Either Edell received it before he died — and it's more than likely he wouldn't have said anything to his wife about something like that — or the letter writer, unlike the murderer, knew he was dead."

"Which means the murderer and the letter writer are not the same person."

They sat in silence for a while.

"I'm thinking about Susanne Jensen," said Beckman eventually.

Tell smiled at the accord between them. "Me too. About her notes from social services."

"Exactly. They said she was dyslexic. Molin said there were upper -and lower-case letters all mixed up."

Tell braked suddenly as a hare shot across the road. He smacked the wheel with his hand.

"But how does she fit in? Susanne Jensen, the sister of one of the attackers from 1995. What the fuck has she got to do with all this? I mean, it was her brother who . . . Did she send him a threatening letter as well? And if so, why? Plus she came to talk to you, didn't she? About what Olof had said when he was drunk. If she'd been trying to get money out of Edell and Molin, would she really want to draw the attention of the police to the case and risk being found out herself?"

501

"Maybe she's suffering from a guilty conscience and wants to put things right. Sinners must pay, and so on. Or maybe she was in need of money for a fix when she wrote those letters. Or maybe she was raped at some point and thinks —"

"But Maya Granith wasn't raped."

"Maybe Susanne didn't know that. And it wouldn't be so surprising if she re-evaluated the whole thing now her brother's been murdered, would it? Obviously she wants the murderer to be caught. And she might think that the business with the money is now covered by the statute of limitations."

Tell sighed.

Beckman found a forgotten packet of throat sweets in the glove compartment and took two. The chewy mass stuck between her teeth.

"What are you thinking?" she said, poking at her mouth with a fingernail.

Tell didn't reply straight away, but he nodded to show that he'd registered the question. "I don't actually know," he said in the end. "It's just a feeling I've got. That time is important. As always, but now more than ever."

Beckman accepted his less than exhaustive answer and instead thought about what they might get out of the trip to Bengtsfors. Whether she ought to try to convince Tell to contact their colleagues in the local force before they got to Sven Molin's farm. Whether she ought to ring home and say that she was probably going to be late again tonight.

The familiar excitement wasn't really there, presumably because for once she didn't know where she was with Tell. She accepted that he could be temperamental in stressful situations and sometimes over-keen on prestige, but over the years she had learned to tackle these issues.

When she had first joined the group, she had secretly been pleased to detect behind Tell's harsh facade — he sometimes demanded an unreasonable amount from his subordinates — a team leader who was fair, self-critical and had a greater insight into relationships than he was necessarily willing to reveal. But recently she hadn't recognised him. He had seemed distracted by something he was keeping from the team.

She glanced at him out of the corner of her eye. He had been running his hand over his head, removing any vestige of a hairstyle, and his eyebrows protruded over his narrowed eyes, making him look annoyed and dejected.

"Is anything wrong?" she ventured at last. "Anything else, I mean?"

The car veered on to the verge as he leaned over to switch the radio on. The sound of some pop anthem was quickly throttled as Beckman turned down the volume. He glanced at her.

"Sorry, I didn't hear what you said."

"I said, is anything wrong?"

When he still didn't reply, she leaned back in her seat and sighed.

"You have a few minutes before we get there. I might not be able to help you, but I can always listen. If you want me to."

The bend of the exit road was sharper than he expected. The tyres screeched as they passed a garage with its lights off.

"It's just that I . . ." She searched for the right words. "You seem to have had a lot on your mind recently. Like now, for example. I can see that something's weighing you down." A look from Tell made her add, "I mean, apart from the case."

Now it was Tell's turn to sigh.

"Nothing gets past you, does it? If you really want to know, I was thinking about a chat I had with Ann-Christine the other day . . ."

He was putting out a feeler. If she knew what he knew, she would pick up on it. At the same time he was reluctant to reveal what he had been told in confidence. He had never called her anything but Östergren before, or possibly "the boss", ironically putting some distance between them. Ann-Christine was the person behind the professional role.

Beckman's expression told him that she knew as well, and suddenly it became distressing for them both. *Ann-Christine*. As if she had lost some of her authority as soon as she confided in them and exposed her human frailty for the first time.

"The worst thing is that I feel so . . . inadequate," he said eventually.

"Because you're afraid?"

"Because I feel . . ." He thought for a second. "Because I feel something is expected of me. But I don't know what. I don't even know what to say to her."

504

"What makes you think she expects more of you than anyone else?"

"I don't know if I think that . . . Can you just check that we're heading in the right direction?"

Beckman checked her printout and directed him on to a gravel track at a dark crossroads.

"In your capacity as a colleague, or as a friend?"

"How the hell should I know? Both, maybe. I've worked closely with her for a long time so . . . We've always made a good team."

"You think you're going to miss her."

"For fuck's sake, Beckman!"

He took a bend unnecessarily quickly, and Beckman reached out for a grab handle on the dashboard.

"You're forever putting words in my mouth, do you know that?" Tell snapped. "Is that something they recommend on your bloody psychology courses?"

She opened her mouth to reply, but changed her mind and focused on the road ahead.

The air went out of him with a sigh.

"I feel like a clumsy child. And the worst thing is that my first thought was about the vacancy, when she . . . leaves. Not that I want it, but the fact that I'll have to make that choice. Isn't that terrible?"

Beckman slowly shrugged her shoulders.

"What was your second thought?"

"That I hope I don't end up in the same situation, knowing there's nothing that can be done. Knowing I've got maybe a year left. A year of pain, perhaps."

He slammed his hand against the wheel once again and gave a humourless laugh.

"You can hear the way I'm talking — she's going to die, and it's still all about me."

"Do you know what I hear? I hear someone who's fairly egocentric, wallowing in his guilty conscience. You are, honestly! Sometimes I think it's as if you walk around carrying some kind of imagined guilt. Maybe you don't even know where it comes from, or why. But it seems to be bloody exhausting."

She fell silent for a moment. When she went on, she lowered her voice.

"I don't think you should blame yourself just because death frightens you. Isn't it only human to react selfishly when you're confronted with your greatest fear?"

"You mean my greatest fear is death?"

"I don't know. Is it? If it is, you're not the first person to feel that way. And I've thought of something else, Christian. It would be good if you didn't get angry again."

He gave a wry smile.

"You probably don't need to say much. To Ann-Christine, I mean."

"No, maybe not."

"I mean it. What makes you think that anything you say will change her situation, how she feels? It would be a bit presumptuous to think you had that power."

She paused to give him a chance to respond. His silence gave her the courage to continue.

"But I have noticed one thing. Since you, or rather we, found out that Östergren was ill, you've been avoiding her — at least, that's how it seems to me. It's

506

as if you can't cope with being in the same room as her. Isn't that true?"

"If you say so, it must be true."

His tortured expression took the sting out of the sarcasm.

"I think that's much much worse," Beckman went on quietly but undaunted. "You don't need to have all the right words to be there for a friend, but you do need to bloody well *be* there."

It was so long since Tell had cried he wasn't sure if it really was tears that were beginning to throb behind his eyelids. Bloody Beckman. It was so typical of her, thinking she knew it all. She knew nothing about the mess in his life, or why he couldn't look Östergren in the eye. She talked about being there, hiding behind the right words, the empty phrases, the psychobabble. As if it was her strong point. And yet she —

"Stop!" she yelled.

He hit the brake so hard he thought he had strained his calf muscle.

"Back up a few metres!"

Triumphantly she pointed to something at the side of the road. Among the trees a car gleamed in the headlights. Somebody had taken the trouble to park there instead of at one of the passing points along the road. There was only one reason for that: somebody had wanted to hide it.

He switched off the engine. The map confirmed that Sven Molin's place ought to be very close by. Instinctively they lowered their voices to a whisper.

★ ★ ★

The farm consisted of a low metal-covered annex and an older house, which was virtually in darkness when they arrived on foot, their torches switched off. Between the two buildings misshapen clumps of grass forced their way up around the wheel ruts where the earth was compacted.

They didn't make a sound, apart from the faint swish of Beckman's jacket. The lamp on the end of the annex cast a pool of light in front of it, with a blurred reflection of the glowing globe in the glass of the veranda. If anyone was home, they were sitting in the dark.

As if by silent agreement they had both taken out their service weapons. Nor had either of them suggested out loud that they should leave the car beyond the bend, but here they were, with neither a vehicle nor the light from their torches, trying to make as unobtrusive an entrance as possible.

A rustling in the bushes behind them made them jump. Beckman spun around, her gun pointing in the direction of a shed.

When it was quiet again and their breathing had more or less returned to normal, they carried on towards the house.

"Take the back," mouthed Tell, walking slowly up the steps towards the front door. He leaned over the fence and peered in through the window. A kitchen lay in darkness, with only the digital displays on the fridge and microwave visible. The place seemed dead.

He lowered his pistol and replaced it in the holster. The garden was a shadowland in a pitch-black sea. He

508

couldn't see any movement and didn't hear another sound until Beckman appeared around the side of the house, moving through the long grass. She too had put her gun away.

"Seems quiet," she whispered. "There's nobody here."

"Molin's probably done a runner."

Tell met her at the bottom of the steps. The moon emerged from its hiding place behind a cloud, extending their field of vision.

"Shall we take a look around before we go?"

Beckman nodded and walked towards the annex. She could see Tell moving around the perimeter of the garden.

As the tension eased she realised her feet were freezing; they were actually starting to hurt in the cheap trainers she had bought on impulse the week before Christmas. She was desperate to get home, to the children and a hot bath. A glass of wine.

The door was locked. She peered inside. By the glow of a fluorescent bulb she could see rows of cages piled on top of one another and the mink inside.

"If the activists want to get in, they will," she muttered with satisfaction after she had tugged at the iron grille covering the window.

Then she heard rapid footsteps in the grass behind her, the muffled sound of breathing, and before she managed to draw her gun someone was pulling at her jacket. It was Tell. He was pressing a finger to his lips and there was a desperate look on his face.

"Bloody hell," she hissed. "You nearly frightened the life out of me."

"This way," he whispered, pulling her with him.

Her heart was in her mouth. A few seconds later she was trying to think clearly as Tell stared at her with an encouraging expression. He was shining his torch at the back of the shed.

A rucksack was propped against the wall, with a well-thumbed map poking out of the outside pocket. A neatly folded sweater lay on top of it. A pair of binoculars was balanced on the sweater, and the remains of a fast-food meal were a couple of metres away.

Beckman turned to Tell with a look he interpreted immediately.

"Of course he's coming back: he's left the binoculars and . . . He's not far away . . ."

The words died on his lips as a twig snapped not far off in the forest.

Tell clamped his jaws together. As quietly as possible they moved over to a dense clump of fir trees just a few metres away.

Here I am again, Beckman said to herself as she grabbed the sleeve of Tell's coat, thinking that the beating of her heart could be heard for miles around because it was threatening to smash through her chest. Terrified and unreasonably euphoric in equal parts.

Later they would discover that the man had a pistol in his jacket pocket and a hunting knife in a sheath on his thigh. However, he wasn't even close to getting either of them out when they jumped him.

CHAPTER
FIFTY-SIX

The chair was flimsy, with a plastic back. Presumably the table was fixed to the floor. It didn't matter. He didn't have the strength to hurl it at the locked door. Considerable anger was necessary for such a feat, and he was no longer angry. And when it came to strength, if it had ever been contained within him, it had run out through his feet, into the moss, there in the darkness next to Sven Molin's house. When his arms were forced behind his back by the tall red-faced man that, in his confusion, he had mistaken for Caroline.

He had taken into account that this might happen. Perhaps not exactly like this, but that he might be caught before he had completed his task. He had quickly adapted to the new situation without wasting time and energy on cursing himself for his carelessness, for moving too far away from his camp in an attempt to cure his restlessness. For leaving behind clues, unforgivably, that had given him away and delivered him straight into the arms of the police. The mistakes of an idiot, an imbecile, ruining months of preparation. He could hear Solveig's voice in his head: *What have you done, Sebastian? Your sister would never have failed like you.* And she would have been right.

He had offered no resistance, but had cooperated as much as possible without answering their questions. The brief cryptic message he had prepared but not expected to need was sent with a couple of practised clicks on the mobile phone in his pocket.

He knew she would understand.

Afterwards, while they were waiting for the circus to get under way, he had dropped the mobile where he was standing. Of course it would be found later when the area was searched, but by then it would be too late. He had pushed it discreetly into the damp soil with his foot.

When the car arrived and the female officer carefully guided him into the back seat, he felt able to indulge himself with a secret smile.

The inspector looked as if he had stepped straight out of a crime film — tall, with a crumpled suit and a three-day beard. Then there was the short fat one with a low forehead, the waistband of his jeans somewhere down below his beer belly. The mannish old bag with the police logo on her sweatshirt. They all believed he would be an easy nut to crack. They had hauled him ashore like a fish in their net, and would hardly need to get started on their good cop/bad cop parody before he broke down, allowing the truth to seep from him like air from a punctured tyre.

In fact he hadn't settled on his strategy as he sat in the small windowless room. His silence was a passive rather than a conscious act, and had nothing to do with a refusal to admit what he had done.

The ridiculous little team clearly had a plan for situations like this, each one with a designated role to play. Beer Belly, uninspired and unprofessionally aggressive, but too stupid to recognise the solution to a problem even if it was staring him in the face. Old Bag, seeking eye contact and trying to get him on side. The Suit alternated between playing the good guy, offering cigarettes and fetching sandwiches, and slamming his fist on the table and demanding answers.

None of this was going to make him talk, since nothing they said was of any importance to him. If there was one thing he had acquired, it was the ability to leave his body, to transport his thoughts to a peaceful place where no one could reach him, their voices coming and going in an unintelligible blur of sound.

In the windowless room he had lost all concept of time; he knew only that a large part of the night had passed.

Out of sheer curiosity he considered trying to explain how it had all happened. To see if they understood. He wasn't afraid of going to prison as a result of his confession; he almost expected to end up there sooner or later.

Several times he opened his mouth to begin speaking, but closed it again when he realised that his words would not penetrate through the interference. From time to time the roaring sound filled the entire room. Only when the Suit leaned across the table could Sebastian make out individual words.

"You murdered the wrong man, didn't you, Sebastian? You intended to murder Thomas Edell, because you think he tried to rape your sister Maya that night twelve years ago. Thomas Edell, Olof Pilgren and Sven Molin."

The Suit pressed the palms of his hands against the surface of the table so that his fingers turned white.

"Because it was dismissed as an accident and because there was no proof, because they said she could just as easily have tripped and hit her head on a sharp stone. As if she'd suddenly taken leave of her senses and run straight into the forest and the darkness of her own free will, throwing herself headlong into the snow to die. Because the police did such a bloody useless job."

Sebastian could feel their eyes burning against his skin. The roaring had stopped and the words were hurling themselves mercilessly at his eardrums; it was impossible to defend himself.

"Because she ended up in a coma and died, thanks to those three vile men. And so you dedicated yourself to doing what the police ought to have done: asking questions, drawing conclusions. Finding out who was behind it all. And once you knew, you embarked on a campaign of revenge, to avenge your sister. Thomas Edell, Olof Pilgren, and Sven Molin, isn't that right? But you failed, Sebastian. You only managed two, and one of those turned out to be the wrong man."

Sebastian Granith's sparse fringe was plastered against his forehead. Slowly he raised his head and met Tell's gaze.

There was nothing there that Tell could interpret.

"You didn't know you'd murdered the wrong man, did you, Sebastian?" Tell was speaking more quietly. "You've only just found that out, haven't you?"

The air between them was almost too thick to bear.

"You thought he was Thomas Edell because it was Thomas Edell's farm and his name was on the sign and he was married to Lise-Lott Edell. Not so strange, is it? You shot him in the head and drove over him several times, until he was spread all over the ground. How could you know he wasn't Thomas Edell? How could you know that the man you'd just squashed was in fact Lars Waltz, Lise-Lott's new husband, who'd never been anywhere near your sister?"

The uniformed policeman came to Tell's rescue before Sebastian Granith's hands fastened around his throat. He had hurled himself across the table, just to put a stop to the words pouring out of the inspector's mouth.

He sank back into his chair. "Just give me five minutes," he gasped.

Tell waved the uniform away with a gesture towards the door. Drops of sweat flecked the green-painted floor as Sebastian shook his head. The sound of his sobbing rose and fell like a guttural song.

Half an hour earlier Tell had considered breaking off the interview and continuing the next day. Now the night was almost over, and Granith's defence was collapsing.

"Five minutes," Tell agreed eventually.

For a decade he had beaten himself up. Ten long years of grovelling before he finally understood where the blame really lay. As soon as he had gained that insight, it had been like lifting a dusty veil from his eyes, allowing him to see clearly for the first time in years. Sometimes it had felt like floating.

"I did it. I killed them."

Granith had spent his five minutes sitting with his arm across his face. Now his expression was again empty, so disturbingly blank that Tell almost thought he could see his own reflection in it.

However, behind the reflective surface, Olof Pilgren continued to die. Over and over again his skull cracked and his internal organs burst as he was crushed between the garage wall and the grille of the jeep. It was the only sequence in Sebastian Granith's memory worth anything. Whatever happened, nobody could take that away from him. If he concentrated hard enough on the images burned into his retina, it would help him to get through this.

"The only thing I regret is that I didn't get the third one."

"You mean Sven Molin."

Tell leaned back and stole a glance at his watch. As soon as possible, he reminded himself, he needed to check on how they were getting on with finding Sven Molin. Presumably he was terrified and hiding in some cottage somewhere. Or he was somewhere else altogether, blissfully unaware that his life had been in danger, in which case he would come home eventually. The local constable watching the house had the job of telling him the danger was over, if he hadn't done so already.

Getting a confession had been easier than Tell had dared hope. The boy was obviously a nervous wreck, even if he seemed calmer once he started to describe how he had gone about killing the two men. But that was usually the case with criminals. Somewhere deep inside the human soul lay the hope that if you confessed your sins, you would be forgiven. He even seemed slightly excited about his crimes, as if he actually thought he had done something positive. A well-intentioned avenger, correctly apportioning blame. And in a way there was an element of reason in his particular brand of twisted logic: a life for a life. His sister's life.

From time to time, although rarely, a murderer succeeded in arousing feelings of empathy in Tell.

He shook off the notion, stood up and pushed his chair neatly under the table. It was dawn and he intended to go home. Knock back a glass of wine and hope it would help him to sleep well. It would be the first time for ages.

CHAPTER
FIFTY-SEVEN

When the telephone woke her she felt as if she had only been asleep for a few minutes. She had spent the night drifting between the living room and the kitchen, drinking tea that became more and more insipid and listening to music that usually calmed her nerves: Rickie Lee Jones, Manu Chao, Rebecka Törnqvist. Towards morning she had brewed a large strong espresso which she drank in small sips, curled up on the sofa. *No point trying any more*, she had thought, but obviously sleep had been lying in wait, and had crept up on her when she was least expecting it.

As she reached across the low table for the phone, she knocked the dregs of the cold coffee over her sleeve.

"Oh fuck. Hello?"

"Hello?" There was no mistaking Hanna's gravelly voice. "What's the matter with you? Got a hangover?"

Seja got up so quickly that everything went black. She flicked ineffectually at the coffee on her sweater with the back of her hand then wobbled and sat down again.

"Hi. Yes, or rather no. I haven't. But I bloody well feel as if I have. I hardly slept a wink last night."

"I sympathise."

In the pause that followed from the other end of the line, Seja recognised the sound of a lighter as Hanna lit up, took a deep drag and cleared her throat.

"Are you busy?"

Seja laughed.

"Not at all."

An asymmetrical brown stain had appeared on the pale green fabric of her sweater. Between her feet more coffee was soaking into the wooden floor.

"OK. I've been thinking about you a lot since we met up. It's been such a long time since we used to hang out and . . . All that business with . . . well, your research, or whatever you want to call it . . ."

Seja rubbed the palm of her hand over her eyes to try to stave off an incipient headache.

"I know, Hanna. I know it must have seemed strange to you. I didn't mean for you to get dragged in."

"No, no," Hanna protested, "don't start with all that stuff. What I wanted to say was . . . well, I know you asked me to trust you and to respect the fact that you couldn't tell me any more. But it struck me afterwards that Björn — you probably don't remember him, he was a couple of years younger than us. I still see him from time to time. On a completely platonic basis, that is."

"Right, but who —"

"His wife won't let him meet up with female friends, particularly when it's an old flame, so we've met in secret a few times and had a coffee in town. All perfectly innocent, as I said."

"But what's he got to do with —"

"Well, what I was going to say is that Björn is a friend of a guy who was really close to that girl — the one in the white leather jacket, Tingeling. Her name was Maya, by the way, the one who disappeared. It's a small world."

"Hanna . . ."

The headache definitely had her in its clutches now.

Hanna giggled nervously, but immediately became serious again. "I realise I wasn't supposed to talk about this with anyone, but it's done now, even if I didn't know enough to say anything at all, really."

"What did he say, this Björn?" Curiosity began to edge out her irritation.

"He didn't say anything; it was just that he recognised her alias and remembered that she used to hang out with John back then — that's the other friend. Björn said John was the last person she was friendly with, so to speak. They were in the same class, or something. I've got his phone number."

"Whose? John's?" Seja realised she was holding her breath.

"Exactly. If you're interested. I thought you seemed to need to poke about in all this old stuff to find some kind of closure."

"Give me the number."

After once again fending off Hanna's questions about what she was doing, Seja sat there with the number in front of her, hastily scribbled in the margin of the Saturday supplement of *Göteborgsposten*.

Christian Tell's anger at the fact that she had overstepped the mark was fresh in her mind. She knew the right thing would be to swallow her pride and go down to the police station, where he would be sitting in all his self-righteousness. Hand over the information and go home. Not that she had anything other than the telephone number of a person who might have known Maya over ten years ago. It probably meant nothing, in which case she would have humiliated herself unnecessarily.

On the other hand, it would be a good way of showing that she realised she had to respect his point of view. That she could be trusted. Somewhere in the depths of her disappointment a hope was beginning to grow, a wish that things would be good between them. Even if she would have liked him to take the first step and seek her out. But the telephone remained silent.

After making herself a fresh cup of coffee, she sat down at the desk.

The folder Tell had found, with the unfinished texts and the blurred pictures of the body at Thomas Edell's workshop, was neatly inserted between the course material for her upcoming exam on ethics and journalism. She still hadn't started her preparation. She switched on her laptop and keyed in her password.

Saturday's paper was close enough for her to be able to see the numbers. She picked up the phone and decided to give it a go. If the conversation yielded anything of importance, Tell would be the first to know.

John Svensson answered after the first ring.

CHAPTER
FIFTY-EIGHT

According to Tell's watch it was quarter past seven when he left the department, but he didn't give it any thought. Despite his longing for wine and bed, he had ended up drinking coffee with Beckman and Karlberg. They also seemed to be harbouring a subconscious reluctance to go home. Maybe the need to sum up events was stronger than the need for sleep.

Whatever the reason, they often got together after finishing off one of their more demanding cases. They would rummage in the cupboard and find a forgotten packet of biscuits, then sit there dunking the biscuits in their coffee as they went over the various phases of the investigation. Perhaps it was what top management referred to as debriefing.

Afterwards Tell's office had refused to let him go, with its accusing piles of paper and the flashing light on the answering machine. What should have been half an hour's tidying to calm his nerves before he went home had got out of control. Certain people might accuse him with some justification of not taking the administrative aspect of his work seriously enough. However, nobody could say he wasn't effective once he got going.

He walked past reception now, finally ending his working day when most people were just starting. The clock on the wall made him realise his watch must have stopped at some point the previous evening — at quarter past seven, in fact. Behind his eyelids felt like gravel, and his longing for bed was no longer theoretical but physical in the form of spaghetti legs and a total lack of strength in his arms. Even his briefcase felt heavy, and it had just got heavier. Before he left the office he had grabbed the top layer of a dangerously high pile of the case summaries, circulars and memos that constantly poured into his in tray. Reading them all would have been a full-time job. He now intended to use some of them as an excuse to stay at home for a day or two. To catch up.

"Christian!"

Seja reached him in just a few strides. After hesitating for a fraction of a second, she reached out one arm and hugged him gently. She smelled faintly of vanilla. He stiffened and she must have registered it, because she quickly took a step back.

"I've been trying to get in to see you for half an hour. This place is like a fortress," she said in an attempt at a joke.

Neither of them smiled.

"It isn't," he replied tersely. "I asked them not to put through any calls and not to let anyone in. I was busy —"

"Are you busy now?" she interrupted him nervously, pulling a strand of hair out of the loose knot at the back of her head. "Because if you're not I really need to talk to you."

"Yes, I am busy."

He watched her winding the strand of hair around her fingers. A childish action that suddenly irritated him. Earlier he had been feeling tired but satisfied; that feeling had vanished the moment she thoughtlessly pressed her body against his. The lack of sleep over the past few days made the anger that had been simmering in the car on the way up to Bengtsfors boil over.

"I'm usually busy when I'm at work, oddly enough. And if I'm not busy right now, I'm bloody exhausted, so I'm going straight home to get some sleep."

"I understand." She hesitated. "It's just that I'd really like to talk to you about —"

He lost his last scrap of patience.

"Listen to me. I'm absolutely shattered. If you want to see me about something to do with my job, then ring me during office hours. Right now I'm going home."

She opened her mouth with an expression that suggested she wasn't sure if she'd heard him correctly.

"If I want to see you about . . . What the fuck is that supposed to mean? And what if I want to see you about something that isn't to do with your job — what then?"

She moved back a couple of steps towards the door, increasing the distance between them.

Out of the corner of his eye Tell saw a colleague raise a hand in greeting, but he didn't respond. The arm carrying the heavy briefcase was aching, but if he put it down, that would mean he was giving in to her. He didn't want to give her any more time.

"Christian, I realise you're angry with me, even if I do think you're overreacting. Maybe you're right to be angry — what do I know? But in any case I think you could spare me five minutes. You'll be interested in what I have to say."

Deep down inside Tell knew that the woman in front of him had just received both barrels because of a whole lot of issues for which she was not to blame: the way he had let Östergren down, both professionally and personally; his embarrassing inability to deal with the big questions, with life and death, with love. With closeness. That was the nub of the matter: she got on his nerves with her demands for intimacy. Closeness. Just like every woman he had ever known: they had all suffocated him with their desire for fusion, sooner or later.

"I haven't made any demands of you," she said quietly, as if she could read his mind. "I haven't asked you to commit yourself to a shared future, or to tell me everything you do and everything you're thinking. And if you're pretending I have, then you're being unfair. That's why I don't understand why you're so angry with me for not telling you everything."

"There *is* a difference, for fuck's sake."

"No. I'm here now because you wanted me to tell you everything I know. This is to do with Maya, her last two years. I think what I have to say —"

"It's too late now," he said simply. "It doesn't matter any more. It's over."

"As I said, I think what I have to say will interest you."

"I find that very difficult to believe."

He enjoyed spitting out the words, despite the fact that disappointment was instantly etched on her face. By making a big deal of moving the briefcase from his right hand to his left, he managed to avoid meeting her eyes, although he knew it was a coward's way out. Her gaze burned into his back as he left.

A fleeting image of them holding each other close beneath the sloping ceiling in the loft brought tears to her eyes, more from humiliation than sadness. It was too early to talk about a broken heart — they hadn't known each other for long enough. Sorrow over what could have been, perhaps. Over unfulfilled expectations.

He had turned out to be a different person. And she had once again thrown herself head over heels into something uncertain, and had come out on the other side more battered than before. With only herself to rely on once again.

She felt completely alone as she stood there in the middle of the reception area, the doors opening and closing in the morning rush. She felt as if everyone walking past was evaluating her and coming to the conclusion that she was damaged goods, a person who had believed too much. *They were always the most ridiculous.* Those who came running up, full of enthusiasm, like a dog with its tongue hanging out as soon as someone called its name.

The receptionist was a middle-aged woman with bleached blonde hair caught up in combs at the sides.

She winked and smiled sympathetically. Automatically Seja tried a polite smile in return, but it ended up as more of a grimace.

She welcomed the anger when it came surging up from her belly. She pictured the inspector once again — because that was what he was: he was his job more than a man or a person — beneath the sloping ceiling or standing by the fire in her kitchen, too stressed to sit down. His back. The way it had looked when he had strode down the hill outside her house towards the footbridge, his briefcase in his hand. How it looked a couple of minutes ago, when he walked out of the main door of the station.

Men are institutions, one of her tutors had said. It was during a course in basic feminism many years ago. She hadn't understood what the phrase meant, and was too young and insecure to ask. Later she had reconsidered the large dose of questions and answers surrounding women's issues which she had absorbed during a period in her life when she was heavily engaged in such matters. Some aspects had been integrated into her personal viewpoint, some had been rejected. Nonetheless, from time to time she had pondered what her tutor might have meant. And for the first time she thought she was on the way to finding the answer. An institution was a self-evident fact. Something that never had to question itself, which took itself extremely seriously. Detective Inspector Christian Tell.

She might have been able to understand his anger at her failure to pass on her memories of that evening. She could accept that he believed he had the right to those painful memories. She could even accept that she should have put her integrity to one side and talked to him earlier instead of carrying out her own investigation, as he put it.

On the basis of this reasoning, she really had taken his disappointment seriously. She *had* opened up to him in order to try to explain what had been going on in her head that night. Over the years since that night. During the past few days, when she had chosen to wait rather than talking to him straight away.

But he hadn't listened. He'd been far too busy playing the wounded hero struggling in a headwind.

There had been a reason why she had tried to forget the bad feeling she had about Maya's fate. Now it had floated to the surface, the memory of that night was demanding her attention. She would never be able to escape its cold fingers touching her soul, her conscience.

In order to find peace, she had to act. She realised that now. And since all her obligations towards Christian Tell had been wiped out at a stroke, she was free to act in accordance with her own aims. She had the outline of a crime story on her computer, a story she had already begun, and the folder lying next to the massive compendium on ethics and journalism. The exam was in just a few days, and so far she hadn't opened a single book.

But, she thought, *what's the point of being a journalist if you don't write?*

CHAPTER
FIFTY-NINE

It was obvious the hunting cabin hadn't been used for a long time. It had been part of the deal when he bought the farm, but Sven Molin had rarely set foot inside it. He wasn't all that keen on hunting; he felt the physical exertion was disproportionate to the financial gain in terms of meat, particularly since the EU had introduced cheap alternatives to most things. And he had never enjoyed it much either.

The porch floor was rotting, and the front door had swollen and was jammed shut. The evening he arrived he had nothing with which to prise it open, no tools apart from the knife on his key ring. It had been too dark to look for a branch or a sharp stone to lever the door open, but eventually he found a window that wasn't fastened. He wriggled in and landed on the floor with a thud. A well-aimed kick from the inside released the door, after which he stood absolutely still for several minutes.

Breaking the silence went against the grain. The cabin was about as far from civilisation as it was possible to get, and as far as he knew nobody was aware of it; the farm deed of purchase had only mentioned it in a sub-clause. Even the traces left by children who had played there — a doll with no legs and some dried grass in a couple of buckets — looked as if they had been there for many years.

He had slunk through the forest like a hunted animal after loading the pickup and leaving it parked outside the house as a smokescreen while he crept out the back way, taking the ignition key to his neighbour's Saab from where he kept it. He *was* a hunted animal, and if he had managed to suppress this knowledge while he was surrounded by the bright lights and minutiae of everyday life, it came home to him now with full force. Someone was after him, and this someone had presumably found it reasonably easy to track him down, although he had never made any serious effort to cover his tracks; he had never really thought it would be necessary.

The fact that he had cut his losses and left Olofstorp after the Accident didn't really have anything to do with any fear of legal repercussions. He wasn't even sure a crime had been committed; he preferred to think of it as nothing more than bad luck. What he had been running away from was the memories, which grew stronger each time he saw his two childhood friends, or heard their voices, or was reminded in some other way of that nightmarish December night outside Borås.

He had wanted to get away, and didn't think there was much to keep him in Olofstorp. The suffocating concern and trembling anxiety of his parents. The pathetic bachelor flat in the basement of his parents' home, which was nothing more than a boy's bedroom in disguise. His boring job in the warehouse. He

530

wanted to be his own man, and he wanted a family. And with the mink business and Lee he had achieved his goal. He had been happy. He was starting to forget about the Accident, just as he had predicted. It belonged to the misguided kid he had once been, not to the family man and provider he had become.

The morning after the Accident he had thrown up all over the hallway and the steps down to the basement, shaking and crying like a child. His parents had never mentioned it until now, when his father had grimly gone through the facts from which he had drawn his conclusions. He had been perfectly objective, as if none of it would have been of any significance but for the fact that Lise-Lott Edell's second husband and Pilen had been murdered within a few days of each other.

Of course he had never thought it would catch up with him. In one way the timing was particularly annoying. He had finally attained something of value, something to fight for. Now he would be forced to fight.

Every sound outside the cabin made him jump. The impenetrable darkness increased the panic which he had felt all day. Keeping hold of his gun at all times, he crawled around on all fours so he couldn't be seen through the cabin's single window. He didn't dare to use the forest for his bodily functions; instead he used one of the buckets that the children had left behind. The food he had grabbed in leaving soon ran out.

It wouldn't take long for him to lose his mind. Unless he starved to death first.

Since his mobile phone had no clock, he quickly lost all notion of time. His parents' number flashed silently on the display at regular intervals, interspersed with a withheld number which he presumed belonged to the police. They had left a message on his voicemail asking him to go to the nearest police station immediately. That could have been days ago or hours ago, he had no idea. He didn't trust the police, and he certainly didn't believe they could protect him from a lunatic.

From the start, giving himself up had been unthinkable. His thoughts had gone round and round in circles. Would his part in the incident be seen as manslaughter, aiding and abetting an attempted rape, or refusing to cooperate in a police investigation? Would the incident be covered by the statute of limitations, twelve years later?

As time passed it became more a matter of fear, but a different kind, more primitive. He would have liked the police to be with him in the hunting cabin, as he lay huddled in his sleeping bag, shaking with terror and expecting the deranged avenger to kick down the door at any second. The battery on his phone had almost run out — he would soon have no choice. As he sat there poised to key in the emergency number, a text message came through: "The police authority in Gothenburg has been trying to contact you with regard to a possible threat to your safety. We are now able to confirm that this threat no longer exists, as the perpetrator is in custody. Please contact Detective Inspector Christian Tell on 031–739 29 50 immediately in connection with this matter."

He had to read the message several times before he grasped what it said.

Molin's heart was still in his mouth as he ran, half-stooping, through the forest to the place where he had hidden his neighbour's car. He leapt inside, locked all the doors and took off along the dark twisting gravel track at death-defying speed. Away from the worst twenty-four hours of his life, away from feverish waking dreams of a silhouette looming over him, its arm raised. He would contact the police as soon as he got home.

He screamed as a shadow leapt at the car. For a fraction of a second he stared straight into a pair of terrified eyes. The car struck the back of the deer, and it let out a scream. In the rear-view mirror he saw the animal collapse in a heap on the road; it stopped moving. He would have assumed the deer was dead had it not then struggled awkwardly to its feet and dragged its damaged body off into the forest, emitting long drawn-out cries of pain.

Everything flickered in front of his eyes. He made himself stop the car at the crossroads by the mailboxes. Almost home.

. . . *this threat no longer exists, as the perpetrator is in custody.* The danger was over. He breathed as calmly as he could.

The ghostly cries of the deer seemed to be coming closer. He glanced in the rear-view mirror once more. Behind the car the branches of a dense fir tree were swaying.

For a moment he hesitated, then leaned across and picked up his gun. When he opened the door and got out, the animal's cries sliced through him. It was unbearable. He had to shut it up — it would only take one shot.

He followed the sound, his way dimly lit by the rear lights of the car. He didn't have to go far before he almost fell over the animal. The shot echoed through the forest, and a merciful silence descended. He hurried back. He was only a couple of metres away from the car when he sensed a movement behind him.

The next second he felt a stabbing sensation between his shoulder blades. At first he was surprised, and instinctively twisted his arm back to touch the source of the pain. The second blow caught his wrist. The agony shot up his arm and through his body and brought him to his knees. There was a figure leaning over him and the sound of rapid breathing. His bewildered brain repeated on a loop: *The danger is over. The danger is over.*

CHAPTER
SIXTY

Tell had waited outside the off-licence with the alcoholics, and when the doors opened had bought himself a bottle of Glenfiddich and one of decent red — to celebrate if nothing else — then called in at the local mini-market on Vasagatan. The girl behind the counter was chatting loudly on her mobile phone, but lowered her voice when Tell walked in. He picked up a few DVDs, some crisps and other snacks for a day on the sofa with the blinds drawn.

In the rear-view mirror he could see a traffic warden approaching and a road sweeper slowly clearing the junction between Vasagatan and Viktoriagatan, while the café in Tomtehuset, with its promise of coffee and freshly baked cinnamon buns, was opening its doors for the day.

Tell breathed a sigh of relief as he pulled away without having acquired a ticket; he didn't need another fine, particularly on a day like this. It was crazy to use the car for the short trip between home and work — but he knew that already. He narrowly avoided being hit by a number 3 tram. The driver made an obscene gesture and angrily sounded his horn, but Tell was far too tired to get annoyed.

The apartment had a musty smell when he got home. He kicked off his shoes in the kitchen and poured himself a Glenfiddich, moved in slow motion towards the living room and crash-landed on the sofa.

The end-of-shift siren from Valand woke him several hours later. He glanced at his watch: it still said a quarter past seven. He had slept for a long time, but he still felt tired as well as hot and sticky. The leather sofa was slick with sweat.

Stiff from lying in an awkward position, he hauled himself to his feet and shuffled into the kitchen to find something to eat before attacking the crisps. He ate a sandwich, gazing down on Götabergsgatan and the part of Vasa Park he could see from his window. A gang of youths were shouting as they made their way along Avenyn.

In the old days the drunks had at least confined themselves to Saturday nights, he thought. The noise of the city had never really disturbed him, though, not seriously. In fact he found the silence out at Seja's cottage more unnerving.

He took a shower with a glass of red perched on the edge of the washbasin — he was planning to spend his day off in a pleasant haze of intoxication — while the trailers flickered on the TV screen, introducing Clint Eastwood's *Million Dollar Baby*. He didn't hear the phone until the answering machine kicked in.

"... have reached ... automatic answering service ..."

As he towelled himself dry his recorded voice requested the caller's name and number. He reminded himself to disconnect the landline next time he was planning a day to himself.

The extended tone stopped, replaced by Karlberg's agitated voice. Tell went into the kitchen and leaned over the speaker so he could hear more clearly. The poor quality of the recording meant he had to rewind and listen again.

The second time he played the tape, he had no doubt what the message said.

"Sven Molin has been found dead. Murdered. I've rung Beckman too. Give me a call when you get in."

Tell looked at the bottles over on the draining board, at the useless watch still showing a quarter past seven; according to the clock on the wall, it would soon be showing the right time. He decided to call a taxi.

If he hadn't been so keen to conceal the fact that he wasn't entirely sober, Tell would have laughed at the deathly pale detective waiting for him. If the reason for this meeting had been funny, that is.

"We didn't forget to lock Granith up before we went home, did we?" Tell couldn't resist it, but he pulled himself together when he saw the surprise on Gonzales' face. "OK, OK. This isn't exactly what we were expecting."

He could feel the anger mounting as he took in the scale of what had happened. The shared sense of failure was clearly written on the faces of his colleagues.

"Bloody hell! How the fuck . . ." he burst out before making an effort to think clearly. "Is Karlberg up there?"

Gonzales nodded. "He took the call from Bengtsfors and went there straight away. We were waiting for you so we could check before —"

"Who's spoken to Karlberg?"

"I have."

Bärneflod appeared in the doorway, threading his belt through the loops in his jeans.

"And?"

"Molin was lying there on the road, stabbed to death just a couple of hundred metres from the officer on duty."

"Close to where he lived, then."

"Yes, at a crossroads just before you get to the farm. For some reason Molin had stopped the car and got out — the driver's door was wide open."

"Karlberg thought maybe he'd stopped to pick up the post," Gonzales interjected, "he was only a few metres from the mailboxes. Or he might have hit something. There were brown marks on the front of the car that could be blood. If it's an animal, they should find it before long."

The sound of high heels echoed along the corridor, and Beckman appeared. Her tousled hair indicated that like Tell she had turned the day upside down and been woken by the bad news. "Bed hair," Bärneflod whispered loudly to Gonzales, who didn't move a muscle.

Beckman slumped down next to Gonzales, looking at Tell with an expression that said she couldn't get her head around this latest development either.

"How did it happen?" asked Tell, perching impatiently on the very edge of the chair. "Stabbed, you said? Which means we have a completely different method. I just can't understand —"

"Well, it's a completely different murderer," Bärneflod informed him.

Tell closed his eyes for a second before replying. "Yes, I'm aware that Sebastian Granith can't have murdered Sven Molin while he was locked in a cell. But, bearing in mind the background, perhaps we should consider that it would be a strange coincidence if Sven Molin had been murdered by a total stranger, someone with no connection whatsoever to Sebastian Granith. Wouldn't it?"

"Never say never when it comes to police work. Not unless there's proof," replied Bärneflod loftily.

No doubt that's your intelligent comment for the day, thought Tell. Then he set out his own hypothesis.

"Without taking anything for granted, we must start from the premise that this third murder also has something to do with the fact that Maya Granith, the sister of Sebastian Granith, was probably attacked by Thomas Edell, Olof Bart and Sven Molin. So it's someone who's working with Granith."

"Someone who was also close to Maya," said Beckman.

Tell nodded. "Or is close enough to Sebastian to go along with his campaign of revenge. And of course there's another alternative, namely that Sebastian Granith has confessed to two crimes he didn't commit. That he's protecting someone else."

"Who found Molin?" asked Beckman.

"One of the neighbours," said Bärneflod.

"Have they been questioned?"

"Yes. The local police have started knocking on doors. Not that there are many doors to knock on out there. But one person thought he heard a shot."

"A shot?" said Beckman. "Now I'm getting confused."

"Yes. Molin's rifle was on the ground next to him. He could have felt uneasy; he could have shot at the murderer and missed. How should I know?"

"Right."

Tell could feel his brain revving up, emerging from the alcoholic haze.

"Beckman, you go up and join Karlberg. I'll talk to Sebastian Granith and see what I can get out of him. The rest of you, keep going through Maya Granith's life from when we broke off the other day. The investigation into the accident took place in 1995. Start from there and work backwards. Bärneflod, you can bring me a preliminary report later." He fell silent for a moment. "By the way, has anyone spoken to Östergren?"

Bärneflod looked thoroughly confused. "Isn't that your job? Isn't that why you get paid more than us?"

Tell got up, shoving Bärneflod past on his way out of the room.

"Stop moaning and get on with it."

The door of Östergren's office was closed. Tell decided not to call her at home just yet.

Half an hour later Tell walked into Bärneflod's office.

"I've got Gonzales following up a couple of leads. I thought you and I should go and see Ma Granith."

"Borås, then?"

"Borås it is."

540

"Can't Björkman take it?"

"No, he bloody well can't. This one's ours. Get a move on."

Just as they were passing Landsvetter, the traffic jams started. Tell was forced to slow down and eventually came to a standstill. He swore. They heard on the radio that a lorry had overturned right across the motorway, and the vehicle still hadn't been removed. It would probably be a couple of hours before the traffic was flowing normally again.

After a forty-five-minute wait and countless curses, they were able to crawl along for what seemed like an eternity before turning off at the exit for Kinna and Skene, taking the minor roads towards Borås.

Considerably later than expected they arrived at the address, a relatively central but depressing block of flats. On the second floor the curtains were closed.

They went upstairs and came to a door marked S. GRANITH. A scraping noise from inside the flat persuaded them to wait, even though no one answered at first. Bärneflod hammered on the door with his fist. He pushed open the letterbox and caught sight of stocking-clad feet.

"We're from the police, fru Granith. Could you please open the door and let us in?" After a further delay the key was turned and a woman with messy hair peered out.

"What's it about?" she said with affected surliness, clearly trying to conceal her anxiety. Tell showed her his

ID. When she failed to react he took a step into the flat, followed by Bärneflod. The woman backed away.

Tell had to remind himself that the woman's son had just been arrested on suspicion of murder. She looked terrible: her unwashed grey hair hung in clumps around her neck, and her face looked as if it had been distorted by too much anger, humiliation or perhaps weariness. She was tugging frantically at her sweater, which was much too short — a band of pale wrinkled skin showed above her waistline — and faded tights hung loosely around skinny legs.

"My apologies for the late hour. May we come in?" asked Tell once again.

"You're coming in anyway, aren't you?" the woman spat but led the way into what seemed to be the living room. It was bursting at the seams with an incredible amount of mismatched furniture. Tell counted four tables of different sizes. The policemen squeezed their way past and each sat down on a two-seater sofa. Solveig Granith remained standing at first, as if to say she didn't expect them to stay long. When Tell and Bärneflod didn't appear to take the hint, she sat down on the armchair nearest the window.

"Your son is Sebastian Granith, is that correct?" said Bärneflod, brushing the dust off the back of his sofa with an expression of unmistakable disgust.

The woman nodded peevishly.

"You have been informed that he is being held in custody, and that during the night he confessed to the murders of Lars Waltz and Olof Bart."

Solveig Granith turned to the window without the slightest change of expression.

Bärneflod and Tell looked at one another. This woman wasn't going to be an easy nut to crack. She was probably in shock, but something about her behaviour told them there was more to it than that. Tell decided to get straight down to business.

"As we understand it, your son lives here, which gives us reason to ask where he was on the evening of Tuesday 19 December, and early on Thursday 28 December."

He wrote the dates on a blank page in his notebook and passed it over to Solveig, who squinted at the paper before staring out of the window again.

"Please take your time if you need to give it some thought."

Through a gap in the grubby curtains he could see the neon-lit facade of the building opposite.

"Let me put it this way: on the night between 19 and 20 December last year, did he come home?"

"How the hell am I supposed to remember?" she asked scornfully.

A door closed, and Bärneflod raised his eyebrows, wondering where the noise had come from. Tell stiffened and instinctively placed his hand close to his holster.

"Is there anyone else here?"

Solveig Granith shook her head. Bärneflod glanced at Tell and stood up. Granith chewed nervously on her lower lip.

"OK, I'll ask you this instead," said Tell, seizing the opportunity. "Where were you last night?"

"I don't have to answer your questions," she said without conviction. Her eyes darted between Tell and Bärneflod, as if she expected one of them to agree with her and put an end to the unpleasantness.

"Where were you at the times written on the piece of paper in front of you?"

"I don't remember!" she screamed.

With her eyes wide open and a deranged expression on her face, the feeble woman took two steps forward and stuck her chin out at Bärneflod, who was nearer to her. He was unprepared for her aggression and knocked an ornamental dove to the ground.

Fragments of porcelain flew across the scratched parquet floor, and one shard ended up at her feet. She crouched down with some difficulty and placed it in the palm of her hand. For a second Bärneflod thought she was crying.

"I don't remember," she whispered, placing the sharp fragments she was now collecting in her cupped hand.

"But I'm sure you remember what you were doing yesterday evening," Tell went on inexorably.

He had to repeat the question before she answered. "I suppose I was here. I'm always here."

"Is there anyone who can confirm that?"

"No."

Tell felt a draught across his neck. A window or a balcony door must have been opened in another room. He was now certain that there was someone else there, listening to every word that was spoken. He gestured to Bärneflod to get ready to search the flat.

When Solveig stood up again, Tell decided to put his cards on the table.

"I believe that Olof Bart and Lars Waltz, who was mistakenly assumed to be Thomas Edell, were murdered as a result of the alleged attack on your daughter twelve years ago. That is the explanation your son has given for the murders. At some point during the last twenty-four hours the third attacker, Sven Molin, was also murdered. The problem is that your son was in custody at the time."

"And how is that a problem for me? Or for you?" Solveig Granith was talking to herself. She seemed increasingly distant.

"It's a problem because we don't believe it's a coincidence that Molin has also been murdered. And since your son was under arrest at the time, it means that someone else, somebody who presumably also had strong feelings for Maya, has avenged her in his place. I'm not saying that person is you; I'm simply asking if there is anyone who can confirm that you were at home yesterday evening."

She tugged at the neck of her sweater as if she couldn't get enough air.

"I can confirm that she was here."

The woman who appeared in the doorway had bright red lips and a severe bob, dyed black. Possibly a wig, Tell noted after establishing that she didn't constitute a direct threat. She was tall and wore an old-fashioned grubby suit that had once been expensive.

"And who are you?" Bärneflod was openly scrutinising the woman from head to toe. She may have been in her forties.

"I . . . I help Solveig with the shopping and so on. As a home help," she explained. "I can confirm that Solveig was at home yesterday evening."

Solveig Granith had turned gratefully to her helper, as a distressed child turns to its mother.

"And during the night?" asked Bärneflod suspiciously.

Several things didn't make sense. The fact that the room was in such a mess didn't square with the assertion that Solveig Granith had a home help. Equally, the suit the woman was wearing didn't suggest that cleaning was her job. Perhaps cleaning wasn't included in "and so on".

"Oh, so you work evenings and nights too?" growled Bärneflod after glancing at the clock. He made no attempt to hide his suspicion.

"I do work in the evenings sometimes, yes. People don't only need help during the day," she said unconvincingly. "But yesterday evening I was here for a different reason: I'd left my watch on the draining board. I take it off when I do the washing up and didn't want to be without it, so I . . . rang Solveig to ask whether it was too late to —"

"I stay up late," said Solveig mechanically.

"And what time was this?" said Bärneflod in the same tone as before. He looked at the younger woman.

Her gaze didn't falter. "Around nine. I stayed until a quarter to ten."

Bärneflod grunted as he passed over his notebook and asked her to write down her name and where she could be reached. "Just in case we need to get hold of you."

After a moment's hesitation she bent her head over the notebook, he caught sight of a tattooed snake emerging from the collar of her shirt. He shuddered.

CHAPTER
SIXTY-ONE

Michael Gonzales had made the same exasperated noises as his colleagues during the crisis meeting, but in reality he was excited about the turn the case had taken.

He was young to be working in CID, and at the beginning he had heard the same things again and again. Some people would praise his enthusiasm and pat him on the back; others would banter about him being leadership material. Sometimes the comments weren't so friendly. Not everyone was impressed by the fact he was climbing the ladder more quickly than usual, whether they believed the reason was unusually high motivation or the need to fill quotas. This was a favourite topic among members of the police service who were not burdened with an overly high IQ.

This ill-concealed hostility made him angry and aggressive at first. He had been brought up not to take any crap by his mother, who, while she was as proud as Punch that her son was in the police service, would never allow him to kowtow to anyone to get on. Initially he had gone into battle for her sake. Not that he would define himself as a foreigner — he had lived in Sweden all his life — but the battle his mother had fought against racism since her arrival in the mid-seventies had to count for something. However, it was possible to choose your battles, and Gonzales had got the hang of this after a while. He was positive by nature. Over the years he had developed the ability to use his charm: it could smooth over misunderstandings, disarm his opponents and thus give him control. And so he never became a victim of his own anger.

And he didn't want to be anywhere else; he had always wanted to be a detective. That was why he always had his nose in a crime novel when he was a teenager, and had watched every detective series on TV. He had no problem identifying with the lonely, obstinate and self-sacrificing detective, whether portrayed by Henning Mankell, Colin Dexter or Michael Connelly. That was also why he had applied to the police training academy twice before he finally got in.

Not that the police work he had been involved in so far bore much resemblance to the investigations in books or on TV. During what felt like an endless period on patrol he had escorted drunks to the cells to sober up, intervened in hundreds of domestic disputes, caught speeding drivers, arrested dozens of petty thieves, worked his way through tons of paperwork and filled in reports on stolen cars. But eventually, one day, he was given the chance to tackle something big.

In his mind's eye he had excitedly seen his name printed on his office door, and on his card: MICHAEL GONZALES — HOMICIDE. But he continued to work his way through piles of paper. Carried on writing reports about domestic disputes — the difference being that now they usually ended with one of the drunks being dead.

There was a shortage of car chases, he would say when the little boys in the square asked him about his job. The kids who had not learned to hate the police were still impressed, but those with elder brothers in gangs were not exactly overwhelmed.

"It's smaller than Slavko's," was the response from one of the younger boys when Gonzales showed them his service pistol. This embarrassingly unprofessional moment had cost Gonzales sleepless nights before he decided not to report the boy's older cousin for the illegal possession of a weapon. Applying a logic that was anything but legal, he concluded that the fact that he had been told about the gun somehow took away his right to judge. Easy come, easy go, sort of. Or maybe he was just scared that his colleagues would find out he'd been using his pistol to impress little boys.

Now he took a call that had been misdirected by the exchange, then sat there, doing nothing. The endorphins that had coursed through his system when he heard that Sven Molin had been murdered were starting to dissipate.

Go through everything was the phrase Tell had used. Get to know the person. Gather information, draw together the loose threads. Think around the situation.

Easy for him to say.

Gonzales was no novice when it came to murder enquiries; he was familiar with the structure and approach, which in many ways were exactly the same irrespective of who had killed or been killed. He had worked on a number of such cases during his time with the team.

In the Jeep enquiry he had been given more of a free rein. Though no one had told him so explicitly, he had been trusted to draw his own conclusions and organise the investigative work as he saw fit. And now he was sitting there without any kind of guidance while people assumed he could think for himself.

He had contacted Borås and asked for the case file from the 1995 investigation, which had been called off due to lack of evidence. Nobody interviewed at the time had been able to come up with names of potential attackers, and there was no proof that Maya Granith hadn't left the track of her own accord and simply tripped.

He found a notepad among the piles of paper on his desk, opened it at a clean page and wrote *MAYA* in a circle in the centre.

Start with the year of the crime and work backwards, Tell had said. Gonzales closed his eyes and tried to think about what was relevant in a young person's life, what had been important in his own life. Where you live. What you do. He wrote *job/studies* in the margin. If you're with anyone — a boyfriend? *Boys/mates.*

Apparently she had lived at an address in Borås with her mother. For the last two years of her life she had also had a different address in another part of Sweden — Stensjö. It sounded like the back of beyond. There was some kind of foundation registered there, the Arnold Jansson Foundation for the General Education and Training in Craftsmanship of the Working Class.

551

Since 1999 the foundation had run a training centre for "the development of local craft", but before that the buildings had housed a folk high school and boarding facilities. On the same web page he discovered that Stensjö lay to the north and inland.

Gonzales raised his eyebrows. If Maya had both lived and studied in some backwater for the last two years of her life, it wasn't impossible that the solution was somehow linked to the school or the surrounding area. Sticking a load of people from different backgrounds with different reasons to run away from home into some kind of barracks in the forest — well, that was worse than *Survivor*. Anything could happen.

But what could have happened that was relevant to his investigation? Nobody had been murdered in Stensjö, after all. And the three men who might indirectly have cost Maya her life already had names and faces. He was looking for someone who had been close to Maya and was capable of murdering in order to honour her memory, or possibly to protect her brother.

The telephone interrupted his thoughts once more.

"Michael?"

"I haven't got time at the moment, Mum. I'm working."

He put the phone down gently but firmly. She'd have something to say about that this evening. He got up and started pacing between the door and the desk.

There were only two alternatives, he decided. If three thirty-something men were desperate enough to rob someone, they would hardly choose a teenager, who by definition was likely to be broke — particularly a teenager on her way home *from* a party. No, it was more likely that it had been their drunken intention to rape Maya, otherwise why would they have chased her into the forest? They had planned to hurt her, even if events had taken a different turn and they had left her to freeze to death, unconscious in the snow.

He tried to weave the strands together.

Someone had reacted on Maya's behalf. Who would do that? The family, of course; Sebastian Granith's confession was in the process of being transcribed. An enraged father was Gonzales' next thought, but the official register informed him that her father was unknown. Although he might have been out there, waiting to take vengeance on his daughter's attackers, and possibly on her mother and those around her who had refused to recognise him as the father of his child. The mother, Solveig Granith. Tell's opinion after meeting her was that she was mentally far too fragile to carry out a murder. That was a contradiction in itself, of course, since a normal person doesn't go and kill someone, irrespective of what they have done to his or her family. Or do they?

He stopped himself. His sisters, full of life and joy, passed before his mind's eye; a fraction of a second later they were lying in the snow — left to die because some randy pissed-up bastards had been too scared, wanting to save their own skins, to call for help.

He clenched his fists and erased the image. It wasn't his sister who had been lying there in the snow. There was no reason to start speculating about what was morally defensible or even human. That wasn't his job.

553

He was there to find a murderer. The law could make judgements. He wrote *Boyfriend?* on his pad, then picked up his phone and keyed in the number for the principal at Stensjö. To his surprise there was a person on the other end, not an answering machine.

"I'm looking for information about a student who attended the folk high school between 1993 and 1995. I know it's a long time ago, but . . ."

The woman on the other end of the phone laughed. She had a pleasant voice.

"It certainly is a long time ago. I've only been principal here for eighteen months, so I definitely can't help you. Berit Hjärpe was the principal before me and was involved in setting up the centre, but this is a completely new venture, even though it's backed by the same foundation. There used to be a more traditional folk high school here."

Gonzales thought for a moment.

"Would you be able to put me in touch with someone who was around in 1995?"

"I don't know . . ." She hesitated. "If I can come back to you next week, that will give me time to contact the board. They must have details of the people who were working here at the same time. But I know that Margareta Folkesson, the chairwoman, is on holiday at the moment and —"

"I'm afraid I can't wait until next week," Gonzales interrupted her. "This is a murder enquiry, and it's of paramount importance that the information we're looking for —"

554

"OK," she interrupted gently, and Gonzales immediately regretted the formality of his words. She was actually trying to help.

"You can't think of anyone else who might know more?" he asked in a conciliatory tone.

"I can, in fact," said the woman after a brief silence. "You could try our secretary, Greta Larsson. She's worked for the foundation for ever, and she had a similar role at the school for many years. She might be able to help you."

"Could you put me through to her?"

"She's not working today."

"Then I need her home number."

There was silence at the other end of the line.

"As I said, this is a murder enquiry, and I do have the right to —"

"Yes, OK. Just a moment."

A man who sounded at least a hundred years old answered just as Gonzales was about to hang up. He said that Greta Larsson was out walking by the lake and wasn't expected back for at least a couple of hours, but she had her mobile with her. Did he want the number? He himself was in bed most of the time because of heart problems.

Gonzales took down the number, eventually managed to interrupt the old man by thanking him for his help, and called Greta Larsson's mobile. She answered almost immediately with a shrill "Hello?"

When he had introduced himself she sighed audibly and laughed.

"Oh my goodness, I was so scared. I got this phone because Gunnar, my husband, is so ill, and he has to be able to get hold of me. There's a nurse who comes in every day while I'm at work, but when I'm free I like to go walking."

She disappeared in a torrent of sounds that forced Gonzales to hold the receiver away from his ear so that his eardrum wouldn't burst.

"Sorry, I just had to take off my rucksack, and I was so worried when the phone rang. Nobody else has the number, you see, so I thought —"

"I know what you thought, fru Larsson." He was going to have to take the lead if he was going to get a word in edgeways. "I'm calling because I have a couple of questions about a pupil who attended the folk high school in Stensjö twelve years ago. I will understand perfectly if you can't answer my questions, but I thought I'd give it a try. It would be a great help if you could remember anything at all. Her name was —"

"I have an excellent memory, Constable. If you just wait a moment, I'll sit down on this rock . . ."

She disappeared again in a rush of noise, and Gonzales sighed.

"Maya Granith," he said before Greta Larsson had time to open her mouth.

"Hmm . . . it sounds familiar somehow," she murmured thoughtfully.

This is a waste of time.

"What did she look like? At the time, I mean. I have a good memory for faces. I had all kinds of different roles in those days — study mentor, counsellor. You

556

know what young people are like: their confusion can make them fairly demanding."

"On the photographs I've seen she had dyed black hair and a ring in her nose. I could send you a couple of photos of —"

"No, I remember!" Greta Larsson exclaimed so loudly that Gonzales actually jumped. "Granith, you said! I know exactly who you mean! It was a long time ago, but the reason I remember her so well is that I had a lot of trouble with her, to put it mildly."

"Trouble?" asked Gonzales. He noticed he was clutching the phone in a vice-like grip.

"Yes. I was also in charge of the administration of the boarding side of the school, you see. And she rented a room, stayed there for a while, moved out, then moved back in. I hardly had time to get the paperwork done before she changed her mind again. That's why I remember her so well."

"You mean she dropped out of school, then changed her mind, or . . ."

"Not at all; it was love that caused all her problems. She moved into one of the staff residences, over and over again, to live with our — how can I put it? — caretaker. General factotum. At first it was all sweetness and light. Then there were quarrels and tears and she moved out again. Then it was back to sweetness and light. I have to say that it all took place quite openly, and if you want my opinion, it was rather embarrassing. Stensjö wasn't a big school; everybody knew most things about everybody else. Not that I'm one of those old-fashioned types — even if I am old — who doesn't tolerate tendencies outside the norm, but I mean you don't have to advertise what you do in the bedroom."

She paused for breath.

"But listen to me going on and on! This will be costing the police a fortune, calling me on my mobile!"

"Don't worry, fru Larsson, that's fine. But I don't understand. What do you mean by 'tendencies outside the norm'?"

"She was a lesbian, of course! What did you think I meant? Not that there's anything wrong with that, Constable, but it was just so public! The thing was, the school's old rules and regulations were still in place, which meant that the students who were boarding weren't allowed to have visitors in their rooms, which is why she moved into the caretaker's cottage every time things were going well between them. The school wasn't exactly adopting a modern approach, and in many ways I think we avoided problems by sticking to the old ways. There's nothing that causes as many difficulties as love, Constable. And the students were there to study, after all."

"So you're saying that Maya Granith had a relationship with the female caretaker at the school."

"I am, and it went on more or less the whole time she was at the school. I even remember trying to talk to her once, when she came to me wanting her room back yet again, with her eyes all red from crying after they'd fallen out for the umpteenth time. I suggested it might be better if she concentrated on her studies, something along those lines. I did feel a bit sorry for her — she was a bright girl after all. But she certainly wasn't going to take any notice of me; I expect she thought I should keep my nose out of her business. And she was so deeply in love as well, and love is blind, isn't that right, Constable? You must have seen plenty of that sort of thing in your job over the years — all those *crimes passionnelles*, or whatever they're called."

She became serious once again.

"It wasn't my place to have an opinion, of course, but to be honest I didn't think much of that woman, the caretaker I mean. She was . . . strange in some way. I thought that right from the start. Not just because she had those . . . tendencies. She . . ."

Greta Larsson hesitated.

"What is it, fru Larsson?"

"I don't like to pass on gossip, but it's so long ago now, and if you say it's important to your investigation, then . . ."

"What, fru Larsson? What's important to our investigation?"

"I think she'd been in some kind of mental hospital before she came to the school. You see, I was the permanent secretary to the admissions team and I think there was some feeling that the school ought to take some kind of social responsibility. The charter was formulated mainly during the 60s. I can tell you that opinion was divided as to whether so-called diversity created a positive study environment or not. In my view . . . well, I don't suppose that's relevant any longer. Anyway, there was a testimonial with her application, from a psychiatrist. Of course I had no reason to read it, so I didn't, but I assume it said it would help her

559

recovery if she could spend some time in a peaceful environment out in the country. I remember it clearly because of course she became an employee of the school later on. We were almost colleagues in a way. It felt a bit . . . odd. But on the other hand, this business of psychological problems doesn't seem to be such a big thing any more. These days people decide they have mental health problems at the drop of a hat. It's not like in my day, when there were only three categories: those who were as fit as a fiddle, those with aches and pains, and then the lunatics."

"Do you remember her name?"

"Of course I do! Caroline Selander. I hope you haven't misunderstood me — she might not have done anything wrong — but I don't think I was the only member of staff who felt she was a bit unpleasant. Eventually she resigned and disappeared. That would have been around the time you mentioned — 95, perhaps."

Gonzales was furiously taking notes.

"Fru Larsson, this is very interesting. I'd like to contact you again, if I may. I'd also like you to think about whether there's anyone else that I could contact, just to supplement the information you've given me."

"There are a couple of people I could put you in touch with. But I don't think their memories are as good as mine. I was the spider at the centre of the web, you see. I saw and heard most things."

She laughed again.

"Before we finish, I wonder if you could describe this caretaker to me?"

560

"Yes, of course. She was tall and powerfully built, a bit masculine if you ask me. Tattooed like a sailor, and not just on her arms. She had a snake crawling up her neck, as black as a leech it was — horrible. Short hair, far too short for a woman, but I suppose that goes with the territory. And she wore quite masculine clothes, even in her spare time. She often wore dungarees. Er . . . and I think she had a big nose."

"OK, thank you, fru Larsson. You've been a great help." He hung up. "You really have been a great help," he murmured to himself.

The phone rang, the display showing his home number. He could just picture his mother, smarting from his brusque snub, pressing "Redial" and waiting to give him an earful.

He let it ring.

CHAPTER
SIXTY-TWO

As a child she had visited her aunt in Borås. Apart from those family gatherings, Seja had set foot in the town only once, when she had gone to see a band she quite liked with an untrustworthy boyfriend and a couple of other boys at a frightening bikers' club.

That was typical of what she did in those days; her teenage years were spent with people she didn't necessarily like, going to parties and pubs where she didn't enjoy herself. Listening to music she sometimes didn't even understand, just because that's what you were supposed to do, then listening to different music in secret. Giving boys what they wanted because she was grateful that they wanted her.

She tried looking at it differently. *What an achievement to have finally learned to say no to things you don't really want to do.* No thank you to boring parties with tedious self-obsessed people. No thank you to the perpetual competition to see who owned the most, who could be the coolest, who was the most loved.

If she really had achieved that state of mind.

She was forced to concentrate on her driving for a while. Navigating through strange towns wasn't one of her strong points, and when she finally turned into the right street, it was more a matter of luck than good map reading. She put money in the meter for an hour — she shouldn't need any longer than that.

Seja hesitated before getting out of her car, and allowed herself one final moment of reflection.

She knew there had to be a reason why she had stood outside the bikers' club twelve years before, just as the first snowflakes were beginning to fall. Why she had had a funny feeling in her stomach as she watched Maya leave. Why fate had decreed that she should be one of the first people to see the dead body outside Thomas Edell's workshop.

She had no firm plan. Christian had accused her of having a hidden agenda when she embarked on the relationship with him. She felt unsure now. Had she had an agenda that was hidden from herself as well? Was their relationship — the dizzying rush of happiness she had experienced, the intense sense of loss she now felt — yet another sign? Just one of the many signs that had led her to the same decision: she was going to deal with this story and make it comprehensible. And she was going to do that by writing. The only way she *could* do it was by writing.

Maya had died. Not only because she had been hunted down like a fox, but because no one had come to help her. She could have survived if someone had got there in time, before she lost too much blood.

That's why Seja felt so guilty: because of the disrespect she had shown to Maya. She had been too weak to act on her feelings or to talk to the police about it. The world had shown Maya nothing but contempt by letting the three men who had robbed her of her life remain at liberty. Until now; the murderer had seen to that. The murderer had not been able to tolerate that disrespect. In a way, Seja could understand the person who had taken justice into their own hands. A feeling of envy, irrational and primitive, fuelled the curiosity that had driven her to come here. She was jealous of Maya, who was loved so much that someone had killed in her name. Jealous of the murderer who had chosen to do something with their rage, rather than allowing it to eat away their soul.

She was going to write to get some justice for Maya, thus atoning for some of her guilt. She wanted to write an in-depth crime report. She was a journalist — well, a trainee journalist — but she would write this story from her own perspective, as a participant in the drama. As a member of the cast, albeit with a walk-on role.

She had no idea how to go about it, but in order to portray Maya as she had been in life, she needed to talk to those who had been close to her. She would start with the family, her mother. Then perhaps she could track down Caroline, the woman who had been the love of her life.

John Svensson, the friend of Hanna's friend Björn, had known Maya only in passing when they were growing up in Borås. It wasn't until they both ended up at the same school that they had become friends, close friends, or "as close as Caroline allowed them to be". That was how he had put it. He had talked for a long time about Maya and Caroline. Their love was quite something, he had said.

Standing outside the door of the apartment, Seja took a deep breath. She could still change her mind. She could call Christian, suppress the bitterness she had felt when they parted and make a fresh attempt to get him to sit down and listen. Instead she knocked on the door. It was opened immediately. The skinny woman must have seen her through the spyhole and been waiting for her to knock. This put Seja on edge straight away, and her apology sounded confused even to her own ears.

She said she wanted to talk about Maya. She had been more of a passing acquaintance than a close friend, but she would like some help in clarifying one or two things that had happened.

"I can imagine you must have many questions too. I won't give you false hope — I don't know much — but I . . . I was thinking of writing something about Maya, about what happened. Because I knew her. And because I thought somebody ought to do it. Anyway . . . I just wanted to talk a bit. About Maya."

She stopped. The woman stood there motionless. She might have been listening intently to every word that came from Seja's lips, carefully interpreting the slightest twitch in every muscle of her face, but her gaze seemed fixed on a distant point, as if she was in a world of her own.

"I hope I'm not opening up old wounds, turning up like this," Seja said hesitantly when she got no reaction. "May I come in for a while?"

That seemed to penetrate. The woman disappeared into the apartment, obviously expecting Seja to follow her.

Alone in the hallway she slowly undid her boots. She looked around and realised the woman didn't live alone. There were two pairs of men's shoes on a rack, as well as several pairs of women's shoes far too large for her. On the hall stand hung a red coat that would come down to the feet of someone even as tall as Seja.

There was the scent of smoke, and something that reminded her of cut flowers that had gone off — a rotting smell. Suddenly fear hit her like a well-aimed kick to the small of her back. She had just bitterly reproached herself for ignoring an instinctive feeling in her stomach at an important point in her life, and it was impossible to miss the physical signals now, yet she continued into the gloom of the apartment. It was a typical 70s layout, with all the rooms off the central passageway. Since all the doors were closed, the light in the passageway was dim.

Solveig Granith had sat down in an armchair by the window in the living room. The room took the idea of clutter to a new level. After some hesitation, Seja pushed her way through to a two-seat sofa and sat down opposite her. Solveig turned her face to the window, despite the fact that the curtains were closed. They let in only a thin strip of light which fell across her skinny thighs, over Seja's stockinged feet and out across the parquet floor. The shards of a broken ornament lay scattered in the shadow of the armchair.

"You say you knew Maya?" said the woman in a monotone.

"I knew her a bit," Seja replied. "We met occasionally, said hi if we bumped into each other. We liked each other. I mean, I liked her and I think she liked me. We were quite similar, I think."

The woman turned slowly to Seja. Something was beginning to move in those grey-flecked eyes.

"You liked her?" she said. Her lower lip began to quiver uncontrollably as the tears welled up in her eyes.

Oh my God, thought Seja. *She's still a wreck after all these years. She hasn't got over her daughter's death.* And even if it was only natural not to emerge from such an experience with your life intact, something told Seja that she had an explosive wreck of a person in front of her. All suppressed bitterness and grief. How much hatred could a human body contain, she wondered, without collapsing like a house of cards? Particularly such a frail body; this woman couldn't weigh more than forty kilos.

Suddenly everything fell into place for Seja: *This woman was so still, so detached because she was afraid of falling to pieces! There was so much unresolved hatred inside her that she was afraid she'd burst if she opened up the slightest crack and let what was inside her escape. And she knew something. She knew.*

Seja now understood the reason for her visit: despite the bad feeling she had, she was going to find out the truth. She could feel the adrenalin pumping through her body as she leaned over and took Solveig Granith's hand.

"Yes, I liked her very much. It was difficult not to like her. She seemed to be an honest person."

Solveig jerked as Seja touched her, but didn't pull her hand away. She closed her eyes and allowed the tears to pour down her cheeks, soaking her stained sweater.

They sat like that for a while, with only background noise. Music from somewhere in the building. A neighbour throwing a bag of glass bottles down the rubbish chute in the stairwell. The neighbour's door slammed shut and the key turned in the lock.

A while later Solveig Granith dried her tears with her sleeve. Without a word she got to her feet unsteadily and went into the kitchen, where she started clattering about with the coffee machine.

"Is it OK if I record our conversation? I'll just get my tape recorder."

Seja regretted the words as soon as they came out, afraid that her pushiness might destroy the fragile bridge she had temporarily built between them. But Solveig merely mumbled that it was fine, and yes, she was welcome to make notes too.

In the hallway Seja's jacket lay where she had left it on the arm of a chair, with the recorder in the pocket.

The rotting smell seemed to have grown stronger. She looked around for the source, but found nothing apart from a paper bag pushed underneath a low table in front of the mirror. Dirty clothes protruded from the top of the bag, the edge of a padded jacket, stained brown. *With blood?* Seja pulled herself together; the woman was a nervous wreck, but she wanted to talk.

568

She could hear Solveig returning to the living room. As soon as Seja appeared, she started talking. When she talked about Maya, her earlier restraint disappeared, as if the thought of forgetting her daughter was what terrified her, and the only way to guarantee Maya a place in her memory was to keep going over old ground.

Setting the tape running, Seja quickly lost herself in Solveig's story. Sometimes she felt as if Solveig was talking about her, as if she had been watching Seja ever since she was born, although there were few similarities between Seja's own mother and the woman sitting in the armchair opposite.

It was amazing that this woman, who was obviously not of sound mind, had the ability to paint such a detailed and accurate portrait of her daughter. Idealised, certainly, *but then that's how we choose to treat the dead.* Suddenly Seja had the conviction that Solveig Granith had got to know her daughter after her death, as an attempt to work through her grief.

"I heard from . . . another friend of Maya that she had met someone, someone she lived with for a couple of years before she . . . passed away. Someone she was really serious about. I thought perhaps you might have met her, that you might be able to tell me something about her. I'm interested in her because . . ." Seja sighed. "I'll be honest with you . . ."

The words just flowed; she was temporarily unable to control them. Her fears went to the back of her mind. She was far too interested in Solveig's reactions.

"I've been talking to someone who went to the same school as Maya. He knew her fairly well, and the woman Maya was with, Caroline Selander, he said she loved Maya so much that she seemed to want to own her."

Solveig Granith's eyes darted across the room. Seja assumed she wasn't comfortable with the fact that her daughter had had a lesbian relationship — perhaps this knowledge sullied the perfect image. But perhaps there was another reason.

Seja suddenly remembered the long coat hanging in the hallway. She swallowed. There was no going back.

"I was just thinking, if this woman was so important to Maya, and Maya was so important to her, maybe there's a chance I could talk to her?" Then she added apologetically, "For my story."

Solveig was now extremely worked up: her eyes had narrowed to slits and she was hugging herself. Seja didn't dare to speculate on the cause of Solveig's sudden agitation.

"Perhaps I'd better go," she said, trying to sound calm even though her heart was pounding.

"No, stay!" said Solveig sharply. "I'll ask her." The thin fingers grasping Seja's wrist were cold and possessed an unexpected strength. "I'll call her right now."

"Call her?"

"Of course you can talk to Caroline."

Solveig Granith's tone of voice had changed: she was speaking gently and reassuringly. *My God, she's completely crazy.*

570

Seja didn't dare say no but she really wanted to get out of the apartment. She knew she was too high up to escape through the window. Hopefully the telephone was in the kitchen, so she would be able to sneak into the hallway and grab her shoes when Solveig went to make the call. *The bag in the hallway, the jacket. Blood.*

But Solveig had no intention of releasing her wrist.

"Come with me and I'll ring her now. You might be able to speak to her yourself. Or at least to arrange a time."

Seja nodded, her mouth as dry as sandpaper. She had to think clearly. She was taller and younger than this woman, although insanity might make Solveig the stronger one.

The best thing is to keep calm, to keep Solveig Granith calm. Try to talk your way out of the situation.

Like a mother who has lost patience with an obstinate child, Solveig now pushed Seja in front of her, further into the darkness of the apartment.

Seja's mind was whirling. She tried to turn around to make eye contact with Solveig. Her voice became shrill.

"I mean, I've got her name. I can ring her from home. I . . . it's fine . . ."

They passed the kitchen, where an old-fashioned telephone sat on the table. Seja was just about to make a serious protest, push past Solveig and run out of the apartment, when she yanked open the door to what seemed to be a dressing room.

Seja had no time to react to the darkness before a sharp knee in the small of her back made her fall

571

forward on to something at once hard and soft. Arrows of pain shot up her spine. She managed to turn her head just enough to see the silhouette of another person, just behind Solveig, blocking the light from the hallway. Then she felt a blow to her head, and everything went black.

CHAPTER
SIXTY-THREE

"He's said he killed them, that they deserved it and he doesn't need a lawyer to defend him. I don't suppose he thought there was anything to defend."

Tell and Bärneflod were round the back of the police station, a dreary area with its neglected paving and half-rotten wooden benches. A concrete bin full of sand was strategically placed for those who hadn't managed to give up when smoking was banned in the building.

"So you can't get anything out of him?"

"Not a word. Literally. He hasn't spoken since he confessed. He told his story, and since then he's kept his mouth shut. It's bloody frustrating, I can tell you." Bärneflod let out a long whistle between his teeth. "Who would have thought the little shit could be so cocky — he seemed like a nervous wreck."

Tell lit his second cigarette in five minutes. Since he had taken himself outside to smoke, he might as well make the most of it. In the past he often used to close the door of his office, open the window and lean out, using one of the plant pots as an ashtray — God knows how they'd ended up on his windowsill in the first place. However, since he had found out about Östergren's lung cancer, he had followed the rules and

573

taken the lift down here. That's how banal and predictable he was.

"I don't know if he's cocky," said Tell, thoughtfully furrowing his brow.

He had spent a number of hours with Sebastian Granith. There was no longer any suspicion that he might be protecting another murderer in the cases of Lars Waltz and Olof Bart. Particularly because his fingerprints matched the ones they had lifted from the rented Jeep, and the tyre tracks of the same vehicle had been found at the crime scene. And since the murder weapon had turned out to be the same in both cases, Granith was also tied to the murder of Lars Waltz.

The case of Sven Molin was more difficult. Tell was convinced that Sebastian Granith knew who had killed Molin, but once he had got over his initial shock, he hadn't shown the least sign of distress or given any indication that he might start talking. Tell was becoming increasingly angry at being denied a final solution to the case.

"No," he said after thinking for a while. "He isn't keeping quiet because he's cocky. He's just switched off. It's as if he's sitting there thinking about something else entirely, as if he really can disconnect from reality at will."

"It seems to run in the family," muttered Bärneflod. He looked as if he might well have developed his theory if he hadn't been stopped by a coughing fit that came from somewhere deep inside his lungs. He turned his back on Tell, his whole body shaking, and Tell thumped

574

him between the shoulder blades. For a moment he felt like an actor in a bad comedy film.

"Are you OK? You sound like someone with TB. What were you saying?"

Bärneflod walked inside and pressed the lift button.

"I was just saying that it runs in the family. I got exactly the same feeling with the mother. That she just switched off from time to time — she didn't even notice I was there — and at other times she was all too aware of me. What a psycho. It's hardly surprising he went over the edge, poor kid."

Tell nodded absently. He was heading to the cafeteria instead of his office, since he had the feeling he wouldn't be able to concentrate on anything properly. Bärneflod followed in his wake, still talking. They both picked up a coffee and a cinnamon bun and took them back to the department, where Gonzales caught up with them.

He seemed desperate for company after spending hours alone at his desk. "My wrist is absolutely killing me," he complained. "Don't you think we should have headsets?"

Tell smiled to himself. There were a lot of similarities between Gonzales and his younger self: impatient, enthusiastic and hungry for practical experience. No doubt Gonzales was just going through the first wave of disappointment that the reality of the job fell short of expectations.

"Did you get anything from visiting the mother?" asked Gonzales with a nod to Bärneflod, who took a bite of his bun, shook his head.

"Not much, really. Apart from the fact that she's completely crackers. Pretty unpleasant, if you ask me. I wouldn't want to bump into her in a dark alley."

"OK, well, I have found something. I've been on the phone to —"

Gonzales stopped as Tell held up his hand.

"Hang on. Something else struck me as a bit odd. While we were with the old woman, this girl turned up. Well, I say girl — she was maybe thirty-five, forty. Said she was a home help, but both Bengt and I thought there was something that didn't quite add up, didn't we?"

Bärneflod nodded vigorously. "If she was a home help, then I'm Donald Duck. Her clothes were all wrong, and so was her attitude. And she gave the old woman an alibi for the time of the murder."

Tell nodded. "I'd like to sit down and go through all this in more detail. Is Beckman around?"

"She had really short hair and huge earrings and lipstick," Bärneflod went on. "She looked as bold as brass. And she had a horrible great big snake tattooed on her neck, like some old sailor."

"She had a what?!"

Gonzales banged his knees against the table, gesturing wildly before he managed to express himself a little more clearly.

Just as Tell slammed on the brakes in front of the reddish-brown building, after a slalom drive along the motorway with flashing blue lights, the display on his mobile lit up, showing Michael Gonzales' number.

Tell had noticed Gonzales' disappointment when he was told to stay at the station to find out as much as possible about the woman with the snake tattooed on her neck, and quickly. It wasn't the knowledge that Bärneflod would be deeply offended at the merest hint that *he* should stay at his desk that influenced Tell's decision. However prejudiced and socially inept he might be, there was no disputing that Bengt Bärneflod had over thirty years' experience of this kind of situation. He operated on autopilot these days, apparently unmoved whatever the circumstances and kept a cool head in situations where experienced officers lost it. Whether this was because he was too emotionally handicapped to be affected by other people's crises was unclear, but in the present situation it was irrelevant. Tell had to admit that even though he could get heartily sick of his colleague — and God knows it happened often enough — his presence was always reassuring when difficulties arose.

Of course this visit to Solveig Granith hardly put them in critical danger. At the most there were two women in the apartment, however crazy they might be. It was just that Tell had a bad feeling in his stomach. He also had an inkling that their tactics over the next couple of hours would hold the key to solving this case.

Gonzales briefly confirmed the information he had received from Greta Larsson: Selander had been admitted to a psychiatric clinic on three occasions between the ages of eighteen and twenty-one. He had requested access to her notes, but they could take some time.

"Before that she was in a secure unit for just over a year — until she came of age. She was under a youth care order. Sentenced to psychiatric care by the court at the age of nineteen, for attempted murder. The person she tried to kill was Gunnar Selander — her father. That's all I've got for the moment. Be careful."

The quickening of his heart was familiar from his time on patrol. The sharpened senses and heightened eye for detail. Tell noticed that the handle of the rubbish chute on the second floor was loose, and the door had been left ajar. A faint smell of rotting rubbish filled the landing. It struck him that since he had become an inspector the number of strange stairwells he frequented during the working week had dropped dramatically.

He groped for his wallet in his inside pocket. The weight of the pistol felt unfamiliar but gave him a sense of security, as it always did on those rare occasions when he strapped on his holster. He rang the doorbell, held his ID to the spyhole and waited.

Not a sound could be heard from inside the apartment. He turned and looked at Bärneflod. His hand too was resting on his gun. He nodded.

Tell pushed down the handle and the door opened silently.

On the journey they had gone over the layout of the apartment: the hallway was a narrow passageway with the bathroom straight ahead. The kitchen was furthest away on the left, with the living room next door. They recognised the smell immediately: stale smoke, a lack of oxygen and a hint of overripe fruit.

They found Solveig Granith sitting exactly where they had left her. She was staring vacantly in front of her. Her hands were on her bony knees with the palms turned up. She looked resigned to whatever might happen to her.

Shards of the broken dove still lay on the floor. Tell lowered his gun and gestured over his shoulder. Bärneflod began to search the rooms, looking for traces of Selander, but they already sensed she was no longer in the apartment.

Tell crouched down near Solveig. "Where is Caroline Selander?" he asked calmly.

She gave no indication that she had seen him.

"We will find her, Solveig. It's just going to take a little longer without your help. If you protect her, the only person you're hurting is yourself."

He moved a little closer. Still crouching, he gathered up the fragments of the dove and placed them on the coffee table next to Solveig Granith. Her eyes narrowed and the reddened hands cupped instinctively, as if she wanted to pick up the shards and protect them.

"You can't protect her, Solveig." Tell moved much closer but didn't touch her. "You don't have the strength. And besides, she doesn't deserve it. After all, she's left you here, hasn't she? She didn't bother taking you with her, so why should you risk anything for her sake?"

For a while the only thing he could hear was doors opening and closing, the muted sound of Bärneflod's movements.

She hasn't even fucking blinked.

Suddenly Tell saw in Solveig what he had seen in her son. It was just as Bärneflod had said earlier: they both had the ability to switch off reality when it became unbearable.

"Where is she, Solveig? You haven't killed anyone, have you? All these things that have happened. None of that was you. But until we can talk to Caroline Selander, you're the only one with a motive and no alibi. So start talking, Solveig, if you know what's good for you."

As he uttered the last sentence he heard a shout from Bärneflod, who appeared a second later in the doorway, his gun weighing down his right arm. His expression was grim.

"Come and take a look at this, boss."

Tell dashed into the hallway. The unpleasant feeling in his stomach peaked, and it dawned on him.

Seja and her irrational feelings of guilt and her bloody journalistic ambitions. In the foyer of the police station: of course she had been trying to tell him something about Caroline Selander. She had found out something, but he'd been too arrogant and too tired to listen. Instead he had driven her here. To this dark, stinking, disgusting apartment with these two psychotic . . .

Holding his mobile to his ear, Bärneflod stepped into the corridor and pointed to the smaller room from which he had emerged. A bulb on the ceiling shed light on the grubby brown carpet.

"A woman in her thirties," he heard Bärneflod's matter-of-fact phone voice. "No, no, she's alive. But I think she's received a severe blow to the head . . . Yes, that's right. I think she's actually one of the witnesses we interviewed earlier."

She was lying in an odd position, with one arm bent under her body. At first glance it looked as if her neck were broken. Tell went cold, but then he saw that it was twisted because she was lying on her hair. There was blood in the doorway and underneath her.

Presumably she had been struck on her way into the room, then dragged another half-metre so that she wouldn't obstruct the door. *Nobody bothered to put her in a more comfortable position*, he thought with helpless irrationality. The sinews of her neck were stretched taut in a way that made the whole scene look as if it had been arranged. This vulnerability disturbed him the most: how long had she been lying with her throat exposed in this madhouse?

He sank to his knees and straightened her arm and her head. Her hand twitched as he touched it.

Bärneflod had clearly managed to get hold of the inspector at Borås. He let out an inappropriate whinnying laugh. Tell's anger was channelled into concentrated rage against Bärneflod, who had merely established that Seja was alive before settling down for a nice chat with Björkman.

Bärneflod let out a whistle. "Yes!"

From the conversation that followed, Tell gathered that Bärneflod had information about a vehicle, a camper van registered in Caroline Selander's name.

"Keep it down, for fuck's sake," said Tell between gritted teeth. "And put out a call for the van straight away."

"I know how to do my job, thank you."

Bärneflod was still sufficiently buoyed by the breakthrough not to let Tell's mood get him down.

"We've got the bitch, Tell!"

Seja's eyelids flickered as Tell gently laid her head on his knee. There was blood on his trousers although most of it had coagulated into a sticky mass around the wound in her head.

"They'll be here soon," said Bärneflod, flicking his phone shut. "Have you seen all this?" He gestured around the small room, a dressing room which had clearly served a different purpose.

Only now did Tell notice the meticulous shrine to Maya Granith. The walls were covered with photos of her: as a child, naked by a paddling pool in the garden; as a ten-year-old in shorts, her arms and legs disproportionately long; fourteen years old, her hair dyed with henna. There were banners carrying political slogans and clothes Maya must have worn at different ages. Vinyl records were stacked on a bench along with teenage novels, school yearbooks and music magazines. Posters of bands like Sisters of Mercy and The Cure. One of the walls was papered with poems and pages torn out of diaries.

He moved closer and was able to read her teenage musings.

On a table covered with a lilac cloth stood a dusty bouquet of dried roses. A card protruded from the flowers: *Congratulations on your 18th birthday, Maya.* Above the table hung an enlargement of a black and white photograph in a gold frame. Tell guessed it was one of the last ever taken of her. It was a full-length picture, capturing Maya on a flight of wide stone steps, laughing at the photographer, apparently unprepared but completely relaxed. Compared with the sullen teenager in the adjacent photo, Maya had blossomed into a woman. It was a lovely picture. Tell could easily understand why someone would choose to pray to this particular image.

Bärneflod appeared beside him.

"Horrible, isn't it? A real temple of the dead."

Just as the paramedics knocked on the door frame and stepped into the apartment, Seja opened her eyes.

"Shit," she said as she caught sight of Tell.

CHAPTER
SIXTY-FOUR

Without bothering to explain himself to his colleagues, Tell went in the ambulance with Seja to the hospital in Borås. She was awake, if somewhat confused, suffering from what turned out to be a severe concussion. Flashing his ID, Tell managed to get a doctor's attention remarkably quickly. The wound on Seja's head would need stitches and probably result in a substantial lump.

They hadn't found anything in the apartment that could have caused the injury. The doctor suggested it might be something rough and blunt, possibly a baseball bat. Seja couldn't remember, and despite gentle pressure from Tell, didn't want to talk about what had happened.

"I saw the shadow of a person, then I felt my head explode. That's all I can say. And that's all I want to say right now. I'm grateful that you came with me, Christian, but you can go now. I'm tired and I know you've got a lot of work on."

"Wrong time for pride," he said, mildly reproachful. "Besides, they can manage perfectly well without me for a couple of hours."

He didn't have time to say anything else before a sweaty boy dressed as a nursing assistant stuck his head around the door.

"Christian Tell? I have a message . . ." He leaned forward gasping, his hands on his knees. "I'm sorry . . . I've run across the hospital looking for you . . . You're to ring Karin Beckman. It's obviously important and, I quote, 'bloody urgent'".

Tell ducked out into the corridor, opened his phone and keyed in Beckman's direct line. A nurse walked past, frowning. She pointed meaningfully at a sign on the wall showing a mobile phone with a cross through it. Tell mimed a vague apology.

"Beckman? What's going on?"

"What do you mean, what's going on?"

He realised from the tension in her voice that something must have happened.

"Where are you? Bärneflod said you went to the hospital with Seja Lundberg?"

"Never mind. Carry on," he said.

An agitated man in a white coat was approaching, and he turned towards the wall with the telephone partly hidden by his lapel.

"Caroline Selander has been arrested in Ystad, at the ferry terminal for Poland, and . . ." Beckman's voice broke up.". . . the police down there have searched the camper van and found . . ." Her voice disappeared in a rushing noise.

"For fuck's sake!"

". . . a knife which could well have been the one she used to kill Molin . . . It's been washed, but according to forensics they ought to be able to find traces because the handle is made of wood."

"Good," said Tell. "I'll take over when they bring her in. What did they say about the arrest? Did she —"

"Christian," Beckman broke in, "Östergren collapsed in her office two hours ago. They had to send for an ambulance, and she's been taken to hospital."

Tell stumbled back and leaned against the wall. He felt dizzy and became aware of a bitter dryness in his mouth. *When did I last eat properly?* he thought vaguely. *Was it yesterday I bought that pizza?*

"Hello, Christian? Are you still there?"

He pressed the palm of his hand against his forehead. "I'm still here. How is she?"

"I don't know. The hospital only gives out information to next of kin. Renée had a mobile number for Ann-Christine's husband, but he hasn't picked up since he got the news and took a taxi to the hospital. Oh God. I don't know if I can cope with this."

It sounded as if she was crying, which surprised Tell. He had never thought Beckman had a close relationship with Östergren.

"I'm going outside, Karin. Don't go away."

Tell took the lift downstairs and rang Beckman back from outside the hospital. It seemed as though she had regained her composure.

"Sorry. I don't know what's the matter with me. There's just been so much going on recently. I've left Göran. For good this time. At least I think it's for good."

Tell realised that he was holding his breath as he waited for her to continue. "You don't have to apologise," he said when nothing further was forthcoming. There was a silence between them, a pleasant healing silence.

"Well," she said eventually, "sometimes you do have to apologise. I can be too bloody honest sometimes. It takes it out of all of us, this business of dealing with death all the time. Not just you. Me as well." She blew her nose noisily. "I just want to say that I value our conversations. I know that I can sometimes make it seem as if they're just to help you, but I need them as well."

"It's fine, Karin," he said.

Snowflakes began falling hesitantly on the car park.

"It's good for us to be there for each other." Under normal circumstances he would have reproached himself for sounding inane, but he realised he really meant what he said. "And listen," he went on. "You said Östergren only went in a couple of hours ago? In which case it's hardly surprising if you can't get hold of anyone. It's terrible, Karin, but there's nothing you can do at the moment. You're going to have to wait until tomorrow, whatever happens."

"But what if she doesn't make it?"

"You still won't be able to do anything other than wait."

She laughed and sobbed at the same time.

"You mean, 'Karin, you can't be in control right now. Not of death, anyway.'"

"Something like that, yes."

For a moment he thought she'd hung up, but she continued in a brighter tone: "By the way, Björkman called about something they found in Bart's house. Hidden letters from his sister. Apparently she was trying to blackmail him."

"With what? No, let me guess: she was threatening to reveal what she knew about him and the bikers' club?"

"Exactly. It seems she thought he'd got his hands on money that was hers at some point, and this was her way of trying to get it back."

"Shit. Well, there you go."

He searched his pockets for the slip of paper with Seja's room number. It was probably best to leave now, before it started snowing properly, to avoid getting stuck on the motorway. But he didn't want to hang up before he was sure Beckman was all right. It was very rare for her to lower her guard. If she could understand that it was possible, that it might even do her good, she would do it more readily the next time.

Instead, she was the one who ended the call.

"Go back to Seja," she said. "I'm sure she's waiting for you."

Tell couldn't think of a reply. He stood there in confusion, holding his car keys a centimetre from the lock. He was tired. His head was whirring with so many thoughts, so many questions, but he realised that these were unlikely to be resolved here in the snow that was falling more and more resolutely, covering the tarmac like a soft blanket. He turned uncertainly and surveyed the half-full car park.

Almost every window of the hospital was lit up, with the odd forgotten Advent candlesticks dotted here and there. *People inside those walls are fighting for their lives.*

Dropping the keys in his pocket, he went back through the revolving doors. He didn't take off his coat because he wasn't intending to stay long. But he would at least tell Seja that he was going. And that he would be coming back.

Epilogue

Christian Tell looked around the glassed-in veranda, typical of the single-storey brown-brick house to which it was attached. There were plants everywhere, some of which he recognised from his childhood. The rosary vine, for example — perhaps because its name and appearance were so well matched. Pelargoniums, of course. Just below the ceiling dark green tendrils twisted and twined, so overgrown that it was difficult to see which came from which pot.

It can't possibly be Östergren who has such green fingers, thought Tell; he could picture her office with its empty windowsills.

He could see that the back garden wasn't as neatly kept. The grass had been cut, but the trees hadn't been pruned. The shrubs had been allowed to go wild, and the cypresses grew unchecked. Beyond the lawn he could see the beginning of a grove or a small wood, with Askimsviken somewhere below it.

From the kitchen he could hear Gustav Östergren mildly reproaching his wife for doing too much. She dismissed his concerns with some irritation, only to apologise a second later. Tell smiled sadly. Relationships

590

weren't easy when life was suddenly turned upside down.

She had seemed pleased to see him. They hadn't talked for a while, not since she had been signed off work indefinitely. And not for a while before that either. Tell still felt uncomfortable; his first impulse on seeing the house had been to drive straight past. He hadn't phoned to say that he was coming. It was early. She might still be asleep.

"I can't stay long," had been his ridiculous greeting as a surprised Östergren opened the door. He had pointed at his watch with embarrassment. "You know how it is."

She had stood there motionless at first, looking as if she didn't recognise him in such a different context. Then she said his name and burst into almost exhilarated laughter. This made him happy.

"I just wanted to see how things were."

"If you'd like to go and see how things are on the patio, I'll make us a cup of coffee."

He was wearing a new suit, light grey instead of the usual dark shade. He picked a thread distractedly from his trouser leg, got out a tin of snuff — which was also new — and took a pinch with an unpractised hand.

Seja had given him an incentive: one cigarette-free month and she would take him away on holiday. She hadn't specified the destination, just "somewhere hot". She had no idea how long a month could be. And it was ridiculous for her to even consider paying for them both, given the state of her finances. But he did want to go away with her, he really did. That alone would make this torture worthwhile.

Gustav Östergren came out with a pot of coffee and set it on the table, brushing fallen leaves off the cloth.

"Can I do anything to help?" Tell asked, like a child visiting an elderly relative, and for the first time he was aware of the age gap. Östergren wasn't that much older, but the house betrayed that she was of his parents' generation: the 60s hairstyle in her wedding photo, the imitation-grass flooring in the veranda, the fluffy cushions, the pine coasters.

The whole thing made him feel confused, as if the person he had worked with on a daily basis for so many years had suddenly become a stranger. He had never thought of his boss as being any particular age, neither old nor young, neither a woman nor a person with thoughts and emotions outside work.

He suddenly wondered what it had been like for her to be so remote. If she had deliberately created that facade or if he, like others, had chosen to acknowledge only certain aspects of her.

"Anki, can you bring the sugar?"

When Östergren had mentioned her husband in passing during their most recent conversation, Tell had been surprised that she was married. He had immediately created a picture of the man in question.

It transpired that Gustav Östergren was not the tall elegant retired lawyer or businessman Tell had imagined. It also transpired that Tell had actually met him several years before, at a Horticultural Society Christmas party. Tell remembered that Carina had been delighted with this unassuming man, who resembled a friendly goblin with his wild hair and salt-and-pepper beard, his sparkling friendly eyes, shirt hanging loose and jeans tucked inside his socks. He perched his glasses on his nose to read the date on the milk carton before pouring it into a jug.

Ann-Christine came out with the sugar bowl. It occurred to Tell that he had never seen her move slowly before and he wondered if she was in pain.

"I hope you won't be offended if I go off into the garage for a while," said Gustav Östergren. "It's just I'm working on a little project. I'm making a violin, although there's no guarantee it will ever be finished. You're welcome to come and have a look later on, if you like."

He slipped on a pair of wooden clogs and went out through the veranda door.

Ann-Christine smiled gently. "He just wants to leave us in peace."

"That's impressive, making a violin," Tell replied.

She nodded. "It's always been his dream. And now he's retired — he took his pension a couple of years early so that he could be at home with me — he suddenly has the time to do it."

They were both silent for a while. A magpie landed on the decking outside the window.

"We miss you at work," said Tell eventually.

"Thank you. Actually, I'm not missing the job very much. Not as much as I thought I would, anyway. Everything's relative, after all. I suppose I didn't think I'd be able to cope if I didn't have the job to hang on to. In some peculiar way I thought as long as I was working, I'd stay alive. If I went home it would be like giving up, giving in to the cancer. Waiting for death, I suppose. I couldn't bear that thought. It just got bigger and bigger. You know how it is. You have your work, and that means you know who you are. At work I might not have been the best in the world, but I was competent. At home I'm nothing special. I don't do anything special. Although I have started reading again."

She brightened up.

"When I was younger I used to read all the time. Nothing deep — crime novels, biographies. You know. I've just finished reading a biography of Frida Kahlo, the artist. Fascinating woman. Fascinating life."

"They've made a film about her," said Tell. "With Penélope Cruz. She's a fascinating woman as well. And she doesn't look too bad either."

Östergren laughed. The smile still lingered around the corners of her mouth as she said, "And how are things going otherwise?"

"Well, what can I say? Same old, same old. Bärneflod's wife got it into her head that she should invite the team round for dinner, which Bengt isn't all that thrilled about. He's going round saying it clearly isn't enough, putting up with us from Monday to Friday; now he's expected to have us in his house on a Saturday night *and* supply us with drink."

Östergren laughed again and shook her head. Tell thought he hadn't seen her looking this happy for a long time. He took a biscuit and continued his update.

594

"Gonzales brought in a lad for that rape in Vasa Park, the one where the girl died. The semen matched. And three other girls who've reported rapes over the past year have identified him as their attacker. Once it was clear that we'd got him, he told us that his cousin had been involved as well."

"Horrible."

"Yes, but at least both of them are out of action now. Beckman and Karlberg went off on that course last Monday, the one they should have gone on at Christmas if the Jeep case hadn't got in the way."

Östergren took a bite from a cinnamon bun. She brushed the crumbs off her turquoise jumper carefully. The movement made Tell realise that was another departure; she always used to wear black.

"And that's all sorted now, by the way," he went on, despite a vague feeling that she was only half-listening. "The knife that was found inside the door panel of Selander's car had been wiped, but forensics found traces of Molin's blood on the handle. She confessed when she realised the game was up. Evidently Sebastian Granith and Caroline Selander didn't exactly plan the murders together, not in so many words, but they egged each other on in their mutual desire for revenge: the mother, the brother and the lover. They seem to have had some kind of insane three-way pact. Solveig Granith hasn't been in a fit state to be interviewed so far; she's still in Lillhagen."

"The question is, why did they wait twelve years to murder someone?"

Tell shrugged his shoulders. "There's a awful lot that doesn't add up. I'm no expert, but I've actually been giving some thought to that very question."

"And what did you come up with?"

"I think that separately, however disturbed they were, they weren't capable of murder. Well, Selander has a long history of violence, including the attempted murder of her father. But I think that somehow these three individuals found each other — through their mutual loss — and came to be dependent on each other in different ways. They lived together year after year, getting in deeper and deeper, and that triggered something in each other. Like a secret club of hate, a pact where the dead girl became a symbol for what was missing in their lives. At the end of his interrogation Sebastian Granith said that he had assuaged his guilt. He was satisfied. It seemed as though he had assumed some kind of responsibility for what had happened to Maya — don't ask me how or why — but that the murders were some form of penance. A way of impressing the other two, or perhaps being accepted by them. Over the years he had been driven to a point where murder seemed the only possible course of action." The furrow between his eyebrows disappeared, and he added with a hint of embarrassment, "I don't really know what I'm talking about; Beckman is better at this psychology stuff. I suppose we might never know the answer to some things."

Östergren protested and said it was interesting, which he took as an indication that she wanted him to go on.

596

"Anyway, when she realised we had proof that she was the one who killed Molin, Caroline Selander confessed that Sebastian Granith had sent her a text just after we arrested him. 'Two down — one to go,' something along those lines. He must have pre-programmed his mobile in case he got caught, because he was never left unsupervised. We found the mobile later, after she'd confessed. It had been trodden into the ground where we were standing. It was a bit embarrassing, actually."

"Oh dear."

"Exactly. Anyway, when she got the message she realised he'd murdered the first two. She then saw it as her duty to deal with the last one, and she just went off and did it. She realised it was urgent, that the police knew the background and it was only a matter of time before . . . Well, you get the picture. So she just went out and stabbed him, wiped the knife and took off in her van. They picked her up pretty quickly."

"The police in Ystad?"

"Yes."

"And before that she'd attacked Seja Lundberg?"

Tell swallowed. "Seja Lundberg suspected Caroline Selander because of a conversation she'd had with a mutual acquaintance."

"So she was making her own enquiries, then."

"She was, yes. Selander panicked when she realised Seja was on her trail."

Östergren looked thoughtful once again.

"I read the piece she wrote. It was good. Perceptive."

She leaned over and placed her hand briefly on Tell's, as she reached for the milk.

"But when I asked how things were going, I was really talking about you. How are you?"

"What do you mean?"

She shrugged impatiently. "What do you think I mean? How are you feeling? Are things going well for you? How's your girlfriend?"

He didn't know what to say. Didn't she know that it was all over between him and Carina, or had someone at work got there before him and told her about Seja?

She sighed. "Do you have to look so petrified? First of all, I'm more or less retired and therefore no longer your boss, so you can forget about any repercussions. And secondly, and much more importantly, I'm your friend. At least I thought I was. Perhaps I haven't always been as open as I might have been, but I've always felt that the two of us are pretty much alike. That we understand one another. I trusted you —"

"Yes, but —" he protested.

She raised a finger in the air. "I trusted you to be able to make a judgement about any risks you might be taking as a result of your behaviour. You're perfectly capable of doing so even if you've been treading a very fine line in this case. That's why I was quite hurt that you didn't feel you could talk to me. Instead you avoided me. That was cowardly."

"Yes."

"And childish."

He didn't look up, but he sensed a smile playing around one corner of her mouth. For some reason this made him feel even more vulnerable.

"Absolutely. And since we're on the subject of my lack of backbone, I'd also like to apologise for the fact that I didn't want to see you, or be reminded of you or your illness. It wasn't just this business with Seja. I was just terrified at the thought . . ." He fell silent. A helpless gesture in Östergren's direction said what he couldn't bear to say out loud.

"That I'm going to die soon," she said calmly. "Apology accepted." He could feel her gaze burning into his forehead. "Why are you so angry?" She had raised her eyebrows so high that they had disappeared under her white curls. "Why are you so angry, when I'm not?"

She leaned forward and forced him to look her in the eye.

"I'm going to ask you the same question I've been asking Gustav over these last few weeks. Why should you be angry, when I've stopped feeling that way? I've accepted that I have a year. I have a year to read all those books I'd intended to read when I retired. To sleep late in the mornings. I can use the sauna we built ten years ago and have hardly ever had time to use. Or I can go back to all those exciting conversations I had with Gustav when we were first married, the ones that got lost somewhere along the way as my career took over. I say to him, 'You should be pleased, Gustav. After all, you're always complaining that I never see you.'"

Tell, who thought he was about to laugh, realised to his surprise that there were tears prickling his eyelids.

"And you, Christian, you ought to be happy for yourself sometimes. Be happy, as I am, that you've

599

found somebody nice who can put up with you, and stop wallowing in those peculiar feelings of guilt. Stop letting fear dictate what you do. Stop asking whether you deserve what you get — and just live instead. Live and be happy!"

She swept a pack of cards off the table as she waved her arms. They went everywhere.

And when he thought about it, Tell realised he was happy. Happy that Seja might be in his apartment when he got home from work in the evening. He didn't dare take it for granted, but he thought she probably would be.

"Things are going well with Seja," he said. He smiled as he bent down to pick up the cards.

"There — you see — now you're laughing too," she said, prodding him playfully in the side.

After they had laughed together, a restful reflective silence settled over the room. They watched Gustav Östergren push a lawnmower around the side of the house and park it in front of the cellar steps. The sound of screaming gulls rose as he opened the veranda door. A chilly gust of wind hit their faces. Ann-Christine shivered.

"The wind's getting up," commented her husband, pouring himself a cup of coffee. "Blowing inland."

Tell could actually smell the sea now, through the exhaust fumes from the rush-hour traffic. As a child he had always loved walking by the sea when it was windy.

"And how's the violin?" he asked.

"Let me just finish my coffee, and you can come and have a look."

Gustav dunked a piece of cake in his coffee, popped it in his mouth and reached for a blanket lying by the door. He passed it to his wife, and she spread it gratefully over her knees.

Tell stood up. "Another time, Gustav. I need to make a move."

He took his leave of Ann-Christine Östergren simply and without drama. His heart felt lighter than it had when he had arrived just an hour ago.

Outside the wind was strong and the cypress trees were swaying violently. He decided to take a walk by the sea. After all, he had the time.

Acknowledgements

Thanks to Stefan Ceder (and the rest of the family) for tireless commitment, encouragement and inspiration during the journey. Thanks also to Åsa, Gustaf and everyone else at Wahlström & Widstrand and Bonnier Group Agency who believed in *Frozen Moment*.

Darkside

Belinda Bauer

Shipcott in bleak mid-winter: a close knit community where no stranger goes unnoticed. So when an elderly woman is murdered in her bed, village policeman Jonas Holly is doubly shocked. How could someone have killed and left no trace? Jonas finds himself sidelined as the investigation is snatched away from him by an abrasive senior detective. Is his first murder investigation over before it's begun? But this isn't the end of it for Jonas, because someone in the village is taunting him, blaming him for the tragedy, and watching every move he makes . . .

ISBN 978-0-7531-8888-0 (hb)
ISBN 978-0-7531-8889-7 (pb)

Evil in Return

Elena Forbes

Bestselling novelist Joe Logan walks out into a hot summer's evening in central London. The next day his body is found dumped in a disused Victorian crypt at the Brompton Cemetery. It was no ordinary murder — he'd been tied up, shot and castrated.

Detective Inspector Mark Tartaglia is convinced that Logan's personal life holds the key to his violent death, but unravelling his past proves difficult. Following the overnight success of his debut novel, Logan had become a recluse. Was Logan just publicity shy or did he have something to hide? Then the body of a second man is found in an old boathouse on the Thames — killed in an identical fashion. Can Tartaglia find the link between the two dead men before the killer strikes again? As he soon discovers, nothing in life or death is straightforward.

ISBN 978-0-7531-8872-9 (hb)
ISBN 978-0-7531-8873-6 (pb)